TRULY ETERNALLY MINE

IMMORTAL HOLLYWOOD
BOOK ONE

STORMY O'HARA

For Niobe

ax

Lottie's fangs split through her too-sweet ingenue smile. She'd finally gotten what she wanted. As she bit into my neck, the venom began to soothe my body and mind, and for a moment, I thought I was getting what I wanted too.

The Bite was similar to the effects of the opium I had smoked—it was like falling into an ocean of pleasure so deep, pure and intoxicating that you would happily let it take you to its depths, even if it meant your demise.

It was only when I felt the life force leaving my body that I became aware of something within me trying to hold on to life, kicking and screaming, resisting this path that I had chosen.

But, you see, I didn't want the party to end. I was rich and famous. I had a new woman on my arm each day and another in my bed each night. I moved in the most exclusive circles. I had everything I ever wanted. I was respected, revered, worshipped. In those days I was quite frankly living like a god.

The excess and debauchery of Hollywood in the 1920s was a dream I didn't want to wake up from. I could have imagined nothing like it as a young boy growing up in the poverty of Cheapside, London. No matter how much success I had, how many movies I starred in, how much money I made, that little boy within me still feared it could all end at any moment, and I'd find myself back there again. Cold, hungry, alone.

Lottie's father, Renaud Luelle, was the head of the Fraternity of the Everlasting Rose, and they wanted to recruit me into their exclusive club. A secret society of Hollywood's elite, they offered eternal life in exchange for daylight, silver and one's soul.

Daylight? What of it? My days were spent under artificial light inside sound stages, and Hollywood parties only got kicking after midnight. I was already a creature of the night. My tastes were expensive, and I was more partial to gold than silver, so that was simple. And my soul? What soul? No one reaches the heights of fame I'd reached without a little damnation. I had hurt so many people along the way, I already knew I had no place in heaven.

And so, it had felt like a simple choice.

Lottie was the leading lady in my last five films, and the world loved us together. But she was just as delusional as the fans who would sneak into parties and throw themselves at me, thinking I would fall in love with them. Lottie thought our screen acting meant something, that I couldn't be "that good at acting". But while I had made love to half the women in Los Angeles, I had never been in love with any of them, least of all Lottie. No matter how many women I kissed in front of her, no matter how many chorus girls I took back to my luxury hotel suites, she still thought she could make me hers.

And in the end, I suppose she did.

I did not realize it then, but even if I lived forever, eventually the party would still end.

CHAPTER ONE

oppy

Dear Ms. St Clair,

I'd like to congratulate you on your new position in domestic services at the Montrose Estate. We're very much looking forward to working with you and La Luna Services.

Your presence is requested at a garden party this Friday evening at 5pm at the estate. This is a wonderful opportunity for you to meet other members of staff and learn more about your role. Please note that attendance is mandatory as part of your orientation.

Henrietta Pendleton
Personal Assistant to Max Montrose

I SLIDE out of the car with a quick thanks to my driver and tug on the hem of my short floral dress. When I found the dress at Goodwill last week, it seemed like a decent choice for a movie star's garden party. But now that I'm here, about to walk into Max Montrose's mansion, I'm suddenly very aware of just how out of season this dress is and just how much flesh I'm showing.

I look up at the wrought-iron gates before me and feel completely overwhelmed by the realization that I cannot do this.

I cannot meet the movie star I was completely obsessed with during high school. The man whose posters adorned my walls, whose movies were on constant rotation on my DVD player. I even had a secret scrapbook hidden under my mattress entitled Mr. and Mrs. Montrose. It was filled with cutouts of Max Montrose's face and mine glued onto photos from bridal magazines. An embarrassed flush crosses my cheeks at the thought of it.

I shake my head up at the gate.

I can't meet my movie star crush. I can't work for him, and I definitely cannot clean his house.

And I most absolutely *cannot* spy on him for a cult of religious nut jobs who believe he's a vampire!

I am way out of my depth here.

My dress is way too short.

I can't do this.

Scrambling around in my purse, I reach for my phone to call a ride home. My finger hovers over the button to book the trip when the wrought-iron gates begin to slide open. I look around to try to figure out what's going on, and then I realize that there are three different cameras angled towards me. Someone has been watching me standing here like an idiot this whole time.

Great.

"You're late!" shouts a scratchy voice from an ancient looking speaker beside the gate.

"Sorry!" I call back.

The iron gate continues to slide open like a magic portal that separates the rich and famous from the rest of us.

I take a breath and remind myself why I'm here.

I'm doing this for Aiden.

This gives me just enough strength to step through the gates and onto the other side, where I'm met with a long and steep driveway.

I take two steps forward in my brown vintage platform sandals, but there is no way in hell I can walk up this hill in these shoes. I hold on to a palm tree by the side of the drive as I unbuckle and remove them.

As I walk higher up the drive, sweat starts to form in all the most uncomfortable places. It's a warm late summer evening, and even though I'm dressed for the weather, I'm definitely not dressed for a hike in the Hollywood Hills.

I'm not even dressed for a garden party.

The mansion comes into view, and I have to pause for a moment to catch my breath on two accounts. One, because I'm sweating like crazy, and two, because this is the most beautiful house I've ever seen in my life. Not only is this going to be my new place of employment, but I'm also going to get to *live* here. In a mansion. In Max Montrose's three-story Old Hollywood Italian-style mansion with its glittering white marble columns and high arched windows.

The white stone fountain in front of the house beckons to me. Sticking a hand under one of the cherub's jugs of pouring water, I pat down the back of my neck and my chest to cool myself down, and then one of my shoes drops into the water.

"Idiot!" I mutter to myself as I lean over, praying I don't fall in as I try to grab my shoe.

I'm still shaking my shoe off and walking up the white marble steps when the door flies open and a woman with a lion's mane of frizzy red hair scowls at me. She's just a little older than me, maybe late twenties or early thirties, but she has the look of someone who has their life together, buys their dresses new, doesn't drop their shoes into fountains.

"What on earth?" she asks in what I think may be a hint of a Scottish accent.

"Sorry I'm late," I say, fumbling around as I try to get my dry shoe back on. "The Uber got lost, and then I didn't realize how long it would take me to walk up here."

"Punctuality is essential at the Montrose estate."

"Of course. It won't happen again."

"Mr. Montrose is not big on second chances." She looks down at my one wet shoe like I'm a smelly rescue dog looking for a home, and for a moment I think she's going to send me packing. "Hurry up."

I hobble into the foyer wearing only my one dry shoe, and the space takes my breath away. The walls are painted dark blue with gold gilded edges and covered in what I'm sure is very expensive artwork in gold picture frames. A chandelier catches the light above me, sending tiny rainbows across the dark red and cream Turkish rug.

"I'm Henrietta," the woman says, pulling me out of my daze.

"Max's assistant?"

"*Mr. Montrose's* assistant."

"It's nice to meet you." I stick out the hand not holding my wet shoe. "I'm—"

"Poppy, I know." She gives my hand a quick shake. "Phone?"

"Excuse me?"

"May I have your phone?"

"What? Why?"

"No phones on the estate. You can keep it with you in the staff quarters, but if you are found with a phone anywhere else on the estate, it is a fireable offence."

I reluctantly grab my phone out of my purse, a black fringed bag I borrowed from my roommate Kayla for the occasion, and hand it over.

"It's to protect Mr. Montrose's privacy. I am sure you understand."

I give a nod. I suppose I do. Max Montrose is still a household name even though he hasn't made a movie or been seen out in public for nearly ten years. A photo of him would be worth a lot to the tabloids.

Henrietta opens a large wooden box on the shelf by the door and drops my phone inside.

I'm still holding my wet shoe when she ushers me through the foyer and down a hallway.

"The parlor. You'll be cleaning in here most days," she tells me as we walk into the most stunning room full of plush rugs, paintings, vintage movie posters, chandeliers and price-less antiques.

As I take in the grand piano by the window, the well-stocked bar, the vintage record player and shelves upon shelves of records and pristine cream couch big enough for at least fifteen people, I feel like I've walked into a movie star's mansion.

I have! I have walked into a movie star's mansion!

Under a glass coffee table bigger than my entire bedroom, I notice a tiny black ball of fur. It raises its head and makes a little mew before disappearing into its ball again.

"Awww! Kitty!" I take a step towards the kitten, but Henrietta grabs my arm.

"Please leave the cat alone."

I don't want to leave the cat alone, but I do as she says and follow her through the room.

"Dining room on your left," she says, pointing through an ornate archway to where a gigantic dark wood table sits in the center of twelve velvet-backed chairs, more art, more rugs, another chandelier — this place is exquisite!

And it's going to be hell on earth to keep clean.

"You'll see the rest of the house on Monday." She leads me through a set of French doors that take us out onto a patio revealing steps down to a pool, more steps down into the garden and, far down below us, a view of the city that takes my breath away.

I can't help but let out a gasp. "This is—"

"It's quite something, isn't it?"

There's a marquee set up in the garden below, and I can see that the party is already in full swing. I really am late.

I carefully follow her down the set of stairs that lead to the pool.

"You'll be staying in the staff quarters," she points to a small building to the right of the mansion. "James and I live in the annex down behind the pool room."

Sitting behind marble columns just beyond the edge of the oval shaped white marble pool, the pool room is bigger than any house I could ever dream of living in.

"You can put your other shoe back on now," Henrietta tells me.

I slip my foot into my still soggy shoe and bend over to buckle it up.

But when I'm done, I stand up too fast. These heels are too high, and I'm not used to wearing shoes like this.

I lose my center of gravity and go flying towards Max Montrose's swimming pool.

CHAPTER TWO

I WATCH the guests arrive from my window that overlooks the patio, pool, garden and the City of Los Angeles. Only seven out of eight have arrived so far. Whoever is late will not be returning on Monday. Punctuality is imperative.

The guests do not know this, but this party is a final interview. One that my late guest has already failed.

While La Luna services assure me that they vet their staff thoroughly, I have been around long enough to know that the only vetting worth a damn is my own.

I walk into the ensuite, a black and gold bathroom to rival all others, run a little water on my hands and slick my dark hair back.

Humans tend to find a hairstyle they like in their late twenties and keep it for the rest of their lives. Vampires are the same. We rarely like to change our style from what it was when we were made. I'm no exception. I try to look modern, but I do miss the dapper style of the Roaring Twenties.

Of course, it makes it even more difficult for us to change our style when our hair never grows past what it was on the day we were made. If we try to cut it, it just grows back within a few hours.

I sigh, running my hand over my almost clean-shaven face. It's impossible for me to get a clean shave. I ruffle my hair up just enough so that I'm passable for present times, then make my way reluctantly down the hallway, down the stairs and through the mansion.

I am not at all excited about this evening. I don't enjoy spending time with humans, or anyone for that matter. But Henrietta and James have been on at me about getting some new staff ever since I noticed one of my favorite records was missing, went into a rage and fired my entire team six months ago. I found the record a few days later, berated myself excessively and then sent them all very generous severance payments.

As much as I hate to admit it, they are right. I need assistance to keep the mansion and gardens in good order. There have been plenty of times over the last one hundred years that I have been all alone in this mansion, taking care of everything myself, but I didn't become immortal so I could dust chandeliers for eternity.

I walk into the parlor and see Calliope, Callie as she's affectionately known, the little black cat who appeared one day in the garden a year ago fast asleep under the table. She has twelve cat beds and unlimited couch and bed space throughout the mansion, and yet this is where she chooses to sleep. Over a hundred years later and I still do not understand cats.

She looks up at me and makes a tiny meow, blinks and then curls up into an even smaller ball than before.

I walk through the French doors, and I'm instantly struck by a beautiful derriere sticking up in the air. A short floral dress barely covers it, revealing the soft pale thighs of a woman who's fumbling about with her shoes.

I sense it before it happens. Without even thinking about the repercussions of everyone gathered here seeing me do it, I run at speed towards her, grabbing her wrist just in time to stop her falling into the pool.

Her momentum shifts, and instead of flying into the pool, she flies into my arms.

I know who she is from my research. This is Poppy St Clair. Her most recent employment includes cleaning hotel rooms and working at a bar. My background check also revealed that she's been single for the last year. That shouldn't be of any interest to me as her boss, but the way she feels against me right now—soft, warm, filled out in all the right places, it's the closest I've been to a human woman in years, and it strikes me as quite pleasant indeed.

She looks up at me with big hazel doe eyes, and I am struck by her natural beauty. Brown hair with strands that appear auburn in the early evening sunlight, glowing cheeks dotted with freckles, an intoxicating sweet berry scent and a racing pulse.

It's nothing new for me to have this effect on a woman, but it is something new for me to feel my own pulse slightly raise as I imagine what I would like to do to this woman if it weren't for the formality of this occasion.

CHAPTER THREE

oppy

How to identify a vampire:
Vampires cannot go out in the sun
Vampires cannot eat human food
Vampires cannot touch silver
Vampires feel ice cold to the touch
Vampires are disgusted by the smell of garlic
Vampires cannot come inside unless invited
The Order of Concordia Codex, page 56

WHEN MAX MONTROSE smiles at me, it's like a light is switched on and I didn't even know I was in the dark. Everything around me and within me is suddenly brighter and lighter, more colorful and just *better* in every way. Just when I think no man on earth could be more attractive than he is right now, he slides his sunglasses down and instead of falling into his pool, I fall into the blissful abyss of his bright blue eyes.

His arms are incredibly strong, the hard lines of his chest and abs press against me as I melt into him. Sure, I've been held by a man before, but never like this, never like suddenly my whole life depends on his arms being around me.

He steadies me, bringing his hands up to the bare skin on my shoulders. "Are you alright?" God, I had almost forgotten that in real life he has that killer British accent.

The whole thing is just too much for my human senses. His dark, almost black hair is styled, but a loose wave crosses his brow. He's dressed in an impeccable white shirt, open at the collar to give an expensive but casual look. His sleeves are part rolled up, and his gold watch, which I'm pretty sure is a Rolex worth more than I could make in a million years, catches a glint of sunlight. And to top it all off, the man somehow smells like rain in a redwood forest on a Los Angeles summer evening.

I nod, but honestly, I don't think I'll ever be alright again.

"Perhaps I should introduce myself formally. I'm Max Montrose. Welcome to my home." He removes his hands from my shoulders and steps back, holding out a hand for me to shake like we haven't just been full body pressed up against each other.

I reach out and take his hand. A little cool, but not as cold as the Codex, the Order's weird bible thing, states a vampire's touch should be. And his embrace? Nothing cold about it at all. It was hot. *So hot*.

"Poppy," I finally manage to get out.

"Lovely to meet you, Poppy."

Henrietta clears her throat, and I'm suddenly aware that she's been right there this whole time.

"Please," he gestures down another set of white stone stairs, "join us in the garden for a drink and hors d'oeuvres."

I look down at my shoe, which is still only half buckled. "I just need to—" I wave my hand to my foot.

He gives me a nod and walks down the stairs as if they're covered in red carpet. Max Montrose has the sexy, confident swagger of a very rich and successful man. I can't take my eyes off him as I watch him walk away, his midnight blue pants fitting his waist and behind so perfectly they must have been tailormade for him.

Henrietta follows behind him and then looks back at me with a glare and a gesture for me to hurry the fuck up. I step away from the edge of the pool, crouch down to buckle my shoe and then follow them down to the party.

Kayla and Justin are the only people here that I know, and like me, they are both members of the Order working for La Luna.

Kayla sees me and rushes over. She looks striking in a tight silver dress that complements her brown skin perfectly. It makes her look like a Kardashian and makes me feel even more underdressed for this party.

"Why are you so late?" She plucks something out of my hair. *Great.* "I thought you were coming straight from work?"

"I couldn't get away from a customer who was complaining about the ice melting in their water, and then when I finally got an Uber it got lost and then I had to walk—"

"Oh god, he's coming over!" She flaps her hands at me. "Do I look okay? Do I have anything on my face?"

I shake my head. "You're good."

A tray of white wine floats past, and I grab one, gulping down half of it immediately.

Kayla takes a glass for herself, downing the whole thing before putting the empty glass back on the tray.

Max takes a glass of red from another passing tray and

then stops to speak to an attractive man with dark hair and features and big biceps.

Kayla deflates. "I'm so fucking nervous," she says into another glass of wine that's appeared in her hand. At first, I think she means because he's *Max Montrose,* but then she adds, "So much is riding on this." She means she's nervous about fulfilling her role for the Order.

Kayla is the beauty of our little trio. Her job is to seduce Max, to get as close to him as possible, to find out his weaknesses and secrets.

She frowns out over what can only be described as the most incredible view of Los Angeles that exists. "It's still light," she says.

"That view is really something." I stick my hand into my purse to grab my phone so I can take a photo. But my phone isn't here. It's in a box in the foyer.

Kayla gives me a look. "Poppy, the *sun* hasn't gone down yet."

"Uh yeah, because sunset is a few hours away." I don't get her confusion over daylight hours until I remember. They think he's a vampire, so he shouldn't be able to go out in the sunlight.

"How is he out in the *sun?*" Kayla whispers as Justin appears beside her, wrapping his arm around her waist.

"Get off." She nudges him off her, and he looks pissed.

Justin is the brawn of our group. He's also Kayla's boyfriend. Although Max Montrose has been linked to plenty of women in the past, he's never been involved in any scandals, and his exes only have nice things to say about him. It's highly unlikely he'll be interested in Kayla if he knows she's dating someone else, and so Justin is most definitely not supposed to act like her boyfriend tonight.

We've all had some physical training on how to take down a vampire. It was hilarious, really. We had to practice shooting targets with silver bullets and stake first aid dummies in the heart. But Justin is a trained level four vampire hunter, and that makes him both very nutty and dangerous as fuck. I never complain when I have to clean up after him around the apartment, and at night I always slide my dresser against the door. Just in case.

My job for the Order is to find information. The Order believes that Max Montrose is the head of this thing called the Fraternity of the Everlasting Rose, the oldest and most dangerous vampire society in existence. I'm supposed to find evidence of this fraternity, find out who its members are, where and when they meet, so that the Order can take it down.

Secret societies, vampires — it all sounds like a great plot for Max Montrose's next movie.

But I'm just here to find my brother Aiden, and if that means pretending to believe the Order's bizarre conspiracies, so be it.

Justin and Kayla appear to be getting into a lover's tiff, and so I step away and head towards the buffet table.

I glance over at Max, who's talking to two pretty girls, both dressed in designer outfits. I grab another glass of wine from a passing tray. What's the point of taking an Uber if I'm not going to make the most of the free bar?

I watch as Max laughs politely at something one girl says. His eyes flit over to mine, and I immediately look away, taking another gulp of wine.

"What do you think of these?" A woman with shoulder-length green hair, dressed in a multi-colored sequin jump-suit, holds up some kind of pastry on a fork, eying it suspiciously.

"I haven't had one yet," I tell her.

She shoves the pastry into my face. "Try it."

I take the fork and take a small bite. "It's good."

Her eyes narrow at me, and her green glitter eyeshadow catches the light. "Tell me the truth."

I take a second bite. "It's a little dry."

"Right?" She wipes a hand on a napkin and then holds it out for me to shake. "I'm Trix. Catering."

"Poppy, domestic services."

She lowers her voice. "Have you met him yet?"

I look over to where he's standing now, talking with Justin and Kayla. Justin is laughing his big bro laugh, and Kayla is giggling. I didn't even know she *could* giggle.

"Yeah, I have," I tell her.

"What's he like?" Trix hands me a plate of what looks like salmon and cream cheese on crackers.

"Handsome. Charming. Sexy as hell. He smells like a forest."

She laughs at that. "Of course he fucking smells like a forest!"

I take a bite of the cracker. "Now *this* is delicious."

She grins at me. "It's the only thing on the entire table that's edible. Carrot lox and cashew cheese on garlic chia and flax crackers."

I have no idea what she's just said, but two glasses of wine on an empty stomach have made me ravenous. As soon as I'm done with the first cracker, I stuff another one into my mouth. "This is so good, Trix."

I turn to reach for another wine glass on a tray going past at the same time a piece of lox slides off my plate and lands right onto someone's shoe.

"I'm so sorry." I look up to see who I've dropped it on, and of course—it's Max Montrose.

Oh, my god.

First, I nearly fell into his pool, and now I've dropped food on his shoe?!

He looks down at his shoe and then frowns at me through his designer sunglasses.

I put my plate and wine down on the table, grab a napkin and bend down to clean his shoe, but as soon as I'm down there, another hand appears, swiping the lox away with one napkin, and polishing his shoe with another.

"Thank you, James," Max says.

The man with the lightning cleaning speed looks up at me and gives me a thin smile. He's dressed like a waiter and appears to be in his mid-thirties. He's fairly attractive, with a thick head of light brown hair and kind light blue eyes.

He disappears with the napkins, and I realize I'm still crouching down by Max Montrose's shoes.

I stand up, pulling on the hem of my dress.

Trix shoves a plate into his hands. "Max, what do you think of the carrot lox?"

He narrows his eyes at it. I consider for a moment what the Order told us about vampires — they don't go out in the sun, silver can bind them, they don't eat.

He looks down, and after a moment of hesitation, he takes a cracker and bites into it. When he's done chewing, he licks the corner of his mouth, and I have a sudden urge to throw myself at him and kiss all the carrot lox off his beautiful face.

Yeah, because hot, rich movie stars love to kiss women who drop carrot lox all over their expensive shoes.

"Wonderful," he says, taking another cracker and eating the whole thing. "I don't remember this being on the menu for tonight's event, however."

"I made it," Trix says.

"You made your own food and added it to the buffet table?"

"I did."

He gives her an impressed nod. "Very audacious."

She ignores what I'm not even sure is a compliment and gets back to business. "What are your favorite foods, Max?"

"Let's talk about that on Monday."

"At least give me a place to start."

"I'm not very fussy. I eat mostly plants," he tells her. "If you'll excuse me, I have a few other guests I still need to meet."

"It was so nice to meet you," Trix says, while I stand frozen, still unable to speak or move after what's just happened.

"And you, Trix." He nods at me. "Poppy."

I just give a pathetic smile to his back as he walks off.

The sound of his voice, of Max Montrose's voice saying *my* name, repeats over and over in my mind while I pretend to pay attention to what Trix is saying about the nutritional value of cashews.

CHAPTER FOUR

Max

LOVE DELAYED, one star

Bad acting, bad plot, seen better romance between pigeons outside the cinema than between these two actors. I really hope Max Montrose never tries to make a comeback or makes any movie ever again. He is a disgrace to the art form of cinema! The one star is for Maverick Stone's cameo appearance. Love that guy!
@Filmmmbufff3456

BY THE TIME the sun disappears down into the valley, my guests are mostly drunk, and this is when the vetting process really begins. The best way to truly get to know someone's character is to ply them with just the right amount of wine so that they lose their inhibitions and then just enough food so that they don't get messy.

It's fascinating to watch this group interact with each

other. It appears some of them know each other very well, perhaps too well, considering the way Justin can't remove his eyes from Kayla's backside. Others are meeting for the first time tonight.

Malik is the only one who's not drinking. He will be my new security hire. He's alert and aware of everything going on around him. The drunken antics of the others aren't phasing him at all. When Kayla tries to flirt with him, he simply excuses himself to get another soda.

Julio will be my new head landscaper. When he wanders off with a glass of wine to look at the flowers for forty-five minutes, it's clear his passion for this garden exceeds my own.

Trix is confident and charming, and her brazen act in bringing her own food showed some real dedication to her role. She also speaks to me as if I'm a regular person, which is refreshing. I have no doubt she'll be perfect as my new chef, even if I won't be eating much of her food myself.

But even though I'm trying to continue to observe them all, my eyes keep being drawn back to Poppy. There's something about her that reminds me of the old days. She has a pale, doe-eyed innocent look of a chorus girl trying to get her start in the movies that used to drive me wild. I find that I can't stop glancing at the pale skin at the top of her thighs and imagining what treasure and pleasure lies just inches above her hemline.

I pull my gaze away from her as Henrietta approaches.

"Mr. Montrose," she says. "Are you ready for phase two?"

I give her a nod and then step forward toward the group.

"May I have your attention, everyone?" It takes a moment for my drunk guests to turn and focus. "I'd like to invite you into the theater for a private screening."

There are gasps and oohs and aaahs from some of the women present who are clearly fans of my work. I hear

Justin mumble something to Kayla about my having a big ego. He's not wrong, but his audacity to express it so blatantly on *my* estate is astounding.

I guide the group through the garden, up the stairs, into the mansion and down into the basement. I push open two large wooden doors to reveal the backs of forty plush emerald green seats and a large screen directly in front.

It's a bold move showing one of my own movies, but I need to know how they feel about me as an artist. I will not employ anyone who has no respect for what I do. I also won't employ anyone who has an unhealthy obsession with me.

Poppy, Trix, Kayla and Justin slide into the back row while Sandy and Rachel, the two other women who were hired for domestic services, run straight down the aisle and into seats in the front row, both of them squealing. Neither of them will be here on Monday morning, but I decide to do them a kindness and let them have this cinema experience so that they at least have a positive memory of me and this place.

James hands out bottles of soda (no more wine), buckets of popcorn and cozy blankets to each of my guests. Trix makes a squealing noise when she receives her popcorn as if she's more excited about snacks than she is about me, which I appreciate. Poppy curls up under her blanket, a soft smile on her face, as if she's simply looking forward to watching the movie. I wonder if she's seen it before and what she thought of it. While it was a box office hit, critics panned it, and many members of the public did too, if I'm honest.

I step onto the small stage beside the screen where I've introduced many movies shown here over the years. "The movie you're going to watch tonight may be familiar to some of you. *Love Delayed.*"

Trix's hand shoots up.

"I wasn't planning on taking questions this evening, but yes, Trix?"

"Do you have any plans to make any more movies?" she asks.

"No. I don't."

"Why not?" asks Rachel.

"I'm quite busy with other things these days."

"What other things?" asks Sandy.

"I'm very busy with my non-profit ventures."

"You should make more movies!" Sandy gushes. "You don't look like you've aged a day since this movie came out!"

"You definitely need to make more movies!" Rachel says, clapping her hands together in glee.

Trix gives me a look like she's sorry for asking.

"I had a wonderful career and did everything I set out to do," I say, clasping my hands together. "I'm very grateful for all the opportunities I've had, but I have no interest in acting again."

I look out over my audience and lock eyes with Poppy right as she places a piece of popcorn on her tongue, and I have a sudden urge to be alone with her here, sitting beside her, feeding her popcorn. I'd run my salty sweet fingers over her sweet wet lips. She would suck the flavor from my fingers and look up at me like she wanted to lick more than just my fingers.

Oh dear.

I clear my throat. "James, if you would."

The movie starts to play, and I make a swift exit out of the theater and back up to the patio where I stand in the late evening air trying to gather my thoughts.

"Definitely not Sandy and Rachel," Henrietta says, appearing next to me with a glass of red wine.

"No," I agree, taking the glass from her.

"How many will make the cut?"

"About half."

"What will you do about domestic services?"

"We still have Poppy."

"Poppy? But she was *late!*"

"Yes, but at least she's not obsessed with me."

Henrietta gives me a look. "She hasn't taken her eyes off you all night."

The idea of that warms me inside. "If it doesn't work out, I can always let her go."

She raises an eyebrow. "Just don't forget about the employment contract. It applies to you too."

"That will be all, Henrietta."

She nods and takes her leave, leaving me to sit and admire the view of the city I never tire of.

It has been decades since a woman has entranced me as much as Poppy has in just mere moments spent in her presence.

I take a sip of my wine and find that all I can think of is the idea that on Monday morning Poppy will be here, in my house, dusting my furniture and fluffing my cushions.

The idea appeals to me greatly.

CHAPTER FIVE

oppy

The Secret Princess, five stars

This is a work of pure genius. A must-watch for all film buffs. You cannot understand modern film without experiencing this piece of pure cinematic magic. Leopold Montrose, great-grandfather of that unfortunate hack Max Monrose, is hands down the best actor of his generation. A travesty he never won an Academy Award for his work. Would give it a thousand stars if I could.
@Filmmmbufff3456

The critics hated *Love Delayed*, but it's still one of my all-time favorite Max Montrose movies. The airport, the snowstorm, the one hotel room, the kidnapping drama, the second chance romance!

As I watch the movie *in Max Montrose's private cinema*, I keep pinching myself that this is happening.

I'm at *his* house.

I fell into *his* arms.

"I hate this movie," Kayla whispers to me.

I throw her a look as Max's giant, sexy, beautiful face appears on the screen.

"It's weird, isn't it?" she asks me quietly.

"What is?" I whisper back.

"The sun thing."

"I saw him eat crackers too," I tell her.

Her eyes narrow at the screen. "And yet, he doesn't look a day older now than he did in this movie, which is nearly ten years old."

"I don't think he's a vampire, Kayla. It's probably just Botox," I shrug.

Justin scoffs from his seat on Kayla's other side. "It's a glamour. The food, the sunlight. This is what these creeps do. It's all lies and manipulation."

"They wouldn't send us here if they weren't at least *pretty* sure he was involved," Kayla adds. "And this *was* the last place Aiden was seen. The last place he was sent on a mission for the Order."

My chest tightens at her mention of Aiden. I don't know why he was here. I don't even know for sure that he *was* here. But it's the only thread I have to follow.

"Talk about it later," I say, shushing them as Max's character Roman is about to bump into Laura, the woman he'd been in love with ten years earlier.

As the movie plays, I go to my happy place. The nostalgia hits and takes me back to when life was easier. Before Mom left, before Aiden moved out, before I realized I wouldn't get into college and would end up cleaning hotel rooms for the rest of my life.

The credits roll way too soon, bringing me back to reality,

although reality isn't so bad in this moment, here at Max Montrose's house.

"That ending!" Trix sighs. "Perfection!" She makes a chef's kiss.

James appears and stands at the side of the screen. "We hope you've had an enjoyable evening at the Montrose estate. Mr. Montrose would like you to know it's been his pleasure taking care of you this evening."

Trix elbows me. "I wouldn't mind Mr. Montrose taking care of me. Or this James guy either, for that matter. He's the sexiest butler I've ever met."

James continues, "Please remember to collect your phones on the way out, and we look forward to seeing you on Monday morning for orientation."

I throw off the cozy blanket and follow Trix and the rest of the group out of the theater and back into the foyer upstairs.

"It's going to be great, isn't it?" Trix gushes as we stand in line to get our phones back. "Max and James both seem so nice, so down to earth. For the first time in forever, I'm actually looking forward to work on Monday!"

"He's nothing special," Justin tells her. "Just because he's rich and famous or whatever."

Trix puts a hand on a hip. "Oh yeah? And what have *you* done that's so great?"

I have to hide a giggle at her putting him in his place.

"I've done more than you'll ever know about," he says, stepping forward and grabbing his phone.

"Whatever that means." Trix rolls her eyes and takes her phone back from Henrietta.

"Thanks, Henrietta," I say, taking my phone back.

"See you Monday, Poppy," she says.

I follow the others out the front door and slowly spin

around, taking it all in. It's stunning here at night. Strings of lights run around the palm trees in perfect spirals, and the fountain is lit, making the cherubs look otherworldly. I look back up at the mansion. The middle floor is dark, but one light is lit on the third floor. I wonder if that is where Max is right now.

I'm about to put my phone in my purse and realize I don't have my purse.

"Oh, shit."

"What's wrong?" Kayla asks.

"I left my purse inside."

"You mean *my* purse," Kayla says.

"It'll still be there on Monday," says Justin.

"I can't drive you both here on Monday without my car keys," I tell him.

Kayla sighs, and I run back up the steps.

"Our Uber is one minute away," says Justin. "We can't keep it waiting."

"I think we're going to go out anyway. The bar or something." Kayla gives me an awkward smile and then as an afterthought and not a genuine invitation adds, "Did you want to meet us there?"

"No, you go ahead. I'll just go straight home. I'll see you tomorrow."

"I can wait for you if you want to take a ride together," Trix says as Kayla and Justin wander down the path.

"I'm good," I tell her.

"You sure?"

I'm at the front door again now and relieved that it's still unlocked. "Yeah!" I call back to her. "See you Monday!"

"Enjoy your weekend!" she calls back before trotting off down the driveway like a sparkly disco ball.

I head into the foyer again, and even though there's no sign of James or Henrietta, I still drop my phone in the box by the door.

I walk through the parlor and see that the little fluff ball is now on the white couch. Even though this is kind of an emergency, I can't help myself. I go to the kitten and coo over it.

"Hello little kitty." It looks up at me and yawns. "You're adorable! And you're ruining this beautiful white couch." The kitten mews, stands up with a little stretch and goes into a ball in the other direction, sending black fluff off in all directions. I take my chances and reach out for a gentle pat. The kitten purrs, and I immediately fall in love with the little thing.

"Okay, sweetie, I have to go now, but I'll see you again soon, okay?"

I pull myself away from the extreme cuteness and run down the stairs, praying that my purse is still there as I barge into the theater.

I stop short when I see Max sitting in the front row. He turns to look at me, his handsome features flickering in the black and white light of the screen where a damsel in distress in a huge puffy dress is being pulled away by a classic silent movie villain.

"Poppy," he startles.

"Oh, I'm so sorry." I was so not expecting anyone to be here, least of all *him*. "I—I didn't mean to interrupt, I just—" I take a second to catch my breath. "I think I left my purse in here earlier."

He stands. "Let me help you find it."

"No, that's okay." I slide into the back row where I was sitting earlier. "I don't want to disturb you. Please go back to your movie. I think it's just—" I find the purse wedged under my blanket from earlier. "Got it!" I hold it up to show him.

"I'm glad you were able to locate it," he says.

And suddenly I realize I'm alone with him. I'm alone with Max Montrose. For a second I feel afraid. I don't believe in vampires or supernatural beings, but there's definitely something about him that is more than human.

Max Montrose is the handsomest man I've ever laid eyes on. When he saved me from falling into the pool, he was there *so fast.* His arms around me were *so strong.* His skin is so perfectly clear and even though he must be in his late thirties, he barely has a wrinkle on him.

Botox. And also, *vampires don't exist,* I remind myself.

"Join me." It's not a question. It's a request. Not because he's not giving me an option to say no, but because why the hell would anyone say no to Max Montrose?

I walk down the short aisle and take the plush green seat next to him, realizing just how much this dress rides up when I sit. His eyes sweep over my thighs for just a second, and it's nice to think that he finds my legs worth looking at considering he's probably used to bedding supermodels and other movie stars.

I feel heat rush to my cheeks thinking about him in bed.

"I know what you're thinking." He takes a sip of the red wine sitting on the small table in front of his chair and points to the screen. "We look alike."

Not exactly what I was thinking, but as I look up at the screen, I notice the similarities.

"My great-grandfather, Leopold."

"Oh?"

"He was very popular in his day. You'll notice some posters of his films around the mansion."

"What's the movie about?"

"She's a secret princess, and when the bad guys find out, they kidnap her for ransom. This guy—" he points to his doppelgänger who's wielding a sword across the screen, "—well, he saves her." He gives me a look. "Guess what it's called?"

I shake my head. "No idea."

"The Secret Princess."

"Wow, they really went all out with movie names back then."

"You think they're better now? *Love Delayed* is hardly brilliant."

"Oh, but the movie is."

The corners of his mouth raise and I can't believe that I have made Max Montrose *smile.*

"Can I get you a drink, Poppy?"

Okay, now Max Montrose is offering to get me a drink, and I'm not really sure how to respond to this.

"Glass of wine? Gin and tonic?"

"Um, oh. Yes, okay. Thanks."

I mean, it's not like I can say no!

His eyebrows draw together. "I do apologize. I have made the assumption that you'd enjoy spending time with me. Do you have somewhere else you need to be?"

I shake my head. There is literally *nowhere* else I'd rather be.

"Please don't let me keep you if you need to go."

"I can stay, if you want."

He gives me a sexy smirk. "I do want."

Oh, my god.

"A gin and tonic sounds great," I say.

He grabs his phone and starts texting. "Won't be long."

We both go back to watching the movie and I find myself getting pulled into the story of this princess who's pretending to be a chorus girl so that she can have a life of her own while Max's great-grandfather, who is incredibly handsome, even in black and white, does anything and everything he can to save her.

James appears rolling a gold vintage drink cart down the aisle until he reaches us. He gives me a look of disapproval and then prepares my drink.

"Gin and tonic," he says, putting the drink on the small glass table between me and Max. "Your wine, sir," he says as he fills Max's glass with red wine.

The wine is very red, and I have a sudden flashback to my training when they told us that vampires often drink blood while pretending it's red wine. I don't know why I'm thinking about this now. Max walked around in the sun and ate regular human food all night. There is nothing about him that suggests he's undead!

Maybe it's the low light, or the fact that I'm the only guest still here, or maybe it's that I joined a cult to find my brother and after six months of thinking they were all completely batshit crazy, they somehow still managed to get in my head.

I suddenly have to know if he's drinking wine or blood.

"Actually," I say to James. "Could I try the red wine?"

Max and James exchange a look. "Of course," James says, "Let me bring another glass for you."

"That's okay." I reach out and grab Max's glass. He looks horrified, and I'm not sure if it's because this is such a social faux pas or if it's because I'm about to drink *actual blood*. But I need to know. And so, I take the glass and inhale the scent of —*wine*.

I take a small sip, and it tastes like—*wine*.

Max can go in the sun, eat crackers, and he drinks *wine*, not blood.

It's not like I ever really believed the Order about this whole vampire thing, but it still somehow feels like relief.

Max looks at me curiously. "Would you like a glass of wine, Poppy?"

"No, I'm good with the gin actually, thanks." I take a sip to wash away the wine taste.

James does a little bow. "Will there be anything else, sir?"

"No, thank you. That will be all for this evening, James."

"Yes, sir." James disappears and once again I am alone

with Max Montrose, who is not a vampire, but is very definitely rich, handsome and famous, which still gives me plenty of reasons to be nervous about being alone with him.

Max takes a sip of wine as the credits roll. "It used to be all glitz and glamour once upon a time. Now it's all streaming on demand," he sighs.

"People still go to the movies," I say.

"When was the last time you went to the cinema?" he asks, turning to me and looking at me curiously.

I squish my face up in thought. "Apart from tonight? A few years ago, I think."

"And when did you last watch something on a streaming service?"

"Last night."

He leans his head back on the seat. "We used to see a moving picture several times a week."

"When was the last time you went?"

He lets out a laugh. "Oh, Poppy, I haven't left the estate in years."

I knew he'd been out of the public eye for a few years, but I didn't know he'd become a total recluse.

"Really?"

"I don't like the attention."

"You really got into the wrong industry."

He chuckles a little at that. "Oh, don't get me wrong, I used to enjoy it. But just once I'd like to go out and not be mobbed in the street." He takes a breath. "I must sound so ungrateful for all my success."

"No, not at all." I wasn't sure when I finished my gin and tonic, but Max's eyes widen as he sees my empty glass.

"Let me get you another."

"Oh no, please don't bother James again."

"It is his job to be bothered, but I was going to make it myself." He takes my glass and moves over to the drink cart, and all I can think is, *oh my god, Max Montrose is making me a drink!*

He passes the drink to me, and I wonder if he doesn't leave the estate, how many people come to visit him here. He must have friends, other movie stars he spends time with.

"Shall we watch another?" he asks as the screen goes to black.

"*The Letterbox*," I say, thinking of his movie about a magical letterbox that helped two soulmates find each other.

"Oh no, not that piece of rubbish."

I gasp. "That's your best work!"

"If that's my best work, I truly am the worst actor in history."

I laugh. I knew Max Montrose was gorgeous, but I had no idea he was also *funny*.

"Okay then, you choose."

"Well, we've seen something my great-grandfather was in, how about one of my grandfather's films?"

"Johnny Montrose?"

"Ah, so you've read my Wikipedia page?" He raises an eyebrow.

So *not* Botox.

"How about *Stranger in the Dark*?" he suggests. "That was one of my grandfather's best."

He punches something into his phone, and the movie begins.

CHAPTER SIX

$\mathcal{M}$ax

POPPY DRINKS FAR TOO much gin and tonic, and guilt washes over me. She seemed as though perhaps she had somewhere else to be when I invited her to watch the first movie with me. I hope she didn't feel pressured into staying here with me. I know I can be influential even when I'm not deliberately using my influence or a glamour, something I rarely do at all these days unless absolutely necessary and something I would *never* do to her.

But it has been such a comfort to have her here. She's such a gentle creature and her presence has been a balm for my weary soul.

As the credits on the second movie begin to roll, her eyes softly close, her cheeks still flushed from drink, her lips still wet from her last sip of gin.

A powerful urge to kiss her rises up within me. The desire to feel her lips on mine, to run my fingers through her messy hair and press my cool body against the warmth of her naked curves is something I haven't desired with a human in many years. The pull of it takes me a little by surprise. I wasn't sure I could feel something like this again.

It is not bloodlust. I remember that feeling well enough, even though these days I only drink Sybline, a synthetic blood that tastes like wine and keeps the bloodlust at bay.

No, this is something else, something I am not sure I have felt since even before I was made.

This feeling is more human than anything I've felt in so long. An overwhelming desire to be near this woman, to touch her, to kiss her, to hold her, to make love to her. It's not about her blood. It's about wanting her entire *being*.

Bloodlust would be easier. At least I know where I am when I'm feeling that.

Right now, as I stare at her soft lips, I feel that I am adrift. I do not know where I am.

Perhaps I have simply been alone too long in this mansion.

Poppy's head lolls back as she begins to snore gently, and my cold dead heart warms. I haven't seen a human woman sleeping like this for decades. And even then, it did not make me feel like this.

I pull a blanket from the chair beside me and wrap it around her.

I do the gentlemanly thing and leave her to sleep while I go upstairs to my bedroom. I dress in a pair of satin pajamas, lie down on my bed and stare up at the ceiling.

All I can think of is Poppy's pretty wet lips and warm curves, popcorn on her tongue and my fingers in her mouth. I think of waking her in the theater with a kiss, sliding the thin straps of that pretty dress down her shoulders until her breasts are bare. I think of her by the pool bending over in that dress, presenting her ass to me. I think of lifting her skirt, pulling her panties down and fucking her on all fours at the edge of my pool.

I think of her here in my bed, her legs open for me, my cock hard and ready. I think of how delicious it would feel to slam my cock into her repeatedly all night long.

I think of how fucking good I would like to make her feel.

I think of biting her just before we both reach climax, the ecstasy she would feel at The Bite, the warmth of her blood pouring down my throat. The way she would quench the thirst I have been trying to keep satiated with synthetic blood and avoiding human contact for so many years.

I could go down to the theater and get her. She may want me just as much as I want her. She may want nothing more than to come to my bed and join me in my depravities.

I grip the velvet bedspread and tell myself *no*.

But I'm not completely convinced that I will be able to stop myself.

CHAPTER SEVEN

*P*oppy

The Three Truths:
Vampires are unnatural, evil and the creation of the devil
Vampires hoard wealth and resources while others have nothing
Thou shalt not suffer a vampire to live!
The Order of Concordia Codex, page 27

It's nearly eight a.m. when I shove my key into the lock of the tiny downtown apartment I've shared with Kayla and Justin for the last six months.

By the time Aiden went missing, I was the only one left to care. Mom had left us years ago and made it very clear she did not want to keep in touch. I thought about reaching out to my dad, but as far as my father was concerned, from the moment he came out as bisexual, Aiden was no son of his.

Aiden moved out when I was 16. He had been my rock,

my protector, my best friend. I understood why he had to leave, but things were bad at home without him. As soon as I turned 17, I moved into an apartment with Danny. Not out of love, but desperation to get away from my father. Danny was a decent guy, and we cared about each other, but I didn't love him. When he cheated, I was still devastated, but not really surprised. I moved out, but we were on and off after that, neither of us willing to pull the plug on something with no life-force.

But I at least had my own place that I could just about afford. Things were better. I was okay.

Then Aiden stopped calling and texting. I tried every-thing—emails, writing letters. There was no response. I knew something was wrong, so I found someone to take my apartment and drove the 1,755 miles to end up here, at the last address I had for Aiden.

Aiden hadn't been back for his stuff, but he was still paying rent, so Kayla and Justin let me stay. They told me about vampires, the Order of Concordia and how Aiden went missing while on a secret mission at Max Montrose's house one night.

It all sounded crazy, but I couldn't say no to a free room in downtown LA and the hope that only connection I still had to Aiden.

"Poppy?" Kayla's head appears in the hallway. She's dressed in leggings and a tank top and looks like she's just come back from her morning run. She folds her arms across her chest. "And where exactly did *you* sleep last night?"

A grin spreads over my face, and I nearly tell her where I was when I hear voices in the kitchen and think better of it. Of course, I can't tell Kayla I was with Max. *She's* the one who's supposed to seduce him and get all his secrets.

"I was with Trix," I say. Well, technically I *was* with Trix last night, until I wasn't.

"Claudia's here."

Shit.

I take a quick look in the mirror by the door. I don't look too bad considering. Actually, I look kind of refreshed. Even though I slept in Max Montrose's private theater last night, I had the best sleep in ages.

My stomach does a little flip at the memory of last night. The movies, the gin, the wine, Max's handsome face illuminated by the light of the movie screen.

I roll my eyes at my reflection. This is not the time to be swooning over Max Montrose. Especially not with Claudia here. I pat down my hair, wipe some mascara from under my eyes and head into the kitchen.

Claudia is a little older than us, in her mid-thirties, and she's stunning. Sleek black hair, perfect skin. She's always so well put together, and it's only her ancient iPhone and the fact that she always wears the same outfit of striped t-shirt and jeans that give away the fact that she's struggling financially.

None of that bothers Justin apparently, who's ogling her while Kayla scowls at him.

Claudia looks up at me and smiles. "Poppy, I'm so glad you could make it." Her smile falters a little as she takes in my appearance and realizes I'm only just getting home.

Kayla gestures to the takeout coffee cups, paper bags and crumbs all over the table. "I sent you a text to see what you wanted. When you didn't reply, I didn't get you anything. Sorry."

"My phone went dead."

"Poppy." Claudia's smile vanishes. "Your phone must be charged at all times. We need to be able to contact you. If you can't uphold these simple rules—"

"It won't happen again," I say, taking a seat at the table.

Justin gives me a sly smile like he's enjoying watching me

get berated over this, even though I know for a fact his phone lives on ten percent battery.

"It better not," Claudia warns.

There are three levels in the Order. The Outer Order is open to anyone who believes what are called "The Three Truths" listed in the Order of Concordia Codex. The Order is said to be an ancient secret society, but the Codex was only printed in 2010. Justin and Kayla will enter the Inner Order upon the successful completion of this mission. It takes at least three years and a series of tasks and assignments to enter the Inner Order. And the Secret Order? Well, it's secret, so no one knows anything about it. I'm not even sure if Claudia is a member or not.

In the Outer Order we're placed into pods. We're not allowed to meet anyone outside of our pod who's in the Order. This is to protect us, so if one pod gets captured, they don't have information on other members. Jason is in our pod, but he also has another pod of trained hunters he's in.

Kayla clears her throat. "We texted Claudia after the party last night with the information we gathered on Max, and she called this emergency meeting."

"You mean the information you *didn't* gather?" Claudia lets out a small sigh.

Kayla ticks items off her fingers. "He *can* go in sunlight. He eats normal human food. I brushed against him with my silver bangle and *nothing*."

"I saw him eat a cracker with chia and garlic," I say.

"Maybe it wasn't real garlic," Justin says. "Just garlic flavored or something."

"And another thing," I say, hoping to get back in Claudia's good graces.

Claudia looks at me expectantly.

"The red wine he was drinking was definitely wine and not blood."

"How do you know?" Claudia asks.

I wrack my brain for a way to explain what happened and go with a basic truth. "He left a glass on a table, and when I had a chance, I picked it up and took a sip."

"Ew!" Justin makes a face. "That could have been *blood*, Poppy!"

"That's good thinking," Claudia says. "Well done, Poppy."

Justin looks pissed, and I give him a little smirk.

"So, what happens now?" Kayla asks.

"The plan goes ahead," says Claudia. "I'll admit, it's a little strange, but the Order has evidence that he's a vampire. And if the Order says he's a vampire, he's a vampire."

"What evidence do they have?" I ask.

She gives me a stern look across the table. "You know I can't tell you that."

"Can't or won't?"

She takes a sip of coffee from her paper cup. "I can't tell you because I don't know what it is. I don't question orders, and you shouldn't either." There's something dark in her tone, like she knows more about what happens if we don't follow orders than we do.

Claudia is our point person. She's the only person from the Order outside our pods that we've ever spoken to. I wonder now if she also has a point person, and they have a point person, and somewhere way above us all is the actual leader of the Order sitting in some ivory tower with this alleged evidence.

"But according to the Codex, he doesn't tick any boxes, so he can't be—" Kayla starts.

"I understand the three of you have concerns," Claudia says. "And you're right. We need to tread carefully here. It may take us more time to get the information we need. We're also going to need to find out *why* he can go in the sun and how he can eat food. We're going to need more information before we go ahead with the kill."

My empty stomach lurches. Sitting in the theater with Max last night and then replaying memories of his tousled hair and chiseled jaw all the way back home in the Uber, I had almost forgotten the whole point of all this was to actually *kill* him and all the other members of the Fraternity we can locate.

I fold my arms over the floral dress I'm still wearing. "We can't just *kill* someone with no evidence they're a vampire plus a whole lot of evidence they're just human."

Claudia scowls at me. "There *is* evidence. I don't know what that evidence is, but what I *do* know is that it relates to your brother's disappearance. Don't want to find Aiden?"

"Of course I do."

"Then don't let Max Montrose's good looks and charm fool you. You can be glamoured without any idea it's happening."

"I told you," Justin says.

"We go ahead as planned," Claudia says matter-of-factly. "Kayla and Poppy, as cleaning staff, you'll have full access to the mansion. The first phase is to go through everything you can get your hands on. Find out as much as possible. Report back everything — every letter, every phone bill. Send me everything you find, even if you think it's nothing."

"That's going to be hard since we're not allowed to have our phones on us while we're working," I tell her.

"You'll have to find a way around that," she says.

"If we get caught with our phones, we get fired," Kayla says. "Can we really risk that?"

Claudia frowns at the table. "You'll just have to steal any documents you think might be important and put them back later. Report back to me daily via the encrypted text app."

Just then, Claudia's phone pings. She takes it out of her

gigantic shiny black purse that's slightly worn around the edges and frowns.

"What is it?" asks Kayla.

Claudia just gets up and disappears into the closest bedroom — mine.

"This is nuts," I whisper to them. "We can't be part of this!"

Justin narrows his eyes at me. "Are you going against the Order?"

"No!" I take a breath. "I'm just scared we're going to end up *killing* someone!"

"That's kind of the whole point, Poppy," says Justin. "To rid the earth of vampire scum."

"And redistribute wealth," Kayla adds.

"These vampires hoard wealth over centuries while the rest of us have nothing," Justin says.

"Look at Claudia," Kayla says. "Her kid is sick, and she can't even afford to pay his medical bills while these vamps are living in their mansions. It's messed up!" She takes my hand. "We're just getting information, Poppy, that's all."

"Unless one of them comes at you, then you better be ready to shoot that fucker in the face," says Justin.

I shake my head at the ceiling, and Kayla squeezes my hand. "Poppy, you have to trust the Order."

"And what if I don't?"

"Didn't you *read* the Codex?" Justin sticks his finger into the pastry crumbs on his plate and then licks it.

Kayla runs a finger around the top of her coffee cup. "Poppy, the punishment for going against the Order is death."

Of course, somewhere in my mind I knew that getting involved with the Order was a bad idea, but it's only now I'm realizing just how bad of an idea.

Claudia walks back in and stands behind her chair. "There's been a change of plans."

Oh, thank god!

"Justin and Kayla didn't get hired."

"What?" Justin and Kayla say at the same time.

"Wait, what?" I ask.

"That was Henrietta. They have decided they only need a small staff, four instead of eight."

"And *we* didn't get picked?" Kayla looks like she's about to cry.

Claudia shakes her head and looks down at her phone. "They're only hiring Trix, Julio, Malik and Poppy."

Justin looks up from his crumbs. "So, what's the plan now? Because I really wanted to kill that son of a bitch."

Claudia shoots him a look and then turns to me. "It's all up to you, Poppy. Find the information we need about Max and the other members of the Fraternity. Their names, where and when they meet. You do whatever it takes." She drops her old iPhone into her purse. "And Poppy? I really do mean *whatever* it takes."

CHAPTER EIGHT

oppy

Employment Contract between Poppy St Clair and the Montrose Estate

In signing this contract, you agree to adhere to the following:

No phones outside of the guest quarters

Arrive for all shifts at least five minutes before they are due to start

A uniform of black pants and a white shirt or blouse must be worn at all times outside of staff quarters. Women may wear a black skirt no shorter than two inches above the knee.

All communication must go through James Truscott or Henrietta Pendleton. Never speak directly to Mr. Montrose.

No fraternizing with other staff members

No guests on the estate

No moving around the estate outside of working hours

No use of the pool except on Tuesday evenings between six and eight p.m.

Dinner will be served at six in the kitchen each evening. You will take all other meals in the staff quarters.

Mr. Montrose prefers staff members to stay on the estate during evenings when possible. If you need to leave the estate, please make sure you have permission from Ms. Pendleton or Mr. Truscott.

Any difficulty in maintaining these rules of employment will cause immediate termination of your employment.

DRIVING up to the estate under the bright sun of a Los Angeles Monday morning is an entirely different experience than arriving here by Uber on a Friday evening.

James buzzes me in at the gate, and I drive up the winding driveway in under a minute. When I reach the fountain, I check the map of the estate that was emailed to me and then drive down the side of the house, where I find a small parking area. A handful of cars are already parked, and I slip my cranked-out old Jetta onto the end next to a brand-new black SUV.

The time on my dash alerts me to the fact that I've only just made it on time. Grabbing my duffle bag from the backseat I lug it down a cobblestone path to what I hope is the right door for the staff entrance. I shove it open and find myself in a big bright kitchen filled with embossed white cabinets, huge marble countertops and dark wood flooring. I'm not much of a cook, but if I were ever going to have the urge to take up baking, this kitchen would make me do it.

I let out a little gasp before I realize I have an audience.

"Poppy. Nice of you to join us." James stands above a large dark wood kitchen table where my new co-workers are seated, stacks of papers in their hands.

James hands me a stack and gestures for me to sit in the empty chair next to Malik, the dark-skinned, very buff guy Trix couldn't keep her eyes off on Friday night.

"In your employment pack," James holds up more papers, "you'll find maps of the estate, contact sheets, and a contract and NDA to sign. There are specific rules that you must adhere to, or your contract will be terminated immediately. It's important for you to understand these rules before you sign and begin working here. I'll give you some time now to read it through and ask any questions."

Trix's hand shoots up.

"You don't need to raise your hand, but yes, Trix?"

"How will we communicate without our phones?"

"There are landline phones all around the estate, and you can use any of them to dial my cell, contact Henrietta or to call security in the case of an emergency."

Malik taps his pen over the contract as if he's unsure about signing. "What's this about Mr. Montrose preferring us to stay on the estate in the evenings?" he asks.

"We can't legally force you to be here, but it is a security issue to have people coming and going. We prefer you to stay on the estate, but permission can be granted as long as we know when you're leaving and coming back."

Malik's mouth twists like he's considering this carefully.

It makes no difference to me. I have nowhere to go, anyway.

"Malik, if you'd like to stay and chat after our meeting we can perhaps arrange something for your unique situation," James says.

Julio, the guy I talked to for twenty minutes about roses on Friday night, starts signing before he's even read anything.

The contract is straightforward, but I stare down at the tiny text of the NDA for what feels like ages.

"A few final things to understand before you sign," James says, handing me a pen. "Always go directly to Mr. Montrose's assistant, Henrietta or come to me with any queries or concerns. We both live on the estate, so we're never far away. *Never* speak directly to Mr. Montrose unless he speaks to you first."

My thoughts run back to Friday evening. I'm sure Trix spoke to him first, but had I? Had I spoken to him first when I barged into the theater to find my purse? I think I did, but that he invited me to sit, drink and watch movies with him all night suggests he wasn't mad about it.

I bite the end of my pen. James gives me a look and a little shake of his head.

"There is to be no fraternizing with other staff members or members of the household," James adds.

"What do you mean, *fraternizing*?" Trix asks.

"I think you *know* what it means," he says. "But for those who need it clearer, it means partaking in any activity of a sexual nature."

Trix makes a little strangled noise.

"That includes sexual activity with Mr. Montrose."

I make an internal strangled noise at the idea of sexual activity with Mr. Montrose.

If only!

After ten minutes of complete silence apart from the flipping of pages to read the full contract and NDA, we've all signed.

James talks through emergency evacuations and all the other boring things you need to know when you start a new job, and then he guides us out of the kitchen and down a cobbled path which leads to a small, whitewashed house hidden away behind palm trees and shrubs at the side of the mansion.

This is the first time in my life I'm going to live in a house, not just an apartment.

We walk into a small lounge room with three couches, a

TV and walls adorned with more Max, Johnny and Leopold Montrose movie posters in simple frames.

James shows Julio and Malik to their rooms and then opens another door a little way down. "Trix and Poppy, you're in here."

"We're sharing a room?" I ask, a little disappointed I won't have my own space.

"We're sharing a room!" Trix grins at me and wheels in her suitcase.

James' cool eyes settle on mine. "Mr. Montrose has decided that since the others won't be joining us, it would be a good time to renovate the other rooms of the staff quarters. It's beyond time for some new carpet, paint and furnishings."

Maybe I'll get my own room when the renovations are done.

"You have a little time left to settle in," says James. "Poppy, meet me in the kitchen at ten and I'll show you where everything is."

He closes the door, and I look around at the small but cozy room. Two single beds sit on each side of a small window that looks out over a hedge towards the garden. Matching tasseled lampshades sit on each of our nightstands, and above our beds are two framed posters, one from a Leopold Montrose movie, the other from a movie starring Johnny Montrose. A small desk sits under the window, and on the opposite wall is the smallest closet I've ever seen.

"Well." Trix puts her hands on her hips and eyes the closet. "It's not exactly what I pictured when they said I'd be living in a *mansion*. One guy has that whole three-story mansion to himself, and we're cramped down here like mice."

"At least mice get to go out at night," I say.

"The list of rules is intense, huh?"

I sit down on my bed. It's a little lumpy. "When we met Max at the party, he seemed so nice."

"Don't forget he *is* an actor. It's literally his job to make people think he's someone else."

"You know about actors?" I ask her. "Did you date one?"

"Three years of acting school."

"Yeah? So why are you working here and not starring in your own movies?"

"You might not believe this, but it's actually kind of hard to get into the movies. I mean, who knew, right?" She lets out a laugh, but she's clearly not fully over whatever happened to end her career before it began.

"And now you're a chef?"

She shrugs as if being a movie star's chef is no big deal. "I always loved food. I grew up in a home where food was everything. My mom was always making these epic dinners for the whole neighborhood. I was helping her in the kitchen before I could talk." She opens the closet and frowns into it. "So, when my acting career went to shit, I decided to go to culinary school and try all over again with a new dream."

"I can relate to the dreams not working out part," I say, opening my bag.

"What dreams died for you?"

"How long have you got?"

"Okay, start by telling me how you got into the glamourous life of cleaning Hollywood mansions."

"I moved out here about six months ago. I was cleaning hotel rooms in the mornings and working a bar in the evenings, but I had some friends, Kayla and Justin. They were here on Friday."

She nods in recognition.

"They work for La Luna, and they hooked me up with this job."

She starts throwing clothes out of her suitcase. "Where are those two?"

I look up at the poster of Leopold Montrose above my bed. He really looks like the spitting image of Max.

"Kayla and Justin? They didn't get hired. Max only wanted the four of us."

"Don't you mean *Mr. Montrose?*" She laughs, pulling a woolly scarf out of her suitcase, which she will most definitely not need in this heat. "What did you do before you moved here?"

"Same kind of thing back in Iowa. I used to work at my dad's pawnshop too."

"Oh god, I *love* vintage. Did you ever have clothing come in?"

I nod. "Uh huh, sometimes." I pull out a framed picture of me and Aiden and put it on my nightstand.

"Cute!" Trix leans over my shoulder. "Boyfriend?"

"Brother."

"Straight?"

"Bi."

"Available?"

"Missing."

"Missing?"

"That's why I came out to LA," I tell her. "He disappeared. I came here to find him."

She sits on the edge of her bed. "What are the police doing?"

"Nothing."

"Do you have any leads?"

I just give a noncommittal shrug.

"If there's anything I can do to help, you just let me know, okay? Internet research, stakeouts — I'm here for it."

I give her a smile. "Thanks, Trix."

· · ·

By 9:59, I'm mostly unpacked and waiting for James in the kitchen. He arrives exactly at ten.

"Right, let's get started," he says. He opens a cupboard at the back of the kitchen and pulls out a basket full of cleaning supplies and a very long duster and shoves them towards me.

"The vacuum cleaner is back there too for when you need it," he tells me.

I struggle with carrying everything and follow him through the kitchen and out into the mansion. "You've seen these rooms already." He sweeps an arm across the parlor and dining room. "This is where you'll start today. Over there," he gestures beyond the dining area, "is the guest bathroom, which also needs to be cleaned."

"James," I start. "This is a lot for one person. We were meant to be a crew of four, and now it's just me. How exactly do you expect me to do the work of four people?"

He lets out a resigned sigh. "I've completely reorganized the cleaning schedule. Usually, the cleaning staff would clean every room daily, but because it's just you, you'll be cleaning each room once a week. It is far from ideal. You'll need to do an exceptional job, and a quick dusting of each room on Saturday as well."

"I didn't notice Mr. Montrose's bedroom on my list."

He gives me an annoyed look. "Mr. Montrose doesn't allow anyone into his private suite."

"Oh? So, who cleans those?"

His eyes glaze over. "I do."

"Oh right, sure, okay."

He hands me a pile of paper, which I struggle to hold with all the cleaning supplies. "This is a list of everything that needs cleaning in each room. There will be extra tasks at times, also. If you do need anything at all, call me from one of the house phones. Just dial three and you'll reach me."

I get the feeling that James definitely does not want me to call him.

He disappears, and I struggle with my basket, duster and papers and take a few more steps into the parlor. It's such a beautiful room. So much light and so many beautiful things. The entire house is just incredible. Sure, I'm just the cleaner, but I think I might enjoy getting to spend my days in such a beautiful place.

The black kitten appears out of nowhere and begins winding around my legs.

"Kitty!" I drop everything I'm holding and crouch down to give her a pat. She purrs very loud for such a little thing. It's the most adorable purr I've ever heard in my life. "I wish I could pat you all day, but I have to clean your daddy's house."

She lets out a little mew and then wanders off like she totally understands me.

James' list is long and right up the top is dusting. I begin gently moving the heavy ornaments around—gold tigers, silver birds, empty vases, dusting under and around them. A pretty green glass vase catches my eye, and I think how nice it would look filled it with flowers from the garden and moved to the coffee table. But moving things around is not on the list and I really need to not fuck this up. I'm not under any illusion that I'll find anything here about a secret society of vampires, but if this really was the last place Aiden was seen, maybe I'll still find something here that will lead me to him.

As I dust and move more empty vases around, I realize there isn't a single plant in the house. No flowers, no pot plants, not even a cactus.

There's a lot to do in this room, but when I get to dusting the record collection, I can't help but take a little extra time exploring some of Max's favorite music. As my fingers tip toe across the titles, I find myself imagining him here in this room with his guests, listening to these records. I think of all the beautiful people he's spent time with here, all the beautiful women. A sick, jealous feeling hits me right in the gut and I let out a laugh. Of course he's been in here with beautiful women. He's a movie star! He's Max Montrose! What right do I have to be jealous of all the attractive women he's been with? I'm just a cleaner from Iowa.

I take a breath and try to remember why I'm here. This isn't about me and some crush I had on a movie star when I was younger.

This is, always has been and always will be about finding Aiden.

CHAPTER NINE

I THOROUGHLY DISLIKE the first few days with new staff members. Everyone gets lost and confused and the tension is palpable. That's why I much prefer to hand everything over to Henrietta and James and stay out of the way as much as possible.

I have everything I need in my private suite on the top floor of my mansion. A California king bed draped in plush green velvet sits in the center of my bedroom. A TV screen offers a cinematic experience from the comfort of my bed but can be slid away into the bed frame when not in use. The walk-in robe and ensuite ensure I'm always movie star ready. French doors separate my bedroom and my private parlor with its midnight blue velvet couches, a record player and walls filled with records, books, DVDs and videos. I also have a private kitchen and dining area, but even with everything I could possibly need and want, these rooms often feel like a prison. This *life* often feels like a prison. Where can I go? What can I do? Who can I trust?

I take a book from my nightstand, one I read over thirty years ago. Perhaps I will enjoy it again.

I lie down on the bed and stare at the words on the page, but I'm not reading. I'm thinking of Poppy. Just like I have done constantly for the last two days, I think of her soft lips and pale thighs and the way she's waking something within me that has been sleeping for so long.

I try to recall the last time I had such intense feelings, and my thoughts find Gertie, the girl who lived next door to me when I was only thirteen years old. With her wild red hair and even wilder heart, she never even knew she had mine. She exuded life. Always smiling, dancing, running through the streets, calling me to follow her, always saying what was on her mind. Like mine, her family didn't have two pennies to rub together, but she lived life like she had it all. When I ran away at fourteen to join a traveling acting troupe, it never occurred to me to miss my father. I had already been missing my mother for years, but it was Gertie that I found myself thinking of when I was missing home.

But Poppy is not like Gertie. Poppy is a little reserved, unsure of herself, but she is sexy as hell, and I want nothing more than to help her discover just how sexy and desirable she is.

I picture her downstairs right now, dusting my shelves in that short floral dress of hers. But of course, she'd be dressed in her work uniform. Perhaps I could change the uniform and take away the bizarre old-fashioned rule I came up with fifty years ago about how short a skirt should be. Perhaps I need to implement a new rule stating female staff must always wear short skirts around the mansion.

I throw the book over my face. Of course I would never.

But the idea of catching a glimpse of her in that dress again fills me with longing.

I take a deep, unnecessary breath and throw the book onto the floor. This is *my* house, and I don't need to hide up here fantasizing about some pretty girl with a short hemline dusting my shelves!

I take a quick look in the mirror. My shirt is a little crumpled and so I swap it for a new one. I run my hand through my hair. Dark strands fall over my forehead, and I add a little cream to get them to stay. When I feel I look fairly presentable, I make my way downstairs and try to think of a reason to run into her. But it is *my* house, and I don't need a reason to wander around aimlessly!

When I arrive in the parlor, she has her back to me, a duster hanging loose in one hand while her fingers run across my records. And while I am indeed disappointed not to find her in the floral dress, her black pants are tightly fitted and show off every curve.

Dear god.

She doesn't know I'm here. While the Sybline dulls some of my abilities, I still have the power to approach my victims without them knowing. Not that I need victims anymore. And Poppy would certainly *never* be my victim.

She places the duster onto the floor and pulls out an old Elvis record. She touches it so gently, turning it over to see the back. The gentleness of her touch does something to me.

Would she be that gentle with me? Is that how she would run her fingers through my hair or down my cheek? Is that how she would unbutton my shirt, gently sliding it over my shoulders and onto the floor? Would she be gentle as she unzipped my pants, pushing them down as she took my cock in her hand? Would she be gentle then? Or would she wrap her hand around me tight as she could, tugging on my manhood fast, hard and ravenous until I found my release?

This is insanity. I cannot be with a human woman, especially someone like Poppy. My bloodlust has dulled with the fake blood I've sustained myself on for years, but for how long? At any time I could lose my lab technician or supplier, and the insatiable need for blood would once again rule my life.

I couldn't put this beautiful, careful woman in danger.

She deserves something better than me. Better than my damned soul.

She turns around and notices me for the first time. The record slips from her fingers, and I flinch, resisting the urge to speed over there and grab it before it hits the floor. I'd bought that record in 1963 during Johnny Montrose's heyday, and it has sentimental value to me. It should be hidden away in my suite upstairs. She stumbles and then throws herself to the floor to catch it before it falls, thank goodness.

"I'm so sorry, Max—Mr. Montrose," she says, looking up at me. "It's just that this collection is incredible. I couldn't help taking a look." She's clearly flustered by my arrival, and to know I have this effect on her, well. It's quite wonderful.

She slowly stands, and I catch a glimpse of her white bra through the buttons of her blouse.

How I would rip that blouse off her. I wouldn't be gentle like her touch on my records. I'd be rough and hungry with her. I'd rip her clothes to shreds to get to her naked body, to feel every inch of her nakedness against mine. I'd rip her panties to pieces to get inside her.

I have an insatiable need to know what kind of panties she's wearing under her clothes. Is she wearing full cotton briefs? Or a sexy scrap of black lace?

It wouldn't matter to me. It wouldn't be on her long.

Now I'm the one who feels flustered.

She turns and slides the record back into its slot. "These records must be worth millions," she muses.

"They won't be worth anything if you put your fingerprints all over them." I know it's terribly rude. And the way her face drops when she looks back at me, I can see I've caused some hurt.

But it is better to hurt her a little now. Better for her to know her place, and for me to remember mine. Better to make her feel like this now than to get too close. Better to be rude and put her at a distance now instead of accidentally murdering her in a fit of passion later.

CHAPTER TEN

oppy

"*From tipping hundreds of dollars at restaurants to using the proceeds from his movies to start non-profit organizations to help animals, the homeless and the arts, Max Montrose is considered one of the nicest and most philanthropic movie stars of all time.*"
Max Montrose Wikipedia page

I pile my plate high with delicious looking salads Trix has left out for us in the kitchen. I balance a huge hunk of sourdough bread on top and then stomp down the cobblestones towards the staff quarters.

My encounter with Max has been replaying over and over in my mind all day. I'm mortified that he caught me going through his stuff (some spy I'm turning out to be!) and when I fell on the floor to try to save the falling record, I must have looked so ridiculous!

But mostly I'm just trying to figure out why he was so rude to me after how friendly he'd been with me on Friday night. It was like he was a completely different person.

I angrily take a bite of the bread and walk into the empty lounge room. A laugh drifts from an open door to my right, and I follow it out into a cute little outdoor area. Mismatched retro patio furniture sits under string lights hanging in the palm trees above. The sky is that pretty California pink that always makes my heart feel a little lighter. A reminder that even though it took Aiden going missing for me to do it, I made it out of my hometown. Trix, Julio and Malik are sitting around a bright pink table covered in beer cans and empty plates.

"Poppy!" Trix grins at me and gestures with a beer for me to sit on the orange plastic chair next to her. "You're going to love the grapefruit and soy chunk salad," she says, pointing to my plate.

"It sounds weird," says Malik, eyeing up a strange-looking chunk on his fork, "but I think it's changing everything I knew about food."

Trix laughs a little too loudly. "Oh, it's just a few little things I threw together."

Malik smiles back at her, and she giggles.

"You made the bread too, Trix?" asks Julio, taking a bite of what looks like half a loaf on his plate.

"Of course!"

"This is the best meal I've had in months." Julio tells her. He turns to me. "Beer?"

I'm not usually a beer drinker, but I could use something to take the edge off this big day. "Yes, thanks."

He reaches into the cooler by his side, grabs a beer, cracks it open and hands it to me. He hands Malik another soda. "Trix, do you need a top-up?"

"I'm good," she says, holding her can up at him.

"So how was your first day, Poppy?" Malik asks.

"Don't ask."

"The first day at a new job is always tough," Julio says. "It took me two hours just to sort through all the tools in the gardening shed."

"The security system is a disaster," Malik says. "When James told me it needed upgrading, I didn't think he meant upgrading from *videotapes*. It'll take weeks to upgrade."

I eat my salad as I consider this information. A weak security system is definitely the kind of thing I should tell Claudia about. But I need to tread carefully. I somehow need to figure out how to give the Order just enough information so they think I'm useful here, but not so much that I get fired from this job or get anyone killed.

"The gardens are a little unkempt," Julio says. "But it's going to be fun fixing them up. I spent most of the day weeding, but I'm excited about what I can do here. James wants me to tackle the tennis courts later this week."

"There's a tennis court?" I ask.

He nods. "It's down behind the annex. It's a little overgrown back there, but if I can get them cleared out, James says we can use them."

"But only between four and six on Tuesdays?" Trix waves her own slice of bread around.

"It's weird, right?" Julio says. "Just one guy lives here. I haven't seen him use the pool or even leave the house all day. What difference does it make if we use it?"

"It's so different from what it was like here on Friday," I say.

"We were guests on Friday," Trix reminds me. "Now we're the help."

"Speaking of the party," Julio starts, "what happened to the other cleaners and the handyman guy?"

"They didn't get hired," I tell him.

"At the party Max spent most of his time talking to James or Henrietta," says Malik. "But he was watching us the whole time. There's a reason the others didn't make the cut."

"What do you think was the reason?" Trix asks.

Malik puts his drink down. "That Justin guy gave off a weird vibe. He was too into himself. The girl he was with—"

"Kayla," I tell him.

"She was too into Justin, and they had toxic relationship written all over them."

"How did you know all that?"

He shrugs. "I'm good at figuring people out."

"Okay," Trix leans back in her chair and gives Malik a flirtatious look. "Do me."

He nods. "You're great at cooking, but you have other talents you feel need to be shared with the world. You're smart and talented, and while you're positive and hopeful about the future, you're also scared about not living up to your full potential."

Trix's mouth drops open. "Well. Shit."

Everyone is silent for a few moments. Me and Julio exchange looks like we hope he doesn't do us next.

"Impressive," I tell Malik. "You have a real skill."

Malik looks at me intensely. "Max was watching you more than the others, Poppy."

I let out a gurgling sound around a mouthful of grapefruit.

"Why would he be looking at me?"

"Why wouldn't he be looking at you?" Julio asks. "You're gorgeous."

"Uh, thanks?"

"Just to be clear," Julio continues, "I'm not hitting on you. I don't even bat for your team. But I can still appreciate an attractive woman, and Poppy, you're very attractive. Don't you think, Malik?"

Malik shrugs. "Sure."

"Thanks for the compliment, but I'm not delusional enough to think a movie star who could have literally any woman in the world would choose to look at me."

Julio rolls his eyes.

"And anyway, he was a total jerk to me today."

"What? Why? What happened?" asks Trix.

"He got upset with me for touching his records."

Trix giggles. "Oooh, he doesn't like other people touching his things. Imagine how possessive he'd be about his women!"

I'm not really into the idea of possessive men, but I can't stop my mind wandering into a scenario in which Max goes into a rage about another man touching me.

I take another swig of beer and finally start feeling the buzz kick in. "This dinner was wonderful, Trix."

"There's cake in the fridge for dessert. I'm still trying to figure out what Max wants to eat. He says he eats mostly plants, but what does that mean? Only plants? Sometimes he wants a steak? James was hardly around at all today, so I just winged it and went for salads, bread, soup and cake."

"Did he eat any of it?" I ask.

"Why wouldn't he eat it?" Trix gives me a weird look. "I mean, I didn't *see* him eat it, but James took plates of everything up to his suite on the third floor."

"What does he use that whole top floor for?" Julio asks.

I shrug. "Beats me. James cleans Max's top floor suite, so I'll never get to see what's up there."

"Oh," says Trix, wiggling her eyebrows, "I have a feeling you'll get to see what's up there, Poppy."

"Whatever," I tell her, rolling my eyes. "I'm not even interested in him."

"Not interested in a sexy, hot, rich movie star?" Julio asks. "Yeah, right."

"Fun to joke about, but don't forget about the rules," Malik says, like there is any chance in hell of me and Max *fraternizing*.

"No sexual relations with Mr. Montrose," Trix says in a bad British accent.

"Was that meant to be James or Henrietta?" Julio laughs.

"I thought you were an actor?" I ask with a laugh. "That accent was terrible!"

"Okay, wait. Give me a second. I'll try again." Trix clears her throat and this time she sounds exactly like Henrietta.

"Oh, woah!" Julio gasps. "That was perfect!"

They carry on laughing, trying out accents and talking about their day and the mansion, while I continue analyzing my brief encounter with Max in the parlor.

But the more I think about it, the more the memory starts to turn into a fantasy.

Instead of Max telling me off about the record, he grabs it out of my hands and gives me a dark look like he wants to devour me. He throws the record to the ground and then grabs my waist, his fingers pressing into me hard and strong. He pulls me towards him and kisses me so hard he's practically fucking me with his tongue.

"I want you," he growls into my ear once he's able to pull himself away from my lips for a moment. "Get naked and lie down on my couch."

It would be rude to say no, so I take a step back and unbutton my blouse, revealing my white lacy bra. Max looks at me like he's never seen breasts before.

"Bra off," he demands.

I take it off and he practically drools at my breasts. "Fuck, Poppy. You are the sexiest maid I've ever had." He steps towards me, placing his cool hands on my breasts, massaging gently and then pinching both my nipples at the same time, sending me into a frenzy.

"And I want to have you in every way," he adds.

His hands reach for the button on my pants and within seconds his finger is finding its way to my clit—

"Poppy?"

Trix's voice brings me back to the present.

"You okay? You look at little—hot."

"I'm just a bit warm out here," I tell her. "I think I'll go take a shower.

And when I'm all alone in the shower I get back to my fantasy.

I'm naked on Max's couch while he towers above me in his suit pants and shirt, giving me a dark, smoldering look like he can't wait to make me his.

He unbuttons his shirt and then slides it over his shoulders, revealing sexy, strong, ripped muscles that I'm desperate to run my fingers over. And then he slides his pants off until he's naked before me.

"I'm going to fuck you now," he tells me as I rub fast and hard on my clit.

I'm so fucking close.

I open my legs for him, and he grins.

"I'm going to make this part of your duties," he tells me, settling in between my legs. "I'll get James to add it to the list. Every day after you've cleaned my mansion, you'll open your legs for me and let me fuck you as hard as you can take it."

Holy fuck!

He places his cock at my entrance and grins at me. "Don't worry, I'll be gentle... at first."

I rub my clit faster and harder and my free hand shoots to the shower curtain. I grip it as my body stiffens and prepares for the release.

Max's cock slams into me in my mind and a burst of pure pleasure hits me, starting in my clit and then rushing through my entire body.

I gasp and then sink to the shower floor, smiling to myself.

It's not the first time I've masturbated to Max Montrose, and I doubt it will be the last, but it is the first time it's felt quite so *real.*

CHAPTER ELEVEN

M ax

Poppy St Clair's Domestic Services Schedule*
   Monday: parlor, dining room, first-floor guest bathroom
   Tuesday: library, stairs, hallways
   Wednesday: banquet room, war room
   Thursday: guest bedroom 1, 2, guest bathrooms all
   Friday: basement bathroom, foyer, theater
   Saturday: deep cleaning, various
   Sunday: off
   **Subject to change*

FOR DAYS I agonize over my encounter with Poppy in the parlor. I should have turned, walked back in and apologized immediately. It's not her fault that I find her so attractive, that I can't look at her without fantasizing about ripping her panties to shreds. She didn't deserve to be treated so appallingly.

I'm torn between believing that it is better if she thinks I'm a cad and hoping it's not too late for my apology.

I had always tried to be somewhat of a gentleman. Before I was turned, I always sent flowers and gifts to the women who so graciously shared my bed. Of course, after I was made into a vampire, I went through my murderous phase, all vampires do, but even then, I tried very hard not to kill the innocent. I always went after the worst of humanity I could find. They call this the vegetarianism of the vampire world, and it's very common among those rare few of us who still have some grip on our humanity.

The way I acted last Monday was quite out of character for me and I did not want to repeat it. And so, I stayed in my suite for a week with only Callie for company. I wallowed in my satin pajamas, watched old movies in bed, replied to emails relating to my non-profit activities, all while images of Poppy's gorgeous ass in the air by my pool refused to leave my mind. Her white bra, her soft curves, her hazel eyes that just exude light and life. It's been like watching a rerun on repeat for days on end.

I eventually force myself to shake out of it, to stop acting like a love-sick teenager mortified by one stupid turn of phrase said to their crush.

I will have to find a way to be civil to Poppy, or I will have to fire her. It's the only thing for it.

I shower and dress in a freshly pressed dark blue shirt and black trousers.

"Make your apology and then keep your distance," I tell my reflection in the gold-gilded bathroom mirror before making my way towards the library where I know she will be working this morning.

The library is where I keep all the books that make me

look like an intellectual. I've read all of them. I've had plenty of time, but I have secretly always preferred the cheap crime and western paperbacks kept in my private suite.

The door is open, but I pause at the entrance. Poppy must have only just arrived herself, because she places her basket of cleaning products down in the center of the room and lets out a little sigh as she takes in the enormity of my collection.

My ego inflates at the idea that she is impressed with the endless dark wood shelves filled with classics, first editions and obscure collector's items.

Still unaware of me, she walks past the antique desk and then runs a hand across the old oak research table. She nearly trips over one of the dark burgundy velvet couches. I smile, enchanted by her sweet clumsiness. She rights herself and then steps towards the shelves, running her fingers across the spines of my books. Eventually, she pulls one out and begins to read.

I'm aware that I have been watching her for too long without announcing my presence, but I'm enthralled by her movements. The way her fingers dance gently over my things, the way she slowly and carefully turns each page.

She wears a looser pair of pants today, keeping her figure hidden from my lustful gaze. I also notice the outline of a lace camisole under her button-up blouse. I wonder if she realized after our moment in the parlor that her blouse had shown more than she intended.

Perhaps I need to add a new rule that undershirts are not permitted. No bras either while we're at it. Or maybe I should just walk right over to her right now, rip off her blouse, pull that undershirt off with my teeth, destroy that bra with my bare hands. Hide her clothes from her so that she must clean my house in nothing but whatever panties I haven't torn to shreds yet, and I have plans to tear every single pair of her panties to shreds—

Jesus Christ.

I try to shake it off, but visions of Poppy dusting my shelves in nothing but a pair of black lace panties dance in my mind as she continues to look down at the book, her lips moving slightly as she reads.

Dear god, those lips!

I need to get a hold of myself. I need to apologize. I need to get out of here.

"I wasn't aware I was paying you to read my books." My tone is gruff, and I immediately regret it. I came here to apologize, not make things worse!

She jumps, dropping the book to the floor. She looks up at me with those damn doe eyes. "I'm so sorry, Mr. Montrose," she flounders. "It's just that your library—" she blushes as her eyes flit around the shelves and then land back on me. "I'm obsessed with it."

I'm obsessed too, but not with books! I want to tell her. And then I want to bend her over my antique writing desk, rip those loose pants off and fuck her to kingdom come.

I walk towards her, unable to stop myself from closing all this damn space between us.

"Poppy," I say, closing the gap a little more until we're only a few feet away from each other. "If you can't control yourself around my things, perhaps you are not the right person for this job."

I don't mean it. I don't even know why I am saying it! But perhaps firing her is truly the best thing. I can get back to a life where I'm not thinking about getting this gorgeous woman naked every ten seconds, and she can be free to find and fall in love with a human man and live a normal, happy life.

She bites her lip, and I hope to god that I haven't made her almost cry with my outburst. That was definitely not my intention. I must find a way to keep her at a distance without being such an ass!

But no. It's clear from the way I continue to step towards her even now that I cannot keep away from her. If I can't stop myself from being near her, the only hope I have is that she hates me so much *she* stays away from *me*.

She bends down to pick up the book, and I catch a quick glimpse down the front of her undershirt. It's nothing, just a tiny triangle of pale skin between her breasts. It's just an inch of her skin, and yet I feel like I'm on fire. An unusual feeling for such a cold dead creature as myself.

She places the book back on the shelf and steps back. "It won't happen again."

"You keep saying that." I take another step forward. By the flush on her chest, I can tell our proximity is affecting her just as much as it is me. "And yet these things keep happening."

I want her, and I can tell from her flush, her elevated heart rate, the way her eyes widen, that she wants me too.

Vampires are not mind readers. We don't have to be. We are simply incredibly observant. And right now, my observation is that it would take very little for me to make her mine in every sense of the word.

I lean into her, my lips just inches from her neck and inhale. Her scent is intoxicating. Not just the berry shampoo or body wash she uses, but the sweet perfume that emanates from between her legs makes me want her naked immediately. I want my tongue on her, I want to fucking *taste* her. *Now.*

I exhale, my breath caressing the tendrils of her reddish-brown hair, and I can tell from the way her breath hitches that all I would have to do is ask.

But no. This is too complicated for so many reasons and much too dangerous for us both.

My hand moves of its own accord and sweeps a strand of hair from her flushed cheek to behind her ear. A small gold heart-shaped earring sits in her earlobe, and although she's spectacular in every way, it's the earring that sets my own pulse ablaze. This dainty, tiny thing that she has chosen to wear to work today, even though no one would notice it.

No one but me.

It's the perfect moment to lean in and kiss her. If I kiss her, it would be mere moments before I slam the door shut and have her on my desk, maybe the research table, or perhaps I could sit her on my lap and fuck her in my favorite reading chair—

Get a grip, man!

I take a deep breath, lean in and whisper into her ear, "Get back to work, Poppy."

And then I force myself to take my leave.

CHAPTER TWELVE

oppy

Dearest Leo,

Only you could do justice to the part of Gatsby! If this old thing is ever turned into a moving picture, you must play him!
With warmest regards,
Your friend F

As soon as I get back to my room after my shift, I throw myself onto my bed and let out a groan.

Trix looks up at me from her phone. She's sitting on the floor beneath her bed, which is covered with clothes that won't fit in the closet. Every night before she goes to sleep, she piles them onto the floor, and then when she wakes up, they go back on the bed. "Good day?" she asks.

"The worst!" I throw off my blouse and un-tuck my

undershirt that it's way too hot to be wearing now but seemed like a good idea this morning when it was cooler.

"What happened?"

"Max Montrose happened!"

"What did he do now? Did you touch his *things* again?" She raises an eyebrow at me over her phone.

"It's a bit hard not to touch his things when I'm supposed to *clean* them!"

Trix puts her phone down, giving me her full attention. "Okay. Spill."

"I'm in love with his library. The place is incredible. I've never been in a room so perfect. Whenever I'm in there, I feel like Beauty in the Beast's mansion!"

"Okay, I'm coming with you next time you have to clean in there."

"I was just having a little look around and found a first edition of *The Great Gatsby*."

"Oh, no way! I love that book."

"Me too! And it was *signed!* With a note to his great-grandfather, Leopold." I point to the movie poster above my bed.

She looks at the poster like she's seeing it for the first time. "Jeez, I never realized how much of a hottie his great-granddaddy was. Yum!"

"So then he comes in and sees me reading the book."

"Did you get in trouble?" she grins.

"He said he'd fire me if I couldn't keep my hands off his things!"

"He's got it bad for you."

I ignore her. "I can't lose this job."

"Poppy, you might not want to hear this, but it sounds like the problem is you."

"What?"

"You only get in trouble when you're doing something

you're not supposed to be doing. So just do what you *are* supposed to be doing."

"Great advice, thanks," I groan.

"I wonder when he last had sex."

"Trix!"

"Well, he rarely leaves the estate, right? He hasn't been seen in public for years. The most recent photo of him online was from eight years ago."

"Just because he doesn't go out much doesn't mean he can't invite people over. I'm sure he has plenty of women he can call."

"He's got that vibe though, hasn't he? All tense and itchy like he needs a scratch?"

I pick up a pillow and throw it at the poster above my bed, pretending that Leopold Montrose's face is Max's.

"Looks like he's not the only one who's feeling itchy."

There's no point denying it. It's been nearly a year since Danny and I last had sex, and it wasn't even that good. I'm tense and itchy too. And Max whispering in my ear to "get to work, Poppy" didn't have the effect of my boss about to fire me, but my boss about to stick his tongue down my throat, or in my ear, or anywhere he damn well pleased.

And if he had, I would have gladly let him. I would have let him throw me against the bookshelves and do whatever he wanted with me.

I feel warmth spreading through me at the thought of it.

But he didn't ravage me amongst his first editions. He just walked out.

My phone pings. It's Claudia wanting another update.

Max Montrose is a big, sexy jerk! I nearly type back, but don't.

I've been supplying her with random updates this last week. I took a stack of old bills and letters from a dusty drawer in one of the guest rooms, took photos of all of them and then returned them the next day. I have been feeding them to her slowly, one each day. They are incredibly boring and are all over three years old. The last one I sent was a bill for a plumber who fixed a pipe four years ago.

I type back, "Nothing today, sorry!" and close my phone.

"Why don't you go for a swim?" Trix suggests. "Get it out of your system. You still have one more hour before pool time is up."

"Actually, that sounds perfect." I pull my bag out from under my bed and quickly find my cherry red bikini that I didn't even bother to unpack. "Want to join me?"

She points to her damp hair. "Just got out. The pool is heavenly, though."

I don't waste any time. I change into my bikini, grab a towel, slip into my slides and head to the pool.

When I get there, I take a moment just to pause and enjoy the view. It really is so incredibly beautiful here. The marble tiles beneath my feet, the mansion above me, the gardens all around, the early evening sun shining over the city far below. It's everything Hollywood dreams are made of. I close my eyes, take a deep breath and when I open them again, I pretend for a moment that this is all mine.

I imagine me and Max sitting together on the sun loungers by the pool drinking cocktails James has made for us as we watch the sun go down. We laugh at some private shared joke only we think is funny and then slide into the pool together. His hands dip into the water, reaching for the ties at the sides of my bikini and—why the hell am I thinking about him like this when he's been such a prize jerk?!

I slip off my towel and walk around to the pool steps, slowly lowering myself into the water. It's so cooling and relaxing on my skin after the day I've had — no, the *week* I've had.

I've cleaned hotel rooms before, but the expectations here

are intense. My arms are exhausted from dusting chandeliers, my feet are aching from being on them all day, and my brain hurts from trying to figure out Max Montrose's deal.

I take long, slow strokes across the water and I immediately start to feel better. It's as if the water is washing off this day, washing away Max's bad mood and harsh words. It's just me and the water.

"Poppy!"

I swim to the edge of the pool and look up to see James standing over me holding my towel.

"Pool time is over," he says shortly.

"What?" I check my watch. "No, it's not. I still have another forty-five minutes!"

"Mr. Montrose has changed the pool times."

"Since when?" I pull myself out of the water and scowl up at the mansion.

"Since now."

I wrap myself in the towel. "Seriously? What is his problem?"

James just shakes his head. "Please return to the staff quarters. I'll type up an official notice of the new pool times and get it to you as soon as possible."

"What's the point? He'll just change them again!"

"Mr. Montrose has his quirks," James begins, ushering me away from the pool. "But he pays us well."

"He might pay you well," I say. "But I'm not getting much more than minimum wage by the time La Luna takes its cut."

"I'll ask you to remember that free accommodation in the Hollywood Hills is not to be sniffed at," he says.

I throw my arms in the air and walk off without responding.

CHAPTER THIRTEEN

ax

WHEN POPPY DROPS her towel by the pool, revealing nothing but a skimpy red bikini, my teeth and cock ache in a way that lets me know just how much trouble I'm in.

My earlier attempt at an apology became a moment of strangled sexual tension in which I nearly kissed her and then told her off as if *she* was the one in the wrong after *I* had misused my position of authority over her!

She slips into the water and, dear god she is a thing of beauty as she swims so gracefully up and down my pool.

All I want is to run down there, throw off my clothing and join her. I want to rip that bikini off her luscious body and caress every inch of her, grab her ass and wrap her legs around me, fuck her in the water until she screams my name into the evening sky.

A glass of real blood would fix me, but I have none in the

house. I throw back a glass of Sybline, but it doesn't quite hit the spot.

I call James.

"Yes, sir?"

"Get Poppy out of the pool."

"Why, sir?"

"She's ruining my view!" I snap at him.

"Sir, if I may—"

"You may not."

I hang up the phone, watch as he escorts a very irate Poppy out of the pool and then call him back.

"Apologies, James. Yes, of course you may. What was it you wanted to say?"

"You seem to be out of sorts this last week. Not your usual self. If I may say so. Is there anything wrong?"

"I apologize for my shortness. I have just been—" There is no use lying to James. He may look to be in his thirties, but he has worked for me for seventy years now, ever since the Fraternity forced him into my employ after the uprising. He knows me better than anyone.

"I'm quite affected by the girl," I admit.

"Ah, I see. Can I get you anything? Have a Donna or two brought up, perhaps?"

I feel sick at the idea of being with any woman who isn't Poppy. "No, thank you. I'll—I'll be alright. Perhaps I just need some time."

I pace my room and eventually realize there is nothing else for it.

I lock myself in my ensuite and run a hot shower.

My cock is already firm, but as I step under the water and think of Poppy in that goddamn bikini my cock springs to its full girth. I grip myself with one hand and slam my other hand onto the tiles.

Fucking Poppy!

I imagine summoning her to my room. James brings her up to my bedroom. She steps inside, nervous and unsure. Those doe eyes so pure and confused about why she's been brought to me.

"What are you wearing?" I ask her.

"My bikini," she says innocently.

"Take it off," I demand.

She blinks at me.

"Now."

"I need help," she says, turning around.

I pull the strings around her neck and her back and her top falls to the ground.

She gasps as I run my hands over her naked back. My hands run down to her waist and her skin feels so fucking soft and warm.

"Hands on the sideboard," I tell her.

"The what?"

I guide her, my hands on her waist, my cock pushing into her ass, towards the sideboard. Then I take her hands and put them on the wood.

"Keep them there," I tell her.

I run my hands over her perfect breasts, and I know I'm close.

I pull her hips back to where I want them and then untie the strings at her hips. The cherry red material falls and she's completely naked.

I can feel my release coming as I pump myself harder and faster.

"Open your legs," I tell her.

She does as I tell her and I slide my fingers over her entrance. She's dripping for me, and I know I'm about to come.

Jesus, fucking why can't I get to the good part?

I push two fingers inside her. She's warm, tight and so

fucking wet. I come, my seed spraying all over the tiles while I groan and yell her name.

~

I FEEL BETTER for approximately half an hour, and then I go back to sulking in my bed while watching MacGyver reruns.

AROUND TWO A.M. I get out of my pajamas, dress in a shirt and pants and return to the scene of the crime, the library. I find the book that Poppy was enthralled by—a first edition of *The Great Gatsby*. It was given to me by the author. I barely remember the interaction as I was full of drugs and drink at the time, as I was most nights in those days.

I find myself giving the book a good sniff, as if Poppy's scent will still be on it. It isn't.

Taking the book, I walk through the mansion, out through the kitchen and towards the staff quarters. When I get to her room, I'm unsure of what to do. She's just on the other side of this door, and part of me wants to kick it down and run to her. But I won't go into her room uninvited. That's not a vampire thing, it's a gentleman thing.

I place the book down at the side of the door and hope she sees it when she wakes.

I wander back into the mansion, down the stairs and into the theater. I can't walk in here now without thinking of my evening with Poppy. Perhaps I should have made love to her then and there, before I acted like such a buffoon. We could have had one beautiful evening together. I would have sent her a gift the next day, and then had Henrietta explain to her that I no longer required her services. The coward's way to deal with such strong emotions, but I never claimed to be anything less when it came to matters of the heart.

I choose a silent movie, not one of mine, and I'm only a few minutes in when an alarm pierces through my ears. The alarm hasn't sounded in years, and it takes me a second to realize what it means.

Someone has broken into the estate!

I run at speed out of the theater and up the stairs. I almost knock James off his feet as we meet in the hallway.

"What's going on?" I demand.

"I don't know!"

I run as fast as I can to the security office, and my eyes flick across the screens showing footage from cameras around the mansion. "I don't see anything."

"It must be a false alarm," James says.

Sybline dulls my vampire senses, but not completely, and right now, I'm very aware that something is wrong.

I run out of the office and through the house.

"Sir!" James calls back. "There's nothing out there!"

His words don't ring true. I let my instinct take over and run into the parlor, through the French doors, down the stairs, past the pool and into the garden. Sybline makes me slower, but I'm still *fast*. Faster than any regular human should be. As I jump over a bench and stomp a flower bed, I say a silent prayer that my new staff members are all tucked up and safe in the staff quarters, remembering their instructions to stay inside in the case of an alarm.

When I reach the bottom of the garden, I stop and pause, letting my excellent hearing and sense of smell take over. I can hear every rustle of a leaf, smell every flower, and I sense the intruder is somewhere down by the back fence.

And I can smell... *dog?*

I hear James and Malik running towards me, and I catch Poppy's sweet berry scent from somewhere behind them.

"Get back!" I yell.

"Sir!" James calls.

"Mr. Montrose!" Malik calls out.

I turn, and my eyes are drawn straight to Poppy's.

"Poppy! Get back inside. Now!" I yell out to her.

I'm so busy worrying about her, I forget I'm the target.

The sound of a gunshot rings out, and then another, and it all happens in slow motion. A bullet enters my stomach, and a second blasts through Malik's shoulder. We both hit the ground, and I hear a woman scream.

Poppy.

CHAPTER FOURTEEN

Poppy

I SCREAM as the shots ring out, and both Max and Malik go down.

I start to run towards them, but Trix suddenly appears and holds me back. "There's a shooter out there, Poppy!"

I wriggle out of her grip. "Call an ambulance!" I break free and run towards Max.

"I'm going after the intruder!" James calls. He runs into the bushes at the edge of the estate, and I'm left alone with two bleeding men.

"Shit! Shit! I don't know what to do!"

"Help Malik," Max tells me, clutching his stomach.

"But you're—"

"I'm *fine*," he says through gritted teeth. "Malik might not be."

I do as he says, and instinct, or maybe just everything I've learned from watching way too much crime TV, kicks in. I pull the tie out from the pink satin robe I somehow managed to throw on over my shorts and cami set and tie it around the top of Malik's arm.

"I don't know what I'm doing," I say, trying to act calm. "But I think it's just a flesh wound. Just your arm. You're not hit anywhere else, are you?"

Malik shakes his head. "I don't think so."

Max coughs blood as he writhes on the grass.

"Max! Fuck!" I look over at Trix, who's standing there in shock. "Trix, I need you with Malik!"

She shakes her head at me. "I'm not good with blood!"

"Well, too bad, Malik needs you!"

She seems to realize there's no choice and runs towards him. "Malik," she says, grabbing his hand and squeezing it. "You're going to be okay. The ambulance is on the way."

I pull off my robe, scrunch it up and hold it over the wound on Max's stomach.

"You don't have to do this," he says, blood pouring out of his mouth.

Max Montrose is dying, and I can't do anything!

Oh fuck. Fuck fuck fuck!

Oh god. This whole thing is my fault. This had to have been the Order.

I think of Justin back at the apartment talking about how much he wanted to kill vampires.

Two innocent people have been shot, and it's all my fucking fault!

Fuck!

"Poppy," Max gurgles, and I press his wound more firmly.

"What can I do? Tell me what to do!"

"Get me inside. Before the ambulance arrives."

"You need the ambulance."

He shakes his head. "No. No doctors."

"You'll die!" Tears fall from my eyes, one dropping onto his chest. He's been such a dick, but I don't want him to die!

"Listen to me." He reaches out and puts a shaky hand on my cheek. "If you get me inside, I won't die, but if you take me to a hospital, I might."

"What are you talking about?"

"Trust me," he coughs.

The sound of an ambulance in the distance spurs me into action.

I look over at Trix.

"I think Malik is going to be okay," she says shakily.

"I have to take Max inside," I tell her.

"What? Why?"

"I don't know, it's just what he wants."

"Poppy, what the hell?"

I put Max's arm around my neck and help him up, still holding his wound with my robe. He somehow gets upright, but as he does, more blood pours out of his wound.

He puts a little weight on me, but I can tell he's holding back.

"Just lean on me," I tell him. "I can take it."

He gives me a little more of his weight, and I don't know how I do it, but I eventually manage to get him into the parlor and drop him down on the couch. The very expensive cream velvet couch, which is already getting soaked through with blood.

The kitten appears out of nowhere and lets out the tiniest worried mew.

"Lock the door. Close the blinds," Max says.

I do as he tells me, trying not to think about what will happen next.

"You need a doctor!" I yell at him when he coughs up a little more blood.

He shakes his head, pulls my robe away and throws it

onto the rug, staining it with more blood. He rips open his shirt, revealing an incredibly ripped chest and a bloody hole in his stomach.

"Max!" I rush over to him, picking up the robe to hold it back to his stomach, but he pushes it away.

"I just need to—" He sticks his fingers into the wound, and I cringe, but I can't look away. He reaches deeper into the wound and then pulls out a bullet, throwing it onto the floor.

He falls back onto the couch, and I look at the bullet. I recognize it immediately. A silver bullet. It's one of the Order's, and once again I realize. This is all my fucking fault.

I should have done something. I should have stood up to the Order. Told them how insane they sounded, tried to make them understand *vampires aren't real*! I should have gotten far, far away from Justin, Kayla and Claudia. I should have contacted the police and told them about the Order and its messed-up ideas about killing vampires!

And then something strange happens. Max's wound starts healing over. The open skin that was there just a moment ago is closing up and then, within less than a minute, it's fully healed.

"What the—?" I begin. But I already know.

Max Montrose really is a vampire.

CHAPTER FIFTEEN

M_{ax}

"HUMANS MUST NOT KNOW that vampires exist. After feeding, vampires must immediately glamour their victims, making them forget the incident altogether. A failure to do this will result in the Fraternity having to seek out the victim and complete the task. A hefty fine will be placed upon the vampire who is unable to do their duty."

The Fraternity of the Everlasting Rose Handbook, page 87

POPPY'S MOUTH hangs open as she stares at the way my skin is healing over. Of course, it's nice to have her eyes on my naked torso, but I would have preferred her to see me with my shirt off in different circumstances.

I've lost quite a bit of blood, and I feel a little lightheaded, but I'm healing.

If it wasn't for the Sybline, I never would have bled so much. I knew that without real blood I was weaker, but I didn't realize just how weak until now.

A shot like this should have given me just a moment of pause, not resulted in my blood all over the lawn. I should have been able to pull the bullet out before anyone even saw me do it. It would have instantly healed and looked like nothing but a graze. I should have been able to walk away as if nothing had happened.

But I'm not so strong right now and judging by how bad I still feel even now the bullet is out, it may take hours for me to fully heal from this.

Fucking Order and their silver bullets.

Silver won't kill us, but it can slow us down. If I hadn't been able to get the bullet out, I'd have lost even more blood. I wouldn't have died, but silver poisoning can occur if silver is left within a vampire's flesh for too long and it can be rather uncomfortable.

It almost happened to me once. A round of silver bullets hit me after a night out at a club in West Hollywood shortly after I was first made. I lay in an alley for a week before a friend from the Fraternity found me.

It is rare for a vampire to be attacked like this. The last time this sort of thing was happening was during the uprising in the fifties. But that was vampire against vampire, vampire against fae, and it wasn't vampires or fae I could sense out by the back fence tonight, it was fucking wolves. Wolves who once fought alongside us, but for some reason unknown to me, now see *me* as their enemy.

I could have pulled the bullet out of myself on the grass, but I couldn't let Trix and Malik see me heal.

It was easier to have Poppy help me. I will glamour her to forget this as soon as I have the strength.

She stares at me now, her hazel eyes wide, and I realize

for the first time that she's dressed in nothing but cotton sleep shorts and a delicate camisole. Her nipples stand at attention beneath the thin fabric. My cock twitches, and I wince. She gasps, and I hope she thinks I'm in pain from the gunshot, not because I can't look at her without wanting to rip the poor excuse for clothes she's wearing off her perfect body.

"What just happened?" she asks, running a bloody hand through her hair.

"I'm—" I begin. "Well. You saw."

She just stares at me some more.

"I'm immortal," I tell her as Calliope jumps on my lap and begins to purr.

"What?"

"I can't die."

"I know what immortal means," she snaps like I've just insulted her intelligence. "What *kind* of immortal?"

I narrow my eyes at her. "Most people run away screaming at this point. But I'm glad you're not, because I don't have the energy to chase you down and wipe your mind."

"You can wipe minds?"

"In a way." I don't mention that the Sybline actually dulls that ability and now that I've been hurt, I won't be able to even try to glamour her for at least a good few hours.

"What are you?"

I give Callie a little chin scratch, and she kneads my leg. "Vampire," I sigh. What does it matter if I tell her when she won't remember any of this later?

She shakes her head in disbelief. "I don't believe you."

"No? How do you explain this?" I pull my shirt wide open and show her the place where my wound was. I run my hand over it, pushing away some of the blood, tensing my muscles in the childish hope she notices my sculpted abs. "I'm already healed."

"You can't be a vampire."

"Oh? And why not?"

"You go out in the sun!" she exclaims. "You eat normal food! You drink *wine*! You're not, you can't be. I don't believe you."

"Honestly, it's better if you don't believe me."

"How do you go outside? How do you eat *carrots*?"

"You have two choices," I say, glaring at her now.

She folds her arms over her bloodied and very see-through top.

Dear god, if I had the strength!

"You can promise me right now that you will tell no one what you saw here tonight or what I am. I will know if you're lying." This is true. Even on Sybline, my intuition is heightened far above human capabilities.

"What's the other choice?"

Why the hell am I even pretending to give her a choice?

"I can come to your room later tonight when I'm feeling a little better, and I'll glamour you into thinking you saw nothing tonight. You'll think you stayed in your room, scared of the siren. You'll continue to think I'm just a regular human."

She flushes a little, and I wonder if the idea of me coming into her room later appeals to her as much as it does to me.

"There's nothing regular about you," she says.

The corners of my lips quirk at that.

"I just want the truth. Tell me how you can be so… *human*."

"Poppy."

Dear god, I love her name on my lips!

"This is a conversation for another time. I'm a little tired. I need to rejuvenate." I probably should have said sleep.

"If you glamour me into forgetting all this, there won't be another time."

I sigh. "Fine. What do you want to know?"

"How can you eat food?"

"Just because I don't need to eat food doesn't mean I don't enjoy it from time to time. Humans eat plenty of food that isn't just for sustenance, but enjoyment. We do the same."

"What's with the wine?"

"It's synthetic blood created to taste like wine."

"You don't drink human blood?"

"Not usually."

But how I would drink hers right now if she offered! Her sweet blood would bring me back to perfect health and strength in moments, and it would give her that feeling of divine ecstasy so many humans are drawn to us for.

Within seconds we would be ripping our clothes off. My cock would be filling her within minutes.

My gaze must be intense because she swallows.

"How are you able to go into the sunlight?"

I consider carefully whether I should give this one away. But there is no other way. I must glamour her later, for my safety and hers. What does it matter if she knows all my secrets?

"Lizard juice."

She lets out a laugh. "Lizard juice?"

I nod. "Lizard blood, actually. That's just what we call it."

"You all just go around drinking the blood from lizards?"

"Not all lizards. And no. The lab that creates the Sybline also creates a serum made from lizard blood we can inject daily."

"Why are you telling me all this?"

"You asked." I narrow my eyes at her. "And besides, I'm going to glamour you later."

She takes a breath like she's about to tell me something and then thinks better of it.

I lift Callie, put her on the couch and then stand up, walking towards Poppy. I expect her to flinch or back away or even just *run*, but she doesn't.

"You're not frightened of me," I consider, taking another step forward.

She shakes her head. I can hear her pulse running a little faster with every step I take in her direction, but it's not from fear. My abilities are still strong enough for me to know that.

"Why not?" I ask.

"*Should* I be frightened of you?" She blinks those gorgeous hazel doe eyes of hers. "Are you going to hurt me?"

I wish I could tell her no, but the way I feel around her is too much. She makes the monster inside me ravenous for sex and blood in a way I've kept dulled for too long.

"Poppy, thank you. For tonight. Please don't share this information with anyone before I'm strong enough to glamour you."

"What will happen if I do?"

I close the space between us. I feel the urge to kiss her forehead, her cheek, and then her soft lips. But I expect I have blood all over my face, and I've just told her I'm a vampire. This is not the right moment for a first kiss.

There will not be a first kiss, you imbecile! There can't be any kisses!

I ignore my inner monologue and lean into her, the scent of her sweet skin, her berry shampoo driving me wild even in my weakened state. I am weak, but I could still find the energy to make love to her if she only asked. I place my lips close to her ear like I did only hours earlier in the library, and her breath hitches. Oh, how I enjoy the way her body reacts to my closeness. "I don't think you will," I whisper.

Her pulse races, but she doesn't move, and I know she wants this too. Or at least, she *thinks* she wants this. The idea of us is sexy as hell, but the reality of us is impossible.

I take a step back. I must stop playing this dangerous game. Especially now that she knows what I am.

But she's not pulling back. She stays in place, staring at me with those big wide eyes that draw me into her. She bites her lip and looks down at my bare chest. I don't need my full vampire powers to know what she's thinking. *She wants me.* And I think that now that she knows I'm a vampire, she may want me even more.

Fuck. This is even worse.

I've been playing with her, telling myself I will glamour her so nothing in this conversation even matters. But now that she knows, and she's still looking at me like *that*, I'm not sure that I want her to forget.

"If you tell anyone, I'll make sure you never tell anyone else." I don't want to scare her, but sometimes fear is what keeps people alive, and she could use a little of that when it comes to me.

Her eyes flicker with something, not fear, something more like sadness or disappointment that this night isn't going to end with us naked in my bed together.

If she's disappointed in that, I am truly devastated.

She nods and then turns, walking out of the parlor and into what's left of the night.

I want to reach out to stop her, to take her hand, to take her in my arms, to kiss her, to give her what she wants, what *I* want. Instead, I lock the door behind her and watch her gorgeous behind walk all the way back to the staff quarters.

She knows what I am, and she is not afraid.

I fall back on the bloodied couch as Callie licks some of the blood from my hand.

"What are we going to do about her?" I ask.
Callie purrs extra loud.
"Oh, you like her, do you?"
She lets out a little mew.
"You and me both."

CHAPTER SIXTEEN

oppy

It's only when I return to my room that I spot the book sitting outside my door. The signed first edition of *The Great Gatsby* that I was reading when Max told me off in the library.

I carry it into my room, holding it close to my chest and wondering what it means. He must have been here earlier. He must have left it here for me. Or maybe he just had James do it. I place it on the nightstand and then go take a shower.

I wash off Max's blood and try to scrub away whatever insane reality I have stumbled into.

Vampires are real. Holy shit.

I had thought that Aiden had gotten himself into a *cult of crazies*, not, well, shit, whatever this is!

Visions of blood pouring out of Max's stomach flash through my mind, and then the healing. The way his skin just totally *healed over*.

I think of the way he said *vampire* like it was not something that would rip apart my whole reality.

Then I think of the shooting. Someone was out there tonight who knew that the security was weak. I hadn't given the Order that information, but *someone* knew. And they shot not only Max but Malik, an innocent human!

"What the fuck is going on?" I say to myself as I scrub my skin.

And then my mind decides to think the worst.

If the Order is right, if vampires are real…

But I can't let my mind go to a place where Max Montrose could have hurt Aiden. Max wouldn't. Whatever kind of creature he is, he is not a *killer*.

No, Aiden is still alive, he has to be. But he's not just involved in a cult, he's been hanging out with real life vampires.

I use so much hot water that it runs cool and so I get out and change into a clean set of PJs, throwing my bloodied ones into my washing bag, and get into bed.

I check my phone and see a message from Trix. She's at the hospital with Malik, and he's going to be okay, thank God.

I should absolutely text Claudia. I should one thousand percent tell her about this. If she finds out about what happened here tonight and knows I didn't message her, she'll be so pissed. Now that I know the Order has been training assassins to kill vampires, *who do in fact exist*, I seriously consider Kayla's words over coffee the other morning. If I don't do what I'm here to do, the Order could hurt me.

They could kill me.

Justin wouldn't hesitate. If he thought I had turned against them, I know he's crazy enough to do it.

I stare numbly at the app for a long time until my phone

slips out of my hand onto the floor. I make no effort to pick it up.

I just lie there, replaying the events of the night over and over again. Max bleeding out on to the grass, him calling *me* to help him. Why *me*? The woody, metallic scent of him as I helped him walk through the gardens and up into the house. The way he leaned in close and how for just a second, how I was dumb enough to think that maybe he was going to kiss me.

I toss and turn for what feels like hours, and eventually, when I see Trix is still not back, I consider switching on the light and getting stuck into *The Great Gatsby*, but in the end, I decide to make the most of my alone time. I slip my hand into my pajama shorts and work on easing out my tension.

As soon as my fingers reach my clit, I exhale and think of Max.

We're in the library this time. I'm looking at his books, and I feel him walk up behind me. "I want you to stop touching my books," he growls. "And start touching me." He lifts my hair, drapes it over my shoulder and then places a kiss on the back of my neck. Turning me around, he pulls me in for the most delicious, sexiest, sweetest kiss.

It's not enough to get me where I need to go, so I take the fantasy further.

His hands slide down to my waist. He pulls me close, and I feel him hard against me through his designer pants. He puts his hands on my ass and lifts me up like it's nothing, carrying me to the desk in the center of the room. He places me down, rips open my blouse and then grabs the straps of my bra, pulling them down and freeing my breasts.

"I would very much like to be inside you," he growls into my ear as he runs a thumb over my nipple. "I think I may die if I can't fuck you right now."

"You can't die," I tell him.

He chuckles and suddenly I'm no longer in my work uniform, but in the floral dress I was wearing the first night I was here.

He pushes his hand up the skirt of my dress and rips off my panties.

"Never wear these in my presence," he commands.

His fingers find my clit and suddenly it's him doing this to me, not me doing it to myself.

I can feel my release approaching just as his fangs appear. Not exactly what I was expecting, but I'm too close not to go with it.

He sinks his fangs into my neck, my body tenses, and then the best orgasm I've ever given myself rushes over me. I continue to ride it out, writhing and moaning, still thinking of Max's fangs inside me.

I decide to analyze this fucked-up fantasy later and close my eyes, finally slipping off into sleep.

IT ONLY FEELS like a few minutes later when my phone rings and I wake to sunlight streaming through the curtains I'd forgotten to close last night.

"Hello?" I answer.

"Poppy."

Oh shit.

"Claudia?"

"What the hell happened there last night?"

"You tell me," I say, sitting up with a yawn. "Was it the Order? Because it was a total shitshow."

"Where are you?" she demands.

"In my room."

"Never talk about the Order in the house!"

"No one's here," I assure her.

"Never call me from there."

"You called me!"

"Call me back when you're somewhere else."

"Where am I supposed to go?"

"I don't care. Just get off the estate."

"I can't. They don't like us leaving on workdays."

"Go sit in your car or something, just call me back imme-diately!"

I end the call. I'm in no hurry to get back to her, so I take my time dressing for work, perfecting my eyeliner flicks and putting my hair up in a cute messy topknot with some loose tendrils. It's only when I'm putting on some coral lipstick that I realize I'm doing all this for Max.

I roll my eyes at myself in the mirror and wipe the lipstick off, but my lips are still a little stained.

"He's never going to be interested in you like that, dumb-ass," I whisper to myself. "*He's* a movie star and *you're* a cleaner. Just keep it in the spank bank."

I take my phone and walk down to my car, all the while still thinking about Max and the events of last night. Watching him bleed out all over the couch squeezed my heart in ways I wasn't really prepared for. Yes, sure, the guy is sexy as hell. No one can deny that. But how I felt when I thought he might actually die? I was *scared.* Not scared because he's *really* a vampire, but scared that I would lose him.

Not that he would ever be mine to lose.

I get into my shit box car, a stark reminder of just how far removed I am from this movie star world and call her back.

"Poppy," Claudia answers.

"Yeah."

"What's going on?"

"Was it the Order?" I ask her.

"Yes."

"Because they fucked up. Royally."

"Don't act like this isn't on you, Poppy."

"Excuse me?"

"If you'd given us this information instead of Malik—"

"*Malik* told you?"

"Of course! He called us because he needed support in setting up the new system. The real question is why didn't *you* tell us?"

For a moment I think Malik is in on it, that he's a member of the Order. But no, he would have just told them about the security issues because he needed more staff to help him.

"I didn't know," I lie.

"It's your job to know."

"I gave you all the information I had."

"Are you sure about that?"

I pause and hope it's not obvious I'm considering how to answer. "Of course."

"What happened to Max? Did he get shot?"

I tug at my heart earring and try to think about what to tell her. "Yes."

"Is he dead?"

"No."

"Poppy, tell me what happened." She's losing her patience with me now. "We got news a staff member was taken to hospital, but two people were shot. If he was shot, the silver bullet should have killed him."

"From what I saw, it only just scraped him."

"Justin said he shot him right in the stomach."

"You sent *Justin*?"

"We had a chance, so we had to take it."

"You don't even have any evidence that he's a vampire!"

"No thanks to you."

I bite the inside of my mouth. "I've been trying!"

"Why didn't Max go to the hospital?" she asks.

"He didn't want the media attention. He called a doctor to come see him here." More lies.

"You were there?"

"Yeah, I was, and I could have been shot too."

"You saw it? His wound?"

"Kinda. It didn't look so bad."

"Fuck, we didn't even get him."

"Malik was nearly killed, Claudia. If the bullet had been a few inches over, it could have hit his chest." I take a breath. "Justin could have nearly killed an innocent man. And what happened to waiting until we had evidence? *Two* innocent people could have died on a hunch!"

"Sometimes that's just the cost, Poppy."

"The cost of what?"

"Sometimes there are casualties, for the greater good."

"This wasn't what I signed up for," I say. "I didn't sign up to *die* for this."

"When you join the Order, you put the Order above yourself. Above your life."

Fuuuuck.

She lets out a sigh. "But you're right. Last night was a bit of a fuck-up."

"Claudia, he's not what you think he is," I tell her. This part feels true at least. Whatever he is, Max Montrose isn't a monster. He doesn't deserve to *die*.

"Text me with updates," she says curtly. "And do it *immediately*. I looked like an idiot when I didn't know what had happened there last night."

"Okay, sure."

"Don't forget who you really work for," she says, and then hangs up.

I make a coffee in the kitchen and take it back to the staff quarters where Trix is slumped in an armchair, still in her sweats from last night, staring at a poster on the wall above the TV.

"How's Max?" she asks.

"Just a graze," I tell her, deciding to stick with my lie.

"That was a lot of blood for *just a graze*."

"It looked worse than it was. What about Malik?"

"He's fine." She goes back to staring at the poster. It's one of Johnny Montrose's westerns. I stare at it for a while too, captivated by the spitting image of Max in a cowboy hat and a sexy, determined look staring back at me.

"Are *you* okay?" I ask her.

She shakes her head. "I hardly know him, but I thought Malik was special. We had chemistry. You thought we had chemistry, right?" She turns to me, her expression pleading.

I wasn't sure that I'd noticed any chemistry between them, but this didn't seem like the right time to mention it. "What happened?"

"So, I go with Malik in the ambulance, which Max is paying for, thank god. I hold his hand the whole way there. There's blood everywhere, and I'm telling him he'll be okay. He's squeezing my hand like his life depends on it. He tells me he's so glad I'm there, and I know that something is happening between us." She looks down into her coffee cup. "When we get there, they look at him for ten seconds, tell him he'll live and then leave him there for *hours*. I sit with him the *whole time*. Eventually, a doctor comes and takes out the bullet and puts in some stitches. He keeps telling me he's so grateful for me, blah, blah, blah, and then his *wife* turns up."

"His *wife*?!"

"He doesn't even wear a ring, Poppy! Why doesn't he wear a ring?"

"Married men should definitely wear rings," I agree.

"Right? And the worst part was she was gorgeous, and the

way they looked at each other was just—" she clutches her heart. "That's how I want someone to look at me." She takes a sip of coffee and looks like she's about to cry.

"What's he doing working and living here if he has a wife at home?" I ask.

She shakes her head. "I don't know. Maybe he's getting paid better than we are, and according to his wife, he has *three kids.*"

"What?!"

She just nods at the poster.

"Well," I begin, trying to think of something to say that will help her through this. "You dodged a bullet, Trix. You don't need to get involved with a married man."

She nods. "You're right." She stands up and wipes some makeup from under her eyes. "That's enough moping. I need to get baking."

"Shouldn't you try to get some sleep?"

She shakes her head. "I'm good. And besides, I have a party to cater for."

James sticks his head through the door, and Trix's eyes light up at the sight of him.

"Poppy, we've got a lot to do today. We need you to prepare the war room for a meeting and the banquet room for a dinner."

I exchange a look with Trix and then give her hand a little squeeze, but from the way she's looking up at James, fluttering her lashes, it's clear she's already moving on.

CHAPTER SEVENTEEN

$\mathcal{M}$ax

"VAMPIRE KIND HAS MANY ENEMIES. *There are those who believe that the vampiric ruling class creates wealth inequality due to our talents in glamouring and our eternal nature. What they don't understand is that we are the chosen people. God has chosen us for this life. He has chosen us to rule. Vampires are God's favorite children."*

The Fraternity of the Everlasting Rose periodical, June 1929

HENRIETTA PULLS OPEN THE CURTAINS, sending a stream of bright sunlight into my bedroom. I flinch. I wasn't asleep, just lying on top of the covers. I very rarely sleep at all, but I was resting. Callie, who had stayed with me all night, lets out a very loud meow and jumps off the bed to hide. I don't blame her.

"Henrietta, why?" I sit up and glare at her. "What if I had stopped taking the sun serum? I'd be crust!"

"It's all over the news!" She turns her tablet around, and I see an article about a member of my staff being shot. "And the way *you* walk around in the sun? You haven't stopped taking that stuff since you discovered it."

"Anything about me in the papers?" I ask.

"Not much. Just a mention of how you're a recluse, haven't been seen in years. There's a conspiracy theory doing the rounds that you're dead."

"Good." I slump back on my pillows.

"But obviously this looks bad. Someone being shot on your estate."

"The police?"

"I already spoke to them."

"What did you tell them?"

"Nothing. I put a tonic in their tea, and they forgot what they were here for."

"Thank you, Etta."

She softens at my use of her nickname. "Eventually someone will find the case hasn't been closed and come asking questions."

"Malik is fine. There's hardly a case. How many shootings go unsolved in LA?"

"Too many."

"Any intuitive hits on why werewolves would want me dead?" I ask her.

Her red brows shoot up. "*Wolves?*"

"I'm sure I could smell one out there last night."

"Why on earth would wolves want to come after *you*?"

"That's what I want to know."

Henrietta rummages in her purse for a moment and then pulls out a small crystal sphere. Holding it in her left hand, she closes her eyes and takes a breath. She's silent for a few moments while I wait.

"I see… a small group of them. Misguided. Unorganized. I can't see how they got through my protective wards… but they won't make it onto the estate again. I'll make sure of it."

"Good."

"You'll need to meet with the Fraternity," she tells me. "You'll host a party tonight. I've sent invitations to all active members. Trix is creating a menu, Poppy will prepare the war and banquet rooms."

My heart does a little leap at the sound of her name, at the thought of Poppy preparing my rooms.

"What happened to you last night?" She finally notices the bloodied clothes I'm still wearing.

"I got the bullet out. I'm fine."

"You were shot too? Max!"

"Immortal, remember?"

"You can still *die*, you idiot."

"Not from one silver bullet." I don't tell her how much blood I lost, or that Poppy came to assist me.

"Who saw? Do you need any more tonics? Or are you strong enough to glamour?"

I shake my head. I make it a point never to lie to Henrietta or James, so I just say, "I have it all covered."

She gives me a look. It's difficult to keep things from a witch, but she lets it go.

"The guests will be here at ten-thirty tonight."

Very few vampires take the sun serum like I do. Some will drink directly from a lizard on occasions it's called for, but most vampires believe it to be unnatural. It does have some potential side-effects — dry skin, sunburn, weakness of joints, headaches, death — but nothing that has affected me too much to date. Even if it did, sunlight would still be preferable to a life of perfect skin. The only adverse effect I feel from the serum is that it gives me a different kind of circadian rhythm to most vampires. Since this goes against the natural way for vampires, it can cause tiredness, low mood, and even depression. All things I've had for decades, anyway.

"Thank you, Henrietta."

She nods and takes her leave, leaving me to consider my plans for the day. I will need to find Poppy and speak with her about last night. She seemed to take it all so well, but today may be different. The adrenaline will have worn off, and the reality that she's working for a vampire may be terrifying to her now.

I hope it is. I hope she runs from this place and never comes back. It would be the best thing for us both. No, it would be the best thing for me. The best thing for her would be for me to wipe her memory of last night and then let her go from my employment. That would be the kind thing. Besides, if the Fraternity were to find out that she knows about me, they would either wipe her memories themselves or wipe her from the earth.

But knowing that she knows about me, even if she runs from here and I never see her again, somehow makes me feel less alone.

My feelings must not come into this. I must glamour her today and remove her memory of it all.

I throw my bloodied clothing in the bin and call James to provide me with new sheets. I shower, dress and go to find her.

THE DOORS to the banquet room are wide open, and Poppy is standing on a ladder, reaching up to dust the chandelier above the table. Dust falls onto the table, but I couldn't care less about that. I'm too focused on the gap of skin that appears between her pants and her blouse as it rides up, giving me a perfect view of her soft pale skin. How I wish to touch her there, to grab her by the waist and pull her towards me.

I watch her until she finishes, lowers the duster and looks my way.

Oh, and when she looks my way, how my cold dead heart flutters!

I immediately admonish myself. What a fool I am. To think a beautiful, warm-blooded woman like her would ever want to be with a monster like me.

And yet I don't look away. And neither does she.

We stay there for too long, eyes locked in knowing, in the secrets we share. She knows what I am, and I know that she wants me.

"Hello, Poppy," I finally say. It's pathetic, but it's all that comes to mind.

She takes a step down from the ladder, and it wobbles. I immediately run to her aid, and just as she's about to fall, I catch her in my arms.

She looks up at me with those warm hazel doe eyes. "Hi."

God, how I want her! How I want to pull her into an even closer embrace! How I want to kiss her perfect lips and throw her onto this table, strip her naked and fuck her until neither of us can see straight, dust be damned!

I quickly release her from my grip and step back. "I shouldn't have done that," I say, realizing now just how fast I must have been. How unnatural it would have looked to her.

"You wanted me to fall?"

"Of course not, it's just—I shouldn't have—"

"I already know what you are," she says, wiping her dusty hands on those tight black pants.

"And you're not afraid?" My dead heart hammers in my chest as I await her answer.

She shakes her head, the soft tendrils of loose hair falling from her topknot begging to be pushed aside so that I may kiss every inch of her face.

"Why would I be afraid of someone who saves me from falling?" she asks.

If only she knew how much I wanted to keep her safe, and the safest place I can think of in this moment is with me under the covers of my bed.

I turn and close the doors behind me, leaning against them before I speak again. "Have you told anyone about what happened last night?"

She shakes her head. "No."

"I need to know I can trust you."

"I've seen enough movies to know that I'm a liability to you now, and if you have to wipe my memories, I understand. But I'm not afraid of you."

"No?"

"If you were going to kill me, you would have already. You've had a few opportunities."

I lean my head back against the door. "There's only one thing that's going to keep you safe from me," I tell her.

Her perfect pale neck bobs as she swallows. "What's that?"

"If you keep your distance from me."

Her heart rate is high. She's so nervous. But she doesn't look away from me. "And what would happen if I didn't?" she asks.

I take a step towards her, then another, and another, until I'm close enough to catch the scent of her, *all* of her. I reach out and push back one of the delicious tendrils of hair that begs my fingers to touch it. "Then you would find yourself in all sorts of trouble."

Her breath shallows, but she doesn't move, and just when I think she's about to give in to me, and I into her, she takes a step back. "Then you should probably go."

It's not the response I expect, and definitely not the response I want, but when a woman tells me to go, I do.

CHAPTER EIGHTEEN

"*It is* *with great sadness that we announce the passing of the great Renaud Luelle, former president of the Fraternity of the Everlasting Rose. He will be succeeded by his daughter, Charlotte Luelle who will be inaugurated into the position on the 25th of August at our secret headquarters. All active members are invited to attend.*"

Notice in the Fraternity of the Everlasting Rose periodical, July 1955

The evening begins with canapes in the parlor, and it's all very polite and formal. These things always start this way and eventually turn into complete depravity. There are estimated to be over a thousand vampires in the city, but only 34 active members of the Fraternity.

"Did Lottie give her apologies?" I ask Henrietta as she

uncorks another bottle of blood for my guests, who are quickly getting through the last of my stores.

"No, but she didn't RSVP either."

"Perhaps she didn't receive the invitation," I say, taking a sip from my glass of whiskey. Choosing to drink synthetic blood in a public setting like this would be quite the political statement I am not ready to make.

"We can live in hope, I suppose," she says, passing the bottle to James.

"We need more blood," James tells her.

"They are getting through it. We only have twenty bottles left," she complains.

Maverick Stone, my best friend, whose face is currently on every billboard in LA with his latest movie *Road Rage 6*, places a sturdy hand on Henrietta's shoulder. He sweeps his other hand through his dirty blonde hair and gives her that action movie grin that drives his fans wild. "I'll call my guy. We'll have a hundred bottles here by midnight."

Henrietta smiles up at him, unable to resist his charms.

James shoots me a look. He knows how I feel about the consumption of human blood but keeping these ancient and powerful vampires full of bottled blood is better than the alternative.

"Thank you, Maverick," I say.

He shoots off a text with lightning speed and then looks me up and down. "Nice suit, by the way."

Maverick is dressed in jeans, a t-shirt and a leather jacket, while most of us gathered here tonight are in formal wear. I'm dressed in a dark blue suit and white shirt and tie. Even that feels too casual compared to what some of the older vampires have chosen to wear.

Maverick and I have been friends since he got into movies after he served in World War II. He is possibly the only real friend I have who doesn't work for me.

James passes by us with a plate of hors d'oeuvres. Some vampires refuse human food, but Maverick isn't one of them.

"What is this — fried chicken?" He takes a piece, and as he begins to chew, his eyes light up. "This is the best chicken I've had in decades." He takes two more pieces and shoves them into his mouth.

"It's not chicken, sir," says James.

"What is it?" he asks, taking another off the dish.

"Tofu," James replies.

He immediately spits it out into a napkin. "That's disgusting! I knew something was wrong with it."

I take the last piece off the tray and bite into it. "I do believe Trix has outdone herself with this menu," I say.

"A vampire who eats tofu, give me fucking strength." Maverick rolls his eyes and washes down the tofu he's accidentally consumed with human blood.

I let out a laugh.

"Should you begin the meeting?" Henrietta says, appearing by my side again.

"Without Lottie?" Maverick asks.

"Mr. Montrose is more than capable of chairing the meeting," says Henrietta.

"Very well." I'm about to announce to the room that we will be moving into the war room to discuss the events of last night when Lottie appears in the doorway with James behind her. He takes her fur coat, which is so unnecessary for the weather, throws me a pitying look and then disappears towards the kitchen.

Charlotte "Lottie" Luelle is a very old vampire with too white skin and long platinum blonde hair which she pins up to emulate a twenties style bob. She doesn't look a day over twenty, but she's pure evil.

"Lottie," I say, stepping towards her and taking her icy hands in mine. "Lovely to see you."

"And you, darling," she says, kissing me on each cheek and then taking a good look at me. "Although I don't know why we couldn't have done this at the headquarters."

The headquarters in the cemetery, the location of too many terrible memories, is the last place on earth I'd like to be.

"It keeps us less conspicuous to meet in other locations," I tell her.

Her eyes narrow. "If you say so, darling. Now where is your bow tie?" She's drenched in pearls and pendants and wearing a glittery champagne formal dress. You can take the girl out of Hollywood's golden era… "You look dreadful, by the way," she adds.

I take a breath. "I just fancied something a little more casual this evening."

She pulls imaginary fluff off my shoulder. "I suppose you *were* just shot. Horrible business."

"Indeed."

"Should we get to it?" Maverick suggests.

Lottie casts a disgusted look over Maverick's outfit. "Maverick, for goodness' sake, would it kill you to *try*?" She turns to me. "Lend him a suit, will you, darling?"

Maverick laughs and flexes a bicep. "You think these guns will fit in one of Max's suits?"

She glares at him. "James!" she calls, and he appears at her side within moments. "Find Maverick a suit jacket that will fit him."

"Of course."

Lottie claps her hands. "Let's adjourn to the war room," she announces, her shrill voice cutting through the crowd.

I PLACE THE BULLET, now in a plastic bag, in the center of the table.

"The Order." Brandon Curtis, one of the most influential Hollywood directors and producers of both the golden and modern age, knows exactly what this is. We've worked together on many movies. He still goes by the same name, pretending to be Brandon Curtis the third now. He looks like he's in his early fifties but is much, much older. With his slicked-back blonde hair and three-piece suit, he has never been interested in conforming to modern standards of fashion.

"Why would the Order suddenly become active again?" Maverick frowns down at the bullet.

"Perhaps they have been underground this whole time, waiting for us to become weak," I say.

"We are not weak," Lottie says. "We are stronger than ever."

We all know that's a lie. The Fraternity used to have chapters in every city. We were growing, spreading our influence throughout the world. Now we don't even know what's happening with the vampire community in the next city.

"This is outrageous!" Lottie exclaims. "Why would they be after *you*, Leopold?"

My skin crawls when she calls me by that name.

"Max has very few enemies," Brandon muses. "I suspect this has more to do with vampire kind than Max specifically."

"Then why target his mansion?" Maverick asks.

"Okay, sorry, but like, what *is* the Order?" Juliette Cortez looks both bored and confused as she pours herself another glass of blood, with some difficultly considering the length of her black fingernails. She's about to film another season of a drama on a popular streaming service that has helped her grow her social media to over three million followers. She's a relatively new vampire, only six years old and the newest to our group. The Fraternity has always been interested in collecting famous and influential people, specifically those involved in the arts. For better or worse that now includes stars of streaming and social media.

"The Order was set up during the Middle Ages in England," says Brandon. "It was originally designed to be an order of protection for immortals."

"One immortal from each race or realm served on the council," Maverick continues. "For hundreds of years it kept the peace between our kinds."

Juliette puts her chin in her hand and leans into his every word. Even other vampires aren't immune to Maverick's charms, I suppose.

"Okay, so then what happened?" Juliette asks.

"It became less fashionable to hunt supernatural beings," Brandon says. "Supernatural hunters went underground, and the need for the Order's protection no longer existed."

"Wolves took it over in the eighties. We had a little trouble with them," Maverick says. "Vampires went missing. That version of the Order killed a bunch of us."

"Terrible business," Lottie tuts.

"How did they do it?" Juliette asks.

"All the usual ways," Maverick says. He picks up the bullet and frowns at it. "These are old school. Eighties weapons. No one was ever killed with these."

"Only maimed," I add.

"Well, sure," Maverick replies. "If you get hit with one of these, it *will* slow you down. But it can give them an opportunity to come in with something harder. Crossbow, but only if your bolt is wide enough, stake on the end of a sword, although that only works if—"

"I think she gets the picture," Brandon says.

Maverick continues, "Once vampires got wind of what was happening within the Order, they found those responsible. We killed a lot of wolves that summer."

"And now they're back," says Brandon, rubbing the dark blonde stubble on his chin.

"But why would they want to kill vampires *now*?" I ask.

"It's the pushback against the wealthy." We all look towards Linda McKinley, one of Maverick's leading ladies from back in the fifties. With auburn hair piled high on her head, her neck covered in bright green jewels to match her dress, Linda is another vampire who's barely changed her style since she was at her peak.

"How do you know this?" Maverick asks.

"I was at the club the other night. I heard talk."

"What did you hear?" Lottie demands. Lottie has never liked Linda. She was always jealous of Linda's beauty and success. Linda is currently working in indie cinema and has recently won her thirtieth Oscar. I'm jealous too, I've never won an Oscar, but Linda deserves all her success.

"I heard some Donnas discussing it," Linda says.

"I hate this disrespectful term, *Donnas*," Brandon says. "Can't we just call them what they are?"

"Food?" Juliette suggests.

Me and Brandon are the only ones who don't laugh at that.

"They were having a moral dilemma about how much wealth vampires hoard," Linda continues. "They still enjoyed The Bite but weren't sure if it was still ethical to be bitten." She looks positively bored by all this. "Needless to say, I glamoured them both into thinking our wealth was most definitely a good thing."

Juliette hits a hand on the table. "Why are we sitting here *talking* about this when we should be out there ripping these Order asshole's throats out before they come after the rest of us?"

"We can't just go on a rampage and kill any wolves we

find," Maverick says. "And besides, we don't know for sure it is wolves."

"Who else would it be? Witches?" Juliette's eyes darken.

"They're too busy hexing the government to come after us," I say. Maverick is the only one here who knows what Henrietta is, and I wish to keep it that way.

"But the wolves haven't given us trouble for decades," Maverick says. "And the fae, well—" He shoots me a look. "Maybe they are finally looking for retribution."

"Wolves are very poor, aren't they?" Linda muses. "Perhaps Juliette is right and we should kill them all before they come after us."

"We will figure this all out with as little bloodshed as possible," Brandon assures us all, making me wish not for the first time that he was the head of the Fraternity instead of Lottie.

"And when we do, we *will* rip their throats out," Juliette says, with a blood-stained grin.

I look into the bottom of my nearly empty glass and think of the one person who may still want me dead, even after all this time, but they aren't wolf, fae or witch, they're vampire.

ax

IT'S JUST after two in the morning when Maverick's delivery of blood donors arrives. What was supposed to be a meeting to make a plan for what we're going to do about the Order is turning into a blood orgy in my garden. Great.

No one cares that we still don't have a plan as long as they're all getting a free meal.

I pour myself another whiskey while the others start gravitating towards their chosen Dons and Donnas.

Maverick eyes up a blonde in a tight skirt and then looks back at me. "You look like you could use a little treat, Max. When was the last time you fed?"

"I don't do that anymore."

His dark eyebrows knit together. "*Never?*"

I take a sip of my drink and shrug.

"Sybline isn't supposed to be an alternative to real blood, Max. It's just for those times when feeding isn't practical."

"It's never practical for me."

"After what happened the other night, you're going to need blood to heal. And if they come back for you—"

"I am healed, and they're not coming back," I tell him. "But you're right. If I'd been at full strength last night, I would have been in better form. Maybe I'd have picked up their scent faster, sensed the shot coming and moved out of the way. I may have been able to stop my staff from being in danger. But when I'm on the blood, *I'm* the danger."

"You're one of the most level-headed vampires in this town," he says, beckoning a woman with dark hair towards him. "They're amateurs," he continues. "If they were a genuine threat, they would have staked you."

"How reassuring."

"Whoever they are, they aren't organized. Breaking into your place just to fire a couple of shots? That's not a plan."

"That could make them even more dangerous. A band of werewolves on the loose shooting silver bullets with no idea of what they're doing?"

Maverick claps me on the back. "You'd feel better if you fed from one of the Donnas."

"And blood bond with one of these women? No thanks."

"It wears off eventually."

Last time I drank from a donor, I was still thinking about her blood many months later. We can erase their memories of the experience, but we can't erase the bond feeding creates. It's not so bad for us celebrities. When our donors start dreaming of us and feeling an insatiable urge to give us whatever we want, they can put it down to celebrity obsession. But many think it's love. Even vampires have been known to confuse the blood bond with true love, marry a human and end up in an awful situation.

It's just one more reason drinking from Poppy would make things so complicated. If I bit her, I would never know if her feelings for me were real or if it was just the blood bond.

God, why am I even thinking this? I will never bite her.

"Sooner or later, you're going to need to scratch the itch," Maverick says.

I think of Poppy, of her neck, her thighs, the top of her breasts, all the places I'd like to sink my teeth into.

"I can handle it," I tell him.

The brunette finally approaches, and Maverick gives her a grin. "It's your life, man." He clinks my glass with his, takes the woman's hand and then wanders off toward the blonde he also had his eyes on.

I look around at the debauchery that's about to happen, and my eyes fall on the staff quarters. I see the curtain in Poppy and Trix's room flutter and realize they are watching. They won't be able to get a good look at anything happening here from that far away, but I can always glamour them in the morning just to make sure.

Maverick's two Donnas strip off naked and jump in the pool. He pulls off his shirt and pants and jumps in after them.

At least someone's having a good time.

Another attractive brunette appears above me. "Max Montrose," she says with a flirtatious grin. "I'm Tessa. Would you like a drink?" She pushes her long hair away from her neck and bites her lip. She's a little wobbly on her very high-heeled shoes, and a strong whiff of vodka emanates from her.

Of course, no one is supposed to know about our existence, but there are those who do. Friend and foe. These girls here tonight are definitely friend. Most of the donors are glamoured into forgetting immediately after feeding, but they still have a strong pull towards the vampire who bit them, they still remember that vampires exist, that bites feel like giant orgasms through your veins and where to go to find that feeling. I can tell this isn't Tessa's first time doing this. She knows what we are, and she knows what she's doing, even if she doesn't remember everyone she's done it with.

She also has Maverick's scent all over her. Which, even if I was interested in biting a woman who wasn't Poppy, makes her instantly unappealing.

"You are very lovely," I tell her. "But I'm not looking for anything tonight."

She pouts and lets out a whiny sound. "I'll do anything for a little bite."

This should be exciting. Any other cold-blooded vampire's fangs would extend immediately in this situation. But while I can appreciate that she is very beautiful, I have had enough empty feeding sessions and love-less sex in my existence.

"You may have forgotten all about it, Tessa, since your mind gets wiped every time, but it seems that Maverick Stone has already claimed you."

A coy smile spreads over her lips. "He has?" She wobbles again, and I place a hand on her back to steady her.

"Indeed."

Once a human is claimed by a vampire, no other vampire can feed from them or even touch them without permission from the one who claimed them. And woe be to any human who would get in the way.

Most vampires don't bother to claim Donnas. They can find a new one whenever they like, there is no need for any attachment. But it seems that Maverick has already claimed at least half of the women here. I suspect he'd be more than happy to lend me one of his claimed girls for the night, but not only am I not interested in drinking from Maverick's personal supply, I have no interest in drinking from anyone but Poppy.

Even if I will never drink from Poppy.

But god, how I want to drink from her! It would be pure ecstasy for us both!

Tessa looks over at Maverick, who's drinking from the wrist of one of the women in the pool. He wipes his mouth, grins and then sinks his fangs into the neck of the other girl.

"I'm sure he'd be happy to have you join them," I say.

"Before I do, would you please show me where the bathroom is?"

"Of course." I guide her with my hand on her lower back to stop her from falling over towards the pool room. She wobbles again, and I change course towards the house. This woman doesn't need The Bite, she needs *a* bite. "Perhaps a little something to eat, Tessa?"

After she's been to the bathroom and eaten half a peach pie I find in the kitchen, she returns to the party to join Maverick and the others while I disappear into the theater watching old movies until dawn, once again wishing Poppy was beside me.

CHAPTER TWENTY

oppy

"Poppy. Poppy!"

I pull the blanket over my head. "I'm trying to sleep!" I groan.

"Oh my god, is that Maverick Stone?" a male voice coos.

"Julio?" I pull the blanket down to see Julio and Trix with their faces pressed up against the window.

"Get over here!" he says, gesturing wildly.

I sit up in bed and reach for my hoodie. It's not like I'm sleeping anyway, my mind is too full of Max Montrose telling me that if I didn't keep my distance, I'd be in *all sorts of trouble.*

Did he mean I'd end up drained and dead? Or spread out naked on his banquet table?

"It *is* him!" Julio says. "It's Maverick Stone!"

I scramble out of bed and join them by the window. "How can you tell that's him? He's so far away."

"Oh, I'd know those enormous arms anywhere," Julio says.

"You're a fan?"

"Isn't everyone? He's the perfect male specimen. Sexy, built like a tank, confident. Oh, and don't forget rich and famous."

"Meh," says Trix. "He might look okay-ish, but he's *so* obnoxious."

"What?!" Julio exclaims.

"I can't stand his shit excuses for movies," Trix shrugs.

Julio clutches his heart. "I can't believe what I'm hearing."

I squint into the darkness trying to make sense of the tiny shapes moving around in the darkness of the garden.

"Is that Juliette Cortez?" Trix squeals.

"Where! where?" asks Julio.

"There, at the table in the middle. She's so fabulous," Trix gushes.

"You appreciate Maverick Stone, right, Poppy?" Julio asks.

I shrug. "He's not really my type."

Trix gives me a look. "Of course, you prefer those old-fashioned kind of guys. The open the car door for you kind of guys. The ones always wearing suits even in the middle of a heatwave. Those dark-haired, blue-eyed—"

I nudge her in the ribs. She lets out a loud laugh, and the tiny blob she thinks is Maverick Stone looks our way.

"Keep it down," I tell her.

"He can't hear us from here, we can barely even see him! We need binoculars. Do you have any?"

"No, Trix. I do not have a pair of binoculars."

"Most people wouldn't have a party the day after they were shot," Julio muses.

"Where were you last night, anyway?" I ask him.

"In my room. Where we're all supposed to be at the sound of an alarm if you'd read your information pack," he tuts.

"Maybe if Malik had stayed in his room, he wouldn't have been shot," Trix says.

"Yeah, and you would never have found out he was *married*," Julio reminds her.

"The party is weird," Trix says. "Why bring all these people here when someone just tried to *kill* you?"

"Maybe Max just wanted to take his mind off things," I suggest.

"Well, this will help," Julio says as a group of barely dressed women and a few men walk into the gathering.

"Models?" Trix asks.

"Honey," says Julio, "I don't think they are *models*."

"Oooh, this is so Hollywood," Trix says.

For a second, I think one of the guys who's arrived is Aiden. My heart lurches at the similar build and buzz-cut short hair, but it's not him. Or is it?

The man approaches one of the other female guests that I don't recognize, not that I can really recognize anyone from this distance, and he starts peeling off his shirt.

I stare at the figure for a long time before realizing I'm just imagining things. That's not Aiden. It's just a guy who's about as tall as he is.

My stomach flips as I watch one of the girls approach Max. Even from this distance, I can somehow tell she's stunning. She's thin, with huge breasts and a skirt that barely exists. She practically throws herself at him, and I feel physically sick but can't look away.

He puts his hand on her lower back, leaning into her like he's murmuring some kind of sweet nothing into her ear, and then he walks her up the stairs and into the mansion.

I'm not stupid enough to think I belong at his party, or that Max Montrose would choose *me* over any of these girls, but I don't think I just imagined those sexually charged moments between us.

Did I?

Yes, the answer to that is most obviously yes. I did imagine it.

And if I didn't, if there really *was* something between us, even just a little something in those few heated moments we shared, and he's now off to pay for sex with someone else, or get it free, because would he even have to pay? Well, that stings.

"Is this going to turn into an orgy?" Trix muses.

"Oh god, I hope so," Julio replies.

I draw my eyes back from the mansion, where Max and that woman are now nowhere to be seen, and look back out at the garden, finding the guy I thought was Aiden. And then I realize, even if he's *not* Aiden, maybe he knows where Aiden is. Maybe Aiden came to one of these parties. Maybe that's why he was last seen here.

"I need to get into that party," I say, shoving my feet into my sneakers.

"Poppy, what?" Trix asks. "You can't go out there!"

"I'll just be a minute."

"Poppy!" Julio calls out.

"Poppy, get back here!" Trix yells down the hallway.

But I'm already gone, running through the living area and out into the night.

I start moving towards the party and then pause behind a bush. What the fuck am I thinking? I can't just go over there!

Juliette Cortez catches my eye, and I realize I'm screwed. I signed a contract saying I would not do exactly what I'm doing right now.

But I need answers! Not for the Order, for me.

I try to move slowly backwards towards the staff quarters, but in the process, I trip and land on my ass. I look up, and Juliette is standing above me.

"Who are you?" she asks.

I swallow. "Oh. I'm nobody."

She holds out a hand with long black manicured nails, and I take it.

"You know you're not supposed to be out here, right?" she asks when I'm upright again.

"I thought I saw… um, a friend out here. I just wanted to say hi."

"You're friends with the Donnas?"

"The who?"

She narrows her eyes at me. "Who do you think you know?"

"That guy." I point to the guy I thought was Aiden.

"Oh yeah, what's his name?"

"Andrew," I say, hoping I sound more confident than I feel and that she doesn't know his name. "We went to college together."

"Which college?"

"UCLA."

"You know you can't just walk into a gathering like this and come *say hi* to someone," she says. "It's not really safe for your kind."

My kind? Oh, holy shit, of course! This is a fucking vampire convention, and Juliette Cortez is one of them!

I just look at her blankly, trying not to give away that I know anything.

"Andrew!" she calls out. He ignores her at first, but when she calls his name a few times, he eventually looks our way.

"Come over here!"

Juliette walks towards him and then sends him over to me while she returns to the party.

Okay, I think I like her.

"Do I know you?" the guy asks when he arrives at the bush. Up close, he looks even less like Aiden. He looks out of it, drunk or high, and the bags under his eyes suggest he hasn't had a good sleep in a week.

"No, I just thought you might know my brother."

"Brother? Why?"

"Do you know Aiden St Clair?"

"Aiden?" The guy wobbles a little, and I'm pretty sure I'm not going to get anything out of him.

"Aiden St Clair." I repeat.

I think I see a flash of recognition, but then it fades. "I don't know. I don't think so. What did you say his name was? Aaron? Arlo? Bartholomeewwww?" He laughs.

"Aiden!" I snap. "Do you know him? He would have been at one of these parties about six months ago?"

"Six months ago?"

"Yeah, here, at Max Montrose's estate."

He looks up at the house. "Max Montrose lives here?"

Well, this was a complete waste of time.

"Do I know you?" he asks, like he hasn't been standing here looking at me for the last few minutes.

Just then, James appears beside me. "You can go back to the party," he tells the guy. "And you—" he glares at me, "— need to get back to your room. *Now.*"

"Am I fired?" I ask with a sigh.

"That's up to Mr. Montrose."

"Maybe you don't have to tell him."

"If I don't, one of them will, and that will be worse."

James walks me back to my room, and when he sees Julio and Trix staring out the window, he clears his throat. "I'm sure I don't need to explain to you the seriousness of all this."

"Seriousness of what?" Trix asks, launching herself into bed.

"I was never here!" Julio walks swiftly out of the room.

James bids us a quick "Goodnight," and leaves me to

agonize over my future at the estate and wonder what the hell Aiden was doing at one of these orgy parties at Max Montrose's house.

oppy

"WHAT WERE you doing out of your quarters the night of my party?" Max's bright blue eyes glare at me over the antique desk in the library.

His eyes are striking as always, but it's the pot plants that have appeared in the room that really take me by surprise. There are now eight huge plants dotted around the room making this room feel even more like a sanctuary than it already did.

I've just finished another day of intense cleaning and I'm sweaty and exhausted. It's been days since the party, and while part of me was happy flying under the radar in the hope it meant that James had decided not to tell Max, another part of me had missed Max's sexy glare and gruff words.

Tomorrow is my day off, and I was just about to go and

get ready for a night out with Trix when James arrived in the staff quarters telling me I'd been summoned.

My belly did a little somersault at the idea of being told off again, but my brain is pretty sure this time I'm getting fired for real.

"I thought I saw someone I knew," I tell him, shifting my weight from one foot to the other, having completely forgotten how to stand upright.

"You think that's a good enough reason to ignore the rules and put yourself into—" he takes a pause. "Hollywood types take their privacy very seriously."

"I signed an NDA."

"You also signed a contract stating that you *would not* wander the grounds of the estate after working hours." The way he looks at me has me imagining him standing up, pulling me into him with a hot kiss and then throwing me down onto the desk, spreading my legs wide—

No, Poppy. This isn't the time to think about that.

"I'm sorry," I mutter.

He sighs. "Poppy." My stomach flips as he says my name. "I don't want to hear that word from your lips ever again." His eyes move to my lips for a second, and I can't help but wet them.

"Honestly, I just thought he was someone I knew."

"Juliette told me you said you knew him from college?"

"Uh—"

"I read your employment application, Poppy. I know you didn't go to college. Why would you lie to her?"

For a second I consider telling him everything, just asking him outright if he knew my brother, but then I'll have to admit I'm working for the Order, and I can *not* tell him about any of that!

"Because I was embarrassed?" I say. "That I didn't go to college."

He raises an eyebrow. "Do you *want* to go to college?"

"I wanted to. At one point. But I didn't have the grades. Or the money."

"What did you want to study?"

"Veterinary Science."

He raises an eyebrow, and I feel like an even bigger idiot. Why did I just tell him, of all people, about my stupid childhood dream to be a vet?

"Is that still something you want to pursue?"

I let out a laugh. "That dream died a long time ago."

"Sometimes dreams come back around."

"Am I fired?" I ask, just wanting to get this over with.

"Not yet." He stands up from behind the desk, and I'm suddenly aware of just how tall he is. He leans over the desk, and his deep forest scent hits my nostrils, sending memories of moments I've been close to him rushing to my mind.

"But if you want to continue working here, I'm going to need something from you."

Oh god, please let it be sexual favors!

"Anything." My voice comes out way too breathy.

"Re-read your contract, Poppy."

I nod.

"Any more of these incidents, and I really will wipe your memories and send you home. Do you understand?"

I just nod again.

"Now, get back to work." He waves me off with a flick of his wrist towards the door.

"Yes, Mr. Montrose. Thank you, Mr. Montrose," I say, giving a little bow and disappearing out into the hallway.

CHAPTER TWENTY-TWO

Max

I WANDER into the kitchen and look for something to eat, purely for something to do. I check the fridge and see a chocolate cake looking back at me. At first, I'm not sure if I'm allowed a slice, but then I remind myself that this is my house, Trix works for me, and if she's made cake, I may certainly eat it.

I pull the entire cake out, place it on the counter and find myself having a flashback of my childhood, when I could not have even dreamed of a cake like this. We lived off stale bread, dirty water and the occasional potato or piece of offal. Even after all this time, this life sometimes feels like a dream. I slide a knife into the cake and then pause. I'm a beneficiary of several homeless charities and food banks in the city, but I still sometimes find it hard to enjoy food I don't even *need* to eat while so many go hungry. I open the banking app on my phone, deposit ten thousand dollars into one of the charities and then cut myself a slice.

Eating food is different for me now. The taste is better than it ever was. My heightened senses make anything delicious taste even better, but the satisfaction is lacking. Because as much as I try to resist it, there is nothing more satisfying to me than human blood. I eat the cake and enjoy it, but all the while I find myself thinking about blood. *Poppy's* blood.

After the party, I ordered some more human blood for my personal supply. Maverick was right. I can't protect myself, the estate or Poppy without it. Six bottles sit in my private suite, but I have been unable to drink.

I have avoided Poppy again these last few days. I wanted nothing more than to run into her, whisper something into her ear, play my twisted make-believe game of me and Poppy, but it's getting too dangerous.

When James told me he'd found Poppy hiding in the bushes at the party, I was livid. Poppy put herself in extreme danger by not following the rules. I can't even imagine what would have happened if it had been one of the others who had found her. As far as I know, Juliette hasn't said a word to the other Fraternity members about her which I am thankful for.

I only called her into the library after her shift as I needed to know she was safe, to make sure she would stay safe by following the rules here.

Who am I kidding? I called her into the library because I wanted an excuse to see her.

I'm aware of James entering the kitchen from the staff entrance behind me. "James," I say.

"I see you found the cake, sir."

"I hope it was for me."

"Everything Trix makes is for you, even if you don't touch

it," he says. There's judgement in his tone, but I ignore it, as I always do.

"Where have you been?" I ask him.

"I gave the girls a ride into the city."

"Nights out on the town. I remember those. Vaguely."

"When was your last night out, sir?" James asks.

"Please take a slice and join me."

James does as I ask, as he always does, as he has done for many decades now. Working for me is his punishment for a crime he committed against a vampire back in the fifties. The Fraternity needed a fae to punish for the sins of all fae involved, and I was in need of a new butler. His choice was working for me or death. I suspect sometimes he wishes he'd taken death.

"Eight years ago?" James guesses.

"Around then."

"You can still pass," he says.

We've had this conversation too many times.

"Everyone is getting cosmetic surgery these days," he says, taking a seat and a slice of cake. "Do you know one star who isn't immortal, who hasn't had Botox?"

"I can think of a few."

"No one would bat an eye, sir. You could have another ten, fifteen years of work at least."

"Doing what?" I push my now empty plate away. "Playing the father in teen dramas? The love interest in budget Christmas movies? In case you haven't noticed, the Golden Age of Hollywood is very much over."

"Work is work. You always said you enjoyed entertaining and brightening people's lives through your movies. You could still do that, even if the format is different."

I take a breath. "I would be miserable working for a streaming service."

"And yet, you are happiest when you are working."

"Happy is an overstatement."

"You are much easier to deal with when you're working, how about that?"

"I'm always open to the right project," I lie.

"There is a stack of over three hundred scripts on your desk in your private office. Is there really nothing there that interests you?"

"Not much interests me anymore."

"Ah, but not *nothing*."

Of course he's noticed. I'd be a fool not to know that he knows about my infatuation with Poppy.

"The only thing that interests me is something I need to stay as far away from as possible."

He raises an eyebrow.

"You know what would happen," I tell him.

"No, I don't. And neither do you. Your bloodlust is under control. You are not the same man you were when we first met. And god knows you deserve some love and a little light in your life."

I let out a loud "Ha!"

"The girl could be good for you. The way you look at her, the way she looks at you. I've never seen you connect with another human in such a way."

I slide my plate back towards me and take another slice of cake.

"What is it about her, if you don't mind my asking?" he asks.

I chew on a bite of cake while I consider my response. "It's… unexplainable. There is just something within my soul that recognizes something within hers."

"So it's not just those tight pants she wears?"

I glare at him across the table. "Never speak of her like that again."

He lets out a laugh and then presses his lips together. "But surely it helps that she's pretty."

"Pretty? She's beautiful! She's exquisite! She's a dream!"

James gives me a knowing smile as he takes another bite of cake. "If you feel this strongly about her, you should definitely do something about it."

"You approve of my getting involved with the staff?"

"No. But I can see that the way you feel about her is different. If it was just about getting your end away—"

"James!"

"I apologize, sir. What I meant to say is that love is always scary. There is always a danger of being hurt or hurting someone."

"But for most people, that hurt doesn't end with someone getting accidentally drained or murdered by the Fraternity."

James takes another bite. Of course, he has no retort for that.

"Where are the girls tonight?" I ask.

"I dropped them outside Vincent's."

My cold blood suddenly runs even colder. "You did *what*?"

He licks his fork as if what he's done is no big deal.

I can feel the tingle in my fangs that, had I not been drinking so much Sybline, would be an indication they were about to project from my mouth ready to kill somebody.

James has been with me for decades. He has been a good friend to me. But if he has put Poppy in harm's way, I will never forgive him.

I'm at the back door in an instant.

"Sir," he says, standing and looking concerned. "What's the matter?"

"The matter is that you just left the girls at a vampire bar!"

"Plenty of humans go there," he shrugs.

"Yes, to get bitten!"

"They have plenty of security. I'm sure they'll be—"

"You'd better *hope* to whatever god you believe in that nothing happens to her."

I slam the door behind me and speed over to the garage, grab the keys to the Aston Martin and drive.

CHAPTER TWENTY-THREE

oppy

"THIS PLACE IS INCREDIBLE!" I yell to Trix over the live band with full horn section playing modern songs in the style of the 1920s. I feel like I've stepped back in time here. Vincent's is a fabulous art deco style bar that I've heard about so many times but never actually been to until tonight. It's all black and gold furnishings, black velvet curtains, a lot of elegant looking people. Once again, I feel very underdressed in my blue floral skirt and white tank top. It's not cheap to come here, but Trix knew the security guy out front who told the woman at the door to waive the $20 cover charge.

"I knew you'd like it!" Trix yells back before shouting an order of two gin rickey cocktails to the very hot and buff bartender.

"Do you come here a lot?" I ask her.

"I worked here for a couple of months when it first opened a few years back. That's how I know Dave out front."

"Why did you quit?"

She presses her lips together. "I was fired."

"What for?"

She gives a one shouldered shrug, the strap of her gold sequin romper glittering in the light while she watches the bartender shake our cocktails.

I'm about to ask her more about it, but the bartender hands over our drinks, placing a lime wedge onto the lip of the glasses.

Trix hands over the money, but he waves her away. "It's taken care of."

She frowns at him. "By who?"

He thumbs towards a man sitting at the end of the bar. He's dressed in all black—black pants, shirt and black suit jacket. His hair is also dark and he's ridiculously attractive, even if he is giving off some intense vibes.

Trix holds up her drink to him as if to say thanks. I do the same and then follow her to a table in the opposite direction. It's quieter here and slightly hidden from the guy at the bar.

I sit and smooth down my skirt, thankful that it's long enough to cover my thighs from prying eyes. The only eyes I want on my thighs are Max's. Meanwhile, all eyes in the club are on Trix in her short romper and matching gold glitter eyeshadow. Trix is very shiny and not just because of what she wears.

"I hate when guys do that," she complains, sitting down and sipping her drink. "It's like they think they can buy you for the cost of a cocktail."

I take a sip of my drink, and it is *strong*.

"Yeah, me too," I say, even though my bank balance really doesn't allow me to say no to a free drink.

"So," Trix starts. "How was your second week at the Montrose Mansion?"

I let out a laugh. "Has it only been two weeks? Feels like a lifetime."

"Right? We've survived a shooting, a celebrity orgy and you nearly got fired how many times?"

"About eight, I think."

"Anyone else would definitely have been out on their ass by now."

"Not this again."

"I'm just telling it like I see it. Max has some reason he wants you around. He definitely could have fired you after that stunt at the party. What was that about anyway?"

"I thought he was—" I take another gulp, and the gin buzz makes me think telling Trix will be okay. "I thought he was my brother, Aiden."

"Oh, shit. Your brother that went missing?"

I nod.

"Why would he be at Max Montrose's place?"

I shake my head. "I don't know, I just saw the guy and thought—"

"No wonder you went running, if you thought he was Aiden."

"It wasn't, though. It just looked a lot like him from a distance."

"How long has he been missing?"

"Six months."

"Any leads yet?"

"None."

"You were close, right?"

"We were, yeah. He's a few years older than me, but we hung out all the time. At least, until his last few years of school. He started going to parties and bars. He still invited me along, but I never liked that scene."

"What was the scene?"

"Aiden was friends with a lot of…" I try to find the words. "Burnouts, I guess you could call them. People who just wanted to drink, take drugs and party. I thought if I hung out with them, I'd become like them, so I kept a bit of distance. At the time, I still thought I might go to college, so I studied hard but still talked to Aiden most days on the phone."

"What happened with college?"

"I didn't get the grades. Sometimes I think I might as well have been out getting wasted instead of trying so damn hard and failing."

"At least you tried."

"I guess."

"What's he like? Aiden?"

I'm so grateful for the way she asks in the present tense. Like she just somehow knows he's okay, he's still out there somewhere.

"Aiden's great. Girls have always fallen for him. But he's a little wild. A loose cannon. That's part of the reason no one is taking his disappearance seriously. The cops didn't even look. They just said that he probably didn't want to be found."

"But you don't buy it?"

I shake my head. "He's never been the most reliable guy, but he wouldn't stop returning my calls just like that."

"If I can ever do anything to help—" she says.

I nod. "Thanks, Trix."

"Okay." Trix slaps her thighs and stands up. "Another round?"

We hit the bar, and this time when the bartender shakes his head at Trix's money she shoves it at him and forces him to take it.

"I wish I'd done that the first time!" She hands me my drink and grabs my other hand, pulling me onto the edge of the dance floor.

I'm feeling more than a little buzzed now, and my hips start moving to the music all on their own.

"I haven't been out dancing in so long!" Trix says as she spins around, losing a little of her drink on the way.

We drink and dance and sing along, and it's the first time in a long time that I'm not consumed with thoughts of Aiden or the Order. But Max Montrose is still never far from my mind.

We're on our third or maybe fourth cocktail when the hot guy from the bar appears with two more gin rickeys.

"For you and your friend," he says, handing me one.

I know I shouldn't, but I'm drunk and having fun, and I want to be even more drunk and having even more fun, so I hold out my hand to take it. It *is* a free drink after all, but then Trix appears beside me, taking the drink out of my hand.

"We already said no. Twice," she tells him, shoving the drinks towards him. "Why do you think we'd say yes the third time? Because we're not that drunk, jerk."

Trix looks so mad, and the guy is frowning so hard that, for some reason in my drunk state, I find it hilarious and start laughing.

Trix shoots me a look.

"I'm just being nice," the guy says.

"Oh, please," Trix says. "Nice guys *never* have to say, 'I'm just being nice'".

He raises his hands in surrender. "Look, I get that a blue-haired freak like you might not be interested in what I have to offer, but maybe you should let your friend make her own decisions."

My mouth drops in shock at what he's just said to her.

"My hair is *green*, asshole!"

He ignores her and looks at me, his dark eyes turning into pools of warmth that immediately draw me in. This guy is so hot I can't believe he's even interested in me. He was only trying to be nice by buying us some drinks. We should have thanked him and been nicer to him! This guy is *gorgeous*, and he wants *me*! Not Trix, not any of the other beautiful women here, but he wants *me*.

"Why don't we get out of here?" he asks, and it's all I want. To be alone somewhere with this sexy, wonderful, generous man who makes me feel like the only girl in the world!

I'm vaguely aware of Trix calling me back, but I don't care. I don't care about Trix, she's just jealous! She doesn't care about me or my happiness! She's just pissed that he chose me and not her!

He holds out his hand, and I take it with a smile. "I'd love to," I say. "Whatever you want. Whatever you want." And I mean it. God, I would give this man whatever he wanted. My body, my blood, my life.

"Poppy! Poppy!" I hear Trix call.

I turn back and smile at her, giving her a little wave. He pulls me through the crowd. He's strong, and I like it. I feel so safe holding this beautiful man's hand.

And then suddenly, his hand is pulled out of mine as he's shoved into the bar, breaking a row of glasses filled with recently poured cocktails.

"Poppy is mine!" It's a deep growl, a familiar voice that I can't quite place right now. I'm dizzy and confused, and I'm glad when Trix appears by my side to help me get my balance.

"Poppy, honey," Trix says. "Close your eyes and take a deep breath."

I do as she tells me, and when I open my eyes again, I see Max Montrose holding the guy I was about to go home with by the collar. There's a rage in Max's eyes I have never seen there before. His look isn't just dark, it's... *murderous*.

The guy just laughs. "I wasn't aware that she was *claimed*."

"I was going to leave with him," I whisper as I look at the guy again. A moment ago, he looked so hot, and I wanted nothing but to leave with him, to let him do whatever he wanted to me. Now there's nothing I find appealing about him at all.

"Your scent wasn't on her," the guy says. "Well, not enough for her to be claimed."

"You caught my scent on her and still tried—" Max looks like he's about to explode.

The guy's fangs appear, and I gasp.

Max growls at him. "Poppy is mine. I have claimed her. And if you ever touch her again, I will not hesitate to end you with the Certain Death."

The guy lets out a scoffing sound and gives Max a grin. "You think you can end me when your fangs can't even protrude?"

"It's time to go, Damon," says Dave, the bouncer who let me and Trix in for free. "We don't do that here."

"I didn't do anything," he says.

"You glamoured the girl and were taking her against her will. We only feed off the willing here. You know that."

"Sure, you just keep pretending *that's* how it works."

"We don't want to see you in here again," says another security guy.

"And if you don't leave now," says Dave, "we'll report you to the Fraternity."

He rolls his eyes. "Like they have any power anymore."

Max finally lets him go and shoves him towards the security guards. "I will not tell you again."

Damon smirks at Max. "This was a big mistake, Max Montrose," he says. "Very big."

"Get him out of here," Max says, and the two security guards guide him out of the club.

Max turns to us, his eyes dark and furious. "What were you two thinking, coming to a vampire bar?"

"I didn't know it was a vampire bar!" I tell him.

"I didn't mean—" Trix starts.

"You know what? I don't want to hear it," he says, cutting her off. "We're leaving. *Now.*"

We follow him out of the club and onto the street like berated teenagers, stopping in front of what looks like a James Bond car. Max opens the passenger door and gestures for me to get in, but I don't.

"Wait a second," I say. "Did you just *claim* me?" I fold my arms over my chest and glare at him.

"Just get in the car, Poppy. We'll talk about this at home."

Trix lets out a long sigh and climbs into the backseat.

"We will talk about it now," I tell him.

Max folds his own arms over his chest and it makes his arms look huge. "That vampire Damon glamoured you and was about to—" He looks up at the sky, taking a deep breath and then glares down at me. "If it weren't for me, you could be half drained in a gutter by now."

"I wouldn't have let that happen!" Trix calls out from the backseat.

He glares at her through the window. "And what if you couldn't call security in time? What if they were busy dealing with something else? What if you were glamoured too? You'd both be drained!"

Trix presses her lips together and stares out the other window.

"You can't just go around claiming people!" I tell him.

"I claimed you in order to save your life. Do you understand?"

Now it's my turn to go silent.

"Please, Poppy. Just get. In. The. Car."

I do as he says.

He drives us home in silence while I try to process the fact that a vampire glamoured me and could have killed me.

I could have died tonight.

But I didn't. Because Max was there. Because he claimed me. Heat runs through my entire body at the thought of it.

Max Montrose not only saved my life, but he *claimed* me as *his*.

CHAPTER TWENTY-FOUR

"Once a human is claimed by a vampire, no other vampire may feed on that human. A vampire may stake any other vampire who feeds on or attempts to feed on their claimed humans."

The Fraternity of the Everlasting Rose Handbook, page 76

It's been years since I drove off the estate into West Hollywood, but the drive home has never felt this long or this uncomfortable.

I didn't go in there with a plan to claim Poppy, but all my senses were telling me something was wrong before I even stepped into the club. And seeing Damon holding her hand like that, clearly having her under his control, it felt like I was burning alive from the inside.

All these feelings I've been having for her were heightened a thousand-fold in that moment. I couldn't let her go with him. I couldn't let anything happen to her. I couldn't let anyone else *touch* her.

Of course I didn't want to see her drained, but I couldn't think of her under another man either, someone else's lips on her, someone else *inside* her.

Rage boils within me as I pull into the garage and turn off the engine. I take a breath and try to calm myself down enough to speak to Poppy about all this. I turn to her, and she looks back at me, her soft warm eyes showing none of the anger at my claiming her without her permission now.

"You will probably feel a little confused for the next few days," I tell her. There's a strand of hair that crosses her cheek, and I am about to reach out and push it back for her, but I resist. "You may find yourself thinking about Damon, thinking he's desirable. It's just an echo of the glamour. It will fade fast, much faster than a blood bond. You're lucky he didn't bite you."

I'm lucky he didn't bite you.

"What's a blood bond?" she asks. Dear god, she is such an innocent. Someone who doesn't know about blood bonds should never have been at a vampire bar, and I should not be dancing a dangerous, flirtatious game with one so pure.

"A blood bond is what happens when vampires feed off humans," I tell her. "It's a very strong psychic bond. It's hard to break, but it will fade, eventually." I turn to Trix and give her a warning look. "And Trix, I'm sure I don't have to explain to you how important it is that you tell no one about what you saw tonight or that I'm—what I am."

Of course, I knew from Trix's background check that she had worked at Vincent's. I suspected she might know something of vampire kind from her time there, but I thought it most likely she had been glamoured of any memories. But I see now I was wrong. Some idiot vampire, probably with a crush on her, decided to let her remember.

I think about how I should have glamoured Poppy when she first learned what I was. But even that wouldn't keep her safe from other vampires who took a shine to her, and she was so very easy to shine for.

Trix nods. "Of course, you have my word. And I'm so—"

I hold up a hand. "The two of you should get some sleep."

I let them go ahead, following behind them, making sure they do in fact go into the staff quarters rather than god only knows where.

If I've learned one thing tonight, it's that those two are both magnets for trouble.

CHAPTER TWENTY-FIVE

Poppy

Max's voice growling the words "Poppy is mine" runs in circles around my brain all night. I barely sleep. It's my day off, and I wanted to sleep late, but I'm too restless. Too full of memories of being glamoured and Max coming to my rescue.

Trix's bed is empty, and I wonder if she's had the same kind of night.

Just before dawn, I throw a cardigan over my PJs and go in search of coffee.

The kitchen is dark and quiet. I switch on the light and go about making myself an oat latte, just like Trix showed me so that she didn't have to make my coffee every morning.

"Hey." Trix slides onto a bar stool on the other side of the enormous marble counter.

"Latte?" I offer.

"Please."

"Where did you sleep?" I ask as I grab another mug.

"I didn't," she yawns. "I spent most of the night watching infomercials. I think I got maybe twenty minutes during some ruby necklace and bracelet set. I've just been out sitting in the courtyard watching the sky start to lighten."

"So," I begin as I froth more oat milk for her drink. I don't know where to start. "Last night, huh?"

She rubs her hands over her eyes. "Yeah, last night."

I finish making our drinks and then nod back towards the staff quarters. We walk back down the path, into the staff lounge and settle ourselves on the couch with Trix's crochet blanket over our knees.

"I mean, I knew vampires existed," Trix starts, "but I didn't know *Max Montrose* was a vampire. That's a revelation."

"You knew about vampires?"

"Vincent's," she says, pulling her legs up under her. "When I got the job there, I didn't know it was… you know, run by vampires. Or that vampires were even real. I just thought it was a weird vintage goth bar."

"How did you find out?"

"Vampires are experts at hiding what they are. If anyone got suspicious that things weren't quite right there, they'd just glamour them, erase their memories of what they'd seen. Most of the bar staff would just get glamoured every night after their shift to make them think they had a normal working night. So messed up."

"But you somehow remembered. You knew?"

"There was this guy." She lets out a soft laugh. "It's always a guy, right?"

"You hooked up with a vampire?" I immediately want to ask her what it was like.

She shakes her head. "No. I didn't. But I liked him, like

really liked him. You know those crushes where you just can't stop thinking about them?"

I think of Max. "Yeah, I do."

"He was one of the owners, and he had this magnetic energy about him. I was obsessed. Every shift I worked, I'd just be constantly looking around for him." She takes a sip of coffee. "One night after everyone was gone, I heard a noise in the office upstairs. Security had already left, so I grabbed an empty bottle to use as a weapon and went up there to see what was going on."

"I would've just run."

"I should have! When I got up there, I saw him with a woman. His fangs were out and his mouth was covered in blood."

I gasp.

Trix waves a hand around. "She was fine, laughing, loving it. But it was a pretty big shock."

"He didn't glamour you and make you forget?"

"It was weird. It was like he *wanted* me to know. I don't know why. I think maybe it's some vampire kink. They like knowing that you know what they are. Knowing you're slightly freaking out every time you see them. They don't usually want humans to remember because it puts their kind in danger, but fuck, who am I going to tell? No one would believe me."

"What did you do? Did you keep working there?"

"Poppy, the tips at that place were incredible. It sounds crazy to work for vampires, but at the time, I really needed the money to pay off some debts from culinary school."

"So how did you get fired?"

She twists her lips. "One night after work he comes up to me and tells me he wants to drink from me."

"Oh, shit!"

"The crazy thing was that after everything, I still felt so

attracted to him. I wanted so badly to let him drink from me."

"You let him do it?"

She shakes her head. "I couldn't go through with it. I was too scared. So I said no, and you know what he said?"

"What?"

"He said don't bother coming in tomorrow or ever again."

"That's unfair dismissal."

"Like I was going to fight a vampire in court?"

"What a dick," I say.

"Sometimes I think I should have just done it."

"For the tips?"

"I knew a lot of Donnas when I worked there. It's what they call the girls who like getting bitten. It's a play on donors, blood donors. The guys are called Dons. One of my friends there had her mind wiped so many times she was kind of nutty, but she told me that the feeling you get from a vampire bite is like nothing on earth. She said it's better than drugs, sex or even shopping."

"Wow, even better than shopping?" I laugh.

"That's what she said!"

"I'm still curious about it. The Bite. I liked him. A *lot*. He was sexy, rich and powerful. But I was... just a scared dumb human, I guess."

"You probably should've been scared."

She puts her mug down on the coffee table and turns towards me. "Are you scared of Max?"

My face heats and I try to hide behind my own mug.

"You know, now that he's *claimed* you and all," she adds.

"What does that mean?" I ask. "That he *claimed* me?"

"I'm not exactly an expert on this stuff, but I know it means that no other vampire is allowed to feed from you."

My stomach churns at the idea of anyone feeding off me. But then I think about Max's fangs in my neck and the idea of it being better than sex, and it feels more exciting than scary.

"I don't think he would hurt you, Poppy. But... just be careful around him, okay?"

"Okay."

"But if you do let him bite you, I want *all* the hot horny details."

CHAPTER TWENTY-SIX

ax

I WAKE from a deep rest the next morning to Henrietta banging on my bedroom door. I suddenly remember last night. Damon almost taking Poppy, me claiming Poppy, me standing outside the club in West Hollywood as I tried to get the girls into my car.

Oh shit.

I throw my robe over my pajamas and let her in.

"What did they get?" I ask.

She shoves a tablet in front of my face.

"Reclusive movie star Max Montrose in threesome with two girls young enough to be his daughters," I read out loud. I swipe to the next one. "Has-been Max Montrose appears with secret daughter? Oh, for Christ's sake. I'm only nine years older than her!"

Henrietta gives me a look. "The age gap is a little more than that, isn't it, Max?"

I ignore her and read another. "Washed up old hack Max Montrose is seen trying to relive his youth with girls half his age. Wonderful." I hand back the tablet and take last night's glass of Sybline from the nightstand, throwing back a large unsatisfying swig. "I'm done with all this. I don't care. Let them say what they like."

"Do you even want a career anymore, Max?" Henrietta sighs.

"What an earth has ever made you think I care about my career?" I turn and pour myself a fresh glass.

"You know you still have some years left—" she starts.

"Oh, not you too! Yes, yes, so I keep being told. But I. Don't. Care. I'm done. Done with it all and I have been for a long time, Etta." I take a seat at the table by the window and nurse my drink.

"You used to care about how the world saw you, even when you'd had enough with the industry."

"Well, maybe I don't anymore. And they are right. I am a washed-up has-been old hack."

Henrietta sighs. "Max. You are one of the greatest stars of all time. You seem to have forgotten that in the last few years, but as long as I'm working on your staff, I will continue to remind you."

"Perhaps I should let you go, then."

She ignores my threat, as she has been doing for the last six years. "I can do damage control on this, but I still need your permission."

"Fine," I say, staring into my glass. "Is there anything else?" I ask dismissively.

"Get off that stuff." She leaves, closing the door behind her.

I place the synthetic blood wine on the table. She's right. First with the shooting and now with other vampires having notions concerning Poppy, I need to be at full strength to be able to protect her.

But when I'm at full strength, when I'm off the Sybline and back on the blood, I'll become more of a danger to her than ever.

CHAPTER TWENTY-SEVEN

oppy

CLAUDIA: Poppy, where are you?
   Claudia: What's going on there?
   Claudia: I saw you on Hollywood Daily!!!!
   Claudia: We need an emergency meeting.
   Claudia: Meet at the apartment ASAP.

I SIGH and throw my purse onto the passenger seat. The last thing I want to do with my day off is see Claudia, but maybe if we get it done quickly, I can still make it to the vintage market.

I quickly bash out a message that I'm on my way and drive out of the estate, down through the hills and then get stuck in traffic for an hour.

I mash the radio panel to try to find something a bit more upbeat than the depressing ballads that always seem to be playing. I find a station playing one of Taylor Swift's old songs and sing along while I crawl towards the apartment.

The song ends, and the DJ starts talking fast and furiously. I mostly just ignore him until I hear him say "Max Montrose". I slam on my breaks, turn up the volume and listen.

"So, this guy hasn't been seen in public, for like, what? Three years?"

"Three years?" his female co-host laughs. "More like eight, Bob!"

"Get out, eight years? Are you sure, Stacey? Well, where the hell has this guy been?"

"No one knows! He did publicity for his last movie, *Love Delayed*, and then the guy totally disappeared!"

"Well, if I was in that movie I'd disappear too!"

They both laugh manically.

"So, what's his story?" Bob asks. "Why has he appeared now, in that incredible vehicle with those two gorgeous young girls?"

I don't think I've ever been called gorgeous before, especially not on national radio. A smile crosses my lips and then quickly falls again. This may not actually be good. For me, for Max or for my situation with the Order.

"There are a bunch of rumors going around this morning," Stacey says. "Some people are saying these are his new girlfriends, others speculate that they are his daughters, secret love children."

"How old is the guy now?"

"Mid, maybe late thirties?" she guesses.

"The images are a little grainy, but these girls look about mid-twenties to me. Does that math add up to you?"

"Well, I think we all know those aren't his *daughters*, don't we Bob?"

They both laugh again.

"Wait, we're getting something just coming in," he says. "He's just released a statement on social media."

"I thought wasn't on social media?"

"It's his first and only post."

"Okay, okay, what's it say?" she asks.

"He says these women are in his employ and he was simply giving them a ride home when they got stuck out in West Hollywood last night."

"In his *employ*?" she giggles.

"I bet you wouldn't mind being in this guy's employ, huh, Stacey?"

"The picture on his socials this morning is giving *heat*," she says. "Max Montrose, if you're listening, I'm available for hire!"

They both laugh again.

"Max Montrose risen from the dead!" she says. "I for one would love to see him do another movie."

"He's made some amazing movies, hasn't he?" Bob says. "*A Knight to Remember* really was an excellent time travel film."

"*The Letterbox*!" she exclaims.

"Oh yeah, even me, a hardcore action fan could appreciate *that* romantic comedy. A work of genius, truly."

I shake my head. Two minutes ago, they were talking about how bad his acting was and now they're singing his praises. Amazing how fickle people can be about celebrities. Suddenly he's hot and trending and everyone's a fan.

"Well, whoever those girls are, I'm glad they got home okay," Stacey says.

"Oh, me too," says Bob. "Really great to know there are upstanding guys out there like Max Montrose getting everyone home safely."

.   .   .

THIS TIME when I get into the apartment there's coffee and a croissant waiting for me.

"Poppy," Claudia says, beaming at me. "Sit, eat."

I sit in-between Kayla who's also grinning at me and Justin who's eying up my croissant.

I shift my chair slightly away from him now that I know he's attempted murder and pick up my pastry.

"You've got Max eating out of your hand, this is fantastic," Claudia says.

"What? No, I don't. He just gave us a ride home."

"He hasn't left his house in *eight years*," Kayla says. "He could've just booked you an Uber."

"We have some intel that vampires may frequent Vincent's," Claudia says. "Tell us everything about what you saw."

She clearly doesn't know that Vincent's is run by and *absolutely* filled with vampires. I think about that Damon guy and how he was going to take me and for the first time I think I get it. I get why the Order wants them all gone. They are rich, powerful and immortal, and clearly some of them are very fucking dangerous.

But not all of them. Not Max.

Max has had so many opportunities to drink from me, to drain me, to kill me, and he hasn't.

But if I protect Max and the vampires who are trying to live decent lives, am I also protecting the bad vampires who are glamouring and taking humans against their will?

If I tell her what I know about Vincent's, even if I stick with my story about Max not being a vampire, will they follow the threads and come after him eventually, anyway?

I take a bite of the pastry and chew, considering what to do next.

Save the good vampires and let the bad vampires live? Or sentence them all to death?

My eyes flick to Justin and then back to my pastry.

"I really didn't see much," I say. "I was drunk off gin rickeys. I don't remember a lot."

"Poppy, we need you to be on it at all times," Claudia says.

"Can't I just have one night to let loose a little?"

"No," Claudia says. "You can't remember anything from the club?"

I shake my head. "No, not really."

"What else have you got on him?" She says it like he's already convicted.

"Nothing," I say, taking a sip of the coffee that is now cold.

"I'm this close to replacing you, Poppy!" Claudia snaps.

"Max already has some kind of connection with Poppy," Kayla says. "We need her in there. She's our best asset right now."

"You're right," Claudia sighs. "I'm sorry Poppy. It's just that I have the Order breathing down my neck and I—" For a split second I see her tough, confident exterior fall. "I need evidence that he is the head of the Fraternity. A book, a letter, any information with anything alluding to him being a vampire, involved somehow. I need the names of all the other members. I need—" She pushes her hair behind her ear. "I just need this to move forward."

"And what if there is no evidence, because he's *not* a vampire?" I ask.

"If you can't find evidence he's not a vampire, you better find some real strong evidence that he's human."

"What happened to innocent until proven guilty?" I ask.

She lets out a laugh. "Oh, Poppy, you think that's how the Order works? In case you didn't realize it yet, they shoot first, ask questions later. And if we don't give the Order what they want, it will be all four of us with our heads on the block."

There's something about her tone, the way she says *the Order* as if she's not part of it. that makes me wonder if she doesn't want anything to do with any of this, just like I don't.

Justin glares at me. "You better get this right, or this will all be on you."

I put my croissant back in its paper bag. "Are we done here?"

Claudia nods. "I still expect daily updates but get me something better than the pointless bills and letters you've been sending."

"I'll do my best." I stand up, grab the croissant and walk out of the kitchen towards the front door.

I'm just about to close the door behind me when Kayla opens it and hands me my coffee.

"Oh, thanks," I say.

"I don't know what you're up to," she says in a half-whisper, "but you're going to have to give him up sooner or later."

My heart does an extra thump. "I don't know what you're talking about."

"One way or another, Max Montrose is going down. Just make sure you don't go down with him, Poppy." She gives me a straight lipped smile and then disappears back inside.

CHAPTER TWENTY-EIGHT

"*The average vampire will need to drink at least two to four pints of blood a day to sustain strength and immortality. Less than this will result in a tired and ill-equipped vampire. Anything over six pints can create a sensation of being high on blood which is to be avoided at all costs. This makes the vampire act much like a human intoxicated on alcohol, silly and clown-like.*"

The Fraternity of the Everlasting Rose Handbook, page 139

THE THING about my bloodlust returning is that while it means I'm more of a danger to Poppy than I was before, my hunger for her becomes nothing less than insatiable.

It's quite the quandary.

After three days of slowly bringing human blood back into my diet, I am already feeling stronger, hungrier and hornier. These last few days I've been taking numerous showers each day just so I can sort myself out. And every time I think about Poppy as I reach my climax.

It will probably take another week or so before I'm back to full strength, and so I decide that it's better to talk to Poppy now, before the bloodlust fully returns.

I pick up the phone and dial James.

"Sir."

"Where is Poppy right now?"

"She's in the library I believe."

Of course she is.

"Perfect, thank you, James."

I dress in a clean, crisp ivory shirt rolled up to my fore-arms with freshly pressed midnight blue trousers. I style my hair and choose the most expensive gold Rolex from my watch collection. Poppy doesn't seem like the sort of woman who would even know the worth of it, which is refreshing to me, but it still makes me feel confident to wear it.

I stand outside the library and feel butterflies in my stom-ach. I let out a light laugh at the feeling. It's something that I have not felt for a very long time. Is it *nerves*? Excitement? It's uncomfortable, but somehow comforting. My body telling me something wonderful may be about to happen. The door is ajar, and I consider knocking until I remember this is *my* library. I do not need to knock.

I walk in to see Poppy standing on the bookcase ladder dusting the top shelves. She's dressed in those tight pants again, and they stretch over her gorgeous backside as she moves from side to side dusting.

I instantly go into pushing Poppy away mode before I can stop myself. "Nice to see you actually doing some work for once," I say.

She nearly falls off the ladder, and in an instant I'm right underneath her, holding it and bracing myself for her fall. But she doesn't fall. She holds on and just glares down at me.

"I work very hard around here, thank you very much," she says as she begins to slowly make her way down. The closer she gets to me, the further away I step.

"Of course, please accept my apologies. I am very happy with your work, Poppy."

She blinks at my change of tone, her big bright hazel eyes making me want nothing more than to launch myself at her and finally get to see, touch and taste what's under those pants.

"Apology accepted," she finally says.

"I wanted to speak with you about the other night."

"Oh."

It's awkward just standing here, her with a duster in her hand, me with my hands stuffed in my pockets. I'm about to suggest we sit on the couch in the center of the room, but the proximity would be too much. Instead, I gesture to a pair of comfortable chairs by the window. "Please sit."

She puts the duster down, and we sit opposite each other. It's the first time we're sitting together like this, and it's worse than being on late night TV and waiting for the host to bring up the one thing I've told them not to, which they always do.

"About the other night?" she prompts.

"Yes."

"When you *claimed* me." She makes air quotes around claimed like it was something I made up in order to get into bed with her.

I shift in my seat. "Yes."

"To save me."

I want to tell her as much as I wanted to step in and save her from that vile piece of rubbish Damon, that it wasn't the only reason I claimed her. Damon was already about to be removed by security. I didn't need to claim her at all. It was just that in that moment I couldn't do *anything but* claim her.

"It's not very gentlemanly of a vampire to claim a human without their express permission."

"You're just now asking for permission?"

"Let's back up a little," I say. "I want you to understand what it means to be claimed."

"Okay."

"It means no other vampire has permission to drink from you. If they even dare to try, I have permission to kill them. And believe me, Poppy. If another vampire walked in here right now and tried to bite you, I would kill them without hesitation."

Her heart rate rises, and her mouth falls open a little.

"I know I didn't ask for your permission, and that was wrong of me. If you like, I can release you from my claim. But it will be safer for you, now that you are known in the vampire community, to continue to be mine."

A flush of color appears on her chest and moves up to her cheeks. "Oh."

I lean forward and look into her eyes. "Do I have your permission to claim you? To call you mine?" I anxiously await her response as those butterflies start dancing again within me.

"What else does it mean?" she asks. "Aside from the fact that no other vampire can drink from me? Do you like, *own* me? Does it mean *you* get to drink from me? What if I meet another vampire who wants to date me? What if I met a normal human guy but I'm claimed by you? Sorry, I'm asking a lot of questions." She puts her hands over her cheeks, and it's so adorable it makes me want to take her hands away and kiss every inch of her entire face.

"It doesn't have to mean anything more than your protection."

"What does it usually mean?"

"Well, usually… when a human is claimed by a vampire, it means that vampire has permission to drink from them whenever they like, but I will absolutely never drink from you."

"Oh."

"Unless it's something you want," I add softly. *Oh, Jesus, what am I saying?* "The experience can be… quite pleasant for humans."

The flush disappears from her face, and I immediately take that as a no, berating myself for ever even suggesting it in the first place.

"It's actually been a long time for me," I say, leaning back in my chair. "I haven't fed directly from a human for many years."

"Why did you stop drinking from… humans?"

"Because I didn't want to be a monster anymore. Or at least, I wanted to be less of a monster. I can't change what I am, but I can choose to cause as little harm as possible."

"Like some kind of Buddhist vampire?"

Her joke makes me chuckle. "Something like that."

"You don't drink blood at all?"

"I didn't." I pause. "But since the shooting and what nearly happened to you at Vincent's, I've decided to go back to drinking."

"Oh?"

"You see, the synthetic blood takes away the bloodlust, but it also dulls some of my abilities. In order to protect you, I need to be at my full strength. But that also means I'm more of a danger to you, and the others. So, I will need to keep my distance."

"How can you protect me if you're keeping your distance?" I may be mistaking it, my abilities haven't completely returned yet, but I hear worry in her voice, worry at me keeping my distance as if she *wants* me close.

"My claiming of you will keep you safe from other vampires. And as long as you're on the estate, I can protect you here."

She stares out the window, deep in thought.

"And as for your other questions, if you wanted to become involved with another vampire, I would release you immediately. Although I don't recommend it. I try to continue to live as a gentleman as much as I can, but most of our kind are dangerous. Many have no control over their bloodlust at all. As I'm sure you understand from your encounter with Damon."

"What would have happened?" she asks. "If you hadn't arrived in time?"

I don't tell her that most likely, the security guards would have been there in plenty of time, and they would have kicked Damon to the curb. But most likely isn't good enough when it comes to Poppy. "It's best you never find out."

I don't answer her question about what would happen if she met a human man that she wanted to be with. I don't tell her I'd drain any human man that tried to touch her in an instant. I keep that little piece of information to myself.

"I wish that you'd never gotten involved in all this," I say.

She looks back at me, those hazel eyes flickering gold in the light from the bright day outside. "Well, I did."

"And I'm sorry for that. Truly. But my claiming you can help keep you safe. If you consent to it."

She looks out the window again, and I'm filled with worried butterflies that she's going to say no. Not only because I'm worried for her safety, but because I so desperately want her to be *mine*. And maybe I can't have her body, or her blood or her love, but maybe this would be enough. Just a little something, just a little piece of her, tied to me.

"May I claim you, Poppy?" I ask.

She takes a shaky breath. "Yes, Mr. Montrose. You may claim me."

CHAPTER TWENTY-NINE

oppy

"HE ASKED for permission to claim you? Holy shit, that's *hot*!" squeals Trix when I tell her later that night while we're getting ready for bed.

I feel my face get hot for the billionth time today. God, I wish it wasn't, but it was the hottest moment of my life. Even hotter than when he just went ahead and claimed me at the club. The way he *asked* me if I wanted to be claimed by him! I wanted to shout out Yes, claim me! Take me! Make me yours in all the ways you want to! Throw me up against the stacks! Take me, I'm yours!

"Did you ask him about the sex stuff?"

"What?!"

"You know, the sex stuff that goes with claiming?"

"No, I don't know the sex stuff that goes with claiming. You never mentioned that!"

"Oh, sorry. I thought you knew."

"I don't know anything about any of this!"

"Well, you're learning fast."

"What sex stuff?" I demand.

"Okay, so, vampires only claim humans they want to have sex with. Sure, it's about not letting other vampires feed off them, but it also means no other vampire can have *sex* with that human."

"Max didn't mention that part."

But, oh my god I wish he had.

"Well, he is a *gentleman*," Trix swoons. "But Poppy, honey, he wouldn't have claimed you if he didn't want to have sex with you."

"Oh god, please stop," I say, getting into bed and tucking myself in. "If he wanted to have sex with me, he would have by now."

Trix makes an "OooOoOOOOOoooooh" sound. "You're going to give it up for Max Montrose. This is so cute."

"I'm not a virgin!"

"Oh, vampire sex is different. It's like a second virginity."

"You've had sex with a vampire?"

"No. But I've heard it's different."

"Trix!" I laugh.

She sits up on her elbow. "Being bitten would definitely be a first."

"I'm not going to get bitten."

"What about the sex stuff?"

"Or have sex with him!"

"But you would if he wanted to?"

"I'm not talking about this anymore. Go to sleep."

"Poppy, it's totally natural to want to have sex with your movie star vampire boss."

"Goodnight, Trix!"

"If it happens, promise me you'll tell me right away?"

"It's not going to happen," I groan.

"But if it does?"

"Fine. If I ever have sex with Max Montrose, I promise to tell you right away."

"It doesn't have to be right away, like don't reach for your phone right after your orgasm."

I laugh and throw a spare pillow at her. "Go to sleep, Trix!"

"Goodnight, Poppy, sweet dreams."

But I don't have sweet dreams, just dirty ones.

CHAPTER THIRTY

$\mathcal{M}$ax

I SPEND the next week detoxing off the Sybline. The bloodlust is well and truly back, and I can't trust myself to be around humans yet. Especially Poppy. My desire for her blood, her body, her *everything* is so strong — *too* strong. So I hide away in my suite, allowing only James and Henrietta to see me while I try to find myself in what needs to become my new normal. I order some indoor plants for the mansion in the hopes that it will brighten the place up a bit. Not for me. For Poppy.

I tell myself I'm doing well, that I have it all under control. When I feel my desire for Poppy's blood taking over, I take hot showers, work myself to a climax for release, then turn the tap cold to shock myself into remembering that although I've claimed her, she is not really *mine* and never will be.

My awareness is heightened. My hearing is stronger. I

can hear Poppy moving around on the floor beneath me, dropping things and sighing to herself. She often hums as she works, a pretty song I can't quite place.

I've only been on the synthetic blood for a few years, but this process of returning to human blood brings back difficult memories from when I was first turned. The agony of being aware of *everything*. The insane thirst that's never quite quenched no matter how much blood is consumed, and the insatiable desire to *fuck*.

While it's painful and intense and I'm terrified of hurting Poppy or any human for that matter, I also feel more alive than I have in many years.

I hear James and Henrietta making their way through the mansion. They know I can hear them breathing outside the door to my private parlor, but they still knock.

"Come in," I call from my reclined position on the dark blue velvet couch where Callie has been sitting on my chest. She jumps and runs away as soon as the door opens.

"Delivery, sir." James steps inside with another crate of bottles filled with blood. The blood comes from various sources, but the ones I order are from blood banks. I realize that stealing blood that could save lives is morally wrong. But there are worse ways to get it, and we never take rare or much needed blood types. The lab that makes the artificial blood was originally set up by me to create blood that could be swapped for the real human blood we took. It was never part of the original plan for me to drink it myself for so long. But the effects of the product — the way it dulled my blood-lust and allowed me to live a less debauched life — greatly appealed to me.

The company who supplies the blood bank blood to us puts it into wine bottles. It makes me feel slightly less like a villain in a horror movie to drink from a bottle and not straight from the bag at least.

"Thank you, James." He places the bottles on a rack by the bar.

Henrietta hands me a pile of thick envelopes. "More scripts," she says.

I throw the stack onto a table. I have no plan to look at any of them.

"An indie by Palmieri that would be perfect for you."

"Hmmmm?" It's the first time I've been even mildly interested in a project since I retired for good. "Her last two movies weren't bad," I say.

"And they both won Oscars," she adds.

"Ah, the elusive Oscar." I've won plenty of awards during my career and been nominated for sixteen Oscars. I have never won. "Maybe I'll take a look."

Henrietta's eyebrows shoot up into her mane of red hair.

"I realize I haven't thanked you yet, Etta. For the magic you weaved over the situation outside Vincent's."

"That's what you pay me for."

"How did you do it?"

"A witch never tells," she says.

"What was it, Etta? A word weaving spell on the caption?" James asks.

"A sigil on the image?" I ask.

She just smiles. "The intention was to influence the reader of the post to believe that Max Montrose was the most handsome and talented movie star that ever lived. Plus, a little banishing of judgement."

"Yes, but *how* did you do it?" I ask.

"If I tell you my secrets, you may no longer need my services."

"Henrietta, you know you will have a position here until the end of time," I assure her.

James clears his throat. "Will there be anything else, sir?"

"No, thank you, James. Etta."

They take their leave, and I step out onto the balcony taking a deep breath. The air smells so damn *fresh,* and the sun on my skin feels like happiness.

Perhaps things will all work out. Perhaps I could do another movie. Perhaps even win the Oscar. I close my eyes and smile.

When I open my eyes and look down, Poppy is standing by the pool dressed in a towel.

Oh god, is it pool time for the staff again so soon?

She slips the towel down to reveal nothing but that goddamn cherry red bikini she was wearing the last time I saw her down there and had to have James remove her for my own sanity.

If I couldn't handle seeing her like that then, I *definitely* can't handle it now.

She walks towards the edge of the water. Her breasts look as if they are about to break free from the small triangles of material covering them. My fangs tingle. As she turns around to lower herself into the pool, presenting her scantily clad backside, my fangs thrust from my mouth. It's been a long time, and the pain of it is very present. And then the blood-lust kicks in, the insatiable desire to leap out of the window and run to her, grab her, kiss her, bite her, *fuck* her.

I run a hand over the sweat on my forehead.

I need this. Exposure therapy. If I can watch her without running down there to bite her, I will know that I have control. That I can be trusted around humans again.

She begins to swim, and I watch in pain. Teeth and dick throbbing.

I am doing well. I am okay. I am still here, not down there. This is a win.

I grip the edge of the balcony and try to convince myself I'm fine.

She floats on her back, her gorgeous breasts like two lifebuoys calling me to safety. No, this is *danger,* not safety!

It's then that she sees me. I pray she doesn't see my fangs or the bulge in my pants.

And then she *smiles* and *waves.*

It's her gorgeous, sunshine and warmth smile that tips me over the edge. I step back, slamming the balcony door closed behind me. I grab a fresh bottle of blood and down it. It only eases my pain and bloodlust a touch. I crack open another and try to drink, but I remember this feeling too well. When it's like this, the only thing that helps is drinking directly from a human.

I can't. I can't. I can't.

I drink another bottle, aware that I am already exhausting my supply of this blood that was given to save lives, not for monsters to drink.

I rip off my shirt, which is now splattered in blood, and dress for a different occasion.

ax

EVEN AS I arrive at the club, this time wearing a hoodie, baseball hat and dark glasses, I already know that this is a really fucking bad idea. But I couldn't stay there cooped up in my suite, bloodlust raging while Poppy wandered around in a bikini in my garden!

"What can I get you?" asks the girl working the bar. She's human — pretty, with short pink hair and bee-sting lips.

I look up at her from under my hat. "I'm looking for Donna," I tell her. The old code for what I want.

I see a look of recognition in her eyes, and she smiles. "Of course. Can I get you anything else while you wait?"

"Whiskey," I tell her.

She pours me a drink. "On the house." Then she disappears, and I turn to watch the crowd while I sip my drink.

The clientele tonight is mostly human. I spot a vampire, an older man dancing with a young man on the dance floor.

A few other vampires are dotted around watching, but no one appears to be using glamours or trying to pull any tricks like Damon did last time I was here. But it's still early, I suppose.

The pink-haired bartender appears at my side. "Hi, I'm Donna," she says with a smile.

"Oh, right."

I've done this a million times but tonight feels different. I'm nervous. More nervous than she is. Her breathing is calm, her heart rate is slightly elevated, but she's comfortable. She's used to this.

I follow her past the bar to a small room out the back. It's low-lit and decorated much the same as the club in a hodge-podge twenties style — couches and armchairs, piles of cushions for comfort, dark rugs to hide the bloodstains. She closes and locks the door behind us, then takes my hand and guides me towards a worn leather couch. Of course, it's easier to clean.

"Do you do this often?" I ask her.

"I'm a Donna, not a blood whore," she says, mildly offended.

"I didn't mean to suggest that you were, it's just that you seem very calm for someone who's about to be bitten."

"I enjoy it," she says as she takes off her sweater, revealing a skimpy tank top that gives me easy access to all her pulse points. "Where should we start?" she asks. "Do you just want blood or sex as well?"

I run a hand over my face. "I'm not sure," I tell her.

"We can go slow." She slides up beside me and offers her wrist with an easy smile.

And even though my bloodlust is through the roof and that primal part of me wants nothing more than to bite and fuck this woman, all I can think about is Poppy in that goddamn cherry red bikini!

I jump up from the couch. "I'm sorry, I… I can't."

"Did I do something wrong?" she asks, genuinely worried this is all her fault.

"Not at all. You are lovely, really. I just… I've changed my mind. That's all. How much do I owe you?"

She shakes her head. "You didn't drink, so you owe nothing."

I pull out a couple of hundreds and hand them to her. "I sincerely apologize."

She looks at the money and then laughs. "Everything they say about you is true, huh?"

"What do they say about me?"

"That you truly are a gentleman."

But a gentleman is the last thing I feel like as I drive back through the Hollywood Hills, desperate to see Poppy and ask her if she's willing to be claimed by me in *every* way.

CHAPTER THIRTY-TWO

oppy

I KNEW Max was watching as I dropped my towel and walked towards the water. I could feel his eyes on me. And I was glad about it. I *wanted* him to look at me. I may not have the body of a model, but my curves are still in the right places.

As I take a shower and rinse off after my swim, all I can think about is Max watching me by the pool in my bikini.

But when I smile and wave up at him, instead of scowling and disappearing inside the mansion, he lifts his hand and waves back. Then, a few moments later, he runs at vampire speed straight towards the pool. He rips off his shirt and strips down to his boxer briefs before sliding into the water and towards me. He reaches around me, but he's not going in for a hug, he's untying the straps of my bikini.

My bikini top floats away and suddenly his mouth is on my breast, his fangs nuzzling at my nipple.

"You are mine," he whispers, reaching down for the ties on my bikini bottoms.

I reach my climax before he's even gotten me fully naked, his words *you are mine* repeating over and over as I come.

It takes me a second to remember where I am — not naked in the pool with Max, but in the low-pressure shower that often runs a little hot and cold in the staff quarters.

But no matter how many times I self-climax thinking of Max, it's not enough.

It's a warm night, and my shower orgasm has given me a boost of confidence and so I pull out the floral dress and give myself permission to feel pretty for once after days on end of black pants and white shirts.

I follow the smell of burgers out into the outdoor area and find Trix over a grill, laughing at something Julio has said.

"Poppy, you're just in time! There's a choice of mushroom, bean or sticky cauliflower burgers."

"Mmmm, mushroom, please."

She places a gigantic mushroom onto a bun and then points at the table in the center of the chairs. "Condiments and salads are over there."

Julio grins through a bite of burger. "I highly recommend the macaroni salad."

"Oh, that sounds good." I pile my plate high, grab a soda from the cooler and take a seat.

"Could I get a second bean patty?" Malik asks.

Trix grabs one off the grill and practically throws it on his plate. She's clearly still not over what happened, or rather what *didn't* happen between them.

Malik has only been back a couple of days, but I'm surprised he came back at all. If I had been shot, I don't think I ever would have returned. Whatever he's getting paid must be worth it.

"Trix, you have outdone yourself," I tell her, taking a bite of my burger.

"I can't really believe Max would eat burgers, though," Julio says. "Wouldn't he be on some movie star macro diet?"

"Last week I had some extra time and baked a cake," Trix says. "When I looked for it the next morning, only a quarter of it was left."

Julio laughs. "I can just imagine Max, James and Henrietta sitting around in the kitchen eating an entire cake *Golden Girls* style."

"Right?" Trix giggles. "I was kind of hoping it would be the four of us eating it."

"That does sound fun," I say.

"I'll make another one," Trix promises.

"Next time make two," Malik tries to joke, but Trix doesn't find it amusing.

"How are things going with you, Poppy?" Malik asks, switching his focus to me.

"I think I might finally be starting to find my groove here," I say.

"Plus, Max hasn't been seen all week, so he's not around to tell you off," Trix says.

I give her a look over my mushroom burger.

"It's still crazy that you're the only cleaner on staff," Julio says. "Surely a place like this needs at least ten people cleaning every day."

"It's not so bad. I'm not even allowed on the top floor, and a bunch of rooms don't even get used, so they just need dusting and vacuuming once a week."

"I still feel like he's riding you," Julio says.

I spit out a little piece of mushroom and it lands by my feet.

"But exactly who here *wouldn't* be okay with Max Montrose riding them?" Trix asks with a laugh.

"Me," says Malik. "But, if I swung that way, I've got to admit, the man would be pretty high on the list."

"I would be more than okay with it," Julio says.

I'm picking up my chewed mushroom bite from the ground when James appears out of nowhere.

"Poppy," he says.

"Uh, yes?" I say, sitting up with the chewed piece of food in my fingers.

"Mr. Montrose requests your presence."

I look over at Trix, whose eyes go wide, and then I look back at James.

"What for?"

"When Mr. Montrose requests your presence, you don't ask 'what for'".

"Can I at least—?" I point to the last few bites of food on my plate.

"Very well."

He stands there and watches me finish the last few bites of my burger and my macaroni salad, while Trix, Julio and Malik sit in silence as I chew.

When I'm done, I thank Trix for another amazing meal, drop my plate in the kitchen and then follow James up to the second floor. And then we're standing at the bottom of the staircase up to the third floor. Where I'm not usually allowed to go.

"Where are we going?" I ask.

"Mr. Montrose's private suite."

I nearly trip on the first step upwards. "I thought no one was allowed up here."

"No one *is* allowed up here… unless personally invited by Mr. Montrose."

We reach the top of the staircase and walk down a white and gold-gilded hallway. Paintings, posters and old black and white photos adorn the walls up here but I don't have a chance to look at them as I follow James to a set of ornate double doors.

He's about to knock when Max opens the door. "Thank you, James. Poppy," he says, giving me a small nod. He dismisses James with a "That will be all" and then opens his arm to invite me into the room.

Like the rest of the house, it's heavy on antiques and plush furniture, but this room feels warmer somehow. It feels lived in, like these items are meaningful to him and not just for show. There are also plants dotted around, giving this room an aliveness that so much of the mansion doesn't have. Callie looks tiny as she sleeps in the very center of an L-shaped dark blue velvet couch. French doors open out onto the balcony, and the warm night air fills the room with a promise of plenty more hot summer nights still to come.

"You summoned me?" I try to make it sound like a joke, but it comes out squeaky.

"Yes, yes," he says. I don't miss the way his eyes fall onto the short dress I didn't realize I'd be wearing in front of him tonight. "Please sit." He gestures to the couch but doesn't sit himself. "Can I get you something to drink?"

"Uh, sure." I take a seat at one end of the couch so as not to upset Callie, but she stirs and stretches, giving me a look like I've ruined her sleep. She jumps down and goes to lick herself by the door to the balcony.

"Gin and tonic?"

"Thanks."

"I apologize if I've made an assumption. Would you prefer something else? It's just that this is what you drank on our first night together—I mean, that night we—oh hell. I am very much making a mess of this, aren't I?" He stands there holding the bottle of gin and looking tentative, his usual confident movie star swagger nowhere to be seen.

I just give him a nervous smile of my own. "Gin and tonic is great."

He turns around and goes about making my drink. "I do apologize for my demeanor this evening," he says, pouring a big shot over ice, followed by a small dash of tonic. He hands it to me, and when I take a sip, I'm glad it's strong.

He opens a bottle of wine and pours himself a glass. This wine looks thicker than the wine he was drinking before. Of course. This is the real stuff. This is *blood.*

He's about to take a sip and then doesn't, placing it back down on the bar.

"Mr. Montrose," I begin. "Is everything okay?"

"While I do enjoy the way my formal name sounds on your lips, please feel free to call me Max in this private setting."

My heart does a little leap at the idea that he *enjoys* his name on my lips. I wonder if he'd enjoy something else on my lips. "Is there something you need from me?"

His expression is pained as his eyes settle back on his glass. I realize now that he's struggled to meet my gaze since I arrived here.

"Poppy, I—"

"Yes, Max?"

He runs a hand through his dark hair, messing it up a little at the back. "Well. Ah. How to put this." He picks up the glass again but doesn't drink. "I have a proposition for you."

"Okay."

It's only now that he makes eye contact, and when he does, it is *smoldering.*

"I went to Vincent's tonight," he starts. "You see, after the shooting I knew I needed to get off the synthetic blood. But I had mixed emotions about it. I felt I might be more of a danger to you than a help. But after the situation with the vampire Damon and my claiming you, I realized the best thing to do was to reclaim my abilities."

"Okay," I say, even though I already know all this.

He begins to pace. "And in order to do that, I had to start drinking again. Blood. I've been drinking blood, Poppy." He grips the glass in his hand.

"Well, you're a vampire, aren't you supposed to?"

He glares at me and then laughs. "You are not disgusted by this?" He holds up the glass. "This is human blood, Poppy. It's what sustains me. It's what I *need* in order to be who I truly am." He takes a beat. "It's what I need to keep *you* safe." He gestures, and the blood swirls in his glass. "We steal it from a blood bank," he says with a sigh. "But it doesn't quite hit the spot in the way that—" He squeezes his eyes closed. "—In the way that drinking directly from a human does."

"You want to bite me? Is that why I'm here?"

He laughs. "If only it were that simple!" He paces again a few more times before stopping to look directly at me. "Since I got back on the blood, my thirst has been very — present. Tonight, I went to feed at Vincent's. There are always willing humans."

"Why are you telling me all this?"

"Because I couldn't do it." His brows knit together in a tortured way that makes me want to run my fingers over his brow and release all his worry.

"Why not?" I ask.

"Because—" he drops to his knees in front of me and his eyes flicker to my bare thighs. "I was there, about to bite a lovely woman, but all I could think about—" he puts the glass of blood down on the coffee table and then places his hands on either side of my thighs before staring into my soul. "— was you."

"Because you claimed me?"

"Poppy, I didn't just claim you to protect you. I claimed you because I *wanted* you. Every part of you."

A laugh escapes my mouth. This is too crazy, too unreal. This can't be happening. Max Montrose here, with his hands just inches from my thighs, gripping the velvet of the couch, telling me he *wants* me?

It's too ridiculous. Too crazy. Too completely impossible.

He stares up at me. "You are *all* I have been able to think about since you got here."

"But you've been such a—"

"Yes, I know, and I can only apologize." He sits back on his heels. "My inappropriate behavior towards you was merely an act of self-preservation, or rather preservation of *you*." He rubs his hands on his own thighs. "I could hurt you. And I would never forgive myself if I did."

"But you wouldn't," I tell him.

"Poppy, I would try my absolute damnedest never to hurt you." His eyes flicker to my thighs again. No, not my thighs, *in-between* my thighs, and then back to my eyes. "But the thing is, if we — if anything were to happen between us..." He grips his legs, a strong, powerful grip that I wish was on my thighs, pulling them apart... "There can be no future for us, and this is something you would need to understand beforehand."

I'd spent so long fantasizing about him, but I hadn't really considered how a relationship with a rich, sexy, movie star vampire would actually *work* in real life.

And of course, it couldn't.

"I need to be upfront with you about that. If anything happened between us, it would just be—"

"Just sex?"

"No, god, no! Poppy! I don't just want sex with you. I want *all* of you!" He reaches for my hands and grips them tightly. They're slightly cool, but large and strong and I immediately feel so safe in his hands. "I want to have sex with you, of course I do, but I also just want to hold you." He squeezes my hands. "I want everything with you. I want to stay up all night talking to you. I want to watch every movie ever made with you. I want to play you the music that I love and listen to your playlists. I want to show you all my favorite places and see all of yours. I want your heart, your soul, your mind, your everything."

Holy shit!!

No one has ever spoken to me like this, no one has ever said words like these to me, and I can feel my heart aching for more, more of his words, more of *everything* with him.

"But it could only ever just be… *for now*."

"You're a vampire, and I'm a human," I say dumbly, like he doesn't already know this.

His eyes penetrate mine. "I want to claim every part of you, Poppy."

Oh, my god.

"Starting with your perfect, sweet lips." Still holding my hands, he stands up, pulling me up and into him. I feel his heart hammering in his chest, and mine is pounding even faster.

He gently runs his thumb across my bottom lip. "Dear god," he says. "How are you so perfect?"

I let out a little laugh. "I am *so* far from perfect."

"To me, you are perfect." His thumb moves across my cheek now as he takes my face in his strong, cool hands. "Do you want me to claim you, Poppy? In every way I know how? Body, blood and soul?"

I nod and then eventually find my voice. "Yes," I whisper.

His lips find mine, and a firework goes off in my belly. His kiss is soft and slow, cool and confident. Of course, he has done this millions of times before, but this feels like a once in a lifetime kiss. His tongue slowly parts my lips, and the feeling of his tongue inside me opens me up to wanting more of him. I want to be filled with every part of him. His tongue, his fingers, his fangs, his cock, I want it all inside me, *claiming* me.

I have never been kissed like this before, and I suddenly feel like I'm in one of his romcoms, the leading lady being swept off her feet by the handsome British gentleman who kisses like his life depends on it.

I'm completely breathless when he pulls away.

"Poppy," he says, resting his forehead against mine. "That was — *wow*."

"I agree," I say, with a soft giggle.

He steps back, takes my hand and places his lips onto it, lingering for just a moment, and I can't believe that a kiss on the hand can be so fucking erotic!

I'm trembling at the idea of what comes next. Sex? Biting? I'm open to all of it with him. "What now?" I ask breathlessly.

"Now, I bid you goodnight."

"Wait, *what?*"

He's saying goodnight? Now?

"I don't want to rush things with you, Poppy."

"What if I *want* to rush things?"

He chuckles and twists his fingers through mine. "I need to make sure you are safe with me. And that means going slow. Right now, here like this, I still feel I have control of myself, but if we go any further tonight — I can't guarantee your safety, and I need to be able to trust myself with you."

I frown up at him.

"Poppy, if I knew without a doubt that I wouldn't hurt you, I'd be fucking you senseless within the next five minutes. And that dress, damn it to hell, how many times I have thought of you in *that dress!*"

A smile crosses my lips. Lips that *Max fucking Montrose* just *kissed*!

"Are you happy with this, Poppy? Will this arrangement? Will you be mine in every way? Will you be willing to let me bite you? Are you willing to have sex with me? And will you take things slowly with me?"

A rush of pleasure rushes to my lower belly.

Max Montrose wants to fuck me. Me!

"I should mention that although we would have no future, as long as our arrangement lasts, I would expect you to only be mine. You would not be able to be with another man, human or vampire, or I'd kill him."

My heart feels like it's about to leap from my chest onto his vintage rug.

"Well?" he asks, a worried look in his eye that I will say no.

"Of course," I reply. "As long as you promise me one thing."

"Anything."

"That even if I have to wait for it, you promise that one day you *will* fuck me senseless." I'm surprised at the boldness of my demand and immediately wonder if I've overstepped, gone too far, that I'll turn him off by throwing myself at him like this.

"On one condition," he adds.

"What's that?"

He runs a finger over the plunging neckline of my dress. "That on that night, you wear this goddamn floral dress."

CHAPTER THIRTY-THREE

Max

I watch her walk out of the room, and I am completely in awe of her. Her beauty, her innocence, her willingness to be mine. She turns at the last moment and looks back at me.

"Goodnight, Max," she says softly.

"Goodnight, Poppy."

I listen to her footsteps as she walks down the hall and down the stairs. How I want to call her back, to run after her, to bring her back into this room, to take her soft, warm hand and lead her through the doors into my bedroom. How I want to gently lay her down on my bed and do everything that I want with her!

Get a hold of yourself, man!

I straighten up and brush invisible crumbs from my shirt. I *must* control this desire. I *must* learn how to keep my cool. If I can't let her walk out of my room without running after her, grabbing her and taking her right here and now, I will never be able to trust myself with her.

So I find the will to deal with the pain, and I somehow manage not to let the desire take me.

This time.

I take my glass of blood, step over Callie, who's now sleeping in the middle of the floor, and walk out to the balcony. I close my eyes, breathe in the warm evening air and feel myself regaining control.

Until I catch a glimpse of Poppy walking the path from the kitchen to the staff quarters.

She stops mid-step as if she can feel me watching her, and perhaps she can. Or perhaps she's thinking what I'm thinking — about running back to me. And if she did, I would not stop her. If she came back to me right now, I would not tell her to go. I would throw her onto my couch and lift that damn dress and—

That's enough now!

She doesn't turn around. She just continues on her way, disappearing into the staff house.

I stay there for a time, sitting on the balcony searching for stars in the light pollution, remembering a time, nearly a hundred years ago, when they were so much brighter.

But Poppy is my star now, and I only have to close my eyes to see her brightness.

I drink two more glasses of blood and then take another cold shower.

CHAPTER THIRTY-FOUR

Poppy

TRIX IS ALREADY asleep by the time I get back, and I'm relieved that I don't have to give her any details. I don't want to share this with anyone just yet, maybe never. It is too special, too intimate, too magical. I don't want the shine from our night to be diluted by talking to anyone else.

But as excited as I am about the possibility of more nights like tonight, more moments with Max, more kisses, more sexy promises, the gnawing guilt inside me over my association with the Order, fake or not, is making me feel physically ill.

How can I be with Max if I'm lying to him about who I am and why I'm really here?

I have no doubt at all that he is not the monster Claudia and the Order have made him out to be. He is truly a gentleman in every way. He could have ripped my dress off and taken me right then and there tonight.

I wish had had!

He could have bitten me, he could have *killed* me. But he didn't. Because Max Montrose may be a vampire, but he is not a monster.

My mind is made up. I can no longer be a part of any plot to hurt him, and as soon as I can, I will tell him the truth.

If you tell him the truth, he will never look at you like that again. He will never kiss you again. He definitely won't fuck you senseless!

I shake my head and try to silence my annoying inner voice because I *have* to do the right thing.

I grab my purse and phone and walk to my car, hitting call on Claudia's number as soon as my car door is shut.

"Poppy?" It sounds like she's out at a bar. "Nice to hear from you! You have something for me?"

"Not exactly, but we need to talk."

"If you have something for me, let me know. Otherwise, I can't really talk."

"It's urgent."

She sighs. "I'm at Vincent's following a lead."

"I'll be there soon."

I know I'm not "supposed" to leave the estate on a work night, but I can't stay another night here until I make things right.

I drive down to the gate. Malik is sitting in the gatehouse looking bored as hell until he sees me and his eyebrows shoot up. "Poppy, it's so late. Where are you heading? I don't see you on the list. Did you get permission from James to be out?"

"It's an emergency," I lie.

"Is everything okay? Can I help?"

I shake my head. "It's a *boy* emergency. My friend has just been dumped. She's stuck at a bar with no money and no way to get home."

Wow, I'm really getting good at lying to everyone.

"Can't you just book her an Uber or something?"

"She's drunk and crying, and I think she just needs a friend right now."

"Sure, you'd better get going. I'll tell James where you are." He presses the button, and the gate opens for me.

"I won't be that long," I tell him.

"Call if you need anything."

"I will, thanks."

I drive out of the estate and down the hill, the gnawing in my stomach growing now with the lies I just told to Malik, but it's not like I can tell him the truth!

I have to park a few blocks down from the club to get a space. The looks I get as I walk down the street in my way too short floral dress and platform sandals make me walk fast.

When I reach Vincent's, Dave gives me a wave. "Kind of surprised to see you back, Poppy."

I just shrug. "Well, here I am."

He gestures for me to go in and tells the girl on the door to waive the cover charge again.

The club is heaving tonight, but I spot Claudia quickly. She's sitting at the bar chatting to — *shit*, Damon! I thought he was banned from this place?

I walk to the far end of the bar, order a coke and then hide behind my hair until I see him eventually slide off his chair to go bother some other poor human. Then I make my way over to Claudia.

"Poppy. What's going on?" she asks, taking a sip of a blood red cocktail that I really hope contains no actual blood.

"What's your lead?" I ask.

She flicks her hair, and it slides over her leather jacket. "Nothing concrete, just trying to figure out if this is a vampire bar."

"Oh yeah? And what do you think?"

"Jury's out."

I give a nod and take a sip of my drink. Claudia can't even spot a vampire when there's one right in front of her.

"What's all this about, Poppy? Why are you here in the middle of the night?"

"I want out," I tell her.

She glares at me. "What? Why?"

I pause. "I just do."

"I'm going to need more than *I just do*."

"Okay, well. First of all, two people got shot."

She makes a face like she knows that was bad.

"Also, we still have no evidence that Max is a vampire. We also have absolutely nothing linking him to Aiden's disappearance."

"That's exactly why we need you, Poppy. To *find* the evidence."

"I just don't think there's anything to find."

She narrows her eyes at me. "Something happened. With you and Max."

Fuck.

"No," I say, looking into my drink and not meeting her eye.

She throws her head back and laughs. "Oh, this is perfect. All this time we had you pinned as the quiet, plain girl who would fly under the radar while Kayla would seduce him."

"Am I that undesirable?"

"Poppy, you're cute in your way. But Max Montrose? He's not exactly in your league, is he?" She keeps laughing, and I draw spirals in the condensation on my glass waiting for her to be done.

"Poppy." She grabs my hand. "This is fantastic."

For a split second I think maybe she's happy for me, that

I've found such an amazing guy and that he's into me too! But no, that's not at all what she's saying.

"Now you can get *really* close to him. Do the job Kayla was supposed to do. You can find out everything for us."

I pull my hand away. "I'm not doing that."

Her expression turns dark. "It's not a choice, Poppy."

"You can't force me to spy on him!"

"You're right. I can't. The Order can't either, but if you go against their orders—" She finishes her cocktail and smacks the glass on the bar. "You find that evidence or they will kill you, Poppy."

Kayla had tried to warn me before, but I'd never taken the threat all that seriously until now that I'm seeing the look on Claudia's face. She's scared. And that gnawing feeling? It's starting to tear a hole in my insides.

Claudia throws a couple of dollars on the bar and then turns to me, placing a hand on my shoulder. "I guess we're both in deeper than we realized. But trust me on this. There is only one way out of the Order. And it's not through quitting."

She pats my shoulder and turns to walk away.

I'm about to follow her when I see Damon heading my way. I walk in the other direction, going deeper into the club. I follow a back hallway that I know from the last time I was here leads to the bathrooms. The walls here are covered with Polaroid photos of Vincent's customers. Big nights out, smiles and drunken kisses. I guess the thing about vampires not showing up in photos is bullshit. Duh, of course it is. Max Montrose is in plenty of photos!

I'm about to walk into the bathroom when I suddenly spot a familiar face on the wall.

Aiden.

He was here. He was hanging out with vampires. Of course he was. He was working for the Order too. But there's something about the look in his eye, and the way that the girl in the photo is looking at him, like she'd do anything for him, go anywhere with him, like she's completely under his control.

Oh *fuck*.

CHAPTER THIRTY-FIVE

ANGELS AROUND US

Owen: I have been burned a thousand times.

Sarah: What is life if it isn't being burned over and over again but still choosing to face the fire?

Owen: For once in my life, I think I would like some water.

Sarah: What if that's not what your soul signed up?

Owen: Why would my soul sign up for any of this?

Sarah: Fire burns, but it also illuminates.

I DON'T REST MUCH, especially once I get the message that Poppy has left the estate on some kind of "boy emergency". Is she seeing someone else? Has she gone to break up with him now that I've made my intentions towards her plain? I try to trust that if it's anything, it's the latter. Even so, I toss and turn in my California king that suddenly feels too big now that I think of the space Poppy could be taking up in it.

My mind won't stop coming up with scenarios for where Poppy is, or who this boy is. I could try to track her or have Henrietta do it. Is she in trouble? Is she with another man?

I need something to soothe this fire within me. I throw the blankets off, switch on the light and grab the Palmieri script. It is different from anything I've done as Max Montrose. Edgy, a little dark and depressing, it's the story of a depressed alcoholic who meets his guardian angel in the form of a check-out clerk. It's not the usual romantic comedy I'm known for, instead it's smart, quirky, strange. It's the sort of movie I never would have been offered before, and I wonder if Henrietta has done more to my Instagram account than she's let on. I find myself getting into the script, but I'm still relieved when I hear Poppy's car return to the estate. I message Malik to confirm it's her, and when he does, I feel some of the tension leaving my body. But still, I can't stop wondering where she was and who she was with.

I sigh. Trust has never been one of my strongest traits.

I want to see her again as soon as possible, but not just in the library or the parlor while she works. I want to take her on a date. I used to be known for my extravagant wooing of women. But taking Poppy to a fancy restaurant in LA is absolutely out of the question. I couldn't care less about how the public perceives me. In another twenty years no one will remember Max Montrose, and if cinema still exists, perhaps I'll start over again as a new face on the scene. Or maybe by then I really *will* be done. I don't know.

What I do know is that I care about Poppy too much to give the paparazzi any more interest in her.

I decide to prepare a magnificent meal for her in my own private kitchen. James will be given instructions to check on us occasionally just to make sure Poppy is safe.

Of course, I have already told him that if he ever sees me hurt Poppy, he is to shoot silver bullets straight through my brain and heart and then go ahead and stake me.

James wouldn't have it in him to kill me, but I hope he would slow me down with the bullets enough for Poppy to get to safety.

It has been years since I attempted to cook, but I want to make her something truly wonderful.

A little after sunrise, I make my way to the main kitchen, hoping to bump into Poppy on the way, but I don't see her. Perhaps she is still sleeping. A vision of her sleeping in my theater that first night we met appears in my mind. So soft, so perfect.

"Max!" Trix calls out from behind a high-speed blender that looks to be pureeing something that looks like chocolate mousse. She switches it off. "Sorry, Mr. Montrose," she corrects.

"Max is fine, truly."

"Oh shit, and I spoke to you first."

"It's fine."

"Well, what can I do for you, *Max*?" She wipes her hands on her apron. "Can I make you something for breakfast?"

I shake my head. "No, thank you."

Her eyebrows pinch, and then she puts her hands on her hips. "You don't even need to eat, do you?"

"No."

"Okay, so why am I even here?"

"I don't *need* to eat, but I still enjoy the occasional bite."

She raises an eyebrow.

"Bite of *food*," I say. "And whatever that is," I gesture to the mixer, "looks delightful."

"You want some now?"

"Please." I slide up onto a bar stool and watch as she

places two scoops into a glass bowl. She sprinkles dark chocolate on top and slides it over.

"It won't be fully set yet, but it should still taste okay."

I take a bite. "This is heavenly," I tell her. She watches as I proceed to finish the whole bowl.

"You enjoyed it."

"Very much."

"You ate the cake too."

"I enjoy sweets."

"You should have said, I can keep the fridge stocked with cakes and deserts."

"Too much sugar isn't healthy, even for me. The occasional cake will suffice."

She takes the bowl and places it in the dishwasher. "Am I here just to feed your staff?" she asks.

"Mostly, yes."

She appears to think about this for a moment. "That's pretty nice of you."

"You think so?"

"I do. And I'm happy to feed them."

"I'm glad."

"So, what can I do for you?"

"I want to make dinner for Poppy tonight," I tell her.

"Wait, what?" she gasps.

"She didn't tell you?" I had expected Poppy to tell Trix immediately about our kiss, but the fact that she didn't, that she wanted to keep it just between us, warms me.

"Tell me what?"

"That's something that she can discuss with you if she chooses to."

A huge smile spreads over her face. "Oh god, I just *knew* when you claimed her you meant the sex stuff!"

I am mortified, and I must look it because she throws a hand over her mouth.

"Sorry, Mr. Montrose. Max. Not another word about it from me, I promise." She mimes locking her lips and throwing the key over her shoulder.

"What is her favorite dish?" I ask, swiftly attempting to move on from this humiliation.

"Let me think… well, I've seen her enjoy burgers, most food actually, but she's *very* partial to mac and cheese and pizza. Oh, and cookies."

"So, a seven-course gustation menu may not impress her in the way it's impressed other women."

"Honestly, I don't think you need to do anything to impress her."

"It's important to me to do something special for her."

"I can whip up a menu for you for tonight with all her favorites."

"No. I want to make it all myself."

Her mouth drops open.

"You think I can't cook?"

"I think you can probably do anything. Want my secret mac and cheese recipe?"

"You think she will enjoy that?"

"I think she might die if Max Montrose made her mac and cheese."

"That's not exactly the intention."

"Oh god, sorry, bad turn of phrase for a date with a vampire!" She slaps her forehead.

"Don't worry about it. But I'd like some recipes for cookies as well."

"On it," she says with a salute. "I'll email them to you soon."

I'M on my way back to my suite when I catch Poppy's scent

in the library. I have missed this — the ability to smell something so delicious from so far away.

I make my way down the hall and pause at the open library door. Poppy isn't aware that I'm watching her. She goes about polishing surfaces and dusting shelves and while part of me hates that she works for me, that her job is to clean my house, another very primal part of me enjoys it very much when she bends over and gives my antique desk a hard rub.

I love that I'm her boss. That I can tell her what to do, and how I want it done.

"Good morning, Poppy," I say.

She jumps, dropping her cleaning cloth. "Oh! You scared me!"

I chuckle. "I can only apologize for that. I can be quite stealthy."

She bends over to pick up the cloth, giving me the familiar glimpse down her shirt that I have used as inspiration so many times in the shower lately.

"I'd like to request your company for dinner this evening." I only realize after I've said it that it sounds like a demand rather than an invitation. "If you are available."

"I'm available," she says quickly, fumbling with the cloth in her hands.

"Then I shall look forward to seeing you around eight."

"I'm looking forward to it too." She gives me a shy smile, and I immediately want to press my lips to that smile and work my tongue inside her mouth, but she's on the clock, and I have mac and cheese to make.

I give her a nod and leave her to it.

But knowing that she's there, cleaning my house, doing my chores — well! Before I can start preparing our meal, I have to drink two more glasses of blood.

ax

THE MAC and cheese is an absolute disaster.

I work on it all afternoon, and nothing I make is good enough to serve her, let alone impress her. The cookies are even worse.

I have many skills and talents, but baking is definitely not one of them. I don't know why I ever thought this would be a good idea.

I throw everything in the trash and search on my phone for the best mac and cheese, pizza and cookie delivery in the city. The least I can do is order it myself instead of delegate it onto James.

I get ready hours before our date, choosing a blue shirt I've had for many years and a dark pair of pants. I spend forever working on my hair to try to get it right. I choose a gold watch that's slightly less ostentatious than some of my others and then pace my suite until I hear her coming up the stairs right on eight. I'm impressed by her punctuality and hope that the food I have ordered will also arrive in a timely fashion.

I open the door, and her scent of berries, cherry lip gloss and the sweetness of her the perfume between her legs immediately fills the space. She's wearing a different floral dress tonight. This one is white with red roses. It's long, down to her ankles, but the straps are thin, and the cut is low, giving me more than a hint at what's underneath.

"You look beautiful, Poppy." I tell her.

A light blush crosses her freckled cheeks. "Thank you, so do you." She looks me up and down, and her gaze feels like honey as she takes me in. "Do you ever just wear a t-shirt and jeans though?" she asks curiously.

"Would you like me to?"

She shrugs. "I like you like this. But I'm sure I'd like you in anything." Her heart rate rises, and I feel her nervousness. Or is it my own?

"Please," I gesture for her to come in. "Come in, sit, relax."

"This is new," she says, pointing to the Formica diner-style table in the center of the room.

"I wanted to take you to the best diner in the city, but it's not always easy for me to go out. I thought the table would at least make the evening feel more authentic." I pull out a chair for her. As she sits, the long skirt reveals a slit that goes right up her thigh, revealing her legs to me.

Control yourself, man. You can do this.

I turn away and look at the bar. "Drink?"

"Please."

"Your usual? Or something different?"

"Surprise me."

I turn and raise an eyebrow in her direction. "You're open to anything?"

"I am." That shy smile crosses her face, and I turn again,

taking a few deep breaths. I put a drink together for her and pray to the gods of desire to keep me in check.

"Champagne cocktail," I say, placing the glass in front of her.

She takes a small sip. "Aren't these supposed to make you feel kind of silly and sexy?"

"You don't need a drink to make you sexy," I tell her. "Shall we have some music?"

She nods.

"Give me an era."

"Fifties," she says quickly.

"Ah, the fifties." I pull out the soundtrack from one of my movies of that time period. "Do you know this movie?" I hold the record up for her to look at.

"Of course! *Double Trouble* is quintessential Johnny Montrose."

It must be the way I'm holding the record, my own face on the album cover right next to my own face that makes her mouth drop open.

I give her a grin. "Ah. You didn't realize?"

"Holy shit," she whispers before throwing a hand over her mouth.

I chuckle. "Took you long enough."

She jumps from her seat and grabs the record out of my hand. "This is — this is — *you!*"

"Yes, sweetheart. It's me."

She spins in a slow circle, taking in the movie posters all around us, both from my years as Johnny Montrose and Leopold Montrose.

"Leopold Montrose," she whispers to herself. The sound of my *real* name on her lips is nothing short of a miracle.

I place the record on the turntable, and the crooning sounds of the 1950s fill the space. When I look back towards her, she looks at me like *I'm* the miracle.

"You're *him*. You're Johnny Montrose."

"Yes."

"And—"

I nod. "Leopold Montrose."

"You did all this, all these movies, all this great work."

I laugh. "Some of the work was greater than the rest."

"No, no. It was all great — all of it." She takes another circle of the room and then stops. "There's a gap in your CV," she says. "What happened between Johnny and Max?"

"Theater," I say, pointing to a poster of Shakespeare in the Park, New York City 1976. "I wanted to go back to my roots, work on my craft. I also did a stint on a sit-com in the eighties, but I'd prefer not to talk about that." God, that awful sitcom went on for four years, and while I enjoyed it at the time, it has dated very badly.

"You're amazing," she says, shaking her head like she can't believe all I have done.

I pour myself a glass of blood and gesture for us to sit at the table. "The food will be here soon," I say.

She sits, and then nervously fingers the stem of her glass. "Max, I have to tell you something," she starts, her pulse racing.

"Is it about where you were last night?"

"You knew I was out?"

"Poppy, I know everything that happens on the estate."

She swallows. "I went to see someone to talk about a situation that I don't want to be part of anymore. It's — complicated. And if I tell you the truth, you won't feel the same way about me and—"

"Is there someone else?"

"No! God, no. Nothing like that."

"Then I don't want to know."

"I've done something. Something I'm not proud of, and before anything else happens between us I need to tell you—"

I shake my head. "No." I lean over the table and take her soft, warm hand in mine. "I have done things. Awful things. Things you would hate me for if you knew. Things that would horrify you and send you screaming from this mansion. Things that caused me to hide away here drinking synthetic blood instead of being out there in the world causing harm." I take a sip from my glass of blood and watch for the change in her expression, but there is none. Only fear and worry about what *she* has done.

"What if we just start over, right now?" I suggest.

"What do you mean?"

"Everything we have done until this moment is in the past."

"But I—"

I cut her off. "All that matters are the choices we make from tonight."

"I really should tell you this." She bites her lip.

"I don't care about your past, Poppy. I don't care about the men you've been with or the lies you've told or the people you've hurt. All I care about is being with you now."

She's about to open her mouth again when there's a knock at the door.

"Come in," I say.

James appears with four large food bags and three pizza boxes. I send him away with a thank you and place the bags and boxes on the table between us.

"I heard you liked mac and cheese, pizza and cookies?"

A grin splits her gorgeous pink lips. "You heard correctly."

"And I've heard this is the best in the city."

POPPY RECLINES on the couch next to me, biting into her third cookie. Her expression looks positively orgasmic, and I cannot wait until it's *me* putting that look on her face instead of these damn cookies. I take one for myself, and it is indeed a very good cookie.

"Is it true that Elvis was up for the role of Bobby in *Double Trouble*?"

"Ah, that old rumor. Nothing in it, I'm afraid. If it were true, I have no doubt Elvis would have been given the role over me. He was always the better actor."

"What was it like in those days? Did you go to parties with Elvis and James Dean? Did you drink whiskey with Frank Sinatra?"

I smile as I take another bite of the cookie and then wash it down with a sip of whiskey. I like that she's interested in this, that she wants to know about my past. Of course, I will never tell her that I bit one of Elvis' band members in a rage of bloodlust at a party once or that Frank Sinatra was partial to The Bite now and then. "I knew them in passing," I tell her.

"What was Elvis like? Really?" she asks, giving Callie a chin scratch as the cat appears beside her.

"Charming. An absolute gentleman. The kind of man who would give you the shirt off his own back."

"Was he—?"

"A vampire? Elvis?" I let out a chuckle.

"He really could be alive and well and living in Las Vegas," she considers.

"He'd more likely be hiding out on a ranch in Montana or somewhere equally remote."

"You never thought of doing that?" she asks. "You preferred to stay in LA?"

"I used to have houses all over the world. A penthouse in Paris, a farmhouse in Tuscany…" All these things I *used* to have. So much for impressing her.

"How many houses do you have now?"

"Just the one."

She's quiet for a moment as she swirls her drink around.

"You're disappointed. I'm not as rich as you expected."

"What? Oh, no! Just surprised. Some people have this idea of — people like you. That you hoard wealth and property while others are living on next to nothing."

"I have battled with that. Not so much in the beginning when I was young and dazzled by the bright lights of fame and fortune. But later I realized I wanted to use my wealth to make a difference."

"Your charity work."

"Yes. I run twenty-six charities. I don't have any other properties now, but I still have investments. I keep the things that are making me good money, and I use that money to help where I can." I take a sip of blood and once again wait for her reaction, the horror in her eyes. But there is none.

"I try. Of course, I can always do more," I say, placing my glass on the table and moving to face her. "I would like to put you through veterinary school."

"What?" She nearly chokes on her cookie.

"One of my charities is an animal shelter in the city. I took it on after Calliope came into my life. I never thought much of animals until she showed up, but now I couldn't imagine life without her. Perhaps you could work some volunteer shifts there in exchange for the cost of your tuition."

She shakes her head. "I don't understand what you're saying."

"I think you would make a wonderful vet," I tell her. "The way you are with Callie—"

She looks down at the cat, who's now nestled into her side on the couch between us.

"You are good in a crisis. On the night of the shooting, you ran straight out to see if you could help. You took control of the situation and did what needed to be done. And when I pulled the bullet out, you didn't look away."

"I was scared shitless that night."

"You didn't act like it."

She shrugs. "It doesn't matter anyway. I didn't get the grades."

"You could study, retake your exams. But only if it's something you wanted. I don't want to push this on you. I only thought if you wanted—"

"Oh, I do, I still want to... It's just a very big thing. Offering to help me."

"Why don't you think about it?"

She nods. "Okay. I will."

In truth, I don't know how this would work. Would I give her an allowance? Would she live here in the staff quarters? In a guest room? In *my* room? Would I be her boyfriend? Lover? Sugar daddy? And how would all this work when there is no future for us as a couple? But I want to help her, and I know that in helping her do this, she will help so many animals like Callie.

"How did you find Callie?" she asks, and I'm grateful for the change of topic.

"She appeared in the garden about a year ago."

"A year? But she's so small, I thought she was a kitten."

"I'm not sure where she was before, but I suspect she didn't eat enough food to help her grow. When she showed up here, I called Henrietta to bring a cat carrier and take her to a shelter. But when I looked up shelters, I was horrified to find out how many animals were being killed in them."

"And you couldn't let her go?"

I shake my head. "No. She had my heart after just a few hours of being in my life." I nearly add *just like you*, but thankfully, I stop myself. "And then I decided I needed to open and fund my own no-kill shelter."

Callie seems to hear us talking about her. She purrs and nudges Poppy's leg. Poppy shifts in her seat and the slit of her dress falls away, her entire thigh on show. I force myself to look back up to her eyes.

"So, now that you know that most of my money goes to charity, does it change the way you feel about me? I still have the means to keep you well looked after, but if you're looking for someone with a private jet or a castle in Scotland, you may have better luck with someone like Maverick Stone."

"I'm not interested in you for your money," she says bluntly.

"Ah, so it's the fame then?" It's meant to be a joke, but this conversation always gets on my nerves. Until this moment, I hadn't let myself think that she might only be interested in me for these things that so many other women have fawned over. Yes, I've had my choice of women, but not one of them ever truly wanted me for *who* I am, only for *what* I am.

"Honestly, the fame thing is actually kind of inconvenient."

"Oh? How so?"

"Well, we can't go on a normal date like normal people."

"I'm not even a person," I say, taking a sip of blood.

Something like fear flashes through her eyes, and I think she's going to run. She's realizing now what she's doing, that dating a vampire is dangerous and stupid. She would be right to run. I wouldn't blame her if she did.

But she doesn't run. Instead, she lets out a roar of laughter. "You're not even a person!" She giggles uncontrollably for a few more moments, and I find myself just grinning at her like an idiot.

"Can I get you anything else?" I ask when she's finally finished with her outburst. "I could have James heat the pizza if you fancied some more. Or perhaps another champagne cocktail?" She's already had three, it's probably enough, but I still make the offer.

She closes her eyes. "I can't eat or drink another thing."

She turns her head to the side and then opens her eyes and smiles at me. "This was wonderful."

"It was."

"And I know you said we should take it slow," she says, turning her body towards me now. "But all those champagne cocktails are kicking in."

She keeps sliding over towards me, gently nudging Callie off the couch, and I don't stop her. I don't stop her when she straddles me, the slit in her dress riding up the top of her thigh, and I don't stop her as she pushes her hands into my hair.

"Is this too much?" she asks.

I close my eyes. Yes. It's too much. It's much too much.

"No."

She leans into me, her warm, soft breasts pressing against my chest as she kisses my cheek, my jaw, and then she makes her way down my neck. I know she can feel me getting hard between her legs, and I know I should stop it. Tell her that's enough for tonight, but I just don't have the strength.

She kisses me on the lips firmly, confidently. I definitely gave her too much champagne. But I kiss her back, matching her mood. There's no softness tonight, no hesitation, just slightly drunk and confident Poppy. And while I find her shy side very appealing, this is also very nice.

I reach up to the straps of her dress and toy with them in my fingers.

"Pull my dress down," she whisper-begs.

My fingers shake as I run them under her straps. *Ridiculous.* A vampire of my age shaking at the thought of seeing this woman's breasts. I have seen breasts before!

But not Poppy's. Not the breasts of this woman who has occupied every corner of my mind since she arrived at my mansion.

I slide the straps down over her shoulders but no further.

My fingers make circles on her bare shoulders as I consider what to do next, how far I can go with her tonight.

She gives me a dirty smile as she reaches for the top button of my shirt. At first, I consider stopping her, but she's seen my naked chest before, so I let her keep going, right down to the last button. She opens my shirt, and her eyes widen as she takes in my body. The lust in her eyes has me pulling her closer now, and as I press my lips to hers, I feel that tingle in my incisors. I pull away just before my fangs appear.

She grins at me, running her hands gently over my chest. It's that gentle touch I imagined as I watched her touching my things, and now she's touching me and it's sending me into a frenzy.

"Poppy," I say, taking her hand in mine and stopping her from continuing. "We need to stop."

Her eyes soften. "Why?"

"It's too much. I can't lose control with you. My fangs are about to—"

She kisses my neck. "I want you to lose control," she whispers.

"You don't know what you're asking for," I tell her.

"I do," she says, even though she absolutely doesn't.

She gently kisses me on the lips. "I want you to do whatever you want to me," she says, grinding harder into me now.

I can feel the dampness between her legs through my clothes. God, she must be so wet for me. My fangs finally push through. The pain is gone, and I feel a rush of adrenaline and desire.

She gasps and pulls back from me slightly, just enough for me to know that despite all her advances tonight, she is terrified. Just like she should be.

"Go," I tell her, squeezing my eyes shut. "Leave!"

"You're in control," she tells me. "You won't hurt me."

"You don't know what I'm capable of," I growl as I reach for the straps of her dress, this time I grip them hard and tug them down to just above her breasts. I pause, frozen. I want nothing more than to release her gorgeous full breasts from this dress and take them in my hands and my mouth.

"If you were out of control, you'd already have my dress off and your fangs in me by now," she tells me. I'm still frozen, so she reaches up to her straps and pulls them down herself, her breasts now free and perfect and beautiful and right *here*.

"Poppy, you are so beautiful," I moan as I take both her breasts in my hands. God, she feels amazing. "You're so soft and wonderful."

She lets out a giggle as I take her breast into my mouth, gently biting her nipple. I can hear the blood rushing through her veins, faster and faster.

"Is this alright?" I ask.

"It's better than alright," she says, fingering my hair as she lets out tiny little moans while I alternate between gently pinching one nipple and biting the other.

She arches her back, and I know if I don't stop soon, I won't be able to. Even now I don't know that I have the strength. Poppy is beautiful and kind-hearted and — I pull my head and hand back and catch my breath. Here she is, straddling me, her breasts right *here* in my face, she's begging me to keep going, and I'm *stopping*?!

Perhaps I have more strength than I think I do.

I take a breast in each hand and make circles around her nipples. Her head tilts back, and she lets out a sigh.

"I want nothing more than to make love to you right now," I tell her. "I want you naked. I want to be inside you—" I nibble at the top of one breast, being careful not to catch my fangs on her skin as she murmurs something that sounds like an agreement.

"Do it!" she exclaims. "I want you, Max. Please!"

I pull back again and hold her bare shoulders, forcing her to look at me. "Is this what you really want, Poppy?" I show her my fangs.

"Yes, Max. Yes," she purrs, blinking at my fangs like they are nothing. No, not like they are nothing, but like they are *everything*.

I nibble at her breast again and then look back up at her. "You want me to bite you? You want me to drink from you? Truly, Poppy? Is this what you really want?"

"Yes," she whimpers. "Please!"

It takes everything within me not to bite her, not to take her blood.

"This is enough for tonight," I tell her.

"Max, no!"

"Poppy, please." I reluctantly slide her dress back over her perfect breasts, already missing the sight and feel of them, but knowing it's the right thing to do.

"If we stop now, I'm one step closer to knowing I'll be in control when we do make love. And the sooner I can prove to myself I have control, the sooner we can be together and not have to stop."

She bites her lip and nods. "So, this is goodnight?"

"Yes."

"That's what you want?"

I shake my head. "No. It's not what I want, but it's what I must do."

She's all flushed and pink, her lips puffy from kissing, desire in her eyes. As soon as she leaves, I know I will take a shower and rub my shaft so fucking hard thinking about her, attempting to give myself some kind of moment of relief. I wonder if she will do the same thing. Perhaps I should make sure of it.

"I want you to go back to the staff quarters now," I say,

dropping a gentle kiss to her forehead. "And then I want you to take off this dress while you think about me taking it off you. I want you take off your bra and your panties and imagine that it's me. I want you to take a shower, and I want you to think about me in that shower with you, down on my knees, worshiping your pussy with my tongue. I want you to bring yourself to climax as you think about me biting your inner thigh and drinking from you while you reach your peak." Her face is flushed, and her eyes are wide. "Can you do that for me, Poppy?"

She swallows, her throat throbbing, her pulse beating me into agony as she nods.

"And what will you do for me?" she asks.

"I'll promise you that one day, when I can trust myself, I will do it to you for real."

CHAPTER THIRTY-SEVEN

Max

"Getting high from human blood is considered quite the faux pas in vampire high society circles."

The Fraternity of the Everlasting Rose Periodical, November 1928

After Poppy leaves, I masturbate thinking about finishing our evening in a different way and I drink so much blood to try to quench my thirst that I end up high. I haven't been this high on blood since the early 2000s, and I'm absolutely wired. My pulse is at triple speed, and I can't just sit around here like I do every other night. I have to *do* something.

But what?

I run at vampire speed through the mansion down to the garage. It's only when I get behind the wheel of my Aston Martin that I realize one of my staff members could have seen me blurring through the place. Being high on blood stops you caring about that kind of thing, but I really should be more careful.

I start the car, wave maniacally to Malik at the gatehouse and find myself driving down this hill that I know like the back of my hand. Driving on a blood high is not a problem. If anything, it makes us better drivers. We're even *more* aware when high.

I don't know where I'm going. I just know that I need to go *somewhere* and do *something.*

I keep driving until I see the exit to Malibu. Of course. The beach will fix me. I used to come down here all the time, but I haven't been to the beach in too long. Not since the last time I came to one of Maverick's parties over a decade ago.

A different kind of hunger takes over. I'm going to need snacks.

I screech into an empty parking lot outside a supermarket with bright neon lights. I grab a pair of sunglasses and some cash from the glove box.

The lights are so bright, it feels like my eyeballs are being assaulted. Blood highs make *everything* feel brighter, bigger, louder, for better or worse.

I go about grabbing snacks — three boxes of Twinkies, four bags of chips, eight sleeves of Oreos and a carton of 24 sodas. I have a sudden urge to buy something for Poppy. I want to buy her anything and everything she could ever need and want! But what does she need and want? I feel like a fool as I wander around a place like this looking for something for her. I barely *know* her, and yet already I know I *want* to know her on every level of her soul, mind, being and body.

Chocolates are cliché and embarrassing, but flowers? Well, flowers are always a good idea. As I peruse the flower section, I am disheartened by how pathetic they all look.

"Can I help you there… sir?" asks a young store clerk who

is probably too young to have even heard of me, but there is some recognition on his face.

"Do you have any other flowers?"

"Sorry, no."

"Just these then," I say, holding up my snack haul.

"Got the munchies, sir?" The kid gives me a knowing look as he scans my purchases.

I hand over a hundred. "Keep the change," I tell him.

"You serious?" he asks.

I nod and place another hundred in the charity pot on the counter.

"Woah!"

"Enjoy your evening," I tell him.

"You too, sir!" he calls back.

The warm, fuzzy feeling of knowing I've made his night carries me back to the car where I rip open a bag of chips and eat like a lion devouring a lamb. I let out a groan when I get to the end of the bag. I had forgotten that eating while high was the closest thing I could get to the way human food tasted before I was turned.

I inhale a box of Twinkies, in part enjoying the experience of the taste of them, but also somewhat regretting that I hadn't taken myself to a decent restaurant to eat while my taste is both heightened and human.

I wash it all down with a soda and then call James.

"Sir?" he answers groggily.

"Were you sleeping?"

"No, sir. I'm always wide awake at two in the morning waiting for you to call me with some inane request."

I ignore him. "I need flowers."

"Certainly, sir. What kind?"

I pause for a moment, trying to think of the type of flowers that Poppy would like. Roses are so overdone. She needs something different. Peonies? Tulips? "Two dozen dark red dahlias," I decide.

"And to whom should I send them?"

"Just have them delivered to the staff quarters and as soon as possible."

"It may be difficult to get them there at this hour."

"I'm sure you can find a way," I say. "You always do."

"Of course, sir."

I finally arrive at the beach and park. Grabbing what's left of my snacks I walk down to the beach and drop onto the sand. I eat a sleeve of Oreos and remember that although eating while high feels incredible, it also slows the body down and results in the high wearing off faster.

I receive a text from James to tell me the flowers are on their way. Of course they are. James truly is a wonder.

I sit and watch the waves, enjoying all the sensations of the beach — the scent of salt and sea air, the calming, rushing sound of the water, all the while wishing I'd had the presence of mind to bring Poppy here with me. I grab another bag of chips. No, I could never let her see me like this! A high vampire on the beach eating *chips*! How very uncivilized!

I consider how I'm going to make love to her. How can I keep myself in control? I wonder if it's possible to micro-dose Sybline. If I have just a little before I'm with her it could take the edge off and allow me to be more of a gentleman with her. I replay our last encounter, and a smile spreads over my lips. I suspect that Poppy may not always *want* me to be a gentleman with her.

I eat and drink and watch the waves until sunrise, all the while thinking of all the ways I intend to be ungentlemanly with Poppy.

CHAPTER THIRTY-EIGHT

Poppy

I WAKE the next morning to find a massive vase of dark red dahlias next to my bed. I can't help but giggle and kick my legs around in bed.

It wasn't a dream!

I was slightly drunk when I got back to my room, but of course I did as Max asked. I got in the shower and thought about him between my legs, biting me and drinking from me while I worked myself to climax, and it was *hot*. Of course, I'm a little nervous about him biting me in real life, but I'm also curious. *Very* curious.

"You had sex with Max Montrose," Trix accuses, standing above me dressed in her workout clothes.

"No," I tell her.

She points to the flowers. "Those are sex flowers." She pulls on a sweatshirt. "I brought them in for you, by the way, just in case you thought he was Edward-Cullen-ing you by creeping around your room at night."

"Thanks. Creeping in here would be extra weird since it's your room too."

"Right?" She grabs one of her legs and starts stretching. "So? Give me the details!"

"No details. We're… taking it slow."

She gives me a look like this is a foreign concept for her.

"His choice or yours?"

"Definitely his. He's worried that he won't be in control with me."

"How old is he, anyway?" she asks.

"Mid-thirties?"

"Poppy. How old is he *really*?"

"Oh! Uh, I don't know!"

He's never mentioned anything about a life before Leopold Montrose, so I assume that's who he was when he was turned.

I check Leopold Montrose's Wikipedia. "I think he was born in… 1894? Wow, that's weird to think about."

"Now, like I've said, I'm no expert," she says, stretching the other leg. "But vampires that old rarely have self-control issues." She takes a sip from her water bottle. "I need to shower, but there's a note too." She points to the envelope under the vase.

Poppy,

Thank you for spending your evening with me last night. I thoroughly enjoyed our time together, and I would very much like to have the honor of your acquaintance again this evening if you would be amenable.

Please arrive at eight o'clock this evening at the theater.

I look forward to your company.

Yours,
Max

YOURS,

Max Montrose is *mine?*

I hold the note to my heart and take a deep breath.

God, is he really *mine?* He's claimed me and *of course* I am his without question, but the idea of Max Montrose being *mine?*

I jump out of bed and dance around the room for a minute before I realize that I still have to go to work.

MY DAY GOES SLOWER than any other day that's ever existed, and it feels like a decade until I'm sitting out in the courtyard with the crew eating spicy noodles and counting down the last few hours until I can be with Max again.

I was looking for him all day—in every doorway and hallway. He wasn't there, but he *will* be there tonight at the theater, and I'm so looking forward to recreating our first night together, this time hopefully with more kissing!

"Max has so many weird requests," Trix says. The mention of his name has me suddenly paying attention to the conversation for the first time since I sat down.

"Yeah? Like what?" Julio asks.

"This morning he asked for a cold brew and a packet of Twinkies."

Laughter erupts.

"Twinkies?" I ask.

"If I was a multi-millionaire, I would ask for something more than Twinkies," Malik says.

"Billionaire," Trix corrects.

"I'm sorry, what?" I ask, almost choking on a noodle.

"Poppy, it's like you haven't even spent twenty hours online searching him."

"That information wasn't on his Wikipedia page."

"It won't be on there," she says. "You have to go this website that tells you the net worth of celebrities. And according to that, he's well and truly cashed up."

"Where's all his money then?" Malik asks. "This place is nice, but it's not worth a billion dollars."

"He gives it to charity," I tell them.

"Sounds like him," says Malik.

"What kind of charities?" Trix asks. She grabs her phone and starts searching.

"An animal shelter, the arts, homelessness, some kind of medical research, a bunch of stuff," I tell her.

She gives me a look.

"He told me about some of it. I looked up the rest."

"I wonder what else he's into," Julio says. "You know, like other weird requests the guy might have, and if there's any I can help him with?"

Trix laughs, and I feel my face heat. She looks up from her phone and says, "Well, Max is a gentleman, isn't he? That means he's probably an absolute freak in the sheets."

Now my face is on fire.

"How many women do you think he's had?" Julio asks. "Movie stars can get it whenever they want it, and if I got it whenever I wanted it, I'd be having it all the time."

The realization that Max is incredibly experienced in that department suddenly hits me. I have only been with my ex Danny, and none of my encounters with him were exactly toe-curling. Maybe it's me. Maybe I'm bad in bed. There's no way I can compete with the movie stars, models and who knows who else Max has slept with. I put my fork in my bowl, unable to eat another bite.

· · ·

I WEAR a short pale blue dress, put my hair up in a messy bun and flick out my eyeliner. I consider my reflection in the mirror, still unsure of what it is that Max sees in me. Who am I to date someone like *Max Montrose*?

I walk out of the bathroom and into the bedroom, where Trix is sitting on her bed reading a brick of a romantasy novel.

I strap on a pair of chunky black sandals and check myself in the full-length mirror.

"You look *smoking*," she says, looking up at me. "If Max can control himself around you tonight, there's something wrong with him."

I give her a half-smile.

"Are you nervous?"

I shake my head. "No, I'm just wondering if—" I sigh. "Why does he want *me*?"

"Oh girl, stop that kind of thinking *right now*, do you hear me?"

"But seriously, it's Max Montrose! He could have anyone! Why me?"

She puts her book down. "Because you're fucking awesome."

I let out a laugh. "Sure."

"Don't be down on yourself. There are enough people in the world who can do that for you. You're pretty, and your body is banging, and you're nice and so much fun to hang out with. The real question is why isn't every single guy in the whole world into you?"

I throw my arms around her. "Thank you, Trix."

She squeezes me for a moment and then lets me go, giving me a considered look. "You just need one more thing." She searches around in a makeup bag for a minute and then hands me a lipstick.

It's a deep dark red color, not a color I'd usually wear. "It's the same color as the flowers," I say.

"I've never worn it. I bought it when I had dark hair, but with my green hair it makes me look like a Christmas tree! It will be perfect with your coloring and that outfit. It's yours if you want it. Keep it."

I try it on, and she's right. It works.

"It's the perfect color for a vampire's girlfriend," she tells me.

I take a deep breath. "I have to go."

Trix puts her hands on my shoulders and looks me in the eye. "Poppy. You've got this. Don't be nervous. You absolutely deserve to have sex with a sexy, rich, movie star vampire."

I let out a nervous laugh.

"Say it," she demands. "Out loud."

"I absolutely deserve to have sex with a sexy, rich, movie star vampire," I tell her and try to believe it.

But I'm not sure I do. Last night I should have told him. I should have told him who I really am and why I'm here. But all that talk about leaving the past behind, admitting we'd both done bad things but they don't matter now — well, I'd almost convinced myself it was okay.

But it's not.

And so, I decide I will definitely not have sex with Max Montrose until he knows the truth.

CHAPTER THIRTY-NINE

ax

I PACE the length of the theater waiting for Poppy's arrival. I have taken a small dose of Sybline along with a large serving of blood bank blood, and I feel relatively calm. A little nervous and excited to see her, but my vampire urges are as under control as possible given the circumstances.

At least, they are until she walks into the theater in a little blue dress that clings to her hips in perfect ways and dark lipstick that I immediately want to smudge with my fingers, my tongue, my everything.

"Poppy," I say, walking towards her. "You look stunning. As always."

She looks down at her dress. "Oh! Uh, thank you."

I close the space between us, taking her chin in my hand, raising it so she's looking up at me with those hazel golden-flecked eyes. And then I tell her again.

"You. Look. Stunning."

"Thank. You." She gives me a shy smile, but I can tell she still doesn't believe me.

It pains me to think that she doesn't know how beautiful she is.

"You are the most gorgeous creature I have ever laid eyes upon."

She lets out an uncomfortable laugh and tries to look away. I move my hand from her chin to her cheek, forcing her gaze to mine. "You find it hard to take compliments."

"I haven't been given that many."

"I find that hard to believe. Your ex-lovers must have showered you with compliments."

She lets out a loud "ha!" and shakes her head. "Not really. No."

"In that case, your ex-lovers sound like appalling excuses for men."

"You say it like you think there were so many."

"There weren't?"

She shrugs. "Not really. I've only had one serious boyfriend."

"Well, he sounds like a cad." I lean into her and add in a whisper. "I can take care of him for you, if you wish."

Her laugh is nervous, and I wonder if the threat was too much. I am usually very opposed to killing humans, but if someone hurt Poppy, I would absolutely tear them to pieces.

"That won't be necessary," she assures me.

"Let me show you how a real man should treat a woman." I slide my fingers over her shoulder, down her arm and take her hand. I slowly bring it towards my lips, giving it a gentle kiss.

"Max, before we — I need to tell you—" Her pulse is running so high.

I place a finger on her deep red lips. "Poppy, no.

Remember what we said last night? There's nothing you need to tell me. Really."

"But I—"

I lean into her, taking her face in my hands and kissing her lips just to keep her quiet. I don't want her to reveal her secrets to me. I don't want to have to reveal mine to hers. I want nothing to change this moment.

"I don't want to hear it," I tell her as I wipe away a little of the lipstick I've just smudged.

I guide her towards our seats at the front. "I've organized for James to bring us food in a little under an hour. There is champagne, beer, gin and tonic, or would you prefer something else?"

"A little champagne?"

I walk to the drink cart and fix her drink. "What would you like to watch this evening? I have the new Maverick Stone movie. It won't be in theaters for another month."

"*Date with a Disaster*," she says.

I let out a laugh. "Oh, Poppy, no. That was one of my worst movies."

"It was *brilliant*," she says. "Funny, charming, and I related *so* much to the main character."

The film's premise was that the female lead was a complete mess who fell in love with my character, a Type A straight-edge guy who planned and organized everything in life. It was not my best work, but it was a huge box office success and became somewhat of a cult classic.

I let out a resigned sigh. "If it's what you want, it is yours."

She grins like I've just given her the world. I hand her the champagne and place a bowl of pink salt popcorn on the small coffee table I have set up in front of us for our food when it arrives.

I scroll through the app on my phone to locate the movie.

"You could text me, you know," she says. "I mean, if you ever wanted to get in touch."

I look up at her, and she looks uncomfortable again.

"You didn't like my handwritten note?"

"Oh, I loved it. And I forgot to say! I adored the flowers. Thank you!"

"My pleasure. I'm glad you liked them."

"And the book. I never said—"

"Read it at your leisure," I tell her with a smile, glad that it made her happy.

"I can give it back when I'm done."

"It's yours," I assure her.

"Mine? To keep?"

"Yes, gorgeous. It's yours to keep."

"Oh. Well, I don't know if I can accept such a gift. Not when it's signed." She takes a large gulp of the champagne.

"You're uncomfortable," I say.

She nods.

"First of all," I say. "To answer your earlier question, I prefer not to communicate using my phone. Texting and social media — they're not really for me."

"Oh. Okay."

"Now, what can I do to make you more comfortable? Is it the theater? Would you prefer to go somewhere else? Or is it me? Are you worried I can't control myself?"

She shakes her head. "It's nothing like that. I just… I guess I'm not used to being treated like this. For example, this is *real* champagne, isn't it?"

"Of course."

She takes another large gulp, almost finishing the glass.

"I understand," I tell her. "I've had lifetimes to get used to this life, but it wasn't always like this for me. I was born in England at the turn of the last century. It was an abysmal time. Everyone was poor. My whole family would share one measly potato for a meal if we were lucky. We'd often go days without food."

"It must have been something to go from that to… all this."

"When I became famous, I suddenly had everything I ever wanted — fame, fortune, women. It was truly wonderful. For a time. I never wanted to live in poverty again. And then I was given an offer of eternal life. I could keep working, I could make more and more money. There would be no limit to the wealth I could have if I could live forever." I turn towards her. She looks truly interested in this story, and so I continue with my monologue. "But one thing that you realize quite quickly when you amass such wealth is that it means very little if you have no one to share it with."

"You have James and Henrietta," she says.

"James is my butler, and Henrietta and I have a good working relationship, but that's all."

"James is more than a butler."

I raise my eyes to hers. "It is complicated between me and James." I say no more about it. Poppy does not need to know about the uprising, the vampires and fae who were murdered, or the fact that James is not just my butler, but a fae bound to me by a vampiric curse for his alleged part in it all. "Are you ready for the film?"

She nods, but I can tell she's still struggling to relax here with me tonight. At first, I thought it was just fear of being alone with me, but it's not that. Something is weighing on her mind.

I hit play, and the movie begins. My own face appears on the screen, and I start speaking in an American accent, talking about a big business deal. I have no interest in watching this. But I do have a great deal of interest in the beautiful woman beside me.

I slide out of my seat and down onto the floor, kneeling by her feet.

"Let me take off your shoes."

"What?"

"You'll be more comfortable."

Her breath hitches, but she lets me take one foot in my hand. I reach for the buckle on her shoe, and I'm struck by just how perfect her legs are. Of course I have seen them before, but not as close as this. I run a finger around the edges of the buckle, and she giggles, kicking her leg and showing me a glimpse of the white lace panties she's wearing.

Dear god.

"Ticklish?" I smile up at her.

"A little."

I unbuckle the shoe and let it fall to the floor. Her bare foot now in my hand, I gently stroke her instep. She flails around as laughter echoes off the walls and into my heart.

"Oh stop, stop!" she laughs, and I never want to stop. Her laugh is music to my dead ears. It has been too long since there was any laughter in this mansion, and now that I know what it sounds like, I never want to stop hearing it.

"Max!" She giggles. "Please!"

I grin up at her and do as she asks, placing her foot down on the plush carpet. I unbuckle her other shoe, but this time instead of a light stroke, I press more firmly. This gets a tiny little moan out of her, and the sound goes straight to my incisors.

But I'm alright. While my desire to bite her is still there, *always* there, it is under control. I'm not going to bleed her dry. All I want right now is to take away all her tension and worry, to help her feel good.

I place a soft kiss on her ankle, and she makes that heavenly moaning sound again. I will never get enough of that sound! I want to hear it again and again, even louder. I want to hear what she sounds like when she reaches her climax, and I want to be the man to give it to her.

I begin to very slowly and gently pave a path of soft kisses from her ankle to her calf, then over her shin, around her knee and then I find myself at the inside of her thigh. I grip the top of her thighs with both my hands.

"Open your legs for me," I command her.

Her pulse rockets, and she instantly opens her legs, giving me a better look at those white panties.

I move my hands to her inner thighs. "You can open wider than that," I tell her.

She pushes her legs apart, and the way she immediately does what I tell her is such a fucking turn-on. My cock is already rock hard for her.

But tonight is not about me and my desires. It's all about her.

"Your legs are so damn sexy," I tell her, running my fingers up her inner thighs.

She takes a deep breath. "Thank you." And this time I believe she takes the compliment.

I place a kiss on the inside of one thigh. My fangs tingle, but I'm in control. I won't bite her. Not until she wants me to. God, I hope she wants me to, not tonight, but one night very soon.

"Is this alright? Or should I stop?" I ask her.

"If you stop, I will kill you," she says.

I'd like to see her try, but I do as she asks, and I continue making gentle kisses up her thigh.

CHAPTER FORTY

 oppy

His hand pushes my dress a little higher while cool lips caress my thigh, and I am just about ready to fall apart right here and now. Never have I felt so turned on. As soon as he unbuckled my shoe, I was done for. And then when he told me to open my legs, holy shit!

I had intended to tell him tonight, or at the very least, before we had sex. But does this count as sex?!

"Shall I keep going?" he asks between gentle kisses.

I could stop him. I could tell him now. I could just blurt out the truth, but—

His lips creep a little higher, closer to my throbbing clit and I just do not have it in me to tell him to stop!

This doesn't count. This isn't full-on sex!

"Keep going," I plead. "I mean, only if you want to," I add.

Danny tried using his tongue on me a couple of times but

never really enjoyed doing it. I don't want Max to feel like he needs to do anything he doesn't want to do.

Max places a firm hand on my calf and looks up at me with a flirtatious smile. "Poppy. There's nothing I want more right now. I want to taste, lick and touch your center until you're completely satisfied."

I feel my *center* become even hotter and damper than it already was.

"But if you would rather I didn't, if this isn't the right place and time, you say the word and I will stop."

I let out a breath. "No, I want you to, of course I do! I'm just a little nervous about you being down there. I don't have a lot of experience with — this."

"Well then, let me change that for you." He places another gentle kiss near my knee and then continues to kiss his way around my inner thighs as pools of wetness form in my panties.

"I promise I won't hurt you," he says, grazing his teeth over the sensitive skin of my thighs.

But all I can think about is the fantasy from my shower, the one where he bites me on the inner thigh while I climax, and right now all I want is for him to bite me! I want to feel the ecstasy of his bite. I want to know that he wants me, my body, my blood, all of me.

But Max isn't about to bite me. I can tell he's got other plans for me this evening. His hands slip up the sides of my dress, and he firmly grabs my waist, pulling me down so that I'm right at the edge of the seat.

Oh god, is this really happening? Is Max Montrose going down on me in his private theater while we're watching A Date with a Disaster?!

He grips the lace waistband of my panties, and I let out a gasp.

He pauses and looks up at me.

"What if—what if I'm—" Thoughts of all the other women he's been with suddenly flood my mind. The beautiful women who probably get waxed and bleached and—

I throw a hand over my face.

"You're nervous about me seeing you?"

I keep my hand where it is and nod.

"Poppy. I want to do this because it's *you*. Not because of how you look or taste, but because I want to do this *with you*."

I remove my hand and look down at him.

"You know I have super senses. I've smelled you before."

"Oh, god, what?"

He lets out a chuckle. "The day you fell into my arms in the pool, I could smell every part of you." He traces a line up my thigh with his tongue. "That day in the library, your scent was so strong. Berries, floral perfume and a pussy so sweet I could barely control myself."

He runs a finger around the edge of my panties. "Poppy, sweetheart, you smell like heaven."

"I do?"

He smiles up at me. "Yes, you do. And I'd like nothing more than to taste you. If you'll allow me."

"I'll allow it," I say with an exhale.

He doesn't hesitate. In one quick motion, my panties are off and on the floor.

He grips my inner thighs and opens my legs. "Open wider, gorgeous," he says. "Let me see you."

My pulse is racing, my pussy is throbbing, and I nervously do as he asks.

"Your pussy is divine," he says, tracing a finger around my entrance. "And your smell is incredible." He presses his thumb to my clit, and I let out a moan at the same time he does.

And just like that, all my insecurity dissolves. He starts to make small circles on my clit with his thumb while I pulse with heat and anticipation of what's coming.

It only takes a few seconds before I feel like I'm already about to explode. Max seems to sense this, and he slows down his movement. He removes his hand for a moment, and I push myself into the air in search of him.

"I'm still here, beautiful," he says before he kisses a circle over where his fingers have just traced.

"I need you," I groan.

"You'll have me," he says and then his tongue traces a long slow line over my opening and towards my clit where he languishes for a few moments before repeating the slow stroking motion.

And I am in. Fucking. Heaven.

I open my eyes, looking down at his roughed-up dark hair I now realize I have been grabbing, and I can't believe that's *him* down there, that it's *Max Montrose* down there between my legs. And then I look up at the screen where the movie is playing, and he's *there*. A close-up of his handsome, perfect, beautiful face as he broods over the disaster of a girl he's falling in love with.

He's there on the screen and he's here licking my pussy, and holy shit I'm going to—

"Sir, the Chinese takeout has arrived," James' voice booms from the back of the theater.

I cover my face with my hands and attempt to pull myself up in my seat, but Max doesn't stop. He sucks my clit into his mouth like we're the only two people in the world.

I let out an involuntary gasp.

"Sir?" James calls again.

Max swaps his tongue for his thumb and grins at me while he rubs my clit back and forth. "Thank you, James," he calls out while he continues pleasuring me. "Please keep it warm and I'll let you know when we are ready for it." He's talking to James, but he's grinning wickedly at me.

"Certainly, sir," James calls back. "Do you need anything else?"

"No, thank you," he says, taking my clit between his finger and thumb and giving it a gentle squeeze. I can feel my orgasm building, and this time I know nothing will be able to stop it. Once again, Max pulls back, leaving me right on the edge.

I hear the door close as James finally gets the hell out of here, and I can't decide if that was potentially mortifying or just incredibly fucking hot.

"I do apologize for the interruption, Poppy," he says. "Please rest assured that James is very discreet."

"Uh huh, okay, sure," I say, wriggling in my seat.

"Would you like me to continue?" he asks, full well knowing I will probably die if he doesn't.

"He could have seen us," I gasp.

"He didn't see anything. Don't think about him. Think about *me*."

And suddenly James' interruption is the furthest thing from my mind as Max grins that movie star smile at me and pushes a finger inside me. "Be here with me, Poppy."

I let out a moan and push myself into his hand. His mouth moves back to my clit, sucking and pulling on my bud while one steady, strong, long finger pulses in and out of me. My eyes open, and his handsome face appears again on the big screen in front of me. He's up there on that huge screen, and he's down here sucking my clit and fucking me with his finger and my whole body tenses up. I grip his hair, Max Montrose's beautiful fucking dark hair, and feel myself tighten around his finger like my pussy wants to hold on to him forever!

My whole body convulses, and I come. Really. Fucking. *Loud.* And I don't even care who can hear us.

CHAPTER FORTY-ONE

Max

FEELING POPPY COME around my tongue and finger is pure bliss. I haven't done this with a woman for so long, and I'm grateful I haven't lost the skill. Sex and blood have been linked for me since I was turned, but this is the first time I have been able to do this without biting my partner. It's the first time I've wanted to do this *without* biting my partner. But with Poppy it's different. With her, it's not a blood thing, it's a *Poppy* thing.

She continues to ride the waves of her climax, and I ease off slightly, continuing to suck her perfectly sweet bud while I feel the deliciousness of her pussy squeezing around my finger.

Just when I thought human pleasures were behind me!

Her legs suddenly relax down around me, and I know she is done. I place a gentle kiss on her center once more, and she shudders. I wait a moment and then slowly remove my finger, even though I want nothing more than to keep it there inside her forever.

I wipe her wondrous juices from my mouth onto my forearm and sit back on my heels to admire my work. Poppy's face and chest are flushed. She breathes deeply, and her pulse slows. She appears to be in absolute sexual bliss, and I can't help but feel my ego inflate at the sight of her like this. *I* did this to her.

I gently press my thumb to her clit once more. She moans. "Max," she whispers.

"Leo," I say, gently lowering her dress down over her thighs, even though I'd much prefer it if she never wore clothes again. I make no attempt to retrieve her panties. I take the seat next to her, immediately annoyed at the large chairs and how much space is between them. "Come here." I lift her from her chair over to mine and wrap her in my arms.

"Leo?" she looks up at me with those pretty hazel doe eyes, and I am done for.

"I want you to call me by my real name." I inhale the berry scent of her chestnut waves and consider how long it's been since I ate some fruit. I must ask James to bring some with the takeout. "But please only use it when we are alone. Like this." I twist tendrils of her hair through my fingers.

"Leo," she says. The sound of my name on her lips is enough to make me want to smash every remaining bottle of synthetic blood in this mansion and drink from her, only ever from her. For all eternity.

I regret ever telling her that this couldn't go anywhere, that we could have no future. I would do anything to have a future with her. Whatever it takes. I wouldn't care if she aged. Even if she was sixty, I would still want her like I want her now, I'm sure of it.

"You enjoyed it?" I ask her.

She lifts her head and smiles at me. "What do you think?"

"I have to ask, what did you enjoy more? The movie or the lip service?"

She slaps my shoulder, and the warm vibration of her laugh runs through me. "I love that movie, but whatever you did there, it was—" A blush flushes over her cheeks again.

"What was it, Poppy? Tell me. I want to hear how it was for you."

"Honestly? It was the best orgasm I've ever had."

My ego fills the room. "I'm glad I was able to satisfy you, but I'm devastated to know that your previous partners have not treated you in the way you deserve."

She looks up at me. "Honestly? There's only been one."

"Oh?"

"We started dating in high school and stayed together way longer that we should have. I thought about leaving him for a long time, but I didn't know anything else." She shrugs. "Then I found out he was cheating on me, and *he* left *me*."

Anger rises within me. What kind of man would cheat on this goddess?!

"I will kill that bastard," I tell her.

She laughs, not realizing I am deadly serious. "He's not worth it. And anyway, I'm glad he cheated on me. If he hadn't, I might not be with you right now, and I may never have had an orgasm with a man."

I pull my head back to look at her. "He didn't even make you come?"

She shakes her head. "Oh, he tried, he just wasn't — Well, I thought it was me."

I stroke her hair gently. "I'm sad that you have missed out on so much pleasure but knowing that I'm the only man who has made you come makes you feel even more like mine."

"I am yours," she says, smiling blissfully up at me.

Oh, my heart!

"And I hope that I've just proven to you it was *never* you who was the problem in that sexual relationship."

"You did."

She lets out a sigh and relaxes into me while the love story on screen begins to wrap up. Secrets are revealed, lovers are forgiven, and everyone is about to get their happy ever after.

"Of course you must have been with a billion women," she says, her insecurity returning.

"A billion? Hardly."

"You're clearly experienced in that area."

"Honestly, I'm a little rusty."

She raises an eyebrow.

"I haven't done that to a woman in—" I try to think back. "Decades, I think," I tell her.

"Oh, please."

"I would never lie to you, Poppy."

She shifts a little and then rests her head on my shoulder again. "One thing I've been wondering…"

"Ask me anything."

"Why me?"

"From the first moment you nearly fell into my pool, I haven't been able to stop thinking about you. I don't know how to describe it. It's like my soul is drawn to yours."

"I feel the same," she says, and my heart warms. "But women must say that to you all the time."

"Poppy, I meant very little to most of the women I have been with. They want me because of what I am — rich, a movie star, a vampire. Not because of who I am. I know you see something more in me."

She murmurs in agreement.

"Tell me what you liked, so I can do it even better next time," I say. As an actor, I've always found notes useful when it comes to improving my performance.

She lets out a little contented sigh. "It was perfect. Tell me what you like. Next time it's my turn."

I shake my head. While my cock twitches at the idea of it, I'm not sure I'm ready for *that*.

"There is no need for that. I would be happy simply just to please you forever."

"And what if it would please me to please you?" she asks.

"Then I shall have to consider it. But for now, all I want is to feed you the best Chinese takeout in the city and make you watch another old movie with me."

"I guess I can live with that," she grins.

I kiss her on the forehead and then text James to bring our dinner.

CHAPTER FORTY-TWO

oppy

THE NEXT MORNING I'm sleep deprived but still floating on an orgasm-shaped cloud as I make myself an oat latte in the kitchen. Trix narrows her eyes at me over the ton of carrots she's busy chopping.

"You look different," she says, pointing the knife in my direction.

I take my latte and give it a sip, instantly feeling gratitude for the caffeine.

"You *definitely* had sex with Max Montrose this time!"

I shake my head, but I can't stop my mouth from moving into a massive grin.

"Well, you sure as hell did *something* with him." She puts a hand on her hip. "You *told* me you'd tell me everything when it happened!"

"Yeah, but now that something happened, it's kind of too special to talk about." I slide onto the stool opposite her.

"Poppy, I need to live vicariously through you. I haven't seen any action in forever!"

I give her a shrug.

"You didn't have sex…" her eyes narrow at me even more. "You went down on him."

I shake my head.

"He went down on you!"

I laugh nervously as my face heats up. "I'm not telling!"

"I can tell," she says. "You have that freshly licked out by a movie star look about you."

"Trix!" I laugh, covering my face.

She leans over the counter towards me. "Was it good? I bet it was sensational. Just tell me if it was good."

"The best I've had."

"Damn girl! Poppy! I'm so proud of you, and I'm so proud of *him* for doing such a good job. You really deserved that."

I'm still giggling into my hands when James walks into the kitchen. "Morning, ladies." He raises an eyebrow in my direction, and my face is now positively on fire. There's no way he doesn't know that *something* was going on between me and Max last night when he walked in on us in the theater last night.

I take another sip of coffee, trying to hide behind my mug.

"Trix," he says, and I'm glad his eyes are no longer on me. "Mr. Montrose requests a dinner menu for tonight."

"For how many?" she asks.

"Dinner for two is to be served in the banquet room at eight."

My heart leaps at the idea of a romantic dinner for two! My mind is quick to come up with a fantasy where after our main course, Max pushes the plates and condiments to the floor and throws me down on the table, taking me as his dessert, fucking me senseless under the chandelier I just recently dusted.

"I can do that," Trix tells James before turning to me. "Poppy, do you have any requests for what you would like on the menu tonight?"

I'm about to respond that I really don't mind when James clears his throat.

"I apologize for the confusion." He runs a hand over the back of his neck. "But this dinner isn't for you, Poppy."

The happy high I've been on since last night drops like a ball of lead in my stomach.

Trix folds her arms over her chest. "What exactly do you *mean* it's not for Poppy?"

He gives me a pitiful look. "The dinner will be for Max and his wife."

CHAPTER FORTY-THREE

"Vampire law states that vampire couples remain married until Certain Death do you part."
The Fraternity of the Everlasting Rose Handbook, page 208

I HAVE a few hours of good rest and wake smiling into my pillow just after 3 a.m. Knowing that in just a few hours I will get to see Poppy again makes my heart sing.

I take a quick shower and am amused to notice that I'm humming to myself as I do. It's an old song about love and stardust that I no longer remember the lyrics to, but I enjoy the tune. I don't even remember the last time I hummed.

I fix my hair and consider date options for this evening. We've had a date in my suite, one at the theater. How many more can we have on the estate? How can I appropriately woo a modern girl if I never let her leave the house?

I could potentially put a glamour over us so that no one recognizes us and take her to a nice restaurant or bar, but it would take quite a lot of energy to maintain a glamour like that all evening, and I'm still regaining my full strength.

I click my fingers and wink at myself in the mirror. A drive. I'll drive her to a scenic spot in the hills. A starlight picnic. Perfect.

I whistle as I text James to help organize the picnic and walk through the doors from my bedroom into my private parlor.

My whistle suddenly goes flat. "What are you doing here?"

Drenched in jewels and dressed in ivory wide-leg pants, a white blouse and fur coat, Lottie Luelle reclines on the daybed by the window as if it's still 1929.

"How did you get in?"

"Can't a girl just pop in on her *husband*?" she replies with a laugh.

There's always more to her appearances than that. Always some way she would unleash fresh hell on my life when she turned up like this.

I slide my hands into my pockets. "What do you want, Lottie?"

She pouts up at me. The familiarity of the manipulative expression on her pale face makes my stomach turn. It didn't work on me then, and it's certainly not going to work on me now.

"Perhaps I just felt like spending time with you. I told James to organize us a romantic dinner at eight."

"And why would you want to do that?"

She looks offended. "Despite everything, I do miss you sometimes, Leopold, darling."

"No, you don't."

Her face turns dark, and I'm reminded that there is a line I cannot cross with her. She is not only the president of the Fraternity but also my maker and my wife, which gives her more leverage over me than any single vampire should have.

"Don't tell me what I don't feel," she spits.

I look down at the floor for a moment to steady myself and then look back over her. "I apologize sincerely. If you say you miss me, you miss me." I make no suggestion that I miss her.

She runs her hands through her pearls and then thumbs the hideous iron pendant with those strange markings that she's been wearing for decades. "I'm on official Fraternity business."

"I see."

She sits up and scowls. "What does a girl have to do around here to get a drink?"

"This isn't the twenties, Lottie, you can make your own damn drink."

"Ooooh, salty," she says, throwing me a flirtatious look as she bounces up from the daybed towards the bar. "Can I get *you* a drink, darling?"

"No, thank you."

"Oh, you're back on the real blood I see?" She holds up a bottle. "About time you gave up that synthetic stuff. Are you quite sure you don't fancy a tipple?"

I walk over to her and grab the bottle, pouring two large glasses and handing one to her.

"Why, thank you, darling." She clinks my glass, proceeds to down the whole thing and then wipes her mouth, a little blood remaining on the back of her hand. She pours herself another glass and then takes a seat on the couch, right where Poppy had me straddled just last night. I wince and of course, she notices.

"Sit with me, Leopold." She pats the couch beside her.

I take a seat in an armchair a good distance away. "What is this Fraternity business you speak of?" I ask.

"It's come to my attention that you're involved with a human girl."

No one on my staff would divulge that information to Lottie. I rack my brain to figure out how she's aware of something that so recently began.

Then I remember very publicly claiming Poppy at Vincent's.

Damon.

"I presume you spoke to Damon," I say. "You do remember there is a reason for his revoked Fraternity membership."

"Yes. His inability to act with decorum and represent the Fraternity in an appropriate manner." Her glass is empty again and she places it on the side table. "Which is exactly why I'm here."

I raise an eyebrow at her.

"Causing a scene and claiming a human girl in a dive bar in West Hollywood is not an appropriate way for Fraternity members to conduct themselves." She twirls a string of pearls in judgement.

"Poppy is in my employ," I tell her. "I was merely protecting my staff."

She throws her head back and laughs. "Oh, darling. I know you better than that. Do you *really* think you can just hand me an old baloney sandwich like that?" She jumps up again and moves back to the bar, this time clinking glasses and bottles as she helps herself to some kind of cocktail. "It's been decades since you claimed a human. Why now? Why her?"

I sigh and resign myself to the situation. "What does it

matter? You have claimed thousands of men over the years, many of them less appropriate than Poppy."

She turns and glares at me. "How dare you pass judgement on *me*?" She takes a sip of the cocktail and then smiles that sickly sweet smile that works on everyone but me. "I just don't want to see you make a terrible mistake. One that will cost you your membership, your reputation and also ruin your marriage."

Oh, this is rich! What marriage?

When we were first married, I tried. I honestly did. I thought perhaps it wouldn't be so bad. Perhaps I would come to love her in time, as many couples in arranged marriages do. But we have been as good as divorced since she started sleeping with other men on our honeymoon.

But the situation is delicate. She is still the head of the Fraternity, and any vampire who goes against the Fraternity is as good as dead.

I sigh. "I shall be more discreet."

She shakes her head. "You'll end it."

"I haven't broken any Fraternity laws."

"It's not about the *laws* darling, it's about how it *looks*." She walks over and stands above me. "A full member of the Fraternity kicking the beam with his *servant*, indeed!"

"She's not a servant."

"Sorry, *cleaning girl*. Better?"

I just glare at her.

"Darling, it's just what it is, isn't it? You are a big *star*, and while she is quite the little biscuit, she's hopelessly untalented in every way and she's *poor*!"

"What do you mean she's *quite the little biscuit*?" My incisors begin to pulse. How does she know what Poppy looks like? Of course, I can't bite Lottie or even do much to hurt her. She is older and stronger than I am, but I would certainly do my best if she tried to hurt Poppy!

"I make it my business to know what my members are up to." She throws herself onto the couch right beside me. "Perhaps it's time for us to try again, my darling."

"I beg your pardon?"

"Imagine it Leopold, darling. It could be just like the old times." She runs a cold finger down my cheek. "I've been out of the movie business since the eighties, but perhaps it's time for a comeback. I've heard you've been offered the lead in the new Palmieri film. I'm sure I could *convince* them to give me the female lead."

My stomach twists. If Lottie is cast in that role, there is no way in hell I will win an Oscar.

"We're terrible together," I remind her.

"But we make terrific movies!"

"We *made* terrific movies. When audiences wanted insane storylines, hand-painted sets and over the top acting."

Her eyes flash fire. "How dare you insult my acting!"

"You're a wonderful actress," I lie. "But we're not a good fit, on stage or off."

"We were happy. Once."

No, we weren't. I was never happy with her. But I keep up my pretense, anything to calm her down and keep her thoughts off Poppy.

I reach out and take one of her cold dead hands. "We were never right for each other, Lottie. We are far better off as friends."

"Friends?" Her lip quivers. It's almost convincing. Perhaps her acting has improved over the years. "You're my *husband!*"

"Well, perhaps it's time to finally get that divorce." I have asked her for a divorce thousands of times. I don't know why I think this time will be any different. And of course, it isn't.

She just throws her head back and laughs. "Oh, you know I'll never let you go, Leopold." She throws her arms around my neck, and I'm instantly back in 1929, in the crypt, her fangs ripping me apart to make me hers—

I thought immortality would free me — from mortality, from old-age, from losing my looks. I would forever command power as one of Hollywood's elite. I would be Leopold Montrose forever.

But most of all, it would free me from the one thing I feared most of all — death.

But immortality has been nothing but a prison.

CHAPTER FORTY-FOUR

oppy

"SUN EXPOSURE WILL CAUSE BURNS, boils and lesions. If not treated, these can cause weakness of the vampiric body. Light through windowpanes may be tolerable only for the strongest and oldest of vampires but is not advisable for longer than a few hours. All other vampires must be asleep in their coffins one hour before sunrise."

The Fraternity of the Everlasting Rose Handbook, page 67.

"POPPY? POPPY! ARE YOU OKAY?" Trix's voice cuts through the visions of red.

"No! I am certainly *not* okay! He has a *wife*? A wife! What the *fuck*?"

"What an asshole," Trix says. "They are all the fucking same. These hot guys, you can't trust them. None of them!"

James takes a step backwards.

"Oh no, you don't get off that easily," Trix says, glaring at him.

"How am I to blame for any of this?" he asks, taking another step back.

Trix walks right up to him, still holding the knife in her hand. "You could have *told* Poppy he was married! You knew there was something going on with Poppy and Max!"

"I assure you. I did not," he says, looking straight at the wall behind her.

"The very least you could have done was not come in here asking *me* to make a romantic dinner for *them* right in front of her!"

He lets out a small cough. "I didn't actually use the word romantic—"

She points her non-knife welding hand into his face. "You go back to *Mr. Montrose* with a message from me. Tell him there's no way in hell I'll be making a romantic dinner for him and his *wife*!"

James takes a few more steps backward, turns and strides out of the kitchen.

"How dare he!" Trix is livid, but I think I'm just in shock.

"I knew this was too good to be true," I eventually say.

"Poppy! This is not on you, it's on *him* for *lying* to you!"

But I've lied to him too.

"Maybe it's just a marriage of convenience or something?" I suggest.

"Don't even go there, Poppy. There is *no* excuse for this."

Trix pulls out a tablet, swipes away from a carrot cake recipe and heads to Wikipedia. "I don't remember ever seeing anything about Max Montrose being *married*."

"Try Johnny Montrose," I tell her.

"What?"

I just give her a look.

"Holy shit, Max is—?"

I nod.

She quickly searches and scrolls and then shakes her head. "He was linked to a *lot* of women, but no marriage."

"Leopold." His real name catches in my mouth.

"Wait, he's also—"

"Yeah."

"This just gets crazier!" She scrolls for a moment and then nods. "Oh shit. Leopold Montrose was married to Lottie Luelle in 1929." She looks up at me. "And I guess he still is."

She taps on the page, enlarges a photo and holds it up for me.

I just blink at it. "I recognize her from the movie I watched with Max the other night. *Indiana Bliss.*"

"He made you watch a movie he was in with his *wife*? That's fucked up, Poppy."

"She was only in a few scenes."

"Don't you dare make excuses for him!"

I shake my head. "It's all my fault, anyway." A tear threatens to fall, but I blink it away.

"How is any of this your fault, Poppy?"

"Because I'm the idiot who thought that for even a second Max Montrose could be interested in *me*. I'm fucking nobody. I'm his *cleaner,* and she's a star! She's beautiful. She's immortal. Of course they should be together."

"Poppy, *you* are beautiful too, and he's totally into you!"

"He has a fucking *wife,* Trix!"

She holds the knife up. "I could still make the dinner. I could poison her. Stick some silver shavings in her meal?"

I give her a pathetic smile. "I appreciate the offer. Anyway, I have to get to work."

"What? You're still going to go clean this asshole's fucking mansion?"

I shrug. "I said I'd go to work, not that I'd clean anything. In fact, maybe I'll just mess things up. Throw some pillows on the floor, rub some dirt in the carpet."

"If you need extra crumbs, let me know." She finally puts the knife down. "And then tonight we're ignoring the bullshit rule about getting permission to leave the estate and going out to get drunk, party and flirty with randoms."

"Maybe I'll even go home with a human man," I say, smacking my mug on the counter.

She gives me a look. "You can't. You're still claimed, remember?"

Why does the idea that I'm still claimed by him still feel like a light bulb being switched on in my belly?

He's fucking *married*!

I put my mug in the dishwasher and put my hands on my hips. "Then I'll go find him and demand he release me."

Trix makes a fist and punches the air. "You go, girl!"

And I have every intention of doing it. I really do. But I don't. I'm angry at him, I'm pissed at myself, but if I confront him, I know this will all end. He'll break it off with *me*, or worse, he'll tell me all I ever was to him was just his bit on the side.

I walk into the library and drop my cleaning basket on the floor.

Fuck it, I decide, walking straight to the shelves and running a finger across the spines. I'm not working today. I'm just going to sit in here and read. I pull out a very old edition of Jane Eyre.

Callie is sunning herself by the window. I take my book and go join her, throwing myself onto the rug beside her. She seems to like me being here. She makes a little mew and then stretches out even further, presenting her tiny fluffy black belly to me. I give it a little rub as she blinks and purrs. She has a big purr for such a small cat, it sounds like she's about to take off.

"Awww, Callie, you're so pretty!" I coo at her. "What a precious kitty!" She stands up with a stretch and then proceeds to rub her back all around my head. It tickles, and I giggle while I try to pat her from my awkward position on the floor.

Suddenly she hisses, and I pull back. "What's wrong, Callie?" I ask, but she's already disappeared under a chair.

"Reading anything good?" A woman's voice startles me, and for a moment I think, *oh shit,* I should be working, and then I remember Max has a *wife* and I don't care about cleaning his library anymore!

"Jane Eyre." I hold the book up to Lottie Luelle, who's standing in the doorway. She is stunning in every way. Her skin is like glass, her outfit looks like it costs more than I'd make in a year, although the sunglasses and huge white sunhat seem unnecessary for inside. She must be on her way to the pool, which I'm sure *she's* allowed to use any time of day.

She oozes the kind of confidence and sex appeal I could only dream of having. This woman knows she is beautiful. She knows she stops traffic and if she's what I think she is, then she's probably also stopped hearts.

"I'm hardly an expert on cleaning things, but aren't you supposed to be tidying up this place, not lying on the floor destroying eight-thousand-dollar books?" There's something about her. You know she's judging you, you know she thinks you're dirt on her shoe, but at the same time she makes you feel lucky to even be in her presence. Like her judgement is somehow a blessing upon you.

"Just taking a quick break," I say, standing up and brushing down my shirt.

"Quite the little biscuit indeed," she says, eying me up and down.

"Excuse me?"

She just laughs. "I'm Lottie." She reaches out a hand to me, and I really don't want to touch her, but I don't know what else to do.

"Poppy." I take her hand, and it's cold. Not like Max's little bit cooler than normal skin. Her skin is *cold* cold.

"Poppy and Lottie, how cute," she says as she grips my hand too tightly. "We could've been a vaudeville act!" She stamps her foot and waves her free hand theatrically.

"Nice to meet you."

She lets my hand go and a warm smile crosses her face. "You really are very pretty," she says, reaching out to touch a tendril of my hair. I pull away, and she looks pissed.

"Well," she says, removing her hand from my personal space. "I suppose I should at least thank you for keeping my husband warm for me."

I freeze in place.

"But we have no need for you now. I hope you understand."

I just stand there.

"Hello?" She waves a hand in front of my face and then laughs. "Your services are no longer required. Domestically or... *otherwise*."

"Are you *firing* me?"

"Yes, sweetie pie! I'm sure you understand I'd rather not have a cleaning girl my husband has fucked wandering around our estate."

Our estate?!

I open my mouth to tell her we didn't fuck and then decide not to. I won't give her the satisfaction.

"Oh, but before you finish for the day, be sure to launder

the sheets in his room. I don't want any servant juices in our bedchamber."

She gives me a little wave, turns and leaves me feeling about as small as the specks of dust I'm supposed to be cleaning.

ax

LOTTIE BELIEVES that sun serum goes against the natural order of things. And she's right of course, but so does vampirism. Lottie is old and strong and doesn't need to adhere to vampire rules as much as younger vampires, but without a bit of lizard juice, she does need to rest during the brightest part of the day.

I tell her she is welcome to one of the guest suites, but she refuses, instead deciding she will take her rest in my bedroom. She tries to get me to stay with her, but I tell her I already slept a little during the night. She demands I get myself off the sun serum immediately and return to my natural state. I tell her I will consider it and take my leave.

I make my way to the war room, where I've called James and Henrietta for an emergency meeting. Lottie has excellent hearing, and this is the only place in the mansion where she won't be able to hear us.

A shiver goes down my spine at the thought of her in my bedroom, in *my* bed.

While I wait for the others to join me, I run my fingers over some of the many books that are housed here. These books have come from various places over the years, many stolen tomes written by different supernatural orders and organizations over the millennia. They are incredibly useful to have. They can help us understand the way other immortals and supernaturals think and tick. My hand lands on the most recently published Order of Concordia Codex. I'm about to pull it down when I hear the secret knock on the door.

I open the door, and Henrietta bursts in. I close and bolt the door behind her.

"What's the situation?" She throws a velvet bag onto the table and immediately pulls out a deck of tarot cards and a selection of crystals.

"It's Lottie."

She purses her lips.

"She wants us to get back together."

"Oh, no."

Another knock. This time it's James arriving with a coffee pot, cups and some food on a breakfast cart.

"Coffee! Thank the goddess!" Henrietta grabs a mug and helps herself to a cup with a dash of oat milk and three sugars. She then holds up a pastry that appears to have seen better days.

"What on Gaia is this?"

"This was the best I could do on such short notice," James says. "Perhaps some fresh fruit instead, Henrietta?"

Henrietta ignores him, eyes the pastry suspiciously and puts it on a plate anyway.

"Sir?" James asks. "Would you like something?"

"Coffee, please." I rarely drink coffee, but the warmth will be welcome after being in Lottie's icy presence.

I double check the door is bolted. We take our seats, and I fill them in on the morning's events.

"How did she get through the wards?" James asks, throwing Henrietta a judgmental look.

"Uh, maybe because she's the most powerful vampire in the city?" Henrietta spits back.

"Not quite. You're forgetting Brandon Curtis," I tell her.

"He should have been the president," Henrietta sighs.

"We're all well aware of that, but a president can only be removed by Certain Death." I think of what happened to Lottie's father. "And we don't need a repeat of what happened the last time."

"How many vampires were killed during the last uprising again?" Henrietta asks.

"Etta," James warns.

"I'm just asking!"

"Fourteen." I tell her. "It was the largest number killed in one event since the war."

The uprising was awful business. Lottie's father, Renaud, was found to be embezzling funds from the Fraternity to pay for his life of luxury and rare occult artefacts. He had tried to purchase a magical fae item with stolen money. The fae are shrewd and incredibly psychic and don't take kindly to lies and manipulation (even though they are masters of it themselves). This fae passed on word to a member of the Fraternity about what they had discovered. Renaud killed the fae's entire family and the vampire who had discovered his secret, and the Fraternity became split between those who believed in Renaud and those who believed he was stealing their money.

The truth came to light, as it always does. Renaud was given the Certain Death, and Lottie took over as president.

"Let's move on," James says. "And focus on why the wards weren't strong enough." He glares at Henrietta. "Your wards should have prevented this."

"It's very difficult to create wards for a vampire like Lottie."

"Maybe you just need to be better at your job," James says.

"Maybe if *your* security system was better, my wards wouldn't have to be so strong!"

"Enough bickering," I say. "Henrietta's wards are exceptional."

James opens his mouth to speak and then thinks better of it.

"I already told you what I think happened the night of the shooting," Henrietta starts. "They must have had permission to be on the property. Ex-employees, contractors, party guests—"

"It never should have happened," James says.

Henrietta's face turns beet red. "If I could work with my coven, the wards would have been strong enough. But as I'm sure *you* are aware, *James*, if my coven knew I was working with vampires, I'd be as good as dead."

"We've updated security on all fronts now, and that's what matters," I say. "And besides, there is nothing Henrietta could do to stop Lottie entering her own home. Her name may not be on the deed to her house, but as far as vampire law is concerned, as my wife, everything I have is half hers."

Henrietta shakes her head. "How did you let that happen? Didn't you even consider a prenup?"

"You don't tell the president of the Fraternity that you want his daughter to sign a prenup. Besides, she had an insane notion that all my money only came from the movies we did together. She already believed that all my money was rightfully hers."

"Why does she want to come back now? After all this time?" Henrietta asks, shuffling her tarot cards.

"Oh god, not the *tarot*," mumbles James.

"That's what I'm hoping you can tell me, Etta," I say, ignoring him. "I want to know why she's really here. What are her intentions? And, most importantly, what can we do to make sure she doesn't succeed in whatever foul plan she has?"

Henrietta pushes her empty mug, plate and James' arm out of the way and begins placing down cards.

"What do you see?" I ask.

"It's not clear..." she says, making little humming sounds over the cards. "Lottie is always so difficult to read."

"What a surprise," James says.

She shoots him a look and then focuses back on the cards.

"It's not for love..." she says, turning over the Lovers reversed. "But I see there is someone else. She's given her heart to someone new."

"What heart?" James says.

"Then why on earth does she want me back?"

She points to the King of Swords sitting near James' arm. "This is her father. It may have something to do with him. But it can also represent rules, laws..." She pushes James' arm off the table and pulls more cards. "Two of Cups reversed..." she makes some more humming noises while James rolls his eyes. "It appears she may just want to make it look like you are together, to cover up this other relationship."

"For god's sake, why didn't she just tell me that?"

Henrietta taps the Princess of Swords reversed. "Because she's a spiteful, hateful monster?"

James nods. "Well, at least we all agree on something."

"What does it say about Poppy?" I ask, a butterfly running riot in my stomach. "Lottie knows I'm with her and she wants me to end it."

She brings the cards back into a pack, bangs them on the table and starts shuffling again. "Hmmmm. Oh! Oooh. Okay. Now, this is interesting…"

"What is it?" I ask.

"I'm not at liberty to say."

"What does that mean?" James asks.

"Well, there are some things here that the spirits are telling me not to tell you about. They're telling me you have to find this out for yourself."

I slap a hand to the table. "Screw the spirits, just tell me!" I demand.

She startles, pulls some more cards, and then her face falls. "Well, this I can tell you. Poppy's in trouble."

Those words are like a punch to the gut. "What kind of trouble?"

She frantically pulls more cards. "I can't see. It's that block I always get when I try to read on Lottie. It's like it just goes… black."

"What a great lot of use that is," James huffs.

I sigh. "Alright, here is the plan. I'll have dinner with Lottie, see if I can get some information out of her about whoever this person is she's fallen for. Perhaps we can come up with an… arrangement." The last thing I want is another fucking *arrangement* with Lottie, but if a little pretense that we are back together could mean that she gets what she wants, and I could still see Poppy—

But no, Poppy deserves better than this. She doesn't deserve a vampire boyfriend who must remain a secret, not only because is he a celebrity and a vampire but also because he's *married*.

Dear god, it sounds so awful.

I take a deep breath. Of course, it was always going to end this way.

I must end it with Poppy.

"Etta, you can go, but please continue to speak with the spirits and call me if you discover anything else. Do tell them I apologize for my outburst earlier aswell."

She nods. "They say it's already forgiven."

James gives her a withering look.

"And James, please let Poppy know I won't be able to see her this evening." A coward's choice. I should go to her immediately and break it off, but I'm not yet ready to break my own heart.

"Poppy already knows," he says.

"What? How?"

"Well," he looks uncomfortable, and I know I will not like this. "Lottie found me in my office early this morning. She told me she was staying a few days and asked me to organize a dinner for you tonight. I went to the kitchen to ask Trix about a menu and Poppy was there…"

My eyes narrow at him. "What did you do?"

"Well, they thought the dinner was going to be for you and Poppy. So, I told them… that it wasn't."

"And exactly who did you tell them it was for?"

"For your wife."

"Jesus Christ, James!" My incisors pulse, the desire to rip him apart very close to the surface. "You told Poppy I had a *wife?*"

"Well, she *is* your wife."

"No, she isn't! Not in any of the ways that count!"

"Immortals marry for life—"

Henrietta cuts him off. "Your outdated fae views on things do not apply to this situation. Max was coerced into marrying Lottie a hundred years ago. She has never shown him love in any form, ever. And now he's found *love,* and you think he should give all that up for some signature on a piece of paper he was forced to sign so long ago?"

James looks at her as if she's just told *his* girlfriend about *his* wife.

I'm a little choked up by her words. But she is right. Not only did Lottie never love me, but no woman ever had.

Perhaps until now.

Oh hell, is this love?!

My heart swells with the realization that *I love Poppy.*

And I will do anything and everything it takes to protect that love!

Now that Lottie knows about Poppy, even if I agree to her terms, she will not want someone I love walking the earth.

I would rather stake myself than live one more moment under Lottie's control. For almost a century, I have lived under her thumb. I have done as she's asked. I have agreed to all her *agreements*. I have watched in silence as she has corrupted the Fraternity, I have idly stood by as she has killed innocents just for fun.

I will burn down this mansion with Lottie inside.

I will set fire to the Fraternity's headquarters.

I will shoot myself with silver bullets and lie in the sun until I am too weak to move, living in eternal agony if it will keep Poppy safe from Lottie.

I will do whatever it takes.

CHAPTER FORTY-SIX

oppy

I GRAB a pile of clothes from a drawer and throw them into my duffle bag while tears stream down my face. I need to get out of here *now*.

Picking up the stack of books on my nightstand I throw them all into my bag except for one. *The Great fucking Gatsby.*

"Fuck you and your Gatsby shit!" I throw the book at the wall, and the photo of Aiden flies out.

Aiden!

"I'm so sorry," I say, picking up the photo and smoothing it in my fingers. "This was all supposed to be for you."

From the moment I fell into Max's arms by the pool, I lost my fucking mind. Everything was about *him*. I forgot who I was and why I was here, and I feel like such an idiot!

I hold his photo to my chest. "I will find you," I promise him and myself. I put the photo on my bed then grab my phone, ready to tell Claudia all about Lottie.

But something stops me.

No matter how pissed I am at Max, I don't want him *dead*. And if the Order come for Lottie, they'll come for him as well.

A gentle knock on the door startles me.

"Poppy, it's me."

I hate that my heart still leaps at the sound of his voice. That my immediate reaction to knowing he's there is to open the door and throw my arms around him. I hate that even after all this, he's still all I want!

God damn my heart!

I wipe my eyes and then throw open the door. "Your *wife*? Really?!"

"Let me explain—"

I want to leap into his arms but force myself to step back. "What is there to explain? You lied to me! You made me think you were interested in *me* when all this time you were married to *her*?" I cross my shaking arms over my chest. Never have I felt like such a fool. *Of course,* someone like Max would have a beautiful, glamourous, immortal wife! Of course, I would be nothing but a plaything for him! A tear forms in the corner of one eye and I can't stop it from falling.

"I don't love her," he says.

"Oh, so that makes it okay?"

"We were married a hundred years ago." He takes a hesitant step towards me. "I *never* loved her. She forced me into it."

I let out a scoff. "I'm pretty sure a woman who looks like that doesn't need to force anyone to be with her."

"Her father was the—" He looks down at his shoes for a moment before continuing, "He was a very influential member of the vampire community. And to go against their family's wishes would be to risk Certain Death."

"So, what? If you didn't marry her, her father would stake you?"

He gives me a look as if to say, *yes*, this is exactly what would have happened.

"Poppy, I don't love her," he says again, his bright blue eyes pleading. "I love *you*."

All the rage, anger, fear, pain and self-pity I've been holding onto falls away as I hear those words on his lips.

"You barely even know me," I whisper.

"I loved you from the moment we met. That moment by the pool. When our eyes locked, I just *knew*."

"That's a line. No one falls that fast." Except maybe me, because I felt the same way.

He nods. "You're right. It takes time to fall in love. But in that moment, I knew I *wanted* to love you."

Oh god.

"And maybe it will take some time until we're completely there, but I'm very much enjoying falling in love with you."

Oh!

He takes another tentative step towards me. "I don't yet know how I'm going to do it, but I will find a way to free myself from Lottie. And when she's gone from my life, I will come and find you. I will be completely yours, in every way. If that's what you want."

I throw my arms in the air. "Of course it's what I want!"

"I didn't want to pull you into my world," he says. "I wanted more for you. A normal, happy human life. But even after all this time, I am still selfish. Too selfish let you go." He takes my hand and kisses it, his cool lips sending tingles through my entire body. "But I've put you in danger."

"Lottie wants to hurt me." My stomach twists as I think of her perfect beauty, cold hand and cutting words.

"I won't let her. She means nothing, and you mean every-thing to me. Please believe me."

And I *do* believe him. But that annoying voice that's always telling me I'm not good enough for him still pipes up. "I'm supposed to believe that you want me? Some random girl who cleans your house over the most glamourous movie star that's ever lived?"

"Lottie may seem beautiful on the outside, but on the inside, she is rotten to the core. And that is why, even though I love you and want nothing more than to be with you, it's not safe for you here." He notices the bag on my bed. "But I see you're already leaving."

"Lottie fired me."

Anger rises like a storm in his eyes. "She did *what*?"

I don't tell him what else she said. I don't think he could take it.

"I should leave," I tell him. "I—" I decide to tell him the truth. At least part of it. "I need to find my brother."

He sees the photo on the bed and picks it up. "This is him?"

"Yes."

Something dark flickers in his eyes, like he recognizes what Aiden is now. "Don't look for him," he says sharply. "Go home, back to Iowa."

"What? But what about us—"

He takes my face in his hands. "I'll come for you when this is all over. I promise. But for now, I just need to know you are safe."

"But Aiden—"

"I'll find him." He pushes a lock of hair behind my ear, and a twitch of a smile hints at the corner of his mouth as he fingers my gold heart earring. The touch hits me right in my belly.

I shake my head. "I'm not ready to leave you."

"I'll understand if you don't want to wait for me. Mortal

time passes so fast. If you need to move on with your life, if you meet somebody—"

"Nobody will ever compare to you," I tell him, another tear escaping down my cheek.

His thumb wipes it away, and he rests his forehead to mine.

"I've waited lifetimes for you, but now I have to let you go."

"Turn me," I whisper back.

He lets out a soft laugh. "There's nothing I would want more than to spend eternity with you by my side, but you don't know what you're asking."

"I'm asking for forever. With you."

"You would really want that? Forever with me? Will all my — complications?"

I nod up at him as another tear falls.

And then his lips are on mine, his hands tangling in my hair, my hands in his. And I believe him completely. He wants me, he *loves* me. He will come for me when it's safe, I *know* he will.

I kiss him back hard and fast and gasp when I feel his fangs shoot out. He tries to pull away from me, but I don't let him. I pull him closer towards me, running my tongue over the flat edge of his fangs. I'm not scared. I'm excited and turned on, and if I have to leave, I don't want to go until I've felt his fangs inside me.

"Bite me," I tell him. "Before I have to go, I want this. I want a blood bond with you. Please. Do it."

And then he throws me down on the pile of clothes on my bed and begins to unbutton my blouse.

CHAPTER FORTY-SEVEN

$\mathcal{M}$ax

I'm deep in the throes of lust and bloodlust as my fingers tug at the buttons on Poppy's blouse. I want her shirt open. I want her legs open. I want her veins open!

Jesus Christ, I am a monster.

She pushes herself into me, rubbing against my cock that's already hard as fuck, begging for release, begging for *Poppy.*

I want nothing more than to finish what we started so many weeks ago. To make her mine in every way. I want nothing more than to open up a vein and create a blood bond with her so that she thinks about me constantly, so that she dreams about me nightly, so that I'm always the inspiration behind her self-service climaxes.

"Not here," I mumble into her neck. "Not like this."

She rocks herself against me again. "If not now, when?"

She's right. We may be apart for months. Who am I

kidding? It could take years to figure out how to convince Lottie to divorce me. It could take decades before she'd stop coming after Poppy.

In all probability, Poppy may never be safe, and I may never see her again.

And if this is the last time I will ever see her, then—

With one quick movement, her pants are undone. Pulling them swiftly down her soft, pale legs I throw them onto the floor. I move on top of her again, settling myself between her legs, feeling her wetness through the black lace panties she's wearing as she moans into my ear.

She looks like heaven lying here in her underwear, blouse open revealing a white lace bra, panties pooling with wetness, all for me.

"Poppy," I moan. "I want you so badly."

"You can have me. All of me. My body, my heart and my blood."

It's all I need to hear. I gently ease her face to the side and sweep the hair from her neck, my teeth and cock pulsing in unison.

"Are you sure?" I ask one more time.

"Yes."

"Woah, shit! Sorry!" Trix's voice from the doorway has me leaping off Poppy's bed while she pulls her blouse over her bra.

My fangs!

I put a hand over my mouth as I speak. "I sincerely apologize for the intrusion, Trix. This is all highly inappropriate."

"No, no! Please, you two continue. I just wanted to get my —" She quickly grabs a tub of hand cream from her nightstand. "—cream." She gives us both a knowing grin, and then she's gone.

I rub a hand over my face and continue to look at the door. If I turn to look at Poppy lying there in her panties and bra, all flushed from my touch, I will never be able to leave, no matter the consequences.

"I must go," I tell her. "And so must you."

"Leo, please." Her use of my real name almost undoes me. It almost has me turning to her, ripping off her panties, pushing myself inside her and ripping my teeth into her neck.

But my love for her is stronger than my lust.

"I need you to be safe in Iowa. I'll work on Lottie. Calm her down. Give her what she wants. When she leaves again, I can come up with a longer-term plan."

"Are you going to sleep with her?"

"That's what you're thinking about right now?"

She shrugs.

"I'd rather stake myself."

But I'll do whatever it takes to keep you safe, I add silently.

She stands up and moves towards me. I wrap her in my arms and kiss the top of her head.

A flash of Lottie's face appears in my mind's eye, and then I realize, no.

It's Lottie's face at Poppy's window.

Oh fuck.

CHAPTER FORTY-EIGHT

Poppy

MAX GRABS my shoulders and at first, I think he's about to go in for another kiss, but his eyes turn dark and serious and my stomach sinks.

"Poppy, listen to me." There's something in his tone that makes me feel genuine fear for the first time in his presence.

"Stay in your room. Don't leave, okay?" He grabs his phone and starts texting at vampire speed. "Whatever happens next, I need you to trust me." His brilliant blue eyes plead. "Do you trust me?"

My heart pounds. I trust him completely, but he still can't trust me. "Max, there's something I need to tell you—"

He puts a finger to my lips. "Nothing you can tell me could change how I feel about you."

"It might," I mumble into his finger.

He shakes his head. "It won't."

"I'm working for—"

He cuts me off, kissing me quick and hard. "Just promise me you'll stay here, in this room. Pack your things. James will come soon to take you somewhere safe."

"But—"

"There's no time."

And with one more quick kiss, he's gone.

I look out the window and see him rushing through the garden towards the mansion. He stops by the pool where I see Lottie standing by the edge dressed in a flowing satin robe and those enormous glasses and sun hat.

I squint in their direction and see her untying her robe as she walks towards him. I can't see their expressions, but I think they are talking, and I wish to god I hadn't made so much fun of Trix for saying we needed binoculars because we clearly do!

A dagger rips through my chest as I watch them together. He said he loves me, but he's still married to her. Of course, they know each other intimately, better than me and Max ever will. We haven't even had sex, and they must have done it a million times. They've shared secrets and they've shared their life. Even if it wasn't love, it's still *history*.

She slides the robe off her shoulders, revealing a shimmering one-piece swimsuit. She's so glamourous, and as I watch them, I can't help but feel they belong together.

He puts his hands on her shoulders, just like he did to me a few moments ago, and I feel physically sick.

She pulls back, like she's angry at him. He shakes his head and walks towards her with open arms. And then she walks into his arms as hers wrap around him.

What am I watching?

And then he kisses the top of her head, *just like he did to me!*

No. No! He told me he loves me! He said I just had to trust him! This isn't what it looks like!

And I almost convince myself of it until he puts his lips on hers and—

What in the actual fuck?!

I watch dumbstruck as he kisses her, hard and fast.

Just like he kissed me!!

I rub my eyes. This can't be happening.

But it is.

She pulls back from the kiss and starts unbuttoning his shirt — and he lets her. He lets her undress him.

There has to be an explanation for all this. He's *acting*. He's playing pretend with her. He's doing this to keep me safe.

Right?

Right?!

But the way his body leans towards hers as she slides his shirt over his shoulders looks so *real,* how do I know if he's acting now or if he was just acting with me?

He told me to trust him, but that was easier to do when I wasn't watching him kissing *her.*

Maybe this whole thing has just been a game to him. Getting me to fall for him. Getting me semi-naked in my room, having me present him with my neck. Maybe he plays this game with all his staff — some cleaning-girl kink he has. Some fucked up way to spend his immortality.

Fucking idiot Poppy!

I turn around. I have seen enough.

CHAPTER FORTY-NINE

ax

LOTTIE STANDS before me in her swimsuit. Even though she was hailed as the most beautiful woman of the Hollywood golden age, when I look at her all I see is a hundred years of misery. Which is clearly not over yet.

She has lied about refusing to take sun serum. The way she moves in the sunlight suggests she's been taking it for quite some time.

She slides the shirt off my shoulders, and I try not to shudder under her ice-cold touch. She is well aware that Poppy is watching our interaction, and although it is killing me, the only way to keep Poppy safe is to pass this test. So, I don't look towards Poppy's window, I just give Lottie my movie star grin and tell her, "No one possesses beauty quite like yours."

She's not stupid enough to fall for a declaration of love, but she is still vain enough to believe my flattery is real.

"And the sunlight only makes you more radiant."

"Ah, that." She steps back and takes a seat on the edge of the pool, dipping her legs into the water. "I thought I would give it a little try."

"And what do you think? Do you still believe it's an unnatural way for our kind to live?"

"It may have some uses to us, but darling, I think we should both go back to the blessed nocturnal life, don't you?"

My stomach sinks at her words, her assumption that there will be a life we will both share.

I take my phone out of my pocket and then take a seat on a sun lounger, closing my eyes and enjoying the warmth of the sun on my bare chest. I wouldn't give this up for the world.

I give her a smile. "If you wish, darling."

But I would rather die than share my home and my life with her again.

She gives me a sly smile, and it's clear we both know what game we're playing here now. If I don't do as she wishes, she will kill Poppy.

"What was it that you saw in her, anyway?" Lottie asks, kicking her feet in the water.

"In who?"

"Don't play coy with me," she snaps. "That servant girl."

I want to snap back — *she's not a servant, she's the woman I love!* — but I hold my tongue. "Oh, I don't know. Boredom? Convenience?"

"Be honest, darling. It was a fantasy, wasn't it? You liked the idea of screwing the help. Who's next? The girl with the green hair who does your cooking?" She lets out a cackle.

"I'm done with that dalliance. If you wish for us to try again, then I'll commit to you, Lottie. There will be no one but you." I give her a look. "As long as you can say the same to me."

"Of course!"

"No more Dons?"

She laughs at that. "Dons don't count! That was always our arrangement, wasn't it? I think we should continue in that way. You can take as many Donnas as you like. Drink them, fuck them, whatever you like, just promise never to give your heart away."

"And your heart will only be mine?" I ask her.

She hesitates for just a second, but I notice it. "Always, my darling. It will never be elsewhere." She slides into the pool and floats on her back. "Now imagine how it will be when it's you and me again, darling. We can finally bring some class back to vampire society."

Yes, because biting and fucking Dons in the lounge room while your husband tries to sleep upstairs is so incredibly classy.

"It was always meant to be you and me, wasn't it, Leopold?"

"Yes, my darling," I say, my voice colder than her skin.

I won't be able to keep this up forever, but I hope to be able to keep up the pretense at least until James has Poppy somewhere safe.

CHAPTER FIFTY

oppy

"Where are you going?" Trix calls out as I storm through the kitchen with my duffle bag.

"I'm leaving." I tell her, walking to the door.

She rushes over to me. "*Leaving*, leaving?"

I nod and fight back the tears. I just put on new mascara. I also changed into a short jean skirt and white t-shirt, throwing the work blouse Max had just unbuttoned with his strong fingers and pants he'd pulled off me in the trash.

"But I just saw you two going at it—"

"Yeah, and five seconds later he was kissing *his wife* out by the pool."

"What the—?"

"Yeah. And I just — I need to get out of here. I need to find Aiden, I need to—" Tears threaten to fall *again*.

"I'm coming with you."

I shake my head. "You can't just *leave*."

"You think I want to stay here and work for a jerk who treats his staff like that? No way!"

She throws her apron on the counter to reveal a pair of shorts and a t-shirt with a picture of a green avocado wearing a mustache on it. The grinning avocado is the same green as the glitter eyeshadow she's got on.

She shoves her phone in her pocket and follows me out to my car. I throw my bag in the back and drive. The mansion gets smaller in my rearview mirror, and while I know I have to leave all this behind me, I am also devastated at the idea of never coming back here again.

"Where are we going?" Trix asks.

"Vincent's."

"What? I can't go there dressed like this!"

"You look cute," I tell her. "But also, I have all my clothes in the back if you want to borrow something."

She squeezes through the gap in the seats and starts rummaging through my bag. She pulls out the blue dress I wore on my date to the theater with Max. "Can I wear this?"

I suddenly remember the thrill of Max's head between my thighs, his tongue on my clit, the way his finger fucked me at the same time and I—

Trix squeals as I nearly run us off the road.

She throws the dress in the back. "Maybe what I'm wearing is fine."

"Sorry, that was the dress I was wearing when—" I shake my head and take a deep breath. "It doesn't matter now. Wear it if you want."

"Poppy, what the hell happened? When I saw you in our room with Max, the way he looked at you was pure adoration. It didn't *look* like he was just fucking around. I'm hardly an expert on relationships, but he looked at you like he wanted more than just to cheat on his wife with some young hot thing."

"But that's exactly what he did! He *did* cheat on his wife!"

"Okay, so maybe it's not that black and white after all."

"You were so pissed when you found out Malik had a wife."

"Malik never looked at me the way Max looks at you. I don't condone cheating, but maybe there is more to this. Maybe they're separated? Maybe it's a marriage of convenience?"

I grip the wheel a little tighter as I remember him telling me to *trust him*. Telling me that he didn't love *her*, he loved *me*.

"Just for one night, I want to forget about Max Montrose," I tell her.

"So, if we're out forgetting about Max Montrose, why are we going to Vincent's, the place where he claimed you?"

"I know Aiden hung out there. Maybe someone can tell me something. I just want this all to be over. I just want to get what I came here for. My brother."

"Are you new? Where's Dave?" Trix asks a bouncer on the door I don't recognize.

"Yeah. Dave's moved on."

"Moved on, where?" she asks.

"I dunno. You want to come in or what?"

"Yeah. Both of us. Dave usually tells them not to charge us," she adds.

He looks her up and down in her avocado t-shirt. "Twenty bucks each."

"I'll get it," says Trix, handing her credit card over to the woman on the door. "For two."

The woman also takes a good look at Trix's t-shirt before waving us through.

"I can't believe we still had to pay when this place is practically empty," Trix complains, looking around the club.

"It's still early, I guess," I say, making my way straight to the bar.

I pull out the photo of Aiden I took from the wall last time I was here and show it to the pretty pink-haired bartender. "Do you know this guy?"

She looks at the picture like she absolutely knows him. "Are you going to order anything?"

"Jesus, we just paid forty bucks to get in here!" Trix says.

I shoot Trix a look and order two cocktails.

The bartender hands over two gin rickey cocktails I can't afford. I couldn't afford to drink here when I *had* a job!

I reluctantly hand over some cash. "He's my brother," I add, hoping that might get her to tell me something.

"Yeah, he comes in here sometimes."

"When did you last see him?"

"Maybe a couple of weeks ago."

"*We* were here a couple of weeks ago," Trix says. "What if he was here the same night that—" She must realize I'm thinking the same thing.

Aiden could have been here the same night I was drunk and getting glamoured and Max Montrose was claiming me. I was so caught up in my own drama and pathetic crush on a movie star I wasn't even paying attention. He could have been right here in this room, and I didn't even notice!

I'm nothing but a boy-crazy, movie star-obsessed moron.

"Look, no offence," the bartender starts, "but a lot of people come in here because it's discreet. Not everyone who comes in here *wants* people to know about it. And if you're his sister and you don't know where he is, maybe he doesn't want you to know."

"Hey, that's—" Trix starts.

But I shake my head. Because she's right. And I can't believe it's taken me this long to realize.

I throw back half of my cocktail. "All this time I've been putting myself in stupid situations to try to find my brother." I tick the things off my fingers. "I joined a cult. I took a job working for a movie star, which was really just a front to spy on him for the cult. I fell in love with the movie star, who turned out to be a vampire. I got *claimed* by that vampire. Then he turned out to have a *wife* who I'm pretty sure now wants to kill me." I down the rest of my drink while Trix just stares at me with her mouth open. "All to find Aiden when he didn't even fucking want to be found." I shake my head. "Well, you know what? Fuck him. Fuck him for leaving. Fuck him for disappearing. He knew where I was. He could have got in tou*ch anytime.*"

I let out a laugh as I smack my empty glass on the bar. "I was worried sick. I thought he might be dead, but now I think he might be *undead*."

"Wait, you joined a fucking cult?" Trix asks. "And your brother is a *vampire?*"

"I can't be sure," I say, taking the photo in my hands and staring at it. "But he looks different in this photo."

Trix takes the photo and frowns. "How can you tell?"

"I can't, for sure." I shrug. "Oh yeah, I forgot to mention the cult might want to kill me as well."

"I think we're going to need some more drinks here." Trix orders two more cocktails and puts them on her card.

I TELL TRIX EVERYTHING, and while I fill her in, we both somehow get rip-roaring-fucking drunk.

"You're still here," I say, once she knows it all.

"What? You thought I would just leave you here drunk and in danger?" She puts her glass down, only just getting it on the table after it nearly falls off the edge. "Who would protect you if I wasn't here?"

"Max was supposed to protect me. That was the deal, right? When he claimed me?"

"I think we both know there was more to him claiming you than that."

"But he's not here. He's with his wife, and Aiden is out there somewhere just living his maybe-eternal best life without wanting me around. Everyone is living their lives, and I want to live my life too." I jump up from our table and move towards the dance floor. It's now filled with people dancing to some song with depressing lyrics I can't quite place, but the band plays it in a way that makes me want to dance.

And so, I do. And I don't think about Max, or Aiden or Lottie. I just enjoy this moment, throwing my drunk body around in time to the music while the people around me grin and dance and sing along with me too.

I don't know how many songs pass when a cute guy with dark eyes and hair a mess of wild dark curls, bumps into me. "Shit, sorry!" he shouts over the music.

Oooh, he's cute. Not silent movie star handsome like Max, but boy next door you've had a crush on all your life cute. He feels safe and like trouble all at the same time.

"Hey, I like the way you dance!" he says with a cute smile.

"Are you glamouring me?" I ask, feeling woozy.

He laughs. "I don't know what that means."

"Wanna dance?" I ask, even though we're already kind of dancing.

"Yes!"

He takes my hand and spins me around. This guy *knows* how to dance!

"Are you a vampire?" I ask.

He laughs as if he has no clue what I'm talking about. "Am I a *what*?"

"Are you a vampire?"

He shakes his head. "No. Definitely not."

"Then what are you doing here?"

He smiles at me like I'm nuts but still thinks I'm cute. "I met up with some old friends who dragged me in here." He spins me into his embrace, and it feels warm and safe here in his arms. "Finn Huxley," he says.

"Poppy St Clair."

"Nice to meet you, Poppy."

His grin is so warm he must be human. Cute *and* human, and I'm so drunk and Max is at his mansion with his *wife* and—

"Hi, I'm Trix!" Trix appears with two fresh cocktails that we absolutely do not need.

"Finn," says Finn, holding a hand out to Trix.

She shakes it. "Warm."

"Uh, yeah?" says Finn.

"Sorry, but my friend is seeing someone, so I just thought I'd save you the drama."

"Trix!" I shout at her.

"Finn, I'm not seeing anyone. We just broke up. Kind of. I don't even know if we were together, actually. You see, his *wife* showed up and—"

Finn raises his hands and gives me a look like he's sorry he walked into this shitshow. He moves away from us to go dance with someone else he seems to know.

Trix grabs my shoulders, forcing me to face her. "Are you forgetting you're still Max's? He *claimed* you, remember?"

"What? That doesn't work on humans!"

"Uh, yeah, it does, Poppy."

"No. Max said he would only kill a *vampire* who touched me, not a *human*."

"If vampires can kill other vampires for drinking from their claimed humans, just think about what they would do to a *human* who tried to move in on someone they claimed!"

"Oh, right."

"Yeah, so maybe leave the poor human guy alone otherwise Max will have to come down here and murder him."

For a moment I consider it — kissing Finn so that Max will come down here and try to kill him. Not because I want anything to happen to Finn, but because I really, really, *really* want to see Max.

The room starts spinning, and I realize just how drunk, sad and in love with the wrong person I am.

"Poppy," Trix puts an arm around me. "How about some air?"

I nod and let her drag me through the club and out into the garden area out the back. It's decorated with fake hedges, twinkle lights and tea light candles on small round gold tables.

"Oh, it's so cute out here!" I say, rubbing my hand over a plastic hedge.

"You sit here, and I'll go get us some water, okay?"

I nod up at Trix but as soon as she's gone, I grab my phone and search for Max's number. But I don't even have his number. He never even gave it to me.

So instead, I call James.

"Poppy?"

"I need to talk to Max," I say, my voice wobbling.

"He's not available right now."

My chest tightens. Of course he isn't. "Sorry I forgot he's with his *wife*."

"Poppy, are you okay?"

"Just give him a message from me." I wipe tears I didn't even know I was crying from my face. "Just tell him that if he doesn't want me, he should just release me!"

I hang up and try to figure out what next. How to stand up. How to get out of here. There's a fence I could climb. If I knew how to climb a fence.

A minute later my phone rings and it's a withheld number.

"Hello?"

"Where are you?" he demands. "I'm on my way to you." Max's sexy, deep voice is not what I need to hear right now. His voice is like a dagger in my chest, stabbing me with the knowing that I'll never hear that voice in an intimate way again. He'll never again tell me he loves me or that he wants to fuck me senseless. Now he'll just ask, "where are you?" like he even cares!

Wow, I'm really drunk.

"Release me," I tell him.

"What? Why?"

"Because you don't want me!"

"Poppy, what are you talking about? Where are you?"

"I just want to be released!"

"No. I won't do that."

"Why not?" I howl at him.

"Because then you won't be safe."

"I'm not safe anyway!"

"Fuck, Poppy! Just tell me where you are!"

"You lied to me." I can feel the hot tears on my face before I even realize I'm crying again. "You claimed me, and you did all those wonderful things to me, and you made me think—" I take a gasp through my tears.

"I'm coming to get you, Poppy. Just tell me where you are."

"You made me think—"

"What did I make you think, Poppy?"

"That it was real."

"Oh god, Poppy, it was real. It *is* real! I was only

pretending with Lottie, just to keep you safe, so that she didn't try to hurt you! If you saw us by the pool, that's what you saw. I was just trying to stop her from killing you!"

"Oh."

"Poppy, I want you more than you could ever know. You drive me out of my mind. I have never, in all my years on this earth felt the way I feel about you. And that's why I need to come get you right now. Because I tried. I tried to make Lottie think I didn't care for you, but eventually she will find out I was lying to her. If she discovers my true feelings for you, she will hurt you if I don't get to you first!"

"I don't know how to believe you."

"I understand. You've been cheated on before. But I am not the man who did that to you. Please just listen to my voice. And listen to your heart. And know that I love you."

My heart bursts wide open and everything is suddenly clear again. I believe him. Truly. Completely. I trust him. I trust him with my life, and I trust him with my heart.

Max is not Danny. He's nothing like Danny.

"Just tell me where you are."

"You love me."

"Yes. Now where are you?"

"I love you too."

"Poppy, you don't know how glad I am to hear that, but right now I just need to know where you are."

"I have to tell you something. Something that I should have told you from the start."

"You can tell me later."

"No, I need to tell you now, because once you know, it will change everything between us."

"As soon as we're together and you're safe, we can tell each other everything. I'll tell you anything you want to know. I will always be honest with you. Always. Forever. If you just stay with me, I will give you all of me, everything.

All my secrets, all of it. But I need to get to you first. Before she does."

I run my hands over my wet face. "Max, I haven't been honest with you," I tell him, that sick feeling in my stomach going full force. "I've been—"

"Poppy. Just tell me where you are. I can be there in minutes. We can work out anything. As long as we're together everything will be alright."

I take a breath to tell him the truth, the whole truth and nothing but the truth, and then my phone beeps and the call has been cut off.

"What the—?" I'm about to call him back when I realize I can't. His number was withheld. But it doesn't matter now though.

Max loves me.

I feel giddy as I stand up and hold my phone to my chest.

He. Loves. Me.

I grin to myself as I try to shove my phone in my pocket and then I remember, this skirt doesn't have pockets. I look around for my purse, but I can't remember where I put it. Did I even have a purse? I shove my phone down my bra. I stumble a little but manage to right myself. I really need to find Trix and get that water.

Everything is going to be okay. Max is coming to get me. Trix is getting us water.

I turn around to go find her and then everything goes dark.

 ax

"Poppy!" There's no answer. Our connection has gone dead.

I try to call back but it goes straight to voicemail.

Something is very wrong.

"Poppy, it's me, Max. As soon as you get this, call and tell me where you are."

I end the call and furiously text her the same message, so she has my number.

I turn and glare at James who's still standing by the door in the war room, the only place it would be safe for me to call Poppy from.

I glare at James. "You were supposed to take her to safety!"

"Sorry, sir?"

"I told you to take Poppy to safety! To get her off the estate and somewhere safe until she could safely get back to Iowa!"

"I apologize, but I didn't get that message from you, sir."

James is a lot of things, but a liar isn't one of them.

I scowl and check my last message to James.

Message deleted.

Fucking Lottie!

She must have deleted my message!

She must have done it when I had my eyes closed on the sun lounger trying to pretend none of this was happening.

And that means that all afternoon and all evening while I have been acting my ass off to appear to care about her, Lottie knew I was pretending.

Of course, she knew I would see the deleted message eventually and realize what she had done.

But who knows what she will have done by then.

"Sir? What can I do?"

"She's planning something," I tell him. "There's a reason she wants Poppy unprotected."

"But she's been on the estate all day and evening. And I believe she's still here now."

"She never does her own dirty work." I pace for a few moments, running a hand over the back of my neck as I try to figure out my next step, how to get to Poppy, how to get her to safety before Lottie can hurt her.

"Call Henrietta, ask her to find the location of Poppy's call. Then call Maverick and ask him to come with us for backup."

"Us, sir?"

"Yes, James. I need you as well. Meet me in the garage in five minutes."

"WHAT DID YOU DO?" I growl in Lottie's direction. She's taken over my private parlor and suddenly everything here is *Lottie*. Scarves and coats and strings of beads are strewn around the couch and coffee table. Empty wine glasses with little rings of blood in the bottom sit on various surfaces. Some old honky-tonk record I didn't even know I owned and will definitely snap into minuscule pieces when she is gone blares from the speakers.

It even smells like her overpowering saccharine scent.

"Darling, what?" She's changed her outfit about six times today and is now reading a book dressed in nothing but a black slip and a feathered satin robe while she reclines on the daybed.

"Where is she?"

"Where is who, darling?" She looks up at me with those pale gray eyes and bats her eyelashes.

"I told you she meant nothing to me. There was no reason to go after her."

"Who means nothing to you?"

"You *know* who! Poppy!"

She lets out a too high laugh. "If she means nothing to you, why are you getting so flustered?"

"I'm done with the games, Lottie."

She fakes a gasp. "Games? What games?"

I grab the book she's pretending to read and throw it to the ground. I don't care that it's a first edition Mary Shelley.

Her eyes narrow. "I believe *you* are the one playing games, *Leo*." On Poppy's lips nothing is sweeter to my ears than my old nickname, but on *her* lips, it still feels like silver chains dragged down my spine.

The idea that I kissed her for nothing, that I was half naked by the pool with Lottie, all while she *knew* how I felt about Poppy makes me feel sick to my stomach.

I hurt Poppy for nothing.

"Playing house with that little servant is beneath you," she says. "You'll understand as soon as you've had time to get her out of your system. You'll see how ridiculous you're being."

"If you hurt her, I'll—"

She glares those silver daggers at me. "You'll do *what* exactly?"

Fuck walking the fine line. Fuck keeping Lottie happy to keep Poppy safe.

Poppy's *already* in danger.

"I want you out of my house," I tell her.

"Darling, *why*? I thought we were trying again."

"No. I will never try again with you. I am done. Done with your games and your threats and done with you trying to destroy my happiness."

"But, darling!"

I storm out of the room, slamming the door behind me.

"It's you and me, Leo! You and me forever!" her voice calls out to me.

But fuck forever if it's going to be like this.

CHAPTER FIFTY-TWO

oppy

PAIN SHOOTS down my back and into my wrists. My head is pounding, and I feel like I've swallowed a bag of cotton wool balls. I try to open my eyes, but it takes a moment for them to adjust to the low light in this place.

Where the hell am I?

Beneath me is smooth cold stone. Marble. My wrists are bound in chains to a metal ring attached to some kind of ancient looking stone font. Everything is hard, cold and dark. I don't see any windows or doors in the room, only a narrow passageway leading to my right.

I'm about to cry out and call for help until I realize that whoever brought me here, whoever chained me up here, is probably the only one who'll hear me scream.

I scrape through my memories to try to figure out how I got here. Images of Max kissing Lottie flash in my mind, but I'm no longer angry. I'm too cold and nauseous to be angry at him.

Although I *am* angry at myself for ever getting involved in any of this. Why didn't I listen at least one of the millions of times someone tried to tell me I was in *danger*?!

I think back to the club. The girl with the pink hair telling me that maybe Aiden didn't want to be found, the way the truth of that stung my ego and heart like a whip.

Trix! Is she here somewhere with me? Or is she still at the club wondering where I am?

And then I remember the conversation on the phone with Max.

He loves me.

I look up at the stone ceiling above me. Great help that is right now.

But I *cannot* die here, not when Max Montrose is out there somewhere *falling in love* with me!

Lottie. How would we ever be together when he's still married to her?

The truth sinks into my gut. Me and Max can never be together while she's around. But how do you get an evil, powerful vampire out of the picture?

The Order of Concordia.

But they'll kill any vampire in the vicinity. Including Max.

"Fuck!" I pull at the chains around my wrists, but it's no use. I am completely bound.

My memories are still scrambled, but I try to remember what happened just before everything went dark. I hung up my phone and then—

My phone.

I realize that I still have my phone stashed down my bra.

I'm saved!

I wiggle around in the chains, but it's difficult to use my hands. Eventually, I manage to push at the phone with my wrist. After what feels like nearly an hour of struggle, the phone falls to the hard floor, cracking the screen to the point where it's probably unusable.

Shit!

A shadow crosses the corridor and, pulse racing, I quickly push the phone behind the font just in case I can still figure out how to use it.

I'm not ready to see my captor. I don't want to know who brought me here. I don't want to die!

I squeeze my eyes shut and try to pretend I'm anywhere but here.

"Poppy," says a familiar voice by my ear.

My eyes spring open.

"Aiden!"

"Jesus Christ," he murmurs while I wrestle with the chains around my wrists. "You couldn't leave well enough alone, could you?"

"Nice to see you too, asshole!"

His eyebrows shoot up. "How am I the asshole?"

I hold up my wrists and shake the chains.

"Get me out of here!"

He just glares down at me, and I see it in his eyes. He's changed.

"You're a... *vampire*," I say.

He just shrugs like this is no big deal. "Well, at least now you know why I didn't get in touch."

"Aren't you even a little glad to see me?" I ask.

He doesn't answer. He doesn't give me a hug and tell me everything is going to be okay. He doesn't come to my rescue and get me out of these fucking chains. He is not the protective big brother he once was. He is something else now. Something that I don't want to be in this room alone with.

"You shouldn't have come."

"I wanted to find you."

"Don't you think there was a *reason* I didn't call?"

"I thought something had happened, that you were in some kind of trouble—"

He lets out a sigh. "I was trying to protect you, you idiot."

Of course he was. Aiden isn't a monster. He's just been trying to keep me safe.

"From what?" I ask.

"From me." He turns, hearing something that I don't hear.

"Get me out of here," I beg.

"You should have stayed in Iowa."

"No shit!"

"I'll try to talk to her."

"Who?"

"The one who ordered me to bring you here. The President of the Fraternity—" He gives me a look, and I know I'm not going to like this. "My girlfriend."

CHAPTER FIFTY-THREE

M_{ax}

"Witches, werewolves and the fae are the mortal enemies of the vampire. Relationships of any kind between the clans are strictly forbidden under supernatural law."

The Fraternity of the Everlasting Rose Handbook, page 349

I DON'T KNOW what will happen to me now, and I don't care. I can't bring myself to imagine what she may do to Poppy if she finds her, but if something happens to Poppy, I will have no reason to live. And living a life with Lottie in some sick pretend game of house knowing she's the reason I can't be with the one woman I have ever truly loved?

I will never. I will stake myself and end it all before I will exist for eternity like that.

I slide into the Aston Martin, grabbing my gun from the glove box and stashing it in my waistband.

Henrietta glares at James as he takes the passenger seat, leaving her to squeeze into the backseat.

"Maverick is at the Curtis mansion," James informs me.

I start the car and drive out of the estate and out towards Brandon's place. It's been years, but I still remember the parties Brandon Curtis used to host in the fifties and sixties. Pure debauchery. You wouldn't know it to see him parading around in his three-piece suits like he owns half of LA (he does), but the man really knew how to party.

When we arrive at the Curtis estate, Maverick, dressed in low-slung jeans and a t-shirt, and Brandon in a three-piece suit stand at the edge of the driveway waiting for us. Brandon's mansion is slightly bigger than mine, but I do have the superior view. I try not to compare mansion sizes with the man right now.

Maverick slides into the backseat while Brandon has eyes on the front seat.

"James, would you?"

"Certainly, sir." He moves into the back, squashing Henrietta into the middle between him and Maverick while Brandon takes the front seat.

"You're coming too, Mr. Curtis?" Henrietta asks.

Brandon shoots a look at James and Henrietta in the backseat.

"I assume the witch and the fae can be trusted?" Brandon is an old vampire. He's incredibly observant and has been around long enough to know we are not the only supernaturals in the city. Even so, it's quite a skill to have picked up on it when he's only ever seen them in passing before.

"I trust them with my life," I tell him.

"Maverick told me that your girl is missing," Brandon

says. The way he says, *my girl* sends a wave of heat through my body. I want nothing more than for Poppy to be *my girl*.

"We don't know who she's working with," I say. "But we believe Lottie is behind it."

"If it's true that Lottie is part of a plot to kill this human simply because Max has a thing for her, I feel that perhaps it's time for that revolt we've been talking about for some time," says Brandon.

"There's talk of a revolt?" I spin my wheels as I make my way back onto the road. "Why is this the first I'm hearing of it?"

"It's been difficult for members of the Fraternity to feel they could trust you with sensitive information like this, considering you are her husband," Brandon says. The way he says *husband* makes me feel sick, and for the billionth time today, I regret my decision to have ever gotten involved with Lottie or the Fraternity.

But if I had never become what I am, which came with the condition to marry Lottie, I never would have met Poppy. I would never have felt real love.

But at least then Poppy wouldn't be in this situation right now, with her life on the line because of *me*.

Henrietta unfolds a map of the city and places it over James and Maverick's laps in the back seat.

"What the hell is this?" asks Maverick.

"I'm dowsing for her location."

"Fascinating!" says Brandon, turning in his seat to watch.

"What's wrong with your blood bond?" Of course, Maverick would assume I'd have a blood bond with Poppy. If I had a blood bond with her, I'd already know where she was. I'd be *drawn* to her. I'd be able to just let my instinct for blood take over and find her so I could feed from her again.

"I haven't—"

"Oh, Max," Maverick laughs. "You don't date for a decade and then you fall for a human, and you don't even *drink* from her? You're in some serious trouble, buddy."

I'm about to tell him that I have tasted other parts of her that are just as enticing if not more so than her blood, but I choose to be a gentleman about it instead and remain silent.

"Could we have some quiet, please?" Henrietta holds a crystal pendulum over the map and closes her eyes. I go over a bump in the road, and she lets out a yelp. "Max, I need you to pull over."

"I can't stop. There's no time to waste."

"You don't even know where to go. If you stop, I can find that out for you."

The last thing I want to do is stop this car and delay getting to Poppy by even a second, but Henrietta is right. I don't even know if I'm driving in the right direction. I slam on the brakes and veer off the road to stop.

"I need a flat surface," she says. We're still in the hills and at an awkward angle inside the car.

"We can help with that." Brandon leaps from the front seat and waves for us all to join him.

He takes a corner of Henrietta's map and gestures for us all to do the same so that we're holding it flat under her pendulum.

"This is quite something," Brandon says as the pendulum moves of its own accord in Henrietta's hand. "You're not persuading the thing in any way?"

She opens one eye. "Mr. Curtis, if you could please—"

He nods, and we stand in silence, watching the crystal dance over the map of the city.

The pendulum pulls in one direction and then another, and I want to yell out, "How damn long is this going to take?!" But I manage to keep myself and the map steady.

What feels like far too many minutes later, the point of the pendulum hits the map as if a magnet is holding it in place.

We all look down at the point.

I know exactly where that is.

"Vincent's."

CHAPTER FIFTY-FOUR

"I DON'T CARE who you are, you'll have to get in line like everyone else." There's a new bouncer on the door and I don't have time for it. I'll speak with management and have him fired later, but for now I decide that he can be the first person I've glamoured in years.

I take a moment to focus my energy. I probably should have asked Maverick or Brandon to do it, but eventually I find my point of concentration and look into the man's eyes. His entire demeanor changes. His shoulders slouch just a little, and he looks at me longingly. I remember this feeling — to have complete control of your victim.

There's a reason vampires enjoy glamouring so much. Having that kind of control, that kind of power, is intoxicating.

But this man is not my victim. He's just an obstacle.

"My party and I will walk into the club now."

He nods and steps aside.

"Twenty bucks each," says the woman working the inside door.

It's not that I don't have the money, but I just don't have the *time.*

I glamour her too. "The club is free for me and my friends."

She goes extra gooey, almost falling off her chair. She nods and grins at us as we pass.

I make a mental note to send Vincent's the money we owe later.

"Split up," I say. "Call when you find her."

For my own sanity, I have to say *when,* not *if.*

I stride towards the bar and pull up a photo of Poppy from my phone, the one La Luna sent to me with her work experience details.

"Have you seen this woman?" I ask the bartender, a guy covered in tattoos and fresh bite marks that haven't been healed properly. It would take only a second of a vampire's time to heal a wound. Leaving a mark like that is in such poor taste, it makes my stomach churn. Perhaps I won't be sending Vincent's any of my money.

"Uh," he says, clearly still a little out of it from whoever last fed on him. "Yeah, I think she was in here with that green-haired girl." He points to the dance floor, where Trix appears to be having the time of her life.

I storm over to her, grabbing her out of the arms of some blonde-haired vampire in a check shirt and trucker hat and give her a little shake. "Where is she?"

"Huh? Who?" she asks, her eyes rolling into the back of her head.

I glare at the vampire who's been dancing with her. "You glamoured her?"

"Just a bit," he says with a shrug. "She wouldn't dance with me otherwise."

I'm enraged, but I would have to rough him up later. First, I need to make sure Trix is free of his glamour.

"Trix," I click my fingers in front of her face, but she's staring beyond my hand towards the blonde vampire. I drag her over to the bar. "Coke," I say, slapping the counter. To his credit, the bartender pours fast and hands the drink over. Coke can help bring a victim out of a glamour, and when it's ordered here, that's usually why.

I force it into Trix's hand.

"Drink," I tell her.

"What is this?"

"Trix," I say, holding her chin and forcing her to look at me. "It's me, Max. You've been glamoured. Drink this and stay here."

I look at the bartender, who looks like the absolute worst babysitter I could choose right now, but also the only one here.

"Watch her. She's been glamoured."

He nods grimly. "Sure." I see him wave over at security, and I make my way back over to the trucker hat.

"Who are you working for?" I demand.

The guy just laughs at me. "Dude, chill. It's not like anyone got drained."

I punch him in the face, sending him flying into a group of human girls who scream and run off.

"What the fuck, man?" he asks, clutching his jaw.

"While you were here glamouring her, my girlfriend was getting kidnapped. Who paid you?"

"No one paid me, you freak," he says, rubbing his hand over his face. "I just wanted to get it on with that green-haired girl."

"Was she with another girl?"

"She said her friend was in the bathroom. Probably with some other vampire. They're just a couple of Donnas, who cares?"

I punch him again. "Donnas don't need to be glamoured to dance with you!"

"Fuck you!" He lunges at me, but I'm clearly older and stronger than him. As he flies towards me, I simply hold out a fist and he falls to the ground. I don't have time for this shit.

"Nice move, Max." Maverick slow claps at the edge of the dance floor while a group of girls practically fall over themselves. Maverick has never needed to glamour a girl into his arms.

MAVERICK PILES TRIX, who's still dazed and confused, into the back of the car while I berate Henrietta.

"I thought you were taking us to her!"

"This is where she was when you spoke to her on the phone!"

"*Clearly*, I meant I wanted to know where she is right now, not where she was then!"

"Urrrgh!" She pulls the map out of the car and takes her pendulum out of her pocket.

I put my hand over it as I glance over at the club. "Not here. Not safe."

While Maverick and now Brandon know what Henrietta is, if she became known to other vampires, they would either want to use her powers for their own nefarious agendas or just have her killed.

"We can't all fit in the car," Henrietta complains.

"Trix can sit on Maverick's lap," I suggest. "She's only small."

"What? No way!" he says. "Just put her in the trunk. She's out of it. She won't even know."

"Maverick!" I exclaim.

Henrietta glares at him. "Just get in."

They all somehow manage to squeeze in, and I drive just a short way, parking in a lot behind a fast-food restaurant.

Henrietta gets out, and Maverick immediately pushes Trix off him into her spot.

Brandon follows Henrietta and watches with eager interest as she places the map down on the asphalt behind the car.

Trix rubs her eyes. "Where the hell am I?"

"You got glamoured," Maverick says. "Nice t-shirt, by the way."

Her eyes narrow. "*You* glamoured me?"

"I wouldn't waste my time glamouring a Donna."

"I'm not a Donna, you ass! I'm the caterer!"

That just makes him laugh harder. "Whatever, sweetheart, why don't you go back to sleep and let the Supers play?"

"Please don't use that word," I tell him. Supers is an old term from around the fifties used to describe supernatural creatures that suggested superiority. It's outdated and disrespectful.

"It's not a slur, it's just a fact. We *are* superior in every way," Maverick says.

Trix glares at him. "Just because you're famous, rich and powerful, you think you're better than everyone else?"

"No, babe, we're called Supers because we're supernatural." He gives her a grin, and his fangs crack out.

She lets out a scream, and he laughs.

"Maverick, must you?"

He puts his teeth away, but he doesn't take his eyes off Trix. "Want me to glamour her so she forgets what she just saw?"

Trix is still glaring at him when Henrietta's voice calls out, "Santa Monica Boulevard!"

"I'm going to need you to be more specific," I tell her.

"Amazing," Brandon says as the pendulum once again lodges into the map like a magnetic force is holding it to its position.

Henrietta grabs the map and tries to get back in the car.

Maverick sighs, grabs Trix by the waist and pulls her onto his lap again making room for Henrietta in the middle seat.

"What the fuck?" Trix complains, hitting her head on the car roof.

"Just fucking sit still, would you?" Maverick berates her.

"Where are we going?" I ask Henrietta.

"Hollywood Forever Cemetery."

CHAPTER FIFTY-FIVE

oppy

AIDEN LEAVES me here to rot while he goes to "see what he can do" about Lottie, and I fall asleep again. When I come to, I have an even worse headache after sleeping on the stone floor.

When he finally returns, Aiden has a look on his face that I do not like.

"Okay, here's the thing, Poppy."

There's the faintest hint of hope in his words, and I try to make my way up to sitting.

He grimaces as he notices the red welts starting to appear around my wrists.

"Lottie isn't too keen on letting you go."

"What the fuck is wrong with you?" I demand. "Your *girl-friend* has your sister locked up like an animal, and you just—"

"I *told* you I was trying to protect you from all this!" He looks to the entrance of the room or rather *tomb* because I'm pretty sure now that's what this place is. He lowers his voice. "She's on her way to assess the situation."

I frown at him. "If she didn't tie me up here, who did?"

"I did."

"What the fuck?" I kick my legs towards him, but he just moves back.

"Poppy, it's *complicated.*"

"You were always there for me! You always kept me safe, and now you do *this*? I'd take Dad's screaming and shouting over this any day!"

He flinches, and I realize that even though he's a vampire now, his childhood trauma is still there. "I'm not what I was," he says, standing up and stepping back. "When you get… when you get *turned,* your empathy for humans disappears. I do still care about you, but—it's not the same. I'm not the same. I'm not your Aiden."

"Wow, best excuse *ever* for locking up your sister!"

"It's not that I don't want to help you, but you have to understand that these people are my family now."

I swallow around the lump in my throat. Aiden was the only family I had left, but I'm not even family to him now. He's chained me up. And I know, I absolutely know, that if he has to choose between me and them, he will choose *them.*

"And what about the Order? Weren't *they* meant to be your family?"

He shakes his head and continues in a low voice. "I was a spy. From the beginning."

"What?" My head pounds even harder as I try to make sense of all this.

"When I first moved here, I got involved in the scene."

"What scene?"

"The vampire scene. I got bitten and I liked it. I got… *fuck,* okay. I got hooked. Are you happy now?"

"No, not really."

"One night at a party I met Lottie."

"At Max's house." All the pieces start to fall into place. "You were there."

He nods. "As soon as I met her, I just knew. I knew she was the one. She was so elegant, so confident, so classy. She was the most beautiful woman I'd ever seen in my life. She'd had some bad luck with men, never found someone who really got her. When she bit me, it was like we had this soul connection. Nothing felt as good as her feeding from me."

I let out a laugh. Lottie and *Aiden*?!

"She turned you?"

He nods. "She wanted us to be together forever, and it was what I wanted too."

"She's crazy," I tell him. "She's trying to kill me just for falling in love with Max!"

"That's not what this is about. Or at least, not all of it." He takes a step back and pauses like he's not sure he should tell me this. "The Order isn't what you think it is. Lottie's infiltrating it. She wants to rid the city of werewolves, and she's doing it from inside their own Order. It's pure genius."

"*Werewolves*? What the fuck?"

"They're dangerous."

"And vampires aren't?"

"Wolves are different."

"Aiden, listen to yourself. You sound crazy!"

"It's not like she wants to kill them all. She just wants them out of the city."

I shake my head. This is all too much. "Aiden, you have to let me out of here," I tell him.

I don't like the way he looks back at me with his too pale eyes.

Is this my future? Is this what would happen to me and Max? If he turned me, would I turn into a monster with so little empathy I'd hurt the people I love?

"Lottie will be here soon, and she'll decide what to do with you."

"Aiden." My voice is harsh, clear. "She will kill me."

"No. She wouldn't do that. She can be difficult, but she wouldn't—" He shakes his head, but I can see his doubt. It's obvious he's in love with her, but that doesn't mean he's not fully aware of what she's capable of.

"Get me out of here! *Please!*"

We both startle as voices drift from down the passageway. Aiden's eyes shoot to a spot on the wall behind me and then back at me. "There's no way out. And even if there was, she'd outrun us both."

"You're scared of her."

"What? No, I'm not! I *love* her."

"I can tell. It's that look you used to get when Mom and Dad would start screaming. Like you just wanted to run, to get out of there."

"Yeah, well, I have nothing to fear now that *I'm* the monster."

"I'm not scared of you," I tell him.

"You should be." He gives me a dark look, but I know he's still in there somewhere.

"You're still you. Deep down. You're still Aiden, still the same boy who held my hand while plates smashed and doors slammed. You're still my big brother who would do anything to keep me safe."

He takes another step back and shakes his head.

"She's coming."

CHAPTER FIFTY-SIX

"Vampires who are not currently active members of the Fraternity are not permitted on or within twelve feet of Fraternity headquarters. To do so is punishable by the stake."
The Fraternity of the Everlasting Rose handbook, page 364

I stand frozen outside the Fraternity's crypt in the darkness of the Hollywood Forever Cemetery. Shadows of palm trees sway above and perfectly manicured lawns surround me as old memories tighten a vice around my chest.

In recent years, so as not to draw attention to ourselves, Fraternity meetings have been held at our homes. Of course, all members of the Fraternity are rich and powerful and it's easy for us to host such events.

But back when Lottie's father was still alive, meetings were always held here.

This is also where I was turned.

This is where I was kept for three days in agony, thirsting for human blood like I'd never thirsted for anything before.

And so when humans were brought to me, I did what all new vampires do. My new monster instincts took over, and I drained them.

This place represents everything I hate about myself and my murderous past.

I have been here many times since then. I've witnessed many heinous crimes here. But it's my turning that was the worst of all. The way I ripped through their flesh, took every drop of their blood. I will never be able to forgive myself for what I have done. No matter how many glasses of Sybline I drink, no matter how much money I donate to the blood bank. It will never be enough to right these wrongs.

Maverick nudges me. "Max. You have to face it now." Maverick has his own trauma, his originating mostly from the trenches in World War II, but we're not on his battlefield right now. We're on mine.

I swallow and steady myself.

I can do this. I will do this for Poppy.

I step towards the small private mausoleum. Few know that there is a secret chamber inside that leads down to a large crypt. It was created to serve as a place to pay tribute to all the vampiric dead, to host turning ceremonies, and it was also used for more feeding frenzies than I care to think about.

I step through the doorway with Maverick, Brandon, James, Henrietta and Trix behind me like an army of misfit toys — two vampires, a witch, a fae and a human woman in an avocado t-shirt.

"I see you brought the whole gang." Lottie smiles at me

from in front of the secret doorway. "I only just arrived myself, actually."

"Where is she?" I demand.

"Where do you think?" Lottie's smile grows, and I realize, of course, she's keeping Poppy in the worst place on earth. The part of the crypt in which I was turned.

"We'll be taking the girl," Brandon says, stepping into the space.

"My, my, Brandon Curtis! I've always known you had your eye on my job. Good luck getting it." She flounces the fur stole around her neck.

God, does she always have to be so damn dramatic?

"What you are doing goes against the laws of the Fraternity," Brandon says. "You can't kill a human simply because Max is in love with her."

Lottie's painted eyebrows shoot up into her platinum hairline. "*Love?* Oh my, that really does change things, doesn't it, darling? I thought you said she was nothing more than a little plaything!"

"You are the one who said that, not me," I say, stepping forward to make space for the others to enter. "We're here for Poppy."

She waves a hand at us. "First of all, you and you—" she points to Brandon and Maverick, "—are no longer members of the Fraternity." She fakes a pout. "And so, as of right now, you'll need to leave the headquarters."

Maverick and Brandon both look to me. "I'll go in alone," I tell her. "But I'm coming out with Poppy."

"Max, are you sure?" Maverick asks.

"Max." Brandon puts a hand on my shoulder. "We won't be far away."

"Twelve feet at least," Lottie says.

I nod to the group behind me. "I'll take it from here."

Henrietta looks positively horrified, James retains his

regular stoic expression and Trix just looks mad as hell, but they all do as I ask and step back out into the gardens of the cemetery while I take a step further into this nightmare.

Lottie pushes her key into the hidden lock, and the thin entrance opens. I always hated this part, the way you had to squeeze through sideways. I do it now with my breath held, just like I did then, and then begin to walk down the stairs with Lottie at my back. The dank smell of musty old blood brings back flashes of moments I only wish I could forget.

If I get out of here alive, perhaps I'll try to find some kind of vampire therapist to support me in dealing with this.

But for now, I need to put it all in a box in the furthest reaches of my mind. I can not lose myself here. Not when Poppy's life is at stake.

"She's in the old crypt." Lottie says it like she's just telling me which cupboard she put the bread in.

I take the turn to the crypt with Lottie at my back.

"I thought you'd appreciate the *drama* of it all, darling!"

"You always had a flair for the dramatic, Lottie," I say. "But don't you think this is a bit contrived?"

The insult startles her, and for a moment she's speechless. Long enough for me to hear Poppy's breathing and heartbeat just ahead.

My heart feels as if it suddenly starts beating again.

I didn't let myself think it before now — that she could already be dead. But now that I know she's alive, I feel relief flood through me.

She is still alive. Thank god.

Still alive. For now.

CHAPTER FIFTY-SEVEN

oppy

I KNOW my situation is dire and the chances of my getting out of here alive are practically zero, but as soon as I hear his voice from the passageway, a little hope finds its way back to me.

"Max!" I call out, my voice hoarse from dehydration.

A moment later, Max is standing in front of me. My whole body relaxes at his presence, his strength, his everything.

I just wish he didn't look so worried.

"Poppy!" he calls out, rushing straight towards me. He brushes my hair out of my face and looks at me with those clear blue eyes. "Are you alright?"

I'm clearly not anything like alright, but I nod. Because Max is here, and that's the most okay I've felt in... hours? Days? I don't even know how long I've been here for, if it's even night or day.

He kisses my forehead. "I've got you. I'll get you out of here."

I close my eyes and for a moment I'm back in the mansion, on his couch, his hands on my waist, food and drink in abundant supply.

"How touching," says Lottie.

My eyes fly open, and there she is, standing above us with Aiden a few steps behind.

"You really think you love this pathetic excuse for a human, Leopold?" she laughs. "She's so weak, it's disgusting."

He turns to her. "It is not against the rules to fall in love with a human. In fact, while you've been berating me for my conduct, it appears you've taken a new suitor."

"That's just Aiden," she shoots back.

Aiden clenches his jaw.

"You cared enough about him to turn him," Max says. "You've never done that before with any human you took a fancy to."

Aiden's jaw relaxes slightly.

"But I wonder if he knows that only hours ago you were at my house telling me you wanted us to live as husband and wife again, to make our marriage work." He looks up at Aiden. "I'm her husband, by the way."

Aiden's jaw is now made of steel.

Max stands. "Max Montrose," he says, extending a hand. "And you're Poppy's brother, Aiden."

Aiden looks to Lottie as if he needs permission.

"Max, Aiden, Aiden, Max," she says, waving her fur stole around. A lot of things are making me feel ill right now, but wearing real fur? That's sick, even for a vampire.

They shake hands, and I feel like I've stepped into a parallel universe in which my brother is a vampire and Max Montrose is in love with me, and I'm chained to a font in a crypt.

Max turns to Lottie. "If you want to be with Aiden, go right ahead. Just give me Poppy and we'll go our separate ways."

"And how would *that* look to the Fraternity?" she asks. "Divorce is not an option." She walks over and kicks my chains. "And neither is keeping this one alive."

"Lottie," Max growls. "Just tell me what you want. I'll do it. Anything. Just leave Poppy out of all this."

"Oh, but don't you see, darling? It's too late for that. She's *involved* now. She's seen too much."

"I'll wipe her mind. I'll remove her memories of me and you, of vampire kind, of all of this. I'll put her back on a bus to Iowa tonight. I'll glamour her into thinking that Aiden is safe and there's nothing for her to worry about. She can go back to her old life, and we can all go back to ours."

"That's all very gallant of you, Leopold, but there's something you still don't know about her," Lottie says with a shrewd smile.

Max frowns at her, and my stomach churns as I remember what Aiden told me. Lottie infiltrated the Order. She knows exactly what I've been up to this whole time because *she's* been the one ordering me to do it.

"Your little girlfriend here has been working for the Order of Concordia."

Max's gaze turns dark, and all hope I have of him saving me is lost.

"The Order of Concordia no longer exists," Max says, standing up and taking a step away from me. "It was disbanded decades ago."

"That's what they wanted us to think." She takes a step towards him now. "But it was taken over by wolves. And now they want to eradicate vampire-kind from the earth. And this little piece of human trash—" she walks over and gives me a kick in the leg "—is working for them." She lets out a sick laugh. "Imagine that, darling! As if a human girl like her could ever destroy a vampire!"

She kneels down next to me, grips my hair and yanks my head back, forcing me to look up at her.

"Fuck you!" I try to shout, but my throat is at a painful angle, and it comes out raspy.

She laughs. "She certainly has a modern mouth on her."

"Go to hell, you evil—" she cuts me off with a slap to the face.

Her eyes turn black, and then she laughs again. "You know, she might make a useful baby vampire if her allegiance could be turned. Imagine her with brand new bloodlust set on the pack of wolves she's been working for."

"Lottie, please. I beg you. Take me. Do anything you want to me. Move back into the mansion. We can be together again." He whispers the next part, but I still hear. "Please, just don't kill her."

She turns to Aiden, who has regret written all over his face, and then back to Max. "Fine, I will honor vampire law. The human girl is yours. You claimed her, so you decide her fate." She tosses the mink stole over her shoulder. "You can either kill her or turn her. You have one hour."

She spins on her stiletto heel and clicks down the marble floor, with Aiden following behind.

And I'm left alone to die at the hands of the man I love.

ax

"POPPY!" I collapse on the floor next to her and take her bound hands in mine. "Are you alright, my love?"

"No! I'm not alright!" She pulls at the chains, making them rub on the welts around her wrist. "Oh god, you're going to kill me!"

"Poppy, I'm not going to kill you. Please calm down."

"But I — but I lied to you! About being a part of the Order and—" A tear falls to her cheek as I try to pull the chains apart with my bare hands.

The fear falls from her eyes for just a moment. "What are you doing?"

"Getting you out of here."

She thrashes around as if trying to get away from me.

"Poppy, stop!" I grab her wrists and pull them to my chest. "Poppy. I'm not going to hurt you. I'm not going to kill you or turn you. Please try to keep calm."

"I don't understand anything that's going on!"

Another tear falls, and I wipe it away with my thumb. Then I gently and slowly press my lips to hers. I want it to be a promise of what's on the other side of this, but I can't ignore the deep ache inside me telling me that this could be our last kiss.

I pull back from her sweet lips and look deep into her eyes. I don't need to glamour her. What we have is deeper than any glamour.

"Poppy, I love you. And I'm sorry. I am so sorry you have ended up here. This is exactly what I was afraid of. And it's exactly why we can't be together. My world is dangerous for humans. I will get you out of here, I promise. And then I will wipe your mind, and you'll go back to Iowa. For you, this will all just feel like waking from a bad dream. In time it will fade, and you'll feel like yourself again. You won't remember any of this. You'll go back to your regular human life. And one day you'll meet a man who won't cheat on you. I won't promise he'll compare to me in any way, but hopefully he'll at least give you a decent orgasm." My attempt at a joke falls flat.

"I love you too," she says, and my heart fills with warmth and want for this beautiful, fragile human.

A look of despair forms in those hazel eyes I have come to feel so at home in. "But I—" tears spring from those eyes now and a sob retches from her heart. "How can you still love me when I lied to you?" She swallows. "I am — I *was* working for the Order." She tries to put her head in her hands. "But once I knew you, after the shooting, I—" More tears fall from her eyes, and I wonder how long it will take her to cry herself out of them. "I never told them anything about you. I swear."

"Poppy." I take her hands from her face. "I know."

"I swear, I—"

"I *know*."

She looks up at me with mascara-stained cheeks and blinks.

"Poppy, I know."

"You *knew?*"

"Yes, my love. I knew you were working for the Order of Concordia." I take her chains in my hands and try to rip them apart again. "I knew the whole time."

Her beautiful mouth falls open, and all I want is to kiss that mouth and take her home to my bed. But no. We have to get out of this first.

"The company is called La Luna, for goodness' sake. It's a bit obvious for a pack of wolves, don't you think? Of course I knew."

"And you hired me anyway?"

"I wanted to see what they were up to."

"Wait, *you* were spying on *me?*"

"At first." I give up on the chains. I haven't had any blood all day, and I'm not strong enough. I walk around the font to see if there's a weaker link.

"Aiden came to a party just under a year ago as one of Lottie's Dons," I continue. "Something about him was off. I had Henrietta read the situation. She discovered that he was a member of the Order. I've been looking into him and the Order ever since."

"But they shot you!"

"Well, that was never part of my plan. I wanted them to think my security was weak, just to see if they would show up, to see what they were capable of. My mistake was thinking I was strong enough to take a shot after all the Sybline. My deepest regret is that Malik was hurt and that you could have been too." I kick the font, even though I know it won't move. "I had Henrietta read you too. She told me your alliance was with me, not with them."

"She *read* me?"

"Henrietta is a witch."

"There are witches too?"

"Of course. There are many types of immortals and supernaturals in the city."

"Oh, god! I'm so sorry!"

"It's all forgiven." I kiss her quickly on the forehead. "But we don't have much time. I need to get you out of here."

She wipes her own face with the back of a bruised hand. "How can you still love me? After everything I've done."

"Because I know your heart. You're a good person, Poppy. You just got mixed up in a bizarre cult of hateful werewolves. It could happen to the best of us."

"So, werewolves are real, too?"

"Poppy, I don't have time to explain the entire workings of the supernatural world, but once we get out of here, I'll tell you anything you want to know."

"Just turn me," she says suddenly. "Then I won't die, and we can be together forever. Just do it!"

A small smile moves over my lips at the thought of it. Poppy and me for all eternity. All the things we could do, all the wonderful food we could eat, I could show her Rome and Venice and Sydney… I think of all the ways we could express our love for each other. I'd have all the time in the world to watch her beautiful body come apart in a thousand different ways. Eternity with this woman would never be enough.

But this is not the time to be thinking about that.

Never is the time to be thinking about that.

I must stick to my plan to get her out of here, wipe her mind and send her home.

"I will never turn you."

"I want you to! I want to be with you forever, Max."

I shake my head. "Choosing to be turned was the biggest regret of my life. Until I met you. You're the only thing that has brought me any true happiness in over a century."

"Make me like you, Max. I *want* forever with you."

"And I want you back in Iowa with no memory of this mess."

"If you really loved me, you would fight for us. You'd listen to what *I* want. You'd *want* us to be together forever."

A stronger man would stick to his plan. Feign indifference. Pretend not to care for her. Let her go to save her life.

But in the end, I am not that strong. I'm weak. And I fail. Because I know deep in my soul, I can not let her go. I am too selfish.

I take her face in my hands. "Poppy, let's revisit this conversation in one year's time." It's a wish, a dream, to think we'll be together in one year, safe from Lottie, ready to talk about our future. "But for now, my answer is no."

"And what if we both die because you refuse to turn me now?"

"That will not happen. But I am going to need your help to get us out of here."

"How can I help?" she asks, looking up at me with those hazel doe eyes as she rattles her chains against the font.

"I'm going to need to drink from you."

CHAPTER FIFTY-NINE

"I'M NOT strong enough to break these chains without your blood," I tell her.

"Then bite me." She tries to thrust her hands towards my mouth but can only reach so far.

I have wanted to taste her blood since the first moment I touched her. As I embraced her by the pool that very first night, I held her in my arms and I immediately wanted nothing more than to have my way with her in all ways — her blood, her body, her love.

But I resisted. And even when I had her breasts in my hands on my couch and her legs spread open for me in my theater, I tried to be more man than monster.

I pushed down the pain, the passion and the desire, and I kept my bloodlust at bay.

She begged for me to bite her, but I resisted.

But now I have no choice.

I lean in close to her, breathing in her intoxicating scent of warmth, sunlight and life. The scent of my love, my heart, my happiness. I feel a tingle in my teeth and this time, instead of holding back, I relish the relief of them pushing through and meet the anticipation of pleasure.

I look up at her, my fangs bared. "You can still say no. I can still try to get you out of this some other way."

"Do it."

She doesn't need to ask me again.

I trace my fingers over her neck, moving her hair away. She shakes with nerves, her pulse soaring. If I had more time, I would kiss her, caress her, tell her everything will be okay, but time is limited, and so I sink my teeth straight into her neck.

The taste of her is like nothing and no one else. She tastes like berries on a summer day, like hot cocoa on a cold evening. She tastes like a cool swim on the hottest night of the year.

She tastes of life and love, sunlight and happiness.

And all I want now that I'm drinking her blood is to claim her body as well. My hands cannot be controlled as they explore her body while I drink her sweet nectar. I shove my hand under her shirt and bra, grabbing her breast and groaning at the sweet sensation of her blood in my mouth and her breast in my hand.

She moans. "I want you. I *need* you!"

My hands find their way up and under her skirt.

"Yes!" she begs. "I want you to… *fuck me*, Max," she begs. "Please!"

My eyes roll back. The sound of her begging me to take her, the glorious taste of her blood and the feeling of her soft thighs under my hands takes me over. I grip the band of her lace panties and I'm about to rip them off her and fuck her right here and now.

Because there is nothing I would rather do right now than fulfill my promise of fucking her senseless!

But that human part of me shows up just in time, washing guilt over me, reminding me that now is not the time and this is most certainly not the place.

If I can't get Poppy out of here, she may die. We may both die.

That was once something I longed for myself. The end of this infernal life of damnation. But now, the idea of losing Poppy, of missing out on our lives together, it is too much to bear.

I feel the strength and power of her human blood running through my veins, and I know soon I will need to stop—

"Max," she murmurs with a groan of her own pleasure as her head lolls back onto the font behind her.

My eyes flash open, and I have to use all my newfound strength to pull myself from her.

She smiles up at me, her cheeks flushed from the experience. "That was..." she moans as she writhes around in pleasure, her clothes a mess, revealing one breast and her skirt hitched up above her lace panties. "That felt..."

I straighten up her clothes while she whimpers in a pool of pleasure from The Bite.

"We don't have time," I say, kissing her quickly on the lips, a little smudge of her own blood sticking to her lip as I pull back.

I yank on her cuffs, this time with enough force to pull them apart.

She lets out a sigh of relief and lifts her hands, looking at them like she's never seen hands before.

"You're going to need to drink from me now. It will make you stronger."

"I need to drink from you?"

I bite my own wrist and press it into her mouth. I don't

have the luxury of explaining all this to her right now. I can't give her a choice. I need her strong. I need her to be able to run.

She looks up at me with those eyes I want to spend all of eternity gazing into. "Trust me," I tell her. She closes her eyes and drinks. She only needs a few mouthfuls, and when I feel she's had enough, I try to gently pull away.

But she doesn't want to stop. There's a reason vampires very rarely do this. Not only do we not want the world to know just how strong our healing powers are, but the blood is addictive. Even just from having it once.

When humans are bitten, they feel intense pleasure. They feel completely calm, relaxed and incredibly turned on.

When humans drink vampire blood, they feel strong, powerful, immortal. And when they drink from us, they *are*. The amount of blood Poppy's had will make her immortal for a few hours.

Hopefully, that is as long as we need.

"Poppy, my love," I say, finally pulling my wrist away from her. "That's all you need."

"I want more!" A growl escapes her lips as the frenzy takes over. "Give me more!"

Well, I suppose a wild Poppy is better than a dead one.

CHAPTER SIXTY

oppy

"WHILE VAMPIRES MUST DRINK human blood for strength and survival, humans must never drink vampire blood. Any vampire who gives their blood to a human will be sentenced to Certain Death."

The Fraternity of the Everlasting Rose handbook, page 480

SO MUCH INTENSE physical pleasure surges through me. The absolute bliss I experienced at Max's bite was like nothing I've ever felt before. It was like the orgasm I had while Max went down on me in the theater times a thousand! All I wanted to do was open up my veins wider for him and let his teeth sink in deeper, into my body, into my heart, into my entire being. In that moment, I wanted him in ways I never thought it was possible to want someone.

But his blood — it's like I'm drinking the nectar of the gods! With each swallow of the cool thick liquid, I feel myself becoming something greater than myself…

I feel my wrists healing and strengthening. My headache disappears, all aches and pains in my body are gone, and I feel more alive than I ever have before. I feel like some kind of superhero capable of breaking down doors and moving mountains. For the first time in my life, I feel truly beautiful! I feel so *worthy*, special, strong, confident and powerful. I have never felt this kind of power before, and it's intoxicating!

Max pulls his hand away, but I'm not ready to stop. I keep hold of him and beg for more, more of this drug that's making me feel like I am an unstoppable force to be reckoned with!

"That's enough, my love," he says, pulling away from me now. He sucks his wrist, and the puncture wounds heal over. Then he licks a finger and runs it over my neck at the place where he bit me. Mini orgasms go off at the points where his fingers touch, and I feel the wounds instantly heal.

Fuck, it feels good. It all feels so fucking good!

"Let's kill them," a voice that sounds a little like mine growls. "You take the others, but Lottie is mine!"

He chuckles. "I admire your enthusiasm, but I think the best chance we have is to run for it."

"Run for it?" I laugh. "We're not running, we're fighting!"

He smiles that panty-dropping, sexy as hell smile at me, and I launch myself onto him like I'm in heat. I wrap my legs around him, and he holds me up by my ass like I weigh nothing.

I growl into his neck. "I fucking want you so bad!"

He drops to his knees and lays me down on the ground. I don't care that it's freezing cold marble, I just want more of this, more of *him*!

He looks down at me with a soft smile. "I want you just as much," he tells me. "But there will be plenty of time for this later. First, we have to get out of this mess."

CHAPTER SIXTY-ONE

Max

LOTTIE ENTERS the room and laughs as she sees Poppy lying lifeless on the marble floor, blood still all over her throat.

"Well done, darling. I didn't think you still had it in you to kill, but you've impressed me tonight." She turns towards me, her first mistake.

I wipe Poppy's blood from my mouth. "I will admit, I enjoyed Poppy immensely. Her body, her blood. I thought it was love. I thought I could love a human. But I am not human. I am something else, something *more*. And that something more has won out tonight. After all, Poppy was just a donor. But you—" I put my rusty acting skills to the test. "Well, I have been a fool, my darling." I step towards her and place a hand on her cheek. I try to remember our first movie together. I couldn't stand the woman, and yet I made everyone in the country believe we were in love. I can do it again for just a few seconds.

And I can see in her eyes now, deep within her being, beyond the murderous vampire desires, the bloodlust, the jealousy that would make her *kill* for me, that she has always been a fool for me. All these years she has held a candle for me. But it was never love. What she felt for me was nothing like love. She lost her capacity to love when she was turned, if she ever had one. Perhaps she never did. She just wanted the picture-perfect partner, the Hollywood dream. Two silent film stars falling in love and riding off into the sunset together.

I feel sad for her now. A girl incapable of love who was turned into a monster by her own father before she was even old enough to drink.

It is a tragedy, really.

Because for us there will be no sunset at the end of the movie. Just a director somewhere in the darkness about to yell "Cut!"

"Lottie," I say, taking her into my arms. "Can you ever find a way to forgive me?"

She looks up at me and bats her eyelashes. "Do you mean it, Leopold, my darling? Do you really mean it this time?"

"Yes, Lottie. I'm sorry, and I'm asking you for your forgiveness."

She smiles up at me, and in that moment, I don't see the hard, evil monster she's become, but the young girl she once was. So desperate to be loved and adored that she would do *anything*, even give her life for it. A moment of hesitation passes through me. But no. If I have to choose, I will choose Poppy.

Lottie is in pain. She is suffering. But she will only continue to destroy lives and break souls. Poppy is my remedy. She is my heart. I must do this. This is the only way.

"Of course I forgive you, darling," she says, smiling up at me.

I place a kiss on her cheek, and her eyes close.
And then the first gunshot rings out.

CHAPTER SIXTY-TWO

oppy

LOTTIE TURNS TOWARDS ME, where I'm sitting on my knees, Max's gun in my shaking hands.

She screams as she clutches her stomach. But she doesn't fall.

This was the plan. I would pretend to be drained, and when Lottie had her back turned, I would shoot her with Max's gun.

And I wanted nothing more. I wanted to shoot those silver bullets right into her cold, dead heart that was never capable of loving Max in the way he deserved!

But even with this power and rage and invincibility running through me, when the moment comes for me to shoot her, I freeze. With his gun in my raised hand, my soul desperate to get rid of this woman, no, *monster* who would kill *me* rather than see Max happy, I can't fucking do it!

So when the shot goes off, I gasp.

I must have done it! I must have found the strength! Max's blood running through my veins has taken over and given me the courage!

Another shot goes off, and an evil cackle bursts from Lottie's mouth. "You think you can kill me with a couple of silver bullets?"

Another shot fires into her, another and another.

Still laughing, she leans onto the font, holding on with one hand while she pulls the bullets out of her stomach with the other.

This is not like when Max was shot. The bullets have only made her pause, but this was exactly Max's plan.

"Poppy!" Max calls to me. But I think I'm going into shock.

"I shot her," I whisper.

"No," he says. "Not you."

I turn and see James standing behind me, a gun still raised in his hand. His expression is pure hatred and determination.

"We need to finish her," James says, pulling a wooden stake out from his waistband.

"Poppy," Max takes his gun from my hand. "Turn away."

I don't turn. I just stare.

"Turn away!" I have never heard him raise his voice before. The sound rattles me, but I don't move.

"You're going to kill her."

"Yes."

"Can't we just… lock her up somewhere?"

Lottie cackles. "Little Miss Save the Animals wants to save the vampires too! Give me a—" she coughs up a drop of blood, "—break!"

Max glares at me. "Lottie has done unspeakable things, evil things. If I don't kill her now, she will kill you, and James, and everyone I care about. Then once she's made me witness all that, she'll kill me too. Now that she knows what you mean to me. We will live our entire lives in fear, waiting for the moment she chooses to strike." He takes the stake from James, tossing it gently to feel the weight of it in his hands.

"You'll never do it, Leopold," Lottie laughs as she pulls out another bullet. "You never had the stomach for killing. Except perhaps when you were first made. You were fun back then, do you remember, darling? Remember all the humans you drained?"

I try to ignore her words. Whatever Max was then, is not what he is now.

"I am tired of living in fear," he says, as he stalks towards her. "If I let you live, how many lives would you take? Those would all be on my conscience if I let this chance pass me by."

Max rushes towards her with the stake in his hand, but it only takes her a second. She throws him to the ground with a loud crack, and then she's on top of him, holding the stake at his heart.

CHAPTER SIXTY-THREE

ax

THE TABLES HAVE TURNED. I waited too long. The bullets slowed Lottie down, but only for mere moments. She's already back to full strength, and now she's the one holding a stake to my chest.

She straddles me, her mink stole dangling in my face.

It's fitting, really, that I should die here.

I *did* die here. They took my life, my humanity and replaced it with immortality and evil. They made me a monster. And I thought that it was what I wanted, but all it has brought me is misery and despair, a life of reading the same damn paperback westerns, watching the same old movies over and over again.

Perhaps this is for the best. Maybe my death will return some order to the universe.

Lottie won't come after the people I love if I'm dead… will she?

But what choice do I have now? Lottie is stronger than I am, and she is holding the stake.

Oh hell!

She can have my life if that's how this needs to play out, but she can't have Poppy's.

"Poppy, run!" I call out. "Get out of here!"

I see movement in my periphery and I'm grateful that she's taking this moment to run, to get to safety.

I look up at Lottie, and for a second, I think I see her humanity, a moment where she doubts herself, her decision to do this.

"I never wanted to hurt you," she says. I almost believe her. "I only wanted to take down the wolves. Put those dogs in their place. I wanted vampires to run this city once more, like the old days. Remember the old days, Leo?" She gives me a wistful smile, but there was nothing to smile about from those days. Humans drained, wolves hunted for sport, fae murdered.

"I loved you," she says, her pale gray eyes turning dark now. "I never wanted to kill you. It wasn't me who sent the wolves to your door. That was all Claudia's doing. I only wanted information on you. I wanted to know how you were. If you were happy. If you missed me."

My happiness had never been her concern, but I believe the rest. She didn't order the attack on the estate.

Something flashes in her eyes — regret? Remorse? Her brow pinches. "But you never loved me, did you?"

My silence is all the answer she needs.

She raises her arm, and I see in her face that she won't hesitate this time. I've hurt her too much. She would rather see me dead than in love with a mortal.

I have no doubt now. She *will* kill me.

James runs towards us, but Lottie shoves him back with an elbow and a laugh, sending him sliding into the wall.

Thank god Poppy ran. I hope she runs all the way back to Iowa and never looks back. I want her for myself, but more than that, I just want her *safe*.

And then a shot rings out.

And then another, and another, and shots keep coming until Lottie has dropped the stake and slumped over me. I roll her off me and look up expecting to see James or Maverick or Brandon, but it's Poppy with the gun in her shaking hands.

"I — I shot her."

I scramble for the stake and hold it up to Lottie's heart. This time I can't hesitate.

But Lottie just giggles on the floor, already pulling out the bullets. She'll be as strong as ever again in seconds.

Poppy shoots another bullet right into Lottie's chest. "Max, just do it!" Poppy barks. "Now!"

"Gods, forgive me," I say, lifting the stake above her.

"Leopold, my darling," she gurgles. "I am… sorry."

And then the stake is in her heart.

Only it's not my hand that has brought the force down.

James' hand is wrapped around mine as blackness oozes out of Lottie's chest, the sign a vampire has received Certain Death. It's the beginning of the process of decay that will lead to her entire body melting away into blackness.

"James," I say. "You—"

"Of course, sir."

"I thought I could—" I wipe my hands that are covered in black ooze on my pants. "But I—"

"I could see your hesitation, sir."

He's right. I hesitated. Another split second and she may have killed me instead.

"It is done," James says.

I nod. *It is done.*

"In saving my life, you've fulfilled your contract to the

Fraternity. Your debt is paid. You are no longer a prisoner. Please call me Max."

He lets go of the stake at the same time I do, leaving it lodged in Lottie's chest amongst the pearls and gems she was always so fond of that are now becoming covered in the black blood of an immortal's death.

I turn away from the sickening sight and suddenly Poppy runs towards me. She didn't run. She stayed and fought alongside me. What an incredible woman she is! I wrap my arms around her so tight, placing a kiss on the top of her head. "You saved me," I tell her.

She just makes a gasping sound and nudges into me.

"It's all over now," I tell her. "We're safe now. And now that Lottie is gone, we can be together if that's what you still want."

"Of course it's what I want!" she exclaims from somewhere within my embrace.

"Thank you, James," I say, not letting Poppy go. "You saved my life, and Poppy's."

He nods. "Of course, sir… Max."

"Let's get out of here. I've seen enough of this place for one lifetime."

We leave Lottie's body where it is. After all, it belongs here in this crypt now. It will continue to decay and eventually the blackness will completely disappear into nothing but dust.

Lottie is gone. Poppy is safe. All is well.

At least, that's what I think until we walk up the stairs and out into the early dawn of the cemetery only to be surrounded by a pack of werewolves and their human associates holding crossbows at us.

CHAPTER SIXTY-FOUR

oppy

CLAUDIA STANDS at the entrance to the mausoleum — crossbow pointed right at us. On each side of her stand Justin and Kayla and surrounding them are at least ten others I don't recognize. Two dogs sit beside Claudia's feet. No, not dogs, *wolves.*

Fuck.

"Max Montrose," Claudia says, her voice a little shaky. "You're coming with us."

"Ah, the Order of Concordia." Max raises his hands in surrender. "I was wondering when you would show up."

"As the head of the Fraternity of the Everlasting Rose, you are hereby sentenced to death," Claudia stammers.

"He's not the head of the Fraternity!" I say, stepping between her and Max. "Lottie Luelle was the president, but we just killed her."

Claudia looks confused. "*You* killed a vampire?"

"Well, I helped." I cross my arms over my chest.

"Poppy shot her through with silver bullets," Max says. "She slowed her down enough so that we could — well. Perhaps you don't need all the gory details."

Claudia shifts the crossbow that's holding a wooden bolt. It's clearly too heavy for her. "You're a vampire too," she tells him. "And we can't suffer a vampire to live."

One of the wolves growls.

"That's an archaic law to uphold," says an attractive older blond man in a three-piece suit who suddenly appears standing behind Claudia. "I haven't heard language like that for centuries."

There is something about this man, this vampire, that makes everyone stop and listen to him.

"Not all vampires are bad eggs like Miss Luelle there," he continues, pointing to the mausoleum. "Some are upstanding citizens like Mr. Montrose here."

"I'm sorry, but who the fuck are you?" Kayla asks, pointing her crossbow at him.

"Curtis, Brandon Curtis." He holds out a hand in her direction. She glares down at it like there is no way in hell she would touch a vampire's hand.

"You're a vampire, too?" Claudia looks around, clearly worried now about how many vampires she may have to contend with. She clearly didn't plan on this.

"I can vouch for Max Montrose. He's a good man," Brandon says.

"He's a monster!" Kayla exclaims. "You all are!"

"And yet we're not the ones holding the crossbows," Maverick Stone says, stepping up behind Kayla. He takes a wooden bolt from her back and snaps it like a twig.

The members of the Order all exchange looks, but no one drops their weapons.

Maverick waves the broken wood at Claudia. "Max gives

away billions of dollars each year to charity, did you know that?"

Claudia just stares at him for a moment, and it's clear that, like me, she recognizes him from his movies and the billboards all over the city that are advertising *Road Rage 6.*

"It doesn't matter," she says after a breath. "It doesn't matter how good you are, or how many great movies you make. If you're a vampire, you must die."

"Do you understand how insane that sounds?" I ask her. "You can't just kill them! They are good people! You're just following orders, and you don't even know who's giving them!"

Maverick turns to me and then back to Claudia. "Who is in charge here?"

They all look around at each other like no one here actually knows.

"She's meeting us here," says Claudia. "Our leader."

Max and Maverick exchange looks.

"Sorry to inform you of this," says Max, placing an arm around my shoulder and pulling me close. "But you've been had."

"Excuse me?" Claudia says.

"Your leader was the vampire we just killed."

Claudia scoffs. "How could a vampire be our leader? Our mission has always been about killing vampires!"

Max raises a dark eyebrow in her direction. "She was going to destroy your packs from the inside out."

"No," Claudia says. "I don't believe you. She promised us a kill. She told us to come here and kill you."

"She only wanted me dead because I have fallen in love with a mortal." Max holds me tighter, and even though all these crossbows are still aimed at us, I've never felt safer than I do right now, here in his arms, hearing him tell everyone he loves me.

Claudia puts down her crossbow, more out of necessity than anything else, from the way her arm shakes.

"Did you know," begins Brandon, "that the Order's original purpose was to keep peace between our kinds? One member from each clan of supernaturals represented themselves in the Order. It was designed to keep harmony between us all, instead of, well — all this sort of thing." He waves a hand around the group.

"Well, that's not what it's for now," says Justin, aiming his crossbow straight at Brandon's heart. "Don't you think it's disgusting that you all hoard your wealth and positions of power while other people starve and sleep on the streets?"

Brandon raises his hands in surrender.

"We do our part," Maverick says. Kayla turns towards him, and in a second her wooden crossbow bolt is inches away from his heart. His hands raise, but he doesn't look at all worried. He just gives her a flashy Maverick Stone movie star smile.

Claudia nods. "We don't just want to kill vampires for the sake of it. Our mission *is* to bring back balance. We want to re-distribute the wealth so that everyone has what they need."

"And you think murder is the best way to create harmony?" Brandon asks with interest, arms still in the air as Justin stalks towards him.

"Alright," says Max. "So, tell me, Claudia, what is it that you need?"

"Poppy," Claudia says, her crossbow still pointing at Max. "Move away from that abomination."

"That's not what he is! He's not the monster. Lottie was the one who was—"

Claudia takes a step towards me and pulls back her bow. "You lied to the Order, Poppy. I should kill you just for that."

Justin's bolt is now at Brandon's heart, Kayla is one

second away from staking Maverick and every other member of the Order gathered here steps forward and aims their bows at me and Max.

Oh fuck.

Max pushes me behind him and raises his hands. "You are right. I am a monster. All of this really is my fault. I should never have put Poppy in this kind of danger. How about if you just kill me and let my friends go?"

"No!" I rush towards him, throwing myself into his arms. "Max," I warble into his chest. He runs a gentle hand over my hair, and I just can't! I can't accept that this is it, that this is the last time I will ever be in his arms.

"I will always love you," he whispers into my hair. "If I still have a soul and it continues to exist on any plane or dimension, if I continue to somehow exist in any form, I will always love you. But if I have to die so you can live, so be it."

I pull at his shirt as if it's a lifeline between us, like I can somehow stop him from leaving me. If I hold on, I can go with him wherever he will go. Into eternity, heaven, hell, wherever he is, I want to be with him.

"Kill them both," spits Claudia.

"Poppy was glamoured," Max says. "The whole time. That's why she didn't obey your orders. I knew she was working for you, and so I glamoured her. She was under my control the whole time."

Claudia blinks. Of course, it's not true, but if she thinks it is, it may save me.

Suddenly, Trix's voice cuts through. "No, she wasn't!"

"Trix, get back!" Max commands.

She ignores him, stepping up to Claudia with Henrietta at her side.

"I've been glamoured, just recently in fact, and it's nothing like that. Poppy was never glamoured. Those two are in love. Max is a good guy. He could have ripped her throat out the first time we met him. But he didn't. All he did was feed her macaroni, make her watch old movies and make out with her on the couch."

"It's true," James says, stepping out from the shadows now. "Max once called me in the middle of the night and had me spend hours trying to track down dark red dahlias just for Poppy."

"And Max has decided to go back into acting, all because of Poppy's positive influence on him," Henrietta adds.

"You have?" I ask him.

He nods. "Yes. I have."

Claudia falters for a moment at this display of affection for Max. "All so you could gain her trust, vampire! All so you could control her!"

"He never *had* to control me!"

"Some vampires are bad," Trix says. "Lottie wanted Poppy dead because she was jealous, even though she didn't even love Max. And some vampires down at Vincent's are glamouring and biting humans against their will, but it's not these guys here that are the problem."

"I knew there was something going on at Vincent's," Claudia says.

"Max saves animals. He even has a baby cat!" Trix continues.

"Trix," Max says. "This isn't helping."

But the look on Claudia's face suggests otherwise.

"If you want money, he has money," says Maverick.

"You can't pay your way out of this, movie star," she says. But there's something in her tone that suggests even she has a price.

"How much?" Max asks.

Claudia lowers her crossbow again. "A hundred thousand," she says.

"What? You're going to let them just *buy* you?" Justin

turns his crossbow on Claudia. "I should just kill you and take over as leader!"

Brandon has his hand on Justin's neck in an instant. "We're trying to strike a deal here. I suggest you let the lady continue."

Justin tries to speak, but he can't.

"It's for her *child,* you asshole!" Kayla says, pointing her crossbow at Justin. "For his medical treatment. She needs the money, or he'll die. This isn't the time to be principled."

"All I have to do is squeeze," Brandon tells Justin. "Put your weapon down."

Justin's crossbow falls to the ground.

"Is that all you need?" Max asks.

"A hundred thousand for me." Claudia takes a breath. "And I want you to fund the wolves."

"Excuse me?" says Brandon. "You want *vampires* to fund *wolves?*"

"Well, we could use a new headquarters," Kayla says.

"What's wrong with the biker bar in Skid Row?" Maverick asks.

Claudia gives him a look. "Our headquarters are fine. I want a college education for all wolves. Wherever they want to go. If they get in, you pay for their tuition."

"Fine, done," Max says.

"I started La Luna to provide jobs for our community, but there are not enough jobs for everyone. For those I can't hire, you give them paid work at one of your charities."

"Alright."

"Max," Maverick says. "This is a fucking terrible idea. You want wolves working for you?"

"I'll do it," Max says. "But if any vampire is killed by one of your wolves, the deal is off."

"And if any vampire kills a wolf?" Claudia's eyes narrow.

Max takes a deep breath, like this isn't going to be so easy.

"Then you have permission to kill that vampire, but *only* that vampire."

"Hang on, since when did you become the head of the Fraternity and speak for all vampires?" Maverick asks.

"Since now. Lottie has been killed. I was her husband. That makes me next in line."

Maverick raises an eyebrow. "Of course. Well, I guess you can't be worse than the last two."

"We're going to need all this in writing," Claudia says.

"My assistant is right here. She can draft up a contract right now," says Max.

"And I think it may be time for a new Order of Concordia," Brandon says. "And they're all here now. One witch," he nods in Henrietta's direction. "One fae." He turns to James and then to Claudia. "And one werewolf."

"You want us to work together?" Claudia asks. "Even though I just tried to kill you all?"

"Brandon nods. You'd be perfect for the job. Look what you would do for your community, how far you'd go to help them."

"And who will be the counsel for the vampires?" asks James.

"Maverick," says Max.

"Wouldn't Brandon be a much better choice?" Maverick asks, twirling the broken bolt he's still holding in his hand.

"No, because Brandon will be the new president of the Fraternity," Max says.

"You've only held the position for a few minutes," Brandon says. "And you already want to pass it on?"

Max nods. "I'd rather spend my eternity with my love." Max reaches out and takes me in his arms.

And this time, I feel like maybe we will get our happily ever after.

CHAPTER SIXTY-FIVE

Poppy

"You must be exhausted, my love." Max takes my hand and guides me into his exquisite bedroom full of antiques, gilded mirrors, piles of books, a dust-free chandelier and so many pot plants I feel like I'm in a forest.

I take one look at the deep green velvet bedspread lying over the California king bed. I only have one thing on my mind, and it's not sleep.

Max runs his hands over my shoulders. "I'm so sorry about everything. Lottie, Aiden."

I shake my head. "I'm the one who's sorry. I never should have got involved with the Order. I should have left well enough alone."

"But then we never would have found each other." He looks at me with concern in his eyes. "I'm so sorry about Aiden, what he did to you."

"He's not my Aiden anymore. That man who was there

last night — I didn't recognize him. I thought maybe he was still in there somewhere, but I don't know. I think maybe he's gone."

"It's a heavy loss."

I nod. It is. And it's something I will have to process in time. But right now, I don't want to think about him or Lottie. I want to just want to be here now, with Max.

"Young vampires are often the most disconnected from their humanity. Sometimes it comes back."

He pulls me into an embrace. "It's over now, my love. You are safe."

Perhaps it's the effects of Max's bite or his blood still running through my veins, or maybe it's just because *Max Montrose* is finally *mine*. We have each other's hearts, we've tasted each other's blood, and now it's time to complete the holy trilogy.

"Max?" I ask. "Are you ready to make good on your promise?"

"Ah, yes. My promise to… what was it again?" he smirks.

"To fuck me senseless," I remind him, pulling him close and placing a kiss on the light stubble that's always on his neck.

I can already feel him getting firm for me as I press my body into his and I cannot wait until he's inside me.

He raises an eyebrow. "Are you sure you don't want to sleep? Or eat?"

"All I want is you."

"Well," he clears his throat. "I suppose that can be arranged."

I look down at the outfit I've been wearing for the last twenty-four hours. "But first, maybe a shower. Would you join me?"

He shakes his head. "I'll shower in the guest suite and meet you back here."

I step into his ensuite, which is bigger than any other bathroom I've seen in my life. There's a gold claw-foot tub and a huge double shower I can't wait to share with him one day. The cabinets are black with gold edging, and in a matching closet, I find piles upon piles of the fluffiest black towels I've ever felt.

I take my time under the warm water, washing off the dried blood, sweat and tears. I wash my hair with his cedar-scented shampoo, and as the water starts to run clear, I finally feel free. There's no Order to come after me, no Lottie who wants me dead. Just Max taking a shower somewhere else in the mansion as we prepare ourselves for our happily ever after.

When I'm dry and wrapped in the softest towel that exists, I step out into the bedroom and see a breakfast table has been brought in. It's covered in a spread of berries, melon, pineapple and pastries, glass bottles of juice and, of course, champagne.

Then I notice my floral dress on the bed. No underwear, just the dress. I bite my lip. This is the dress I was wearing the night we met and the night that he promised to fuck me senseless in it.

And now he's going to make good on his promise.

I can't believe this is finally going to happen.

I'm going to have sex with Max Montrose!

I put on the dress, my hands shaking with excitement and nerves at what's coming. My stomach flips and flops around like the butterflies in there are doing a mating dance themselves.

I put the towel back in the bathroom and check my reflection in the mirror. I look different somehow. Older, wiser, happier? I smile at myself. "It's all going to be okay," I tell the woman smiling back at me.

Max is still not back, so I grab a bowl of fruit and a glass of champagne to calm the butterflies that are getting out of control. I sit on the bed, which feels somehow both firm and like a giant marshmallow at the same time.

My heart hammers in anticipation of what happens now as I chew on a piece of what tastes like the sweetest pineapple ever grown.

Callie jumps onto the bed and nudges my hand with her tiny fluffy head.

"You really are the prettiest kitty," I tell her before giving her some much-needed chin scratches.

The door swings open, and I look up to see the most handsome man I've ever seen in my entire fucking life looking at me like I'm the most beautiful thing he's ever seen.

He's wearing a crisp white shirt, sleeves rolled up to that perfect spot just below his elbows. A gold Rolex shines on his wrist, and his dark blue pants sit on his hips like they were made for him. Of course, they *were* made for him. His dark hair is still a little damp, and while he's slicked it back, it still curls slightly at the ends and only makes him sexier.

He sits down next to me, his bright blue eyes sparkling with anticipation, lust and… is that *happiness*? It may be the first time I've seen him like this. *Happy*.

Callie jumps off the bed and rubs around his legs before disappearing out into the parlor. Max closes the door behind her and turns to me and smiles.

"Poppy, I'd like you to move in with me," he says.

"I already live here," I say.

"I want you to move into the house."

"Isn't this a bit soon?"

He walks over to the breakfast table, turning to make himself a glass of champagne and give me a view of his firm backside that I'm not mad about.

He turns back to me. "You can have one of the guest suites. You'll have your own space. I'd very much like to help you with your study, if it's something you still want to pursue."

"It's too much," I tell him. "I wouldn't feel comfortable just taking your money like that," I tell him.

He laughs. "Poppy, there is nothing more I would want than to spend my money on helping you to live your dreams. But if it would please you, I'm sure I can find some jobs around the mansion for you to help with."

"Cleaning?"

"Perhaps now and then you could put on those tight pants I so enjoy you in and dust my library shelves while I watch."

My face heats at the thought of it. "And then what?"

"And then I'll rip them off you and finally fuck you in my library like I've thought about so many damn times."

Okay, now my cheeks are on fire.

He sips his champagne and then takes a strawberry from the bowl. He walks towards me slowly, a smirk on his lips as he sits down next to me on the bed. He raises the strawberry to my lips, and I bite into it. The sweet juice runs down my chin and onto his hand.

A smile shines over his face, and holy shit if he isn't the most perfect man that's ever existed.

"Sorry I took a little while. I wanted to drink a little first, just to make sure my bloodlust is appeased before we—"

I take another sip of champagne. "You can drink from me," I say.

"And I will."

How my stomach flips at the way he says *he will* drink from me. How I long for the glorious sensation of his bite! I think of his fangs entering me in the crypt, the way I wanted nothing more than to open every vein, every part of myself to him.

"But I would never want to take too much."

He stands, taking my glass and the bowl of fruit and

places them onto the breakfast table. When he turns around, he looks at me with those shining eyes that have seen so much, but right now are looking at *me.*

"We can wait," he says. I never want you to feel pressured. We have time."

"I'm done waiting," I tell him. I reach for his shirt and pull him down onto the bed.

His hands run down over my hips. "You in that dress," he murmurs as he nibbles my ear. "I wanted you from the first moment I saw your gorgeous ass in the air in this god-damned dress!" He playfully slaps my ass, and I grin at him.

"Are you ready to fuck me senseless now?"

He growls into my neck. "I was made ready."

I move my hair away from my neck and present it to him.

He shakes his head. "Not the first time we're together like this, my love," he says with a gentle kiss to my throat. "I don't want you to be high on my bite. I want to know that you want me, not just for my fangs."

"I just want you, Max. Even before I knew what you were, before I knew about The Bite, I wanted you. Before I even met you, I wanted you."

His hands squeeze my hips as he chuckles. "You were a fan?"

"The biggest fan. I had your posters on my walls. I even had a scrapbook—"

He makes another growling sound as he gently kisses my neck.

"You were my first orgasm."

His fingers run over my neck and down towards the neckline of my dress. "I know."

"I mean, the first time I made myself come, I was thinking of you."

He grins at me and places a soft kiss on my lips. "That's so fucking sexy." He takes a breath. "But how about from now on, instead of just thinking about fucking me, I fuck you for real?"

My pulse rockets and I swallow. "I think I could be okay with that."

"I'll make you feel so much fucking better than okay."

He slips a hand into the neckline of my dress, slowly caressing my breast before giving my nipple a gentle squeeze. A gasp escapes my lips.

"Maybe next time we make love I'll bite you right here." He runs a finger over the top of my breast and then kisses me there as sexy shivers run down my spine.

"Then I'll look forward to next time," I whisper.

"I love that we're already talking about next time," he says with a sexy smirk. "Because I want to fuck you senseless every single day of your long, full life."

"I think I'd like that."

"Then we'd better start now."

He places a firm hand on my cheek and presses his slightly cool lips to mine. He's gentle at first, offering slow, romantic kisses that make me feel weak all over. And then his hand slides back down into my dress, and he's more confident with my breast now, harder with his touch and then rougher and hotter with his kiss.

And I'm melting for him, from the inside out. I'm already so fucking wet between my legs and can't wait for him to be inside me.

He pulls my dress down over my shoulders, exposing my breasts, and he sighs. "God, I wanted you like this, here in my *bed*, in this damn dress, from the second I saw you."

My pussy throbs as he lazily traces circles over one nipple, flicking his tongue over the other.

"Oh, Max!"

"Leo," he says. "Please, when we're fucking, please always call me Leo."

"Leo," I say. He gently bites my nipple, and I cry out, "Fuck, Leo!"

"Oh, you want to fuck?" He looks up at me with a grin.

"Yes!" My hips push into the air towards him, and he grips my thighs.

"Are you ready for me?"

"What do you think?" I ask, knowing he can feel my wetness running down my thigh.

He runs a hand up under the skirt of my dress. I open my legs for him, and he groans as he becomes aware of just how wet I am.

"Dear god," he whispers, running a finger up and down my slick entrance.

"Oh, no, wait!" I throw a hand over my face.

"Do you want me to stop?"

"No, but—! Shit! What about contraception?"

He lets out a soft chuckle. "We don't need it."

"We don't?"

"I have no living sperm, and I am completely healed from all afflictions. I can't catch anything or pass it on. And when I gave you my blood, you would have been completely healed from anything you may have been carrying that you weren't aware of."

"You mean we can just—?"

"If you want me to use something for peace of mind, I can. But it's not needed."

I shake my head, my body trembling at the idea that we don't need anything to come between us.

"Of course it means I can never have children," he adds.

"Would you be okay with more cats?"

He chuckles. "Yes."

He stands, leaving me sprawled on the bed with my dress pulled down below my breasts and pushed up around my thighs.

"God, you look so beautiful like that. Exactly how I imagined you'd look when I fucked you in that dress."

I feel my pussy practically dripping at his words.

He unbuttons his shirt and slides it over his muscular shoulders. Fuck, it's sexy watching him undress. He folds the shirt, placing it over the arm of a chair, and then does the same with his pants, revealing a pair of tight black boxer briefs that already show me how hard he is for me.

He gives me that sexy smirk as he slides them down, and he's now naked. Max Montrose is naked in front of me.

I let out a gasp. I'm not the most experienced girl in the world, but I'm pretty sure this is the most perfect cock in existence. Straight, hard, glistening with desire, and *definitely* a whole lot bigger than I expected.

"Do you like what you see?" he asks, walking towards me.

"I love what I see," I tell him.

He kneels on the bed and pushes my dress up even higher, fully exposing every part of me, except my belly that's still covered in the dress.

"You are so fucking beautiful." He leans down and kisses me gently, soft and slow.

My hips buck and my back arches, my whole body wanting him close, wanting him on me, wanting him *in* me.

He sits up and runs his hands over my thighs. "Open your legs for me, beautiful," he says.

I do as he says and open up for him.

"I know you can open them wider," he says with a grin.

My whole body is throbbing at his command, but I follow his instructions, lifting my knees and opening as wide as I can for him.

He slides two fingers up and down my opening and moans. "Poppy, you are exquisite."

He pushes his two fingers inside me, and I'm gone. I'm so

fucking gone. I buck into his hand, fucking his fingers like they are air, and I can't breathe without them.

He reaches up with his other hand and tweaks my nipple, and I think I'm going to explode, right here and now.

"Not yet, my love," he says, slowing down. "I want my cock inside you when you come."

He slides his fingers out and I let out a whimper at the loss of him inside me.

And suddenly he's right there, his cock at my entrance, and I can't believe this is happening. I'm about to have sex with Max Montrose in his velvet bed in his Hollywood mansion!

He places gentle kisses down over my neck.

"Poppy," he whispers. "Are you ready?"

"If you don't fuck me now, I think I might die."

He lets out a throaty, sexy chuckle, and then he gently pushes his way inside me. He's big, *so* big, and at first it feels like too much, like I might not be able to take it.

"You're so fucking big! Go slow," I beg him.

He reaches down and rubs my clit. "Relax, my love. You can take me."

His finger on my clit and his words of encouragement are all I fucking need.

I open my legs wider and invite him in. I feel myself slowly stretching out around him, and the pleasure of the stretch is fucking glorious.

"Can you take a little more?" he asks, pushing my hair out of my eyes and placing a kiss on my forehead.

I nod. "Yes."

He pushes in further and I stretch around him again, aching now for all of him.

"Can you take all of me now, gorgeous?"

"Please!"

He slowly pushes all the way in, filling me completely, and I gasp. "Oh, Leo!"

And it's like we're made for each other. I've never felt as complete and whole as I do with him fully inside me.

"Oh, Poppy," he moans. "You feel even better than I could ever have imagined. And I've imagined this so many times."

I let out a gasp and then a small laugh as I feel him push even deeper into me.

"You feel so good, Poppy," he groans. "You feel like heaven."

All I can do is moan underneath him as he finds his rhythm, thrusting into me, harder and deeper each time while I find my own heaven.

"Everything alright?" he asks, pulling out a little.

"Better than alright," I tell him.

"Can you take more?"

There's more?!

I have no idea if that's possible, but I tell him, "Yes."

He grips my hips and thrusts into me even deeper. I let out a wail at the ecstasy of this moment, of the feeling of him so fucking deep inside of me.

He promised to fuck me senseless, but while he thrusts into me hard and fast, he's not just fucking me, he's making love to me. Every thrust feels like a confession of his love for me, and I have never felt anything like this. Not even his bite, or the ecstasy of his blood. *This* is otherworldly.

He breathes into my neck and then kisses my mouth — long, slow and deep. His tongue finds its way inside my mouth, and I'm in absolute bliss at the sensation of both his cock and his tongue in me. I want all of him inside of me, forever!

"I want to feel you even deeper," he tells me.

A second later he's holding my legs in the air, thrusting

into me, and it's so deep and glorious that I immediately feel an orgasm begin to build.

"You are mine," he growls, as he continues to make me more and more his with each thrust. "Truly. Eternally. *Mine.*"

My body feels so alive, my heart so open, and the way he claims me with his words while he thrusts into me pushes me to my edge.

"Come for me, my love," he says in that gravelly, sexy voice that I know so well, that I know from *A Knight to Remember* and *Love Delayed* and from our sexy private moments together.

My body thrills at his command. The wave of pleasure hits, and it's like nothing I've ever experienced before. My body spasms and pulses, and the waves crash, but they don't stop at the usual place, they just keep coming.

Max growls into my neck, and I feel his thrusts begin to speed up. His glorious cock hits even deeper now, pushing new waves of pleasure through every part of me.

He lets out a groan, and I feel him releasing inside of me. I grip his back tighter, pulling him into me. *Closer, deeper, more!* He reaches his climax as I ride the last waves of mine, and I know that my life has completely changed.

No other man could ever make me feel this way. Max is my one. My only.

We collapse onto each other, spent.

"I never knew it could be like that," I say, breathless.

"Neither did I." He runs a hand over my cheek. "All this time, and I've never felt like this until now." He takes my hand and kisses it gently before wrapping his arms around me, our naked bodies fitting perfectly together in every way.

"I can't believe that just happened," I sigh, looking up at the gold chandelier above his bed. I can't help the giggle that escapes my lips.

He turns his head towards me and smiles. "Believe it, my love. And you'll need to get used to it, because this is just the beginning of our love story."

CHAPTER SIXTY-SIX

rix

Julio: where are you guys? @Trix, I'm hungry!
   Malik: Is everyone okay? I can't get hold of James or Henrietta.
   Malik: Okay, getting worried now
   Julio: Getting even hungrier now!
   Malik: Make yourself a sandwich, Julio!
   Julio: But it's better when Trix makes it!
   Malik: @Poppy @Trix, just let me know you're okay.
   Poppy: Everything is okay. We'll all be home soon. xx

EMAILS ARE SENT, and contracts are signed. It's a new world order for the supernaturals of Los Angeles, and Poppy and Max go home to consummate their love affair.

But the last thing I feel like doing is going back to Max's mansion to bake a cake he may or may not even eat.

And so, I somehow find myself sitting at a diner across

the road from the Hollywood Forever Cemetery with Brandon Curtis, big-time movie producer, Claudia, the werewolf who just nearly killed all my friends, and Maverick fucking Stone.

I order a veggie burger and fries, but it lacks any flavor. The patty is far too dry, and even a heavy dose of ketchup doesn't help. I munch on soggy fries and stare into four cups of bottomless coffee as I try to process the events of the last twenty-four hours while the others chit-chat about movies and the hottest places to be seen in LA.

"The hilarious thing is you didn't even have the right wood in those crossbow bolts," Maverick laughs.

"What?" I ask, finally hearing something worth paying attention to.

"There are only three types of wood that can kill vampires, and those bolts weren't any of them," he says.

"Max seemed to think they could take him out," Claudia says. "When he was offering up his life for Poppy's."

I grab the salt and shake it over the cold fries in an attempt to make them slightly more edible.

Maverick rolls his eyes at Claudia. "They could still do a little damage if all of you fired at once. But I think he was more worried about Poppy."

Brandon smiles and waves at someone on the other side of the diner. "An old friend I must say hello to. Forgive me." He places a hundred on the table and wanders off. "I look forward to our next meeting."

"I should get home," Claudia says. "Jayden's dad is dropping him off soon." She throws ten bucks on the table, which barely covers her meal, let alone a tip, and then it's just me, a shitty as fuck burger and Maverick Stone.

"I guess you have somewhere to be too?" he asks.

I should make an excuse and get out of here. "Not really."

"What's wrong with you?"

I scowl at him across the table. "What?"

"You've been sitting there like a bunch of vampires and werewolves just tried to eat you." He lets out a laugh like he's so proud of his stupid joke.

"Are you always such an asshole?" I ask him.

"You are a feisty one, aren't you?"

"Maybe for you this stuff happens every day, but for me this shit was kind of crazy!"

"I thought you were a Donna?"

"What the fuck? No! I'm not!"

"You were at the club getting glamoured by that trucker hat vamp."

"Yeah, not really by *choice*."

He rolls his eyes. "Human girls don't go to Vincent's unless they want The Bite. Why were you there if you didn't want it?"

I glare at him, right into his blue-green eyes, the color of water in some tropical paradise. "I was there to help Poppy find her brother Aiden. The piece of shit vampire who was helping Lottie. I *didn't* want The fucking Bite. Especially from that guy. And for your information, I have never even been bitten."

He raises his hands. "Calm down, sweetheart."

"Don't call me sweetheart!"

"Honey? Babe? Baby girl? Sweet cheeks?"

Okay, why did all those feel so fucking good to hear from his mouth?

"My name is *Trix*."

"What's that short for? Beatrix?"

"Yes." I shove another tasteless fry into my mouth.

"Look," he puts his hands on the table. His big, stupid hands that are attached to his bulging forearms, which are joined to his ridiculous biceps. "I'm sorry. It's just that the girls I hang with — they're usually Donnas."

"Yeah, I can imagine," I say, finally ripping my eyes away from his arms.

"You're weird," he says. "But I like it."

"What the fuck is that supposed to mean?"

"There's something about you," he starts. "You're not like other girls."

"Oh, not this narrative." I roll my eyes.

"I mean, you're not…"

"Not like other girls because I'm not *into* you?" I ask, glaring into his eyes again.

He laughs at that and then leans over so close I inhale his clean, saltwater scent. "Oh, baby, you are *so* fucking into me."

A traitorous fire ignites in my belly. *Fuck.*

"You're right," he says, throwing a hundred on the table, way more than the cost of the burrito he didn't touch. "It's been a crazy night. But I'm wired and need to go do something."

I don't think this is an invitation. But still, I ask him, "Yeah, like what?"

"I want blood, and I want sex."

Goddamn, why does that hit me right between the legs?! Traitorous vagina!

"Yeah, well Vincent's opens soon if you want to go get a Donna."

"Sweetheart, I don't have to go to Vincent's for a Donna. My phone is full of numbers."

"I'm sure it is." I throw back the last of my now cold black coffee and get up to go. He's left enough cash to cover my burger, so I don't bother to leave anything.

He grabs my hand and swirls a finger around my palm. "But you're right here."

I scowl at him. "What?"

"If you're up for it," he shrugs.

I pull back my hand and cross my arms over my chest.

"Oh, I get it. It's a convenience thing. Like, why dial a number when there's some girl right in front of you who will drop her panties for you if you just say the word?"

"I haven't dialed a number since the late nineties. That's not how phones work anymore," he says. "And trust me, calling any of those girls would be a hell of a lot easier than this fucking conversation."

I narrow my eyes at him and then turn, stomping out of the diner.

"Is that a yes?" he calls to me when I'm halfway to the door.

I look back over my shoulder at the very sexy, incredibly buff movie star vampire and call back to him — "Sure, why the hell not?"

EPILOGUE

iden

I ARRIVE BACK at the crypt late. Too late. Lottie is lying on the ground with a stake in her chest.

A sob escapes my lips. My maker, my lover, my life, she's gone.

I fall down at her side and grab her hand. "I'm so sorry. This is all my fault. I couldn't stay and watch you kill Poppy. I was a coward. I'm sorry. I should have stayed with you! I'm so sorry! Lottie! My sweet Lottie, oh god!"

Her finger twitches, but no. It can't be. She's been staked! There's no way she's alive. There is already blackness seeping out of her heart.

A gurgling noise escapes from her throat as if she's trying to tell me something but can't speak. I don't know what to do! I don't know how she's even moving!

She makes the noise again, and I look her over.

"Fuck, fuck, fuck!" I yell before deciding maybe I can just
— I yank the stake out of her, and she gasps.

"How the fuck is this possible?" I ask, dropping the stake
down at my side while Lottie gurgles and spasms.

The hole in her chest starts to heal, and I gasp. "What is
happening?!"

A few moments later, she sits up and stares at me. "Aiden,
darling."

"Jesus Christ, fuck! I'm so sorry!" I tell her.

"Sorry?" She tosses her head back and laughs. "Darling!
You just saved my life!"

"How is this happening? How did you survive this?"

She holds up the large metal, bloody-black and now
dented pendant, one of the necklaces she always wears and
eyes it curiously.

"When they put the stake in, it hit this charm. It's made of
iron, you see. My father had it in his collection of occult
curiosities. It was said to have been made by a witch in the
sixteenth century to protect the wearer against curses and
hexes. I thought it was a hideous little thing, but it caught my
eye. It stayed in my dressing-table drawer for many decades.
One day, after my father was killed, I rediscovered it. It
reminded me of him and his passion for these strange pieces,
and so I started wearing it. And I suppose it protected me
after all!" She lets out a laugh. "How about that, darling?"

I gawk as she stands up, brushes herself off and looks
down at me. "Well, are you coming?"

"Coming where?"

"To destroy them all, my darling!"

If you felt the heat with Max Montrose, you're going to catch fire with Maverick Stone!

Forever Undeniably Yours

One night was all they had. One bite was all it took.

Immortal movie star Maverick Stone doesn't do relationships. He has enough demons to last him for eternity, and his insatiable need for blood and sex definitely does not make him good boyfriend material.

So when he meets Trix Delaney and sparks fly, they set some rules of engagement — *no kissing, no calling, never tell anyone, ever.*

Months go by, and Maverick still can't get her off his mind. Nothing and no one can satiate him in the way her blood and body did that night. But with vampires across LA disappearing, and a secret society of the vampire elite suddenly under threat, Maverick is going to need more than fantasies to feed his hunger.

When Maverick's co-star goes missing, caterer Trix is ordered to stand in and play the role of his lover. It's clear their chemistry is undeniable, and it's impossible for Trix to *act like it never happened.*

The blood bond forged from Maverick's bite is too strong, and the vivid dreams that have been plaguing Trix are no longer enough. Soon they're creating a new set of rules and giving in to their desires. But there was one rule they forgot to add to the list — *no falling in love.*

But there's something dark and dangerous lurking in Hollywood's shadows, and the insatiable blood bond they've tried so hard to deny may end up being the only thing that can save them both from Certain Death.

Forever Undeniably Yours draws you back into Immortal Hollywood's dark underworld of love, lust and brooding Immortals.

Will you succumb to the ecstasy of the bite?

Trix and Maverick's story coming November 2025
Pre-Order now:
https://mybook.to/undeniably-yours

Sign up at:
www.stormyohara.com for updates, sneak peeks and deleted scenes!

PLEASE SHARE THE LOVE!

If you have enjoyed this book, please consider leaving a review on Amazon and/or Goodreads, sharing on socials or telling a friend about it!

Tag me on socials so I can re-share and send you some love!

www.instagram.com/stormy.ohara

www.tiktok.com/@stormy.ohara

ABOUT THE AUTHOR

Stormy O'Hara is the alter ego and pen name of a well-known spiritual author who divides her time between writing stories, reading tarot and exploring ancient monuments in the Peak District of Derbyshire where she currently lives.

Stormy believes in the magic, power, creativity and connection of the human heart, soul and spirit and no generative AI is ever used in the creation of her books.

www.stormyohara.com

www.instagram.com/stormy.ohara

www.tiktok.com/@stormy.ohara

ACKNOWLEDGMENTS

First of all, thank you to *you* for taking a chance on a debut paranormal romance author! This is my first adult romance novel and I hope you enjoyed reading this even a teeny tiny bit as much as I enjoyed writing it!

You may think you're just taking time out to read a smutty little vampire book because it makes you happy and perhaps even a little hot, but there is something about the healing power of smut that is rocking worlds, healing wounds and activating the divine feminine in ways I'm only just beginning to tap into! So big love and thanks to you for doing this powerful healing work alongside me!

So of course, my second thank you must be to the divine feminine energy that weaves through all these spicy books, through its authors and readers! We are part of a healing movement and moment, and it's exciting as fuck! Also, thank you to the divine masculine who is healing us in his own special way through this magical work.

Thank you to my beta readers who read a slightly less spicy version of this and demanded more spice! I hope you all appreciate the more detailed fantasies, shower scenes and longer full-on spice moments! To Sonya, Cheryl, Erica, Caz, Louise, Megan and Alexis, you made this book so much better and so much spicier and I'm so very grateful for you, as I'm sure my readers are too!

Thank you to Hannah for all the support you've given to my fiction even before I sat down to write this. Your words of encouragement have truly meant so much!

Thank you to Maria for the activations, the space held and for seeing my vision for this work with so much clarity and faith in me and my ability to do it!

To Gaby, the best beta reader I could possibly ask for! Thank you for all your amazing insights on this book, for your long voice notes that have kept me company on long walks through the countryside. Thank you for your amazing support and your friendship over so many years. I am so very grateful for you.

Nicole, you gorgeous human! Your words of love and support helped bring Stormy and this work to life. You are truly an incredible person, and I'm so blessed to know you.

And finally, as always, thank you to the love of my own life who inspires my male characters, their broodiness, grumpiness, strength, but most of all, their amazingly big hearts in the face of it all. Thank you for supporting all my crazy dreams and not even batting an eyelid when I said I wanted to write spicy vampire romance novels. You are so truly, eternally, mine.